"Richard Kadrey's work has often possessed a dark, satirical edge, but in *The Everything Box*, the San Francisco author allows himself to venture far into the realm of the outright silly. . . . Reminiscent of the comic novels of Christopher Moore, Neil Gaiman or Terry Pratchett."
—SAN FRANCISCO CHRONICLE

"A rolling bouncy-house of a caper tale, *The Everything Box* abounds with quick-witted characters, snarky dialogue, and surreal analogies. If you haven't sampled Richard Kadrey's take on fantasy yet, this is a great place to start."
—CHRISTOPHER MOORE, *NEW YORK TIMES* BESTSELLING AUTHOR OF
LAMB, A DIRTY JOB, AND *THE SERPENT OF VENICE*

"[Kadrey's] books are a romp . . . and they go down like cold lager on a hot afternoon."   —NPR BOOKS ON *THE EVERYTHING BOX*

"Kadrey's simultaneously glib and snide voice [peppers] his story with delightful turns of phrase. . . . *The Everything Box* is a fun read for all of the Kadrey-isms alone."   —*LOCUS* MAGAZINE

The Wrong Dead Guy

THE
WRONG DEAD
GUY

RICHARD KADREY

HARPER Voyager
An Imprint of HarperCollinsPublishers

This is a work of fiction. Names, characters, places, and incidents are products of the author's imagination or are used fictitiously and are not to be construed as real. Any resemblance to actual events, locales, organizations, or persons, living or dead, is entirely coincidental.

Harper Voyager and design is a trademark of HCP LLC.

HarperCollins books may be purchased for educational, business, or sales promotional use. For information please e-mail the Special Markets Department at SPsales@harpercollins.com.

A hardcover edition of this book was published in 2017 by Harper Voyager, an imprint of HarperCollins Publishers.

FIRST HARPER VOYAGER PAPERBACK EDITION PUBLISHED 2017.

Designed by Paula Russell Szafranski

Library of Congress Cataloging-in-Publication Data has been applied for.

ISBN 978-0-06-238958-9

17 18 19 20 21 LSC 10 9 8 7 6 5 4 3 2 1

To Isotope,
who is eating all the burgers

Either he's dead or my watch has stopped.

—GROUCHO MARX

1

The sixth floor of the Department of Peculiar Science looked exactly like an ordinary office in an ordinary office building and not the slightest bit like the home of a highly secret government agency. There were desks, computers, copiers, paper clips, and not a single sentient robot, grotesque monster, or revenant in sight. Those—the ones that hadn't gone home for the day—were on the lower floors, leaving the sixth floor a superb example of the stultifyingly normal.

Except for the break-in.

The room in which the crime was being carried out was completely dark, except for a single spot of light. Charlie Cooper—Coop to his friends—stared at the metal cabinet, adjusted his headlamp, and frowned. "One time I stole a magic coloring book that spelled out the future with pictures of kittens. Seriously. The next president. Super Bowl winners. The whole bit."

"I know, dear," said Giselle, sitting nearby on a step stool.

"Another time I stole a solid-gold bust of Aleister Crowley out of a bank vault protected by vampire bats the size of ostriches. The bust could see the future, too."

"I thought it was the other way around," said Giselle. "Blood-sucking ostriches."

"No. That was when I stole a fortune-telling . . . well, sexual implement."

"You can say 'dildo,' dear. We're all adults."

"It predicted gold futures, though I'm not exactly sure how."

"Yes, you are," said Giselle. She made little moaning sounds.

"Shh," said Coop. "I'm trying to concentrate."

Agent Bayliss, one of the DOPS agents who'd recruited Coop, stood nearby looking extremely uncomfortable, though in the darkness it was impossible to tell if it was because of the current discussion or the break-in she'd arranged. Either way, she was clearly desperate to change the subject as she said, "It sounds like you stole a lot of fortune-telling gadgets."

Coop nodded and wiped sweat from his forehead. "People are crazy for the stuff. I stole a fortune-telling muffin tin. A parrot that would only say 'fuck you' and lottery numbers."

"Yes, dear," said Giselle. "You've stolen a lot of things, and we're very impressed. How is *this* particular crime going?"

"Just fine. Stop talking."

"You're the one who started it."

"Did I?" said Coop. "Well, I just wanted to make it clear that this thing I'm doing now? It's exactly the kind of thing I don't do."

"I'm really, really grateful," said Bayliss.

"You have no idea who's been stealing your office supplies?" said Giselle.

Bayliss shook her head. "None. And I can't bring any from home. It's not allowed. They have hexes that can detect it."

"Why can't you just complain to management?"

"And get audited? Have you ever been audited?"

"No."

"Let me tell you, they don't just search your desk. They search *everywhere*," said Bayliss.

"You mean . . . ?"

"Yes. Wait. You mean . . . ? Eww. No. They just read your mind. But it leaves you loopy for days."

"Oh. Still, eww."

"I agree," said Coop. "Eww. Now please pipe down, both of you."

"Why is it taking so long?" said Giselle.

"The lock is cursed. It keeps melting my damned picks."

"Be careful," said Bayliss. "We can't get caught."

"How much longer do you think it will it be?" said Giselle.

Coop leaned his weight into the lock. "Right about now," he said as the office-supplies cabinet swung open, revealing forbidden stacks of rubber bands and staples.

"Thank you! Thank you!" said Bayliss, giving Coop a quick hug as he stood up.

"You're welcome," he said. "Now, please, don't ever ask me to steal this kind of thing again. It's depressing enough working here, and stealing paper clips makes me not want to be alive."

Bayliss loaded things into a canvas bag. "I understand. Thank you."

Coop sighed. "You know, I once stole a fortune-telling cat from a witch in Salem. She tried charging tourists to hear their future, but the cat wasn't interested. It would only tell you the next time you were going to eat flounder."

"Why didn't you keep any of the fortune-telling things?" said Bayliss. "You might be rich. You might not have gone to . . ." She turned red and stopped talking.

Coop quietly set a pack of Post-its on her pile.

"She means jail, dear," said Giselle.

"I guessed."

"Sorry," said Bayliss.

"I'm a respectable criminal," said Coop, taking off his gloves. "The great toner caper here? No one can ever know about it. Not even Morty."

"I won't tell a soul," said Bayliss.

"Good. *Anyone*. Now let's get out of here."

Coop locked the supply cabinet and led the way back out into the utterly ordinary and completely deserted office corridor.

As they walked back to Bayliss's desk, Giselle prodded Coop in the shoulder. "Why didn't you ever keep any of those fortune-telling toys and bet everything on the World Series? I wouldn't mind a house in France."

Coop shoved the gloves into his pants pocket. "I did. It was a Zune that predicted horse races."

"What's a Zune?" said Bayliss.

"A manic-depressive iPod."

"Why didn't you bet on a race?" said Giselle.

"I did," said Coop. "The horse lost by a mile. Turns out it had a stutter."

"The horse?"

"No. The Zune. That's the last time I ever trusted anything that predicted the future."

Giselle leaned against the partition when they reached Bayliss's desk. "No vacation châteaus for us, I guess."

"Not on a government salary. Of course, I could always start moonlighting."

"I hear the Tooth Fairy is fake, so don't go looking for a fortune in quarters."

"The Easter Bunny is supposed to be loaded, though."

"Only in jelly beans, and banks don't take those anymore."

Bayliss emptied the canvas bag into the bottom drawer of her desk. "Don't even joke about stealing on your own," she said. "You'll end up in the mook department."

Mooks were one of the DOPS's more successful experiments. They were people in the sense that they had two legs, two hands, and two eyes, but they weren't quite people in the sense that they were all incredibly dead. This technicality made it hard to come up with enticing Match.com profiles, but it made them great janitors and hallway picture straighteners.

"Speaking of corpses, how's Nelson doing these days?" said Coop.

Nelson, Bayliss's old partner, had recently entered the ranks of the employed deceased because a few weeks earlier she'd shot him. But she didn't really have a choice. Well, she did in the sense that all sentient beings have free will, but Nelson was going to shoot Coop, so Bayliss shot him. Of course, Nelson filed a complaint against her, but it was dismissed. Still, it didn't stop him from whining to HR when no one came to his funeral.

Bayliss took out some purloined staples and began refilling her stapler. "He's still in the mail room, but he got promoted to night manager."

Coop looked over the empty cubicles. "Ambitious dead people make me nervous. And by 'nervous,' I mean I want to get on a plane to Antarctica."

"You don't think he's the one who's been taking your office supplies, do you?" said Giselle.

"I wondered about that, but no one's seen him on this floor since he got the job downstairs."

"Maybe he's in cahoots with a kleptomaniac rat," said Coop. "Or a ghost. Or a ghost rat. That sounds like Nelson's social circle."

Giselle gave him a look. "I know you're worried, but maybe you should speak to security about getting some wards to protect your cubicle."

"Complain that your wastebasket has become a hellmouth," said Coop.

Bayliss frowned. "That sounds a little farfetched."

"Tell it to Ellis upstairs. He ignored the voices under his desk and now he's infested with imps. He has to wear a sort of demon flea collar and makeup to hide the spots."

"I don't think I know him."

Giselle sat on Bayliss's desk. "Trust me, a demon rash is the most interesting thing about him."

"Bologna on white bread with mayo thinks he's boring," said Coop.

"Good luck with this bunch of supplies," said Giselle. "I hope they don't disappear, too."

Bayliss smiled. "Don't worry. Management just started an office pet program. It's supposed to be a morale builder. I asked for a desk squid. Want to see it?"

"I'll give you a dollar not to ever show it to me or mention it again," said Coop.

"What exactly is a desk squid?" said Giselle.

"They're adorable. Baby Horrid Old Ones. As long as I feed it and keep it surrounded by silver crucifixes, it's my best friend."

Coop took a minuscule step back. "And if you forget to feed it?"

Bayliss arranged Post-its on her desk. "It'll grow up and maybe sort of destroy the world," she said quietly.

Giselle smiled. "Speaking of destroying the world, I'm hungry. Who else is hungry? I'm buying."

"Thanks, but I have to catch up on some work," said Bayliss.

"Okay. Have a good night."

"Good luck with the squid and the supplies," said Coop. "But the squid more."

"Thanks again for everything."

"I'm glad to help."

Giselle took his arm. "Let's go get some flapjacks."

"Do they serve drinks there?"

"At the pancake place? I doubt it."

"Sounds horrible." As they reached the elevator, Coop punched the button for the garage. "I should have kept that magic coloring book. Seeing my miserable future here would be a lot easier with kittens."

"Maybe we should get you that drink before food," said Giselle.

"You're the best."

"I'm smart. If I don't get your mind off the squid, soon you're going to be up all night seeing suckers in the shadows."

"Did I ever tell you about the time I stole a plate of fried clams that could find pirate treasure?"

The elevator doors opened and they got inside.

"Let me guess. The owner got drunk and ate them."

"No. His dog did."

"Ah. Did it at least poop doubloons?"

"No one knows. The last time anyone saw it, the mutt was headed to Vegas in a convertible with a poodle under each arm."

Giselle smiled. "You're the worst liar ever."

When they reached the garage, Coop put a hand over his heart. "I swear. It's why you should never let a dog know your ATM number."

She lowered her eyebrows at Coop. "Or your phone number."

"Too late. I know where you live."

"Be a good boy and I'll let you sit up front in the car like people."

"Woof," he said, getting into the passenger seat. He was all smiles on the outside, but deep inside he was dying a little.

Morty's going to find out about tonight. Phil is going to find out. Who else? Lots of people maybe. Bad news always finds a way out.

As they pulled out onto the street, Coop was already preparing his suicide note.

2

The crew uncrating the sarcophagus worked quietly, expertly, and with what seemed to Gilbert Ferris—the junior museum security guard on duty—just a little bit too much reverence. Yeah, the mummy case, the shiny gold jewelry, statues, and painted canopic jars were impressive, but in the end they amounted to knickknacks and an oversize shoe box for a stiff. If whoever buried him had any brains, they would have hit the sale table at some ancient Egyptian Walmart, chucked in the cut-rate loot, and kept the rest of the gold, or shekels—or whatever passed for money back then—for themselves. It's what Gilbert would have done, what he sort of did do when grandma number two passed and he was in charge of the arrangements. The funeral was nice enough, but not over-the-top. Flowers, a preacher, and a tasteful wake afterward. Yeah, the preacher was a buddy in the Universal Life Church who he was paying in beer, and the wake catering came from the day-old table at Safeway, but it was all refrigerated, so who cares if the salami didn't come straight off whatever kind of animal a salami was? Grandma wasn't a saint, he wasn't Bill Gates, and the money he saved (but still expensed to the family) made for a good down payment on a sweet El Camino he'd had his eye on. Gilbert justified everything by telling his friends that he expected the same kind of treatment when he died. Really, what Gilbert wanted was a Viking funeral, but putting something like that together required a level of concentration he wasn't generally capable of. Instead, he made a deal with his Universal Life Church buddy to put his carcass in a wheelchair, take him to Disneyland, and set him on fire on the log flume ride. It wasn't exactly sailing to Valhalla, but it was cheaper than a casket, more awesome than a funeral, and he'd probably get his picture on TV. That was a way to tag out of life. Not wrapped in sheets and boxed up like a dead cat the way old Harkhuf—the Egyptian stiff—went out.

"Shouldn't you be doing something?"

Gilbert looked around. He'd been so transfixed by the mummy being placed in the display case that he hadn't heard Mr. Froehlich, the museum's head of security, come up behind him.

"Sorry, what?" said Gilbert.

"Shouldn't you be doing something besides gawking?" said Froehlich. He was tall and his breath smelled like instant coffee. "The exhibit will be finished in a couple more hours. Until then, just go someplace and guard something."

"It's Monday. The museum is closed. There's no one to guard anything from."

"Then at least walk around the rest of the floor. The board of directors is in a cost-cutting mood. Nothing to guard against might mean fewer guards and fewer guard jobs. Got it?"

Gilbert did indeed get it.

"Don't worry. I'll find something that needs guarding."

"Tell you what. The surveillance cameras are down in the modern painting wing. Why don't you start there? We wouldn't want anyone walking out with the Kandinsky in their pocket."

Gilbert wasn't quite sure what a Kandinsky was. It sounded

dirty, but the museum didn't have that kind of thing. Still, whatever a Kandinsky was, guarding it was a chance to get away from Froehlich and his coffee breath, and that was good enough.

He shot his boss a quick salute and headed for the elevators.

Upstairs, Gilbert found himself alone. He didn't normally work the modern art area, so he made a quick circuit of the whole gallery. Finding nothing out of place, he was instantly bored. He quietly cursed Froehlich under his breath. At least if he was still downstairs he might be able to sneak out to the loading dock with the mummy movers and steal a quick smoke. But no, he was stuck all alone here with acres of pointless paint squiggles and inscrutable sculptures that made his head ache when he tried to figure out what they were.

The Brian Z. Pierson Museum of Art, Antiquities, and Folderol was falling on hard times. The trust that financed the place was running out of money and the museum's name didn't exactly help when they applied for grants. Sixty years earlier, Brian Pierson's children and lawyers had tried talking him out of including "Folderol" in the museum's name, but he hated the place and wanted the world to know it. For him, the whole project was a tax dodge and nothing more.

To try and not go *buggy*, Gilbert attempted to walk around the gallery backward, hoping it would make the place more interesting. It just made him dizzy and sick to his stomach. He fell back against what was supposed to be a statue of a woman, but that looked more to him like a vacuum cleaner with boobs.

It was because of the museum's rapidly diminishing funds that the board decided to host the mummy exhibit. It was true that Harkhuf wasn't a pharaoh or even a big name in Egyptian history, but he was well preserved and his sarcophagus was impressively gaudy and he was finally *something new*. Sure, he wasn't going to bring in King Tut money, but he was an attraction they could build an advertising campaign around and get a few more tourists and school field trips into the place.

Gilbert rested his forehead against a marble wall. His boredom felt like a headache, then like a fever, then desperation, then it went back to plain old boredom again. After a few minutes of that, he kind of missed the headache and tried to will it back. That just made him dizzy again. What really bugged him was that all this crap that had him wandering an empty gallery like a lost dog was the result of something that had nothing to do with him and, in fact, had happened three thousand years ago. What was it? Gilbert gave up being miserable for a minute and dove into the bong water recesses of his brain trying to remember how the mummy had died.

Murder! That was it. The stiff got himself shanked.

It was kind of cool when he thought about it. But that just made him resent his exile even more.

I could be downstairs with a real live dead Egyptian gangbanger, but instead I'm in the goddamn finger-painting room.

Gilbert angrily paced the floor, stopping short in front of a painting on the wall.

Huh. So, that's a Kandinsky.

It wasn't anything dirty at all. He thought that it looked like a drop cloth. Gilbert turned his head to different angles, but no matter how he squinted, the Kandinsky refused to not look like a drop cloth.

His interest in the painting lasted exactly fifty-seven more seconds. Then he was desperately bored again and it made him sleepy.

Wait. Froehlich said there's no surveillance up here. So, who's to know?

Gilbert looked around and found an alcove at the far end of the gallery where no one could see him from the stairs or the elevator. Stepping inside, he slid down into a sitting position and closed his eyes. In his dreams, he and Harkhuf rode the log flume together at Disneyland, giving the world the finger. Shooting the bird to the Mouse with a mummy. That was a one hundred percent way to get on the news.

The next thing Gilbert became aware of was his walkie-talkie crackling. He fumbled getting it off his belt and nearly dropped it.

"Ferris here," he said.

"Where the hell have you been? I've been calling you," barked Froehlich.

"Sorry. I've been having some trouble with the walkie, but it's working okay now."

"Whatever. Get back to the mummy exhibit. The crew is taking their lunch break. You need to watch the exhibit."

Gilbert checked his watch. "But it's almost my lunch, too."

"Newman called in sick. We're shorthanded, so you'll have to eat later."

Gilbert gritted his teeth. "I'll be right down," he said as his admiration for Harkhuf's Tupac-like death instantly evaporated.

When he got downstairs, Froehlich was waiting for him. The sarcophagus was open and Harkhuf lay on his back, staring with his empty mummy eye sockets at the overhead lights. Gilbert peered into the case. There was only one thing he knew about Harkhuf that was supposed to make him special. Both his arms and his legs were secured to the inner case with a wax seal depicting the gods Set and Anubis. He'd seen something about them online. Like one was the god of death and the other was sort of the Devil. Or maybe he'd seen it in a movie. Wherever he'd seen it, Harkhuf's murder, combined with death and the Devil, reignited his admiration and brought a single word to his lips.

"*Badass.*"

"What? I missed that," said Froehlich.

"I said this guy was murdered and now he's all death's-heads and devils."

"Yes. I suppose that is interesting."

"It's more than interesting. It's *badass*. Harkhuf here is the Ozzy of mummies. That's how they should advertise him. The darkest, hard-corest, most rock-and-roll mummy of all time."

Froehlich looked at Gilbert for a minute waiting for the punch line. It didn't come.

"Oh. You're serious."

"Harkhuf, the Metal Mummy. I'm telling you. We could sell a million T-shirts."

Froehlich nodded, the flicker of despair that lay at the center of his being flaring up like a tire fire. He could think of a dozen occasions when he would have loved to have fired Gilbert. This one made it an even thirteen. But Froehlich knew it was better to put up with someone unqualified to guard a fishbowl than it was to fire him and put the idea that guards were expendable into the board of directors' heads.

"Those are all interesting ideas, Gilbert," he said. "Keep them to yourself for now. We don't want anyone stealing them."

"Sure. I get it," Gilbert said, for the first-ever time not wanting his boss to eat pavement directly in front of a steamroller.

Froehlich patted Gilbert's shoulder. "The crew're all at lunch. I'll be back in an hour. You're on your own till then."

"You're going to tell the board about my ideas?"

"Absolutely. First chance I get," Froehlich said. "Just keep an eye on things here for a while."

"I won't let Ozzy out of my sight."

"Swell," said Froehlich, heading to his car and the bottle he kept under the passenger seat. It wasn't that he necessarily *needed it,* but on a day like this, it kept him from pushing Harkhuf out of his case, closing the lid on himself, and hoping for a swift, deep, dark burial under quiet desert sands.

After a few minutes alone with Ozzy, the Metal Mummy, Gilbert's keen senses took note of two important things: that he was alone on this floor of the museum and that his stomach was rumbling.

Gilbert had a complicated relationship to food. When he was young, his name had transformed from Gilbert to Gill, and eventually—with the cruel cleverness of children—to Fish. Because of this, and despite the warnings from what amounted to a small stadiumful of doctors, he refused to eat anything that had lived in, been raised near, or might have ever glimpsed a body of water. Because of *that,* his diet consisted mainly of fried chicken (chickens lived on farms, they couldn't fly, and they wouldn't know a lake from a Saturn V), hamburgers (for the same reasons as chickens, plus, unlike chickens, cows didn't float, so they'd have no interest in water), and pizza (it was docile, immobile, and, for him, resolutely anchovy-free).

Gilbert took a quick look around just to make sure that no one was nearby. While he was indifferent to exercise and, really, motion in general, he sprinted down one floor to the employee lunchroom, where he purchased a bacon cheeseburger from a vending machine. The microwave seemed to take forever heating the damned thing, so he had to spread on the ketchup and mustard while running back upstairs to Ozzy.

He was panting when he got back, but the exhibit room was still deserted. He took a couple of quick bites of the burger before stashing it on a pile of napkins behind a pillar. His plan was to take a bite or two at a time, make sure the coast was clear, then go back for another greasy morsel. This hit-and-run approach to lunch would also give him time to catch his breath. This was important to him because sometimes when he ran, his left arm hurt like a bitch and he didn't want to look bad in front of Ozzy.

Gilbert went back to the sarcophagus and peered down at the

dead man. As he leaned over the lid, trying to get a better look at Set and Anubis, a glop of mustard he'd accidentally squirted onto his uniform during the mad dash upstairs dislodged itself and fell directly onto one of the wax seals binding the mummy's arms and legs. Gilbert stopped breathing, and for a second, his vision went blank. His chest ached like that time in Little League when a baseball took a bad hop and nailed him right in the nuts. He was perfectly aware that he didn't have nuts in his chest, but whatever was there felt worse every second as he stared at the mustard in the mummy case.

Gilbert ran back to where he'd stashed the burger, which made him feel even more light-headed, and came back with a fistful of napkins. He wiped frantically at the wax seal, removing every trace of mustard. It came off surprisingly easily, but just as he gave the seal one last swipe, he heard a crack. Gilbert looked down into the case. The seal he'd been wiping, the one by Ozzy's right hand, had snapped in two and fallen in on itself, like a collapsed bridge. Spurred by panic and what remained of his vague sense of self-preservation, Gilbert thought fast. He tore off a small piece of his napkin, wadded it up, and stuffed it under the broken seal. The two wax halves, now propped back into place, looked pretty good to him. The crack was barely visible. Gilbert took a step back and checked the room. He was still alone. He relaxed for a solid second before the panic slammed back into him.

The hamburger.

It was the last and by far the worst piece of evidence connecting him to the desecration of Ozzy's corpse.

He went quietly to the pillar where the burger was hidden and wrapped the remaining napkins tightly around it. He wondered for a minute about the best place to ditch the evidence. There weren't any trash cans on this floor, and besides, the smell of grease would give him away.

Froehlich'll flip out if he comes back and I'm gone. But this is a maximum emergency. Time for maximum action.

Gilbert shot finger horns at Ozzy and held the burger behind his back. As he headed for the rear of the museum, back by the sarcophagus, he heard what he told himself was the air-conditioning system coming on. The funny thing was that it also sounded strangely like a low moan.

It was a short walk to the loading dock. The exhibit setup crew was still there, finishing their lunch when Gilbert went by. He smiled to them and sidled up to the big Dumpster at the far end of the dock. Moving the burger carefully around to the front of his body, Gilbert dropped the damning evidence into the piles of boxes and excelsior that almost filled the big bin. As the burger sank beneath the top layer of garbage, his adrenaline dropped a couple of notches and he began to relax. He took a deep gulp of fresh air and burped, tasting microwaved meat at the back of his throat. At that moment, the sweating started again. His chest felt like someone had clamped his insides together with vise grips. Gilbert "Fish" Ferris reached into his pocket for his cigarettes, but never got them. Instead, he fell headfirst into the Dumpster.

Gilbert spent his last few moments on earth under a pile of garbage, staring at the bacon cheeseburger that had done him in, knowing he'd never get a Viking funeral or make it to Disneyland or ever be on TV. As sad as it all was—and on the scale of mortifying ways to die, it was right between "tragic unicycle accident" and "smothered by a blow-up sex doll"—it might have been some small consolation to him if he'd known that the same burger that killed him had done exactly the opposite for Ozzy.

3

It was nighttime in the mail room, but, in the mail room, wasn't it always night? That's how it felt to Nelson and it made his blood boil, or whatever passed for blood in his undead veins and arteries. The funny thing about being dead and still on the payroll was that he didn't feel all that different from when he'd been alive. Sure, he couldn't get drunk anymore and his mind wandered into homicidal rage territory a bit more frequently, but for the most part, it was everyone else who was different. Basically, as a mail-room mook—the lowest of the low, even by mook standards—you could get away with murder. So to speak.

Someone knocked on the door of Nelson's dismal broom closet of an office.

"Excuse me, sir."

Nelson looked up to see Fred McCloud, a mook who'd spent nearly a decade down in the dungeon-like mail room without a promotion, commendation, gold star, pat on the head, or any tangible recognition at all.

All of that made him the best second in command that Nelson could hope for.

"What is it, Fred?" said Nelson in a voice the DOPS *So, Now You're a Manager!* manual called "Supportive Indeterminateness." The manual defined SI as "Encouraging without actually committing to any statement, situation, or idea ever. SI is especially useful to managers of departments consisting of any sentient being, living or undead. Neither is to be trusted. Ever. Hence, commitmentless encouragement."

McCloud went on, "This memo addressed to Ellis on the seventh floor is two days old, but I found it in the hold box."

Nelson took the memo and pretended to look it over. He didn't have to read it. He'd already done that and had slipped it into the hold box himself. God knows what bizarre line of inquiry led McCloud to finding it. Statistically, it was about as likely as a wildebeest writing a paper on a new fusion-reactor design, building the reactor, and then running it with a team of other wildebeests.

"Don't worry about it, Fred," said Nelson brightly. "Ellis has come down with a case of the demons, so we're putting aside some of the less important correspondence until he's shipshape again."

McCloud smiled as brightly as Nelson had spoken.

"Got it. Thanks for the heads-up," he said.

Nelson folded the memo and set it aside. Then he put his index finger on McCloud's forehead and said, "Macho Taco Guy Lombardo."

McCloud's eyes went blank, which was an accomplishment considering mooks' milky-white eyes.

"Forget about finding this memo," said Nelson. "In fact, forget about all of Ellis's mail, memos, and packages. I'll handle them from now on. But don't mention that to anyone. Understand?"

"Sure thing, boss," said McCloud cheerfully.

"Now, you're going to forget this whole conversation, but you're going to remember the orders I just gave you."

"Sure thing, boss."

"One more thing. Did you put the new haul of Bayliss's office supplies where I told you?"

McCloud nodded. "In the bin in the hole behind the filing cabinets in your office."

"Good. When I say the magic words, you're going to feel really good and get right back to work. You're not going to remember what we talked about or the office supplies."

"Sure thing, boss."

Nelson touched McCloud's forehead. "Macho Taco Guy Lombardo."

McCloud's shoulder sagged for a second, then rose back into place. He grinned broadly. "I'm sorry. What did you want to see me about?"

Nelson put a hand on his shoulder and spoke in a tone the manual called "Disinterested Affirmation," which the manual defined as "Apparent interest in a subordinate's duties, but with as little actual knowledge of them as possible, thereby constructing a blissful wall of plausible deniability."

"I just wanted you to know what a great job you're doing and that you should keep it up."

"Thanks. I'll do my best," said a happy McCloud before heading back to the mail room.

Nelson stared after him. He'd have to keep a better watch on McCloud.

Can't have the idiot stumbling over every little thing I'm redirecting. I'll never get anything done and he'll eventually say the wrong thing to the wrong person . . .

Nelson's mind drifted pleasantly to all the ways he could murder McCloud without raising anyone's suspicion. He'd already hypnotized the moron. He could order him to fall into the incinerator where they burned old classified documents. Or stumble into the humongous shredder where they chopped up the documents before they burned them. Or trip under the giant press that mashed the document ashes into little models of the DOPS logo that the agency liked to give to visiting busybodies from Washington.

Or I could just shove a filing cabinet on his head and make it look like it was one of the other mooks . . .

That last idea was very appealing, but became less so the more Nelson considered his position as mail-room manager. Trying to murder Coop was what got him demoted down here in the first place. Another demotion would make his plan even harder to pull off.

He'd already experienced a few setbacks along the way, though nothing he couldn't handle. Other mooks weren't the problem. The problem was when some asshole living person would find out about a wayward missive. They'd find it tucked away in a corner or come looking for something Nelson preferred to hold on to. The good news was that no one ever suspected a thing. Nelson covered up the "mistakes" by passing them off as inevitable mook misunderstandings, something he was working to put a stop to. He'd smile and shrug and apologize, and for the most part, everyone was very nice about it. Really, it amazed him, the things you could get away with when you were dead and seen as just fractionally less incompetent than all the other walking corpses around you. All he had to do was hang on, keep holding back certain letters and packages while pushing others through the system, and eventually *it* would come to him. His Excalibur. His Holy Grail. His first-class ticket to Revenge City.

Then it'll be payback time. Starting with Bayliss. Then Coop.

There was a gentle knock on his door and McCloud poked his head in.

"What is it?" said Nelson curtly, for a moment forgetting the manual's managerial voices.

"There's been a situation," McCloud said.

"What kind of situation?"

"It's Albertson and the shredder."

"Yes?"

"All that's left are his feet."

"Where's the rest of him?"

McCloud glanced over his shoulder and back to Nelson. "Kind of everywhere."

Nelson sighed and picked up a bucket he kept next to the filing cabinet. "Get a mop, a shovel, and some tweezers. We're working overtime tonight."

"I'll tell the others," said McCloud excitedly as he jogged back into the mail room.

Nelson remained in his office for a minute, gathering himself. It wasn't so much having to spend the rest of the night cleaning bits of Albertson out of the shredder and light fixtures that bothered him; it was that now he couldn't murder anyone himself. The manual was very clear on that point. No department below field operations was allowed more than one shredding, decapitation, immolation, or consumption of an employee by a hostile entity—human, animal, or cyborg—per quarter. That included mooks. Limbs flying around willy-nilly ruined budgets and lowered morale. Of course, this lowered *his* morale, but there was nothing Nelson could do about that.

A now mortally depressed Nelson took his bucket out into the mail room knowing absolutely that he couldn't kill any of his employees for another three months.

4

Coop was still drinking his first cup of coffee of the day when Giselle got a text from the DOPS saying that Woolrich, their boss—really, everybody's boss—wanted to see them. Coop experienced the usual stab of cold fear that came whenever he had to meet with Woolrich. The feeling was something like the sinking sensation when you're sent to the principal's office as a kid, only Coop got the adult version. This consisted mainly of a wild search for cash and his passport. The feeling wasn't pleasant, he didn't want to go to the meeting, and he spent the next fifteen minutes trying to figure a way out of it. Giselle was no help. She just finished her coffee and got dressed, ignoring him the whole time.

Hunkered over his third coffee, Coop became acutely aware of her standing behind him.

"No," he said.

"It might not be anything," said Giselle. "Maybe he's inviting us to tea. Maybe it's a promotion. Maybe he's finally giving you your own desk."

"I don't want a desk. I'm a crook. Crooks don't have desks. We have tools and cars and six ways out of town."

"And molls. Don't forget molls," said Giselle, ruffling his hair from behind. Coop quickly brushed it back into place.

"Nothing good ever comes from talking to bosses."

"You were the boss of your little gang and look how nice you are."

"This is different."

"How?"

"I don't have heads mounted on the walls."

Giselle gave him a dismissive wave of her hand. "They're not *people* heads."

"Yet. I swear, every time I see him it's like he's measuring my neck to see how big a plaque he'll need."

Giselle went into the bedroom and came out with three ties in her hands. "Pick one," she said.

"No."

"Why not?"

"If I'm going to die, I'm going to be comfortable. And I'm not going out pretty. In fact, I'm not changing at all. If Woolrich wants to see me, I'm going in my pajamas."

Giselle held out the ties. "Don't be an idiot."

He looked at her, then at the ties, and selected a skinny black one, which he tied around the collar of his pajama top.

Giselle looked at her watch. "I'm leaving in ten minutes. I don't care if you're dressed, naked, or wearing a tutu, you're coming with me."

"You're going to put the whammy on me and trick me into going, aren't you?" he said.

"Fogging minds, making little boys see or not see what I want, is what I do best. And you're right. In"—she glanced at her watch—"nine minutes, we're out the door."

Coop took off the tie. "Fine. But if Woolrich turns me into a mook or a windup toy, you're going to miss me."

He went into the bedroom and grudgingly got dressed. At the

last minute, he took a jacket from the closet. It was dark blue and had a little gold crest on the breast pocket. He hated it. In fact, he'd always hated it and wasn't sure how he'd ended up with it in the first place. It was one of those mystery garments that everybody seemed to have one of in their closet. A gift or a drunken purchase on New Year's. Wherever it had come from, Coop hated it and if he was going to get shot or fed to one of the various horrors on the DOPS payroll, he wanted to make sure that the jacket suffered with him.

As he was finishing dressing, Giselle called from the other room. "And don't bring your passport. There's a chip in it and they'll know you have it. It won't look good."

Coop frowned, bent down, and took the passport out from where he'd tucked it into his sock.

When he came into the living room, Giselle smiled and gave him a kiss, wiping lipstick off his mouth with her thumb. As she straightened his tie, Coop said, "What if Woolrich knows about the office supplies?"

Giselle got her shoulder bag. "Then he'd just want to see you—the crook—and not one of his loyal operatives."

Coop thought for a minute. "That kind of makes sense."

"Of course it makes sense. If Woolrich was up to something, he'd have a dozen unmarked vans outside and goons knocking down the door. Relax. This is nothing," Giselle said.

As they walked to the car Coop said, "But what if it *is* something?"

Giselle tossed her bag into the backseat of the car. "Then you're on your own, sailor. I keep my passport duct-taped under the dashboard."

Coop stared at her.

"Don't worry," she said. "I have one for you, too. But you'll have to learn Portuguese and wear three-inch lifts. Also, a dress, Angélica."

"Oh, good. For a second there I thought you were going to make it hard on me."

The walk to Woolrich's office was through a maze of nearly identical corridors on one of the upper floors of the DOPS building. Giselle knew the way by heart, but Coop always imagined having to track down Woolrich's office on his own and getting lost. He'd never find his way out. He'd wander the halls like a ghost, growing thinner and crazier from lack of food and water. He'd wind up a DOPS legend, a cautionary tale for new recruits. Always stick to the buddy system in the management wing, they'd tell them. And if you happen to stumble across a dazed man in rags eating the stuffing from the hall chairs or swinging from the overhead lights, well, just pretend you don't see him. He's been out in the wild for too long. There's no bringing him back.

When they reached Woolrich's office, Giselle knocked, but didn't wait for a response. She opened the door and pulled Coop inside with her. Woolrich was at his desk, signing a large pile of papers with a gold-tipped Montblanc fountain pen. He didn't look up as they came in, but gestured vaguely to a couple of nearby seats. Coop and Giselle sat and waited. No one said anything. The only sound in the room was the scratching of Woolrich's pen. He signed each sheet importantly, with a flourish, like if he kept going long enough he'd win a prize, thought Coop. He looked at Giselle, but she just shrugged. Finally, he couldn't stand it anymore.

"Don't they have machines for that?" he said.

"What?" grunted Woolrich.

"Signature machines. For people who have to sign a lot of papers. Don't they have machines for that?"

Woolrich stopped writing for a second, tilted his head fractionally upward, and looked at Coop. "Of course, why do you ask?"

"It just seems like a lot of papers. Wouldn't a machine be just as good?"

"For some things. Not for others. And not specifically for this."

Woolrich went back to signing the papers. Coop started to say something else, but Giselle put a hand on his arm and shook her head. Coop mouthed, *What the hell is going on?*

Giselle mouthed, *I don't know.*

One more minute, mouthed Coop.

"One more minute and what?" said Woolrich, putting one last sheet of paper atop the pile on his desk. Capping his gold pen, he took a breath and said, "Well, that's enough dead people for one day, don't you think?"

Coop's brow furrowed. "Those are all people you're going to bump off?"

"Well, it's the end of the quarter. Can't have a lot of loose ends running around, can we?" Woolrich said matter-of-factly. "And *I* won't be *bumping off* any of them."

Coop felt cold. "I hope you don't think we're . . ."

Woolrich leaned back in his chair. "You? Either of you? Don't be ridiculous. Neither of you is suited for it, especially you. I'm not even sure we should let you have sharp pencils."

"Thanks for the pep talk," Coop said. "Can we go now?"

Woolrich shook a finger in the air. "Not quite yet."

The left side of his face twitched slightly. It was a leftover from when he'd been possessed earlier in the year by some ghosts during a labor dispute. Since then, he'd grown a mustache in an attempt to hide the affliction, but it just made it worse. Whenever Woolrich's lip jerked upward, it looked like he'd taught a caterpillar to rhumba. It was a mesmerizing sight and Coop had a hard time not staring. Instead, he focused on the fishbowl on the edge of the desk where a small brain with fins swam gentle laps.

There was a knock at the office door and Morty stuck his head in. "Hi. Is it okay to come in?"

Woolrich waved him in and pointed to a chair near where Giselle and Coop sat. Seeing Morty, Coop relaxed a little. They were old friends and criminal partners. Morty was a Flasher. He could open any lock ever made just by looking at it, a useful skill for a couple of thieves. Sure, Morty was responsible for Coop going to jail a couple of years back, but Coop forgave him. Pretty much. Mostly.

He was still thinking it over.

Morty sat down next to Coop and waved to Giselle. She gave him a little wave back.

"I'm sorry I'm late," he said. "I got lost coming from the elevator. It all looks the same out there. Shouldn't there be room numbers or a map or something?"

"That would defeat the purpose," said Woolrich.

"Of what?" said Coop.

"Of it all looking the same."

"Some kind of security thing, is it?" said Morty.

"Exactly."

"It's a good one. I was debating whether to eat my arms or legs first if I got lost."

"Legs," said Coop. "More meat. If you got lucky, you'd only have to eat one before you found the way out."

"You've thought about this, have you?" said Woolrich.

"Every time I come up here to Narnia."

Giselle cleared her throat. "So, now that we're all here, I'm guessing that you have a job for us?"

"Yes," Woolrich said. "A fairly straightforward one, but one which I thought you'd be particularly suited for."

Woolrich pulled a large folder from a drawer and dropped it on his desk. Coop didn't like the look of it. And he didn't like the word *particularly* so close to the words *suited for*. He thought about swinging blades and death curses and a lot of other unpleasant things designed to hurt and/or kill him.

"What kind of job is it?" he asked.

"A simple theft," said Woolrich. "A local museum has a mummy on display. We'd like to have it instead of them."

Woolrich opened the folder and spread its contents across his desk. There were blueprints, photos of the interior and exterior of the museum, a list of employees with their schedules, and other useful information. Giselle picked up the papers and went through them. Coop stood next to her, trying to see while also trying to stay as far as possible from the murder forms. It's not that he was superstitious. It was more that around the DOPS, death seemed like something you could catch, like a cold or a bullet.

"Get in closer, Coop," said Giselle. "Don't you want to see?"

"I'm fine right here."

Morty held up the blueprints, checking for locks in and out of the museum. Giselle looked over the personnel information. Coop poked a fingertip at the photos, trying to ignore the death warrants and all the trophy heads on Woolrich's walls.

After pretending to study things for a minute, he said, "How soon do you want us to do it?"

"Sunday night makes the most sense. The museum is closed on Monday, so you'll have plenty of time to work."

"Which mummy do you want?"

"There's more than one?" said Woolrich.

"A whole roomful," said Coop.

Woolrich took the photo Coop had been studying and looked it over. He made a face.

"Well, that complicates things. Still, not a problem. I have a special consultant who'll be going in with you. An expert on Egyptian art and artifacts."

"In others words, an amateur," said Coop. "Goody."

Woolrich ignored him and set the photo down on the desk. "You can requisition any equipment you want, within reason.

As I said, it's the end of the fiscal quarter, so we need to mind our budgets."

"Of course," said Morty. "An amateur going in with us and a tight budget sounds like the perfect crime."

"It looks like a fairly simple job to me," said Woolrich. "And I'm sure you'll find Dr. Lupinsky a great help when you're inside."

"I'm sure he will be, isn't that right, Coop?" said Giselle. She gathered up the papers from the desk and put them in her bag.

Coop sat quietly for a minute, thinking. "So, what's wrong with it?" he said.

"Nothing," said Woolrich. "It's a mummy."

"Why do you want it?"

"The thaumaturgic antiquities department requisitioned it. I'm sure they have their reasons."

Coop shook his head. "I've been down there. They have dead bodies stacked to the ceiling."

"It's true," said Morty. "Someone really ought to clean up the place."

"They don't want *any* dead body, they want a specific mummy," said Woolrich. "This mummy."

"They have plenty of those, too," said Coop.

Woolrich leaned his elbows on his desk. "Why are you being such a pest about things?"

"I'm just curious. Why are *you* giving us this assignment? Like you said, it looks straightforward. Someone could have covered it in an email. You only hand out the really big jobs."

"Not always," said Woolrich.

"Always," said Coop.

Woolrich sat back up and opened his hands. "Like you, I'm a humble servant of the DOPS. We go where we're told even if we don't necessarily know why."

"Don't mind Coop," said Giselle. "He didn't get to finish his breakfast. It makes him grouchy."

"Breakfast is the most important meal of the day," said Woolrich.

Coop got up. "Great. I'm going out for waffles," he said. "Who's with me?"

"Not so fast, Cooper," said Woolrich.

"Don't worry. You're invited. You look like a muffin man. Bran, am I right? It helps with the digestion."

"Let me rephrase. Sit down and *calm* down," said Woolrich. "This is an ordinary assignment of an ordinary theft. The reason I'm giving it to you is that I wanted to be here to personally introduce you all to Dr. Lupinsky."

Coop sat back down. Giselle gave him a look that practically left a bruise.

"Whatever you say. None of us knows much about Egyptian stuff, so maybe we could use some help. When do we meet him?"

"Right now," said Woolrich. He shouted at the office door. "Dr. Lupinsky. Are you out there yet?"

Oh, great, he's deaf, thought Coop. "I hope he has a monocle," he mumbled.

"And a pith helmet," said Morty.

Giselle said, "Shh."

The door to the hall opened and a five-foot-tall octopus walked into the room. That's what Coop saw at first. He glanced at Giselle and Morty. By the looks on their faces, it was clear that they were seeing it, too. Coop looked back at the octopus. This time, it looked to him more like a cat. A cat on top of an octopus. Coop closed his eyes, and when he opened them again, the knot of fear in his throat loosened a bit. Just a bit. He realized that the thing wasn't an octopus or a cat. It was a robot with a black-and-white television perched on top, and on the television screen, a thin, young cat paced back and forth. Even though it was obvious that the cat was a video image, Coop got the distinct impression that it was looking at him.

"What a cute kitty," said Giselle. "What is it? Abyssinian?"

"No," said Woolrich. "It's Dr. Lupinsky."

The robot glided into the room on its metallic tentacles. It used one to close the door behind it and held out the other to Morty. Morty looked pale, but eventually he put out his hand to the tentacle and shook it.

Giselle leaned across Coop and said, "Hi. I'm Giselle. Nice to meet you, Doctor."

The robot extended a tentacle to her and the cat sat up. A subtitle appeared across the bottom of the screen.

Purrrrrrr.

The tinny sound of a happy cat came from the television's small speakers.

"And this is Coop," Giselle said.

The octo-cat held out a tentacle to Coop. A subtitle appeared on the screen.

Pleased to meet you. I've heard a lot about you.

Coop shook Dr. Lupinsky's tentacle. "I haven't heard nearly enough about you, doc." He looked at Woolrich. "Why is there a cat on the television?"

A subtitle appeared.

I used to be a cat.

"Of course. It all makes sense now."

Woolrich twitched. "While studying some arcane magic texts, the good doctor transformed himself into a cat. When he died, his ghost entered the nearest viable object. The television. It's all very simple."

"No, it's not," said Coop. "It's all very weird. Why was he a cat? Some kind of mouse fetish?"

Woolrich shook his head. "He was studying Bast at the time, the Egyptian cat deity. The transformation was a mistake."

"Like the television was a mistake?"

"Exactly."

"And this is who you want us to partner with?"

The cat paced excitedly back and forth across the screen. There were more subtitles.

I understand that my appearance can take some time getting used to.

"Good call," said Coop. "No offense, doc, but I don't work with amateur crooks, robots, cats, or televisions. There's no percentage in it."

"That was yesterday," said Woolrich. "For this assignment, not only will you be working with Dr. Lupinsky, I'm putting you personally in charge of his well-being."

"You're fucking kidding me," said Coop.

"What was that?"

Giselle looked at the octopus. "He said, 'I'm looking forward to the job and working closely with Dr. Lupinsky.'"

Woolrich nodded. "Yes. That's what I thought he said."

Coop didn't feel so much like a drowning man as a drowning man wearing a chum tuxedo in a school of sharks. Sharks with tommy guns.

"Okay," said Coop, pulling himself back together. "Let's forget Robocat for a minute. The plans and everything you gave us are fine, but they're not the same as being there. I want to go to the museum and walk the layout."

"Naturally," said Woolrich. "Dr. Lupinsky can come with you."

"No, he can't."

"Of course he can. We spent a lot of money on his legs."

Lupinsky stood on the equivalent of his toes and did a kind of short, metallic soft-shoe routine. When it was over, Woolrich, Giselle, and Morty clapped. Coop shook his head.

"He can't come with us."

Morty leaned forward. "I think what Coop means is that while we're grateful for the doctor's expertise . . ."

Purrrrrrr, appeared on the television.

Morty went on: "As a member of the team, he isn't what you'd call 'low profile.'"

Woolrich gestured to Giselle. "That's why you have a Marilyn."

"I'll handle it," she said. "Don't worry."

"I wasn't."

"What about video surveillance?" said Coop. "Giselle can mess with people's heads, but she can't fool cameras."

"We've already tapped into their system. It will conveniently go down when you're inside." Woolrich reached under his desk and pulled out a small backpack. "You won't want to forget this."

"What is it?"

"The doctor's batteries. Do you think that's a nuclear television? No. It's old. And it takes D batteries."

Coop took the pack off the desk and weighed it in his hand. It felt like a cinder block. "Why can't the cat carry his own batteries?"

A tinny growl came from the television speakers. A subtitle appeared.

Grrrrrrrr.

"Dr. Lupinsky isn't a pack mule," said Woolrich.

"I'm pretty sure we can agree that 'mule' isn't the word anyone is thinking when they look at him," said Morty.

Hisssssss.

"Which isn't a value judgment," Morty added quickly. "In fact, we're all very fond of cats around here. Right, Coop?"

"I'm not," said Coop. "The neighbor's cat ate my hamster when I was a kid."

"You had a hamster?" said Giselle.

"It was my brother's. He abandoned it and I took care of it. Then the cat got in."

"Your poor hamster," said Giselle. "You never told me about it."

"It probably choked him up too much. That childhood stuff sticks with you," said Morty.

"I wasn't choked up. I just don't trust cats."

"He's not a cat!" shouted Woolrich. "He studied at the Sorbonne. He has a doctorate from Harvard. Right, Doctor?"

"He's gone," said Coop.

It was true. The only thing on the television screen was a grainy black-and-white test pattern.

"Look what you've done. Dr. Lupinsky?" called Woolrich. He looked at Coop. "Apologize."

"To an octopus?"

Morty frowned. "A minute ago you said cat."

"Woolrich said he isn't a cat."

Woolrich stood up. "Apologize now or you're fired and we both know what that means."

"I'm off the badminton team?"

"Jail."

"Do it, Coop," said Morty.

"Right now," said Giselle through gritted teeth.

Coop held up his hands. "Fine. Sorry, doc. Here, kitty kitty."

"Stop that," said Woolrich.

Coop looked around. He was outnumbered and the door was too far to run to and, anyway, he'd get lost and Giselle would never speak to him again.

"Hey, doc," he said. "Listen. Why don't you come along and help us case the museum? It can't hurt to have an extra pair of eyes."

The cat came back onto the television screen. It sat down and began cleaning its paws.

Coop looked at Woolrich. "What is that?"

"I think it means he accepts your apology," said Gisele.

"I wasn't apolo—"

Giselle shifted in her seat, discreetly kicking Coop in the leg before settling down again.

Coop looked Lupinsky over. "Do we have to take all of him? Can't we just wheel in the television?"

"You'll want all of him. Would you show them why, Doctor?" said Woolrich.

Lupinsky walked to the wall and kept going, strolling up it and across the ceiling. When he was directly above Coop, he reached down with a couple of tentacles and picked him up.

"Um," said Coop.

Woolrich sat back contentedly. "While Dr. Lupinsky's current situation can be problematic, it also gives him certain advantages. Wouldn't you agree?"

"Definitely," said Coop, dangling several feet off the floor. "Welcome to the team, doc. Can I get down now?"

Lupinsky set Coop gently on the floor and walked back down the wall.

"Thanks," said Coop.

The cat opened its mouth.

Meow.

"That will be all for now, Doctor. We'll coordinate a rendez-vous time so you can all go to the museum together."

As Lupinsky went to the door, the cat stood up and stretched.

It was nice meeting you all. Especially you, Mr. Cooper.

"Coop," he said. "Coop is fine."

See you soon, Coop.

With that, Lupinsky left, quietly closing the door behind him.

"That's it for now," Woolrich said. "You'll need some time to look over the plans and check out the museum. Let me know when you're ready to go and we'll bring Dr. Lupinsky back into the loop."

"Swell," said Coop. Morty picked up the backpack with the batteries and the three of them headed for the door. Just before they went out, Woolrich called after them.

"And Cooper. No more office-supply heists, all right?"

Coop turned white. Giselle pulled him out into the hall.

"You steal office supplies?" said Morty.

"It was a one-time thing," said Coop.

They walked back to the elevators, Giselle in the lead.

"I thought that thing was going to eat you," said Morty.

"So did I," said Coop.

"He's not a thing," said Giselle. "Dr. Lupinsky is a person."

"A very scary person," said Morty. "I wonder what kind of toys cats like?"

"You're not serious," said Coop.

Morty shrugged. "Why make enemies when you can make friends?"

Coop thought about it. "Okay. Put me down for one of those feather things on a string."

"Aw. You forgive him for your hamster," said Giselle.

"Never."

5

If money wanted to take a few weeks off, kick back, and catch some rays, it would do it in Carrwood, a pretty little private community in the verdant hills of north Los Angeles. Carrwood had more security than the Kremlin. Invading rats and squirrels found inside the gates weren't poisoned, but trapped, packaged, and shipped to a small, but well-staffed rodent retirement community outside Palms Springs. To say that Carrwood was affluent was like saying the sinking of the *Titanic* was a bit of a whoopsie.

The community was named for its developer, Joseph Pitney Carr, who made his fortune in real estate and timber, but started out running whiskey from Mexico during Prohibition. In fact, Carrwood itself began as a small vaguely "orientalist" speakeasy called *Báichī De Pìyän*, which Carr had been told meant the Devil's Boudoir.

In reality it meant the Idiot's Asshole.

Carr hid his illicit hooch from the prying eyes of local cops and federal snoops by stashing it in a large cave he had dug out of a local hillside. In 1927, in order to clear land for a new housing project, a real estate developer dynamited a small grove of trees directly above Carr's cave. It cleared the land all right, as the high-octane Mexican gin and bourbon sent a good portion of the developer's real estate investment into the stratosphere. The company promptly went bust and Carr began buying up the land.

He used his speakeasy earnings to build the first mansions in what would come to be called Carrwood. And didn't sell a single one. Frustrated with the real estate racket, Carr put up an ornate fence around the property while contemplating his next move. To his astonishment, people immediately flocked to Carrwood for the chance to live somewhere so exclusive that buyers weren't even allowed inside. Without realizing it, Carr had mistakenly invented the first gated community in Southern California.

After that, Carr went a little fence crazy. Unfortunately, none of those investments worked out. His Riviera-themed pet resort went bust in a year and his gated duck pond was a complete disaster. People couldn't get close enough to the ducks to toss them small bits of bread, so they'd hurl whole loaves over the fence. By most Sunday afternoons, entire flocks of mallards would be laid out with concussions or pinned under piles of sourdough along the shore. Carr discreetly removed the fence and went back to selling inflated real estate to local high rollers. To this day, no duck will land in Carrwood. They'll fly over and shit there, but not a single one will land.

That afternoon in the heart of Carrwood, in a sprawling ranch home on Vieux Carré Lane, six stalwart agents of change had secretly gathered around a marble-topped kitchen island plotting revolution.

The home was owned by the parents of Heather and Dylan Barker. They and the other members of the cabal drank beer and orange juice waiting for Consuela, the housekeeper, to go into the backyard to visit the gardener.

Dylan watched her leave and turned to his sister. "Do you think they're getting it on?"

"Of course they are," said Heather.

"Hot."

"They're married, you moron." Heather rolled her eyes. "You'd know that if you ever talked to them."

"I don't speak Spanish."

"They speak English."

"Huh," Dylan said. "No one ever told me."

Heather pointed a can of locally sourced microbrew at her brother. "That's pure class privilege is what that is," she said.

"Says the girl with the new Mercedes."

"It's a hybrid!"

"With heated leather seats," said Dylan. "You're a vegetarian."

"Vinyl seats have a huge carbon footprint," said Heather.

"Not as huge as your big mouth," mumbled her brother.

Heather threw a handful of imported wasabi peanuts at her brother, but he ducked out of the way.

Tyler, the group's leader, picked up a stray peanut from the counter and put it back in the bowl. "Now that the house is secure, can we get down to business? I think Brad had something to say."

Brad wasn't from Carrwood and found the place both frightening and bewildering. He drove a hand-me-down Honda Civic that was older than most of his fellow revolutionaries. He didn't resent Heather and Dylan's wealth; it's just that it was as alien to him as moon rocks. He was afraid to come into contact with any object or surface in the house in case he accidently marred it. His glass of orange juice sat untouched a good six inches from his hand.

"It's about our last operation," he said. "I think it's great that we liberated all the mice from that medical lab, but they'd all been hand-raised. Remember when we tried to release them into the wild? They just stood there and followed us home to my place. Now I have an apartment full of mice with ears on their backs. I mean, they're friendly enough, but I feel like I have to whisper all the time."

"You know the ears don't work, right?" said Warren, a heavyset young man with a beard that Rasputin would consider unruly.

"Yeah, but it's like they're judging me."

Linda, seated next to Dylan, said, "You need to get out more, man."

"You try dating with an apartment full of Frankenmice," said Brad.

"I have a garage full of glow-in-the-dark guinea pigs, so stop whining," said Warren.

"I'm not whining. My voice just gets high when I'm upset."

"That's pretty much the definition of whining," said Sarah, Tyler's girlfriend. Heather hated her.

"What was your point, Brad?" said Tyler.

"My point is that maybe we need to rethink our procedures."

"Do you have any suggestions?"

Brad squirmed in his seat. He hated being put on the spot in front of Sarah, who had about as much interest in him as she did in the way toilets worked in space. "Yeah. Can't we just liberate, you know, normal animals for a while? One of the mice got out the other day and I thought my landlord was going to call the cops."

"Lucky for us she didn't," said Sarah.

Brad shook his head gravely. "She totally freaked out, though. Started yelling at me in some foreign language that had, like, no vowels. Then she called a priest who did an exorcism. Now the hall outside my apartment is covered in prayer beads and crucifixes. Everyone in the building thinks I'm Dracula. I mean, I don't even eat dairy."

"Fine. Regular animals for a while," said Tyler.

"Don't say 'animals.' They're beings like us," said Linda.

"Won't that get a little confusing?" said Heather. "'Liberating beings' sounds like I want to liberate Warren."

"I'm cool right here," Warren said.

"See? Warren is cool where he is," said Dylan.

Linda looked out the window to the backyard. "Still. It doesn't seem right."

"Let's vote on it," said Tyler.

Hands went up around the kitchen island.

"The motion is carried," he said. "From now on animals will be known as beings."

Sarah cocked her head to the side. "That leaves Warren out. He's definitely an animal."

Warren grinned. "It's true."

Heather stared at Tyler's perfect hands as he sipped his beer.

"Back to our original question," he said. "Does anyone have any suggestions for animals . . . beings we can liberate?"

"What about the zoo?" said Dylan.

Sarah raised her eyebrows. "Are you kidding? Those animals—beings—eat better than some of us do."

"But they should be back home."

"Good luck driving a load of anacondas to the Amazon," said Warren. "When one of them swallows you, I'm not going in to get you out."

"What about bats?" said Brad.

"Too creepy," said Sarah.

"Penguins?" said Linda.

Heather looked at her. "They live in Antarctica."

"My boyfriend works at a 7-Eleven. They have a big freezer in the back."

"Is it three thousand miles wide?" said Warren. "'Cause if it isn't, it's not the same thing."

"I don't think so, but I can ask."

Tyler looked back to Brad. "Since you started this line of inquiry, do you have any other suggestions?"

Brad gnawed on a thumbnail. Finally, he said, "I don't know. I say we lay low for a while, figure out what to do with the mice and guinea pigs, and just keep our eyes open."

"Anyone have any other ideas?" said Tyler. "No? Then let's take a vote. Who's for taking a break and reassessing our methodology?"

Hands went up. Tyler counted.

"That's it, then. We sit tight and look for the right target."

"Do we have to use the word 'target'?" said Linda.

"What do you suggest?" said Dylan.

"'Beingeration.'"

"What?" said Heather.

"'Beingeration.' Like liberating beings."

"I'm not voting on that," Warren said.

"Can we table that discussion for another time?" said Tyler.

Linda crossed her arms and pouted. "Fine."

"If that's all the business for today, let's order a pizza."

"Cool," said Dylan. "What should we get?"

"'Friendmancipate,'" said Linda.

"I was thinking more like mushrooms."

"Like 'friend' and 'emancipate,'" Linda explained.

"We decided no more business tonight," said Sarah.

"How about pineapple?" said Heather.

"On pizza? I live with mutant mice. I'm not going to eat mutant food," said Brad.

Warren nodded. "Yeah. No one wants your freaky fruit pie."

"Besides, pineapples are an invasive species," said Dylan.

Brad made a face. "No, they're not. They grow wild all over Hawaii."

"Then what am I thinking of?"

"We have mushrooms," said Tyler. "Do we want anything else on it?"

"Kudzu," said Dylan.

"They make kudzu pizza?" said Sarah.

"No. That's the invasive species."

"No one wants that," said Linda.

"I know."

"Then why did you say it?"

"I was trying to make a point about invasive species," said Dylan.

"I think it's clear that no one wants to support an invasive species," Linda said.

"I do," said Warren. "I vote for kudzu."

"Don't start," said Tyler.

Warren pounded a fist on the counter top. "I want to friend-mancipate the kudzu!"

Tyler turned to Linda. "See what you started?"

"Sorry."

"Can I just order a separate pineapple pizza?" said Heather.

Warren shook his head. "Pizza is an invasive food. I want a corn dog."

"Shut up, Warren," said Sarah.

He wrapped his arms around himself. "I'm feeling pretty mopressed right now. That's 'mocked' and 'oppressed.'"

"The pizza place doesn't have corn dogs," said Tyler.

"Then I'll eat your imperialist flatbread, but only because I wish to liberate it and all the baby pizzas into my stomach."

"How about olives to go with the mushrooms?" said Tyler. "And if anyone says that olives are an invasive species or a despotic vegetable, I'm burning this place down."

"Technically, olives are a fruit, not a vegetable," said Linda.

"That's it. Someone give me a match."

Heather finished her beer. "This is my parents' summer home. You can't burn it."

"Yeah. Burning a whole house is a bigger carbon footprint than vinyl seats," said Dylan.

Heather glared at him.

"I guess it's mushrooms and nothing else, then," said Tyler.

"How about burritos?" said Warren.

"Shut up, Warren," said Heather and Dylan.

While the others argued, Brad looked past them into the living room, where a television the size of a rhinoceros silently played an ad by a local car dealer, Sheriff Wayne Jr. What caught Brad's eye was that Sheriff Wayne Jr. was shouting about his low, low prices from the back of a weary and distressed-looking llama.

"Hey, guys," said Brad, pointing. "What about this guy?"

6

The morning after their meeting with Woolrich, Coop, Giselle, Morty, and Dr. Lupinsky pulled into the parking lot of the Brian Z. Pierson Museum of Art, Antiquities, and Folderol. They were in a blacked-out DOPS van because it was the only vehicle Dr. Lupinsky could fit in. Coop wasn't pleased. To him and 99 percent of the world, a blacked-out van meant one of two things: cops or serial killers, and both groups were high on his Run Like Hell From list. Still, they'd made it to the museum without law enforcement stopping them to look for dismembered limbs or old ladies wanting them to find their lost cats. And that was good, because Coop had his own cat problems.

Before they got out of the van, Giselle called the DOPS on a secure satellite phone with enough antennae and weird wires trailing from the sides that it looked like a pinup girl designed by extraterrestrial crabs.

"We're going in. Kill the cameras," said Giselle. She noticed Coop looking at her and said, "What?"

"One day that thing is going to turn your brain into lobster bisque."

"Don't be such a technophobe."

"I'm not a technophobe. I just don't trust all those DOPS gadgets."

"It's just a phone, Coop."

"She's right," said Morty. "I have one just like it. They're fine as long as you don't talk too long. Then sometimes you can get a little dizzy."

"That's what I mean," said Coop. "Better check your ears for tarantulas."

"If I have bugs in my head, I don't want to know."

"There are no bugs, Morty," said Giselle. "You just have to be careful because the phone's electromagnetic field can have a tiny effect on your balance."

Morty made a face. "Is that a nice way of saying I have cancer?"

"No. Just don't sleep with it close to your head."

"Good. Because I'd rather have bugs. I've got a cousin who's an exterminator. He'd give me a good rate for a blowout."

"I thought the bug business was a front to get into buildings," said Coop.

"It is, but he has to have the gear to look legit, right? He cleared out the mice on my ex-sister-in-law's brother's farm. Of course, all the trees died, but they're what attracted the mice in the first place, so it kind of worked out for everyone."

"Except the mice," said Giselle.

"They did fine. Moved over to a local college campus. Sure, some got caught by one of the labs and now they have ears on their backs, but they eat good and they're warm at night."

"Kind of like us, right, doc?" said Coop. "Federal mice running a maze for a piece of cheese."

The cat on Dr. Lupinsky's screen meowed.

Don't talk about mice. I'm getting hungry.

"Do you eat, doc?" said Morty.

Metaphorically. They send in video mice sometimes. They don't taste like anything, but they're fun to chase.

Morty said, "My mom would smack me if I played with my food. Here's a big government scientist getting paid to do it."

"I'm sure Dr. Lupinsky does a lot more than play with mice," said Giselle.

Thank you.

"When was the last time you did a field job like this, doc?" said Coop.

The cat stopped pacing for a minute and lay down on its back like it was thinking.

The Tutankhamen tour. New Orleans, 1978.

"Wait. You haven't done fieldwork in over thirty years? How did you wind up on this job?" said Coop.

My legs finally work. For a while, I was on a little flying saucer. That was fun. But it ran off a small fission reactor from Roswell. That put some people off. They used to call me Kittytastrophe.

"That's not very nice," said Morty.

I couldn't really blame them after the incident in the basement.

"This being the DOPS, let me guess. You had a meltdown," said Coop.

The cat put its paws over its face.

Did you know that we don't work in the original DOPS building? That one is gone. Dropped through a small wormhole created by the physics lab.

"They dropped a whole building down a wormhole?" said Giselle.

Dr. Lupinsky said *mrrreeeoow*. Below it read:

I'm afraid so.

"Where did it come out?"

No one knows, but occasionally strange dumping fees appear in the feeds from deep-space radar.

"Got to pay your bills, doc," said Coop. "A bunch of upstanding citizens like the DOPS stiffing an interdimensional garbage dump? What kind of an impression are we making out in the universe?"

"That's probably why UFOs are always probing people you know where," said Morty. "They think it's where we keep our wallets."

Giselle's phone beeped. She spoke into it. "Great. Thanks." She put it in her bag. "The cameras are down. We have the run of the place."

"Let's get you out, doc," said Morty.

He and Coop opened the back of the van and a wheelchair ramp lowered itself to the ground. Dr. Lupinsky stepped gingerly down it to the pavement.

"You doing your Marilyn thing, Giselle?" said Coop.

"Already on mind patrol. No one can see any of us."

"Remember her range isn't infinite, so let's stay together when we get inside," said Coop. "That goes double for you, doc. Someone sees you, they'll think it's *War of the Worlds* and you're here looking for loose change in their asses."

Understood.

Canvas banners hung all over the museum grounds advertising HARKHUF: TREASURE OF THE DEEP DESERT. Coop stopped at the bottom of the front steps, staring up at a banner that spanned the whole front of the building. He said to Morty, "You see the ropes on the right? Some of the grommets holding them in place are loose."

Morty pointed to the other end of the canvas. "There's one over there that's torn."

"Nice," said Coop.

"What's nice?" said Giselle.

Coop pointed. "The banner. It's cheap. The museum couldn't afford to put out the cash for even a big show like this."

"That's good news for us, right?"

"We'll see," said Coop cautiously.

Giselle led the way into the museum, standing next to an oblivious security guard as she walked in the front door. Morty turned and walked backward a few yards.

"That front isn't much to look at security-wise. Take down the power and kill the alarms, I could get in here with a pair of chopsticks and a credit card."

"Speaking of taking the power down, what kind of emergency generator do they have?"

"Let me see," said Morty, staring at the blueprints as they walked.

The group didn't so much walk across the lobby as they did a silent samba. Since no one could see them, it was their job to get out of everyone else's way. Luckily, it was early enough in the day that the crowd was small. Unluckily, everyone there had their noses shoved into museum brochures about the exhibit and weren't looking where they were walking. This forced Coop and his group to be doubly careful. Coop was most worried about Dr. Lupinsky, but soon saw that he didn't have to be. On his octopus legs, the doctor did a respectable Gene Kelly routine around everyone that came his way. He even seemed to be enjoying himself.

I guess thirty years in a basement can make you a little loopy.

He remembered his last eighteen-month stretch in jail, the one Morty was responsible for. By the time he got out, he might have danced a little jig himself, only Morty showed up, and smacking him was just as good.

Lupinsky was first into the Harkhuf exhibit. The room was crowded with mummies, jewelry, pottery, and canopic jars surrounding Harkhuf's ornate sarcophagus in the middle. Coop stopped in the doorway.

"What are you thinking?" said Giselle.

"It's actually kind of impressive. Pretty, even. Kind of, I don't know . . . mysterious."

"Wow. Charlie Cooper getting moony over a three-thousand-year-old dead guy in his underwear."

"Be nice or I won't steal you a snow globe."

"Liar. You always steal a snow globe. It's your signature move in places like this. Al Capone didn't have anything in his vault, but when they open yours, they're going to find floor-to-ceiling snow globes."

Coop went to Harkhuf's sarcophagus to check out the security. "It's L.A.'s fault. When was the last time we had Christmas snow? Christmas ought to have snow."

Giselle stood next to him. "Sentimental is what you are. A sentimental, hamster-loving, snowman maker."

Coop started to say something, but Morty weaved his way through the crowd, with the museum blueprints in his hands. "The emergency generator you were worried about?" he said.

"Yeah?"

"It doesn't exist."

Coop looked at the blueprints with him. "Are you sure?"

Morty slapped the plans with the back of his hand. "This place is a dump," he said.

"I get what you mean," said Coop. "It's like it's daring us not to break in."

"It's an insult to crooks. It's our civic duty to take everything," said Morty.

"I agree."

Giselle held up another DOPS device. It looked like a little satellite dish mounted on a piece of honey-glazed ham.

"What about magic traps and curses?" said Coop.

Giselle shook her head. "Nothing. Morty's right. I say teach them a lesson and take it all."

Dr. Lupinsky stood across the sarcophagus from Coop, gazing inside.

"How about you, doc? Want a whole museum in your office?"

Dr. Lupinsky stood up and swung his kitty television head around the room. The cat sneezed.

Sorry.

"No problem. What do you think of the show? Should we clean it out to teach them a lesson?"

Don't bother. Most of it is junk.

"What do you mean?" said Coop a little nervously.

Besides Harkhuf, there are six other mummies in the room. The ones that are real are in poor condition. From what I can see, at least two others are replicas, and not very good ones. It's the same with the tomb ornaments.

"But Harkhuf is okay," said Coop.

Dr. Lupinsky turned back to the sarcophagus.

He's excellent. The only specimen worth taking with us.

"I don't get it. Why would the museum put up a bunch of third-rate stuff?" said Morty.

"According to you, everything about the museum is third rate. They probably wanted to make their sad little show look bigger and the museum more successful," said Giselle.

I agree flashed on Dr. Lupinsky. The cat on his screen froze. The screen went blank for a second, then flickered back to life. The cat staggered and lay down.

"What's wrong, doc?" said Coop.

I think my batteries are low.

Coop looked at Morty. "Did you bring the batteries?"

Morty heaved the heavy backpack from his shoulder. "Of course. And I carried it in, so you get to carry it out. Right? It's only fair."

"Sure. Whatever," said Coop. "Just get him open."

Morty led Lupinsky to an empty corner of the room. It was a dangerous business, moving through the crowd with several hundred pounds of metal octopus staggering like it was on a motor-oil-and-vodka bender.

When Morty got Dr. Lupinsky to the corner, he pulled the

back off the television and started removing the old D batteries. He handed the used ones to Coop, who handed them to Giselle. "We're still out of sight, right?" he said to her.

"We're fine," she said. "Just don't drop anything."

As she said it, Morty fumbled a couple of batteries, trying to hand them off to Coop. They landed on the floor and rolled all the way across the room. The *crack* as they hit the marble was loud enough to get everybody's attention. Luckily, the batteries rolled away from them, bounced off the bottom of the sarcophagus, and kept going. A guard with sleep-deprived eyes picked them up and put them in his pocket. He looked around for a minute before going back to looking sleepy and bored.

Coop held open the pack with the good batteries for Morty. He took fistfuls, fitting them into the compartment in the back of the television as quickly as he could. When it was full, he closed the door.

Dr. Lupinsky jumped up on his tentacles. The cat on the television ran wildly back and forth across the screen.

A mad purr came from the tinny speaker.

Thank you. That's much better.

"Glad to help," said Morty. "What do you think? Have we seen enough?"

I have. There's nothing of value besides Harkhuf, some of his burial items, and the sarcophagus itself. It's a shame we can't take it, too.

"Woolrich didn't say anything about the box. He just wants the mummy," said Coop. "Less work is good work."

The cat lowered itself on its legs, with its butt in in the air.

I could carry it.

"It won't fit in the van," said Coop.

Morty tilted his head. "I don't know. If we move some stuff around . . ."

"It won't fit," Coop insisted.

Morty straightened up. "You're right. It probably wouldn't fit."

I'd like to come on the robbery.

"Sorry, doc. We can handle the job. You're a smart guy, but you're just a part-time crook. Understand?"

Yes. I understand.

"Let's get out of here," said Morty. "This place depresses me."

"Me, too," said Coop.

The other two agreed and they headed out together. In the lobby, Coop walked away from the group.

"Coop! I don't have you covered anymore," whispered Giselle.

"I'm getting a snow globe."

"Aren't you going to steal it?"

He stopped and looked around the place. "It's just too pathetic for that. I'll meet you at the van," he said, pulling out some cash.

The others went outside and Coop spent twenty-seven dollars on a snow globe with a figure of a mummy inside that looked less like Harkhuf and more like toilet paper wrapped around a rotisserie chicken. It made his bad mood worse. He thought about tossing the thing in the trash but instead he paid for it and palmed a pack of gum on the way out. Morty and Giselle had been right. Robbing this dump was their civic duty. It was like going to the moon. Sure, there weren't any moon people or lakes full of moon water, but it was just what the country needed to feel better about itself. Stealing from a place like this, a place that was just daring them to do it . . . it was what all of them needed. A nice night out breaking the law and knowing there wasn't anything anyone could do about it.

Coop tucked the snow globe under his arm and tore the wrapper off the gum. Maybe things were going to work out all right after all.

Froehlich watched the batteries bounce off the sarcophagus and gently come to rest against the side of his left shoe. He looked around for whoever might have dropped them, but not seeing anyone, he picked them up.

D cells. You don't see these around that much anymore.

They were the most interesting thing he'd seen all day.

After one last look around, he put the batteries in his pocket. That was the last thing the museum needed. Someone tripping, and then a lawsuit, just when the show was taking off. Well, maybe *taking off* was a bit optimistic. But Harkhuf was bringing in the biggest crowds the museum had seen in years.

We don't need the story about a lawsuit eating up time on the news when they should be talking about the exhibit.

That's why he'd worked so carefully with management to hush up what had happened to that idiot Gilbert. Luckily, no one on the loading dock saw him fall into the Dumpster. The body was still limp when Froehlich had it transferred with a load of new trash into the big industrial compactor. Mr. Klein from upstairs had already given him some under-the-table "discretionary cash" to make the problem go away. All he had to do was call a friend in the hauling business and Gilbert would be in a landfill under a ton of debris by the end of the day. There was just one thing that bothered him.

Okay, two things. Froehlich blew into his cupped hand and sniffed. He'd heard some of the guards say that his breath smelled like instant coffee, and the comment had stuck with him. He'd started chewing spearmint xylitol gum. It was supposed to help, but he couldn't tell any difference. The inside of his mouth still smelled to him like a two-day-old coffee filter in a Tijuana cathouse—something, sadly, he knew a bit about.

The other thing that bothered him about Gilbert's idiot death was that it might have been a missed opportunity.

Maybe the museum shouldn't have covered it up at all. Maybe they should have played it up. Turned it into a front-page story. Maybe drop some hints about a mummy's curse. Why not? Harkhuf was a good-looking guy, but he couldn't fill the room himself. No, they'd had to call in favors from small out-of-town museums and even a couple of sideshows to borrow their flea-bitten stiffs. They'd even resorted to renting a couple from a movie prop company.

But the show was still, well, limp in his eyes, and sales at the gift shop were down, not up. Maybe Gilbert had been right about billing Harkhuf as a brutal, heavy-metal mummy. What had he called Harkhuf? Ozzy. Yes. Ozzy, the Metal Mummy. Who would be his next victim? They could build a whole ad campaign around that. Maybe even get some sponsors. If the board liked it, Froehlich wouldn't need to mention that it was Gilbert's idea. If they hated it, he could pass it off as a loser's dying words. But if they liked it, it could change a lot of things for him. Starting with his job. Froehlich didn't want to end his days upside down in a Dumpster. Ozzy could be a good first step back away from that lousy fate. As long as no one ever found out about the fakes.

But what are the chances of that happening?

7

It was over ninety degrees in the Valley, but Sheriff Wayne Jr. was dressed
to kill. A white Stetson with a white leather jacket, vest, shirt,
pants, and boots. The jacket and vest had LEDs sewn into them
so he could light up when they shot commercials at night. It
was a great effect, he thought. The Electric Cowboy meets Elvis.
What's not to love?

Today was an afternoon shoot and it had been going on way
too goddamn long for his taste.

"Action!" said Chris, the director.

Sheriff Wayne took a loping step toward the camera.

"Hi! I'm Sheriff Wayne Jr., blowing away high prices in the
sunny San Fernando Valley!"

He pulled out the two six-guns from the holster he wore low
across his hips, and fired them into the air.

"Yee-haw!"

"Cut!" called Chris, the director. He was a recent USC gradu-
ate who didn't dream about his girlfriend anymore, but instead
dreamed about Kubrick and Scorsese's tracking shots. He had
the day off from running the cameras for porn shoots and was

making a little money on the side working in a broiling-hot parking lot.

"Did you get it this time?" said Sheriff Wayne.

"Let me check the playback."

"Yeah, you do that."

Sheriff Wayne had about had it with the kid, what with his funny camera angles and fiddling with the lights. Hell, he didn't even want the damned llama in the shot. *Probably some kind of animal rights homo,* thought Sheriff Wayne. He bummed a cigarette from one of the sound guys and waited to hear the verdict.

"Well, Sheriff Wayne," said Chris. "Here's the thing . . ."

Sheriff Wayne pulled one of the six-shooters and pointed it at Chris's head. "Here's what thing?"

Chris froze by the video monitor. He wasn't afraid of pissing himself. He'd sweated away far too much water for that. But if he died now he knew that his entire movie legacy would be a second-place prize for a short film at school, and being principal photographer on *Cheerleader Taco Truck.*

Chris put up his hands. "Please . . ." he said.

Sheriff Wayne smiled and reholstered the gun. "Don't be an ass, son. They're fake. You think the insurance company would let me run around with loaded guns out here? Hell, I'd shoot half of my customers. Now give me some good news."

The highlights on Sheriff Wayne's forehead were blown out from sweat, a plane's shadow had ruined the pristine parking lot full of shiny used cars in the background, and, at the last minute, a stray dog had taken a dump by a Prius. All of which Chris knew he could fix with enough beer and his computer.

"Looks great, Sheriff!" he called, giving him a big thumbs-up.

"Good to hear it, Chris. Because the truth is, these guns are real, they are loaded, and I have more lawyers in my family than a bear has pecker hairs. So, what do you say we wrap this up for today?"

Chris started to say something to the crew, but they were already packing up the equipment faster than he'd ever seen before.

"An excellent idea," said Chris. He was smiling so hard it hurt. It was like half of his face was trying to hide behind the other half. He suddenly longed to be back on the set of his first fetish porn shoot, *Forrest Gimp*. There was air-conditioning, pretty girls, free Red Bull, weed, and no guns.

Sheriff Wayne was already walking back to his office. "When can I see a cut?" he called.

"End of the week," said Chris.

"Great. Nice working with you, son. Let's do it again."

Chris waved and called, "I hope your llama gets rabies and bites you."

Sheriff Wayne, who couldn't hear a word, waved and walked into his office.

"What were you yelling about?" said Donna, his secretary. They'd met at an RV show in Tarzana and tested out the sleeping facilities and suspension on several camper models before the weekend was over. Fortunately, Mrs. Sheriff Wayne Jr. never found out. In gratitude—and to keep her around—Sheriff Wayne gave Donna a job answering phones and softening up customers before he came in for the kill. She didn't have a flair for selling, Sheriff Wayne knew, but she had a body that would give a T. rex a heart attack.

"I wasn't yelling, dear. I was saying good-bye to that jackass of a movie director you found."

"He came highly recommended."

"You'd think that someone who shoots skin flicks could work faster."

Sheriff Wayne adjusted his holster on his hips, checking himself in the office mirror.

"Well, some of us like it slow," said Donna, running a patent-leather pump up Sheriff Wayne's inseam. He swatted her away.

"Not while there are customers around. I told you."

Donna smiled and sat up in her desk chair. "Are you sure you should wear those around the lot? People bring their kids. Aren't you afraid you'll scare them?"

Sheriff Wayne adjusted his hat. "Hell. The guns are what brings them in. People like to be scared. Why do you think they like all those monster movies?"

"So, you're the Creature from the Blue Lagoon?"

"Black Lagoon, honey," said the sheriff, adjusting his bolo tie. "And no, I'm not. I'm the law, here to protect folks from monsters like that."

"And sell them hot cars."

Sheriff Wayne looked around and closed the office door. "'Hot' and 'not hot' is a state of mind," he said. "Like that mink stole I gave you. Some would consider that hot."

Donna's eyes narrowed. "You gave me a stolen mink?"

"It was stolen before they even sewed it together. You think the mink gave it up for free?"

"So, it's not stolen?" said Donna tentatively.

"You can't steal something that's already stolen, can you?" said Sheriff Wayne.

"I'm not sure."

"Of course you can't. See? Hot and not hot is a state of mind."

Donna did a rueful little smile. "You could talk Dorothy out of her panties *and* her ruby slippers."

He did a quick draw with his fingers. "And straight into a preowned minivan with room for all the Munchkins she wanted."

Donna typed something on her laptop. "Aha. *The Blue Lagoon* was a movie with Brooke Shields."

"I guess you were right. It *is* a monster movie."

"No. It's about shipwrecked kids."

"Wrong. It stars a model," he said. "Models are well-known devourers of men's souls."

Donna cocked her head. "That include me?"

"Especially you."

"I'm not sure I like that."

Sheriff Wayne came up behind Donna and rubbed her shoulders. "Baby, it don't mean anything. Whatever little smidgen of my soul is left, it's yours to gobble up."

"And not Mrs. Sheriff Wayne Jr.?"

"She's eaten more than her fair share of my soul. And fried chicken. When she bleeds, gravy comes out, and when she farts, she farts biscuits."

Donna crossed her arms. "Is that how you talk about me when I'm not around?"

"Of course not, honey. You're my Brooke Shields. My Blue Lagoon. You're Miss Tarzana RV Queen three years straight."

She turned around and hugged him. "And don't you forget it."

"Never," he said. Gently pulling free of her arms, he turned around toward the doors. "Now go and shake those taters of yours at the customers. Get 'em worked up. I have something to do out back."

Donna straightened her dress and hair in the mirror. "How do I look?"

"Like the Devil herself."

"Just how I like it."

"One thing. Stay away from the llama. It's in a mood today. Liable to spit at anything that gets near it."

"Llamas spit?"

"That they do. And from what I understand, they're quite the marksmen. So, keep yourself and customers away from the mangy thing."

"Aye aye, sir," Donna said, and went out to the sales floor.

"I'm a cowboy, not goddamn Cap'n Crunch," he said.

She shrugged, and he shook his head. He went out the office's other door to the back of the dealership. A man in a Peterbilt hat with gold caps over his front teeth came over to Sheriff Wayne. They shook hands.

"Hello, Lee."

"Afternoon, Junior."

"Don't call me that. It's not my real name. It's made up."

"How come?"

"It makes customers think of families. Makes them feel good."

"Is Wayne your real name?"

"What do you think?"

Lee looked at him. "Then what should I call you?"

"'Sheriff' works."

Lee smiled his metal smile. "Well, Sheriff, today we have an assortment of the finest reconditioned luxury vehicles money can buy. All straight from Texas, where they came from my people in Juarez."

Lee handed Sheriff Wayne a clipboard. "You have paperwork on all these heaps?"

"I've got pink slips and yellow slips. Big slips and little slips. I've got smog certificates, and insurance cards, and original bills of sale. VIN numbers that will check out and brand-new tires on each and every vehicle you see before you."

They walked around the truck loaded with what appeared to be shiny new cars. "You've always done right by me in the past, Lee." Sheriff Wayne turned and shook the other man's hand. "Let's go inside, do some paperwork, and get you your check cut."

Lee smiled. "That girlfriend of yours around?"

"Business associate. And yes, she's with some customers."

He led the way into the office and the two men sat.

"She any good at selling?"

"Why do you ask?"

Lee leaned on the desk and spoke quietly. "I could use a woman like that in my business. Talking to some of the meatheads I have to deal with. Soften them up a little."

"I hate to disappoint you, but Ms. Donna is a dud in the sales department."

"That's too bad. So, what is she good at?"

Lee gave Sheriff Wayne a wicked smile. Sheriff Wayne was about to tell him to shove his smile up his ass when Donna ran in the office and slammed the door. The front of her dress looked like someone had hurled a plate of fried eggs at her.

She panted as she talked. "The llama." *Pant. Pant.* "Some kid let it out." *Pant. Pant.* "It's running wild. Chasing people around." *Pant. Pant.* "And it spit all over my new goddamn dress!"

Sheriff Wayne got up. "Donna, you remember Lee. We were just finishing up some business, but it can wait. Why don't you go into the bathroom and change into some clean overalls from the garage? I'll deal with your dress after I deal with the beast."

Sheriff Wayne picked up a long case from behind his desk and set it on top. Inside was a rifle. He took an odd-looking bullet from a small box and loaded the gun.

"You're not going to kill it, are you?" said Donna. "There's kids out there."

"Calm down. It's a tranquilizer. It'll just put him to sleep until I can get his dumb-ass handler out here. Right now, you go take care of yourself. Lee, you'll be all right here for a few minutes?"

"Take your time, Sheriff. You have any beer?"

"In the minifridge. Donna can show you."

As Sheriff Wayne went out, Donna called after him. "Be careful."

"Always am, darling."

Sheriff Wayne stalked through the salesroom and out into the parking lot with a loaded rifle in his hands, startling salespeople and customers alike. It had been one big shit sandwich of a day. First that John Ford wannabe with the camera, now Lee trying to steal Donna away. And Donna. How was he going to make up for a load of llama spit?

Besides that, he needed a new gimmick. The llama had been a bad idea since day one. What he needed was something new and exotic. Something spectacular. Maybe he could get a big aquarium and put a whale or some sharks out front. No, that was asking for trouble. He'd come up with an answer. He always did. In the end, there was only one thing that was going to make this day bearable.

At least I get to shoot something.

"Please pass the *siu mai*," said Morty.

"Which ones are those?" said Coop.

"The little pork dumplings."

"They're *all* little pork dumplings."

The break-in crew, along with Bayliss, were seated on the floor of Coop and Giselle's apartment. Giselle passed a paper plate to Morty.

"Thanks," he said, picking up a *siu mai* with a chopstick and putting it on his plate.

Coop looked at Giselle. "When you said you were ordering Chinese, I thought you were getting normal food."

"There's more to the world than General Tso's chicken," she said.

"But I don't understand half this stuff. What are these?" said Coop, pointing to a puffy mound of white dough.

"*Char siu bao.*"

"It's a pork dumpling, right?"

"It's steamed."

"Okay. What's this?"

"A potsticker."

"What's that?"

Giselle hesitated. "A pork dumpling."

"But it's fried," said Bayliss.

"See? I win."

"You don't win anything," Giselle said. "You're just complaining because it's new."

"I'm not complaining. I'm confused. I need to be briefed on future culinary experiments. I need charts and blueprints."

"Like at the museum," said Morty.

"Exactly," said Coop. "Display cases and docents."

"I'll get right on that," said Giselle, through a mouthful of egg roll.

"Sorry, Coop. Dim sum was my idea," said Bayliss.

Giselle waved her chopsticks at her. "Don't apologize to him. He's baffled by mac and cheese."

"Only the kind with those little bread crumbs on top."

"Ooo. I like it like that," said Morty.

"Seriously, Coop. Did you grow up eating anything that didn't come from a box or a can?" said Giselle.

Coop shook his head. "Chili dogs were exotic international cuisine in the Cooper residence."

"Not mine," said Bayliss. "My folks were crazy for anything new. I was eating sushi when I was five."

"That's great. How about you, Morty?" said Giselle.

"I didn't," he said.

"Didn't what?"

"Eat," said Coop. "Morty's parents weren't what you'd call nurturing."

"That's not true. Remember in sixth grade that time my dad got me a suit for school pictures?"

Coop set down his food. "Morty, that was a corpse suit. It tied at the back like a robe so the stiff would look good in an open casket."

"That's exactly my point," said Morty. "Dad had to break into a funeral home for it. There's no money in funeral homes. He went out of his way for me."

"The funeral home was next door. The minute people saw you in that suit your dad got arrested."

Morty wiped his mouth with a paper napkin. "I didn't say he was a good crook. But he was a nice one."

Giselle picked up her beer. "Here's to nice crooks. Like us." She looked at Bayliss. "Not that you're a crook, of course. Or you, doc."

Thank you.

The others raised their beers in a toast.

"Stick with us, doc. We'll have you picking six pockets at a time with those claws of yours," said Morty.

I always wanted a second career.

"That's the right attitude. No one wants to do government work forever," said Coop.

Speaking of government work . . .

"Good point," said Morty, spreading the museum's blueprints on the floor between the food cartons. "How do you want to do this, Coop? Go in through the loading dock?"

"That makes sense. It'll be easier getting King Tut out that way." He looked at Giselle. "What about the guards? How many can we expect?"

"On a Sunday, no more than four."

"In the whole museum?"

She flipped through some papers. "They have alarms on the doors and the exhibits, plus motion detectors all over the place. They probably think it's enough."

"We'll need to cut the power to get around all that," said Coop.

"Not a problem. The DOPS has gizmos for that. I'll requisition one," said Giselle.

Coop looked at Morty. They both shook their heads.

"You people really take the fun out of crime," Coop said.

"Sorry," said Giselle. "You'd rather crawl up poles or down manholes looking for the right wires to cut?"

"Oh, man. Those were the days," said Morty, an almost dreamy look on his face.

"What about landlines?" said Bayliss.

"Please tell me we get to cut those," said Coop.

"They'll go out when I cut the power, but if it makes you feel better, go ahead."

"Can I do it?" said Morty.

"Okay. You're in charge of phones."

Is there anything I can do?

"Yeah. We don't exactly have a lot of mummy experience. How do we move it?" said Coop.

Slowly and gently. It will be easier if you carry it on a bodyboard, the kind ambulances use for accident victims.

"Good thinking."

"This is really exciting," said Bayliss. "I've never seen how anyone plans crimes."

"Welcome to the glamorous world of hiding behind Dumpsters at midnight," said Giselle.

"How's the office-supply situation?" said Coop.

Bayliss frowned. "They took my squid."

"What?"

"My desk squid. Whoever it was took it and a bunch of other supplies last night. I wasn't going to mention it."

"Bastards," said Morty.

"I'm sorry," said Giselle.

"Woolrich is onto me. I can't steal any more stuff," said Coop.

"I wouldn't ask you to," said Giselle.

"But I can help set up a trap."

"Really?" said Bayliss hopefully.

"When this is over we'll come up with something."

"Thanks. That would be great."

"You have any pilfering down in your department, doc?" said Morty.

Never.

"How would you handle it?"

Lupinsky held up one of his metal tentacles, opened and closed the metal claw at the end a couple of times with a menacing clank. The cat on-screen hissed.

"That would do it," said Coop.

Thank you.

"Phil says hi, by the way," said Bayliss.

"Tell him hi back. How's he working out as a partner?"

"He's chatty."

"Yeah. That's him."

"I think it's because he gets bored. Even I find following people and collating background information less than thrilling sometimes. I think he misses things like this tonight."

"Come to a few more sessions and maybe we can get you on the crook squad, right, Coop?" said Giselle.

"First we have to catch *your* crook. Then we'll see about making you one."

Bayliss nodded. "First steps," she said.

"Exactly."

What about me?

The cat on Dr. Lupinsky's screen hopped around and purred.

"It's like I said, doc. The body is a problem. If they could make you a thousand pounds lighter, maybe then."

I'll see what I can do.

"Coop, help me clear up the food and we'll get dessert," said Giselle.

"What did you get?" said Morty.

"Pork ice cream."

"You're kidding," said Coop.

"Do you want fried or steamed?"

"Ha ha. That's hilarious. You're hilarious."

"You can tell it's love because he believes everything she says," said Morty.

"That's sweet," said Bayliss.

"It's not sweet. It's diabolical," said Coop. "You're a man of the world, doc. Am I right?"

I haven't eaten food in over thirty years. I'd kill for pork ice cream.

No one said anything for a minute.

"If they make you a new body, you might get them to work on that, too," said Coop.

No shit.

9

At four a.m. Sunday morning, Coop, Giselle, and Morty sat in a DOPS van at the curb outside the museum. In the empty parking lot, a few lights illuminated the carless rows and there was a dim glow coming from the lobby.

"Is that gizmo of yours going to work?" said Coop.

Giselle held up a device that looked like a television remote. It had two buttons: on and off.

"It's never failed yet."

"Then let's get rolling."

Giselle hit the off button. Nothing happened for a few seconds. Then the parking-lot lights began to flicker. A few seconds later, lights began to explode. Neatly, row upon row into the distance, lights blew, scattering glass all over the parking lot. Lights flickered on and off in the museum lobby and, finally, they, too, went out.

Giselle shook the device. "I might have had it turned up too high."

"It looked okay to me," said Morty, smiling.

"Yeah. That was kind of fun," said Coop. "You ought to keep

it. We can use it on the frat boys down the street when they invite friends over for beer pong in the middle of the night."

"Now, now. You were young once."

"No, he wasn't," said Morty. "When other kids had paper routes, Coop was stealing newspaper vans and selling the papers to the delivery boys at half price."

"That's my little entrepreneur," said Giselle.

"It beat bagging groceries," said Coop.

Giselle looked at her watch. "Do you think the guards are suitably confused yet?"

"I think we're good," said Coop. He pointed to the back of the museum. "Why don't you pull us around to the dock?"

Giselle eased the van around the broken glass in the lot until she reached the back of the museum.

"Are you sure you don't want me to go inside with you?"

"Morty and me should be fine. And if that gizmo of yours doesn't work and the lights come on, you're our getaway driver."

"I always wanted to race at Le Mans," she said. "Good luck, you two."

"Thanks," said Morty.

"See you soon," said Coop.

The moment they were out of the van, Morty ran to a box mounted on the wall at the back of the museum. He barely touched the lock and the box sprung open. With a pair of wire cutters, he began snipping away at the phone lines.

"You done yet?" said Coop.

"Yeah," said Morty. "Next time let's break in somewhere with a little class. This is too easy."

"I know what you mean. Got your night-vision goggles?"

"Yep."

"Then let's open-sesame this place and get going."

Morty went up the short flight of stairs to a door on the dock. Again, he touched the lock, and with a quiet click, it opened.

He and Coop went inside and quickly made their way through the dock to the museum's inner door. The night-vision goggles worked flawlessly, lighting up the room in a bright green glow.

Having memorized the blueprints, Morty led the way from the back of the museum to the mummy exhibition. The room was even more impressive in the dark, thought Coop. Like Halloween haunted-house mazes he'd gone through as a kid.

"This is how they could bring in the tourists," he whispered to Morty. "Go for a *House on Haunted Hill* thing."

"Yeah. The junior-high-field-trip bit doesn't do the place justice. Should we leave a note in the suggestion box?"

"I'll send them a valentine."

"Bayliss is right. You're a sweet boy."

"Shut up and help me steal something."

Guards' voices echoed around the museum as they called to each other. Coop and Morty went out onto the museum floor and looked around the corner. Flashlight beams panned around the lobby.

"I guess Giselle's box doesn't work on those," said Morty.

Coop reached into the bag slung around his shoulder. "I knew that thing wasn't all it's cracked up to be." He took out a couple of what looked like black golf balls. "Let's see if these things are any better."

He squeezed each one and threw them in different directions. As the balls bounced away, they crackled and whistled. Blinking lights strobed and buzzed. The guards' flashlight beams followed the sounds. There was more shouting as the guards ran in all directions, trying to find the source of the noise.

"Nice," said Morty.

"Yeah. But let's get moving in case those things crap out, too."

"Always so cynical."

"Not cynical. Scared. It's a good instinct around possibly armed rent-a-cops."

"Good point."

They quickly made their way back to the exhibit room and went to the sarcophagus. From a small backpack, Morty unfolded the bodyboard and set it on the floor. He and Coop got on opposite sides of Harkhuf and slowly slid their hands underneath him. In the distance, guards were shouting to each other.

"On three," said Coop.

Morty nodded.

"One . . . two . . . three . . ." They lifted. Harkhuf didn't budge. They lifted again, but Harkhuf refused to move. Coop looked over the edge of the sarcophagus.

"There's things on his wrists and ankles," he said. "Got your knife?"

"Of course."

"Let's cut him out. I don't know how long those bouncing balls last."

They reached into the case and slit through the wax seals with the pictures of Anubis and Set. Once they did, Harkhuf lifted easily. They set him carefully on the board and Morty started to raise his end. Coop held up a finger. He took something else out of his shoulder bag and set it in the sarcophagus. Morty looked down into the case. It was the mummy snow globe Coop had bought at the museum store.

"You mean, mean man," said Morty, grinning.

"It's like those penny trays at checkout counters."

"Take a mummy, leave a mummy."

"Exactly."

Morty looked around the room. "What do you think? Do we take anything else? Just for fun?"

"I thought about that. The doc said some of this stuff is fake. What if we stole junk? Then we'd be as third rate as these guys."

"You're right. Forget it."

They picked up the board and headed out the back. The guards were still chasing the golf balls.

"Are we really doing this?" said Morty. "Is it this easy?"

"Spooky, isn't it?" said Coop.

They made their way through the loading dock, out the door, and down the stairs. Coop knocked on the side of the van. Giselle stared at him through the window. She rolled it down and said, "What went wrong?"

"Nothing," said Coop. "We've got him right here."

"You're done already?"

"That's what *I* said," said Morty.

Giselle hit the button that opened the back of the van and extended the ramp. They took Harkhuf inside and set him on the floor. Morty stayed in the back keeping an eye on the mummy while Coop got into the passenger seat. Giselle started the van, made a U-turn, and they sped away. When they reached the edge of the lot, she hit the on button on the little box. A few streetlamps flickered on in the parking lot, while others blew sparks into the night sky. Lights came on in the museum, but they were already on the street, heading back to DOPS head-quarters.

Coop and Giselle grinned at each other.

"Is there any beer left at home?" he said.

"Tons."

Morty moved up from the back and crouched between the seats. "I guess Woolrich was right for once," he said. "This was an easy job."

"I told you it was going to be all right," said Giselle.

"Yeah. Woolrich has always been really nice to me," Morty said.

"He hates me," said Coop.

"He doesn't hate you," said Giselle. "He just isn't used to your particular charms yet."

He shook his head. "Story of my life. Let's drop off the stiff and get drunk."

"Best plan I've heard all week," said Morty.

From the back came a sound like a low groan.

"What was that?" said Giselle.

"When we get back, we should tell the garage that this thing needs a tune-up," said Coop.

"Can you imagine if we stalled out with that thing in the back?"

"I can't think of anything worse," said Morty.

From the back of the van, something groaned again.

10

"Did you get the memo?" said Vargas.

"What memo?" said Zulawski.

"*Any* memo! I haven't seen a single one in weeks."

"I'm sure you're exaggerating."

"Am I? When was the last time you got one?"

"Well . . ." said Zulawski. "I'm sure it hasn't been weeks. Let me go and see."

"Yes, you do that," said Vargas, a slight hint of contempt in his voice.

Vargas and Zulawski worked the late shift collecting, cataloging, and occasionally giving ultra-top-level people access to some of the most mysterious and dangerous objects in the DOPS archives. They were known as the Inscrutabilis Unit, a group so secret that its full name—the Extra-Confidential Inscrutabilis Unit—was even more secret, so that if someone happened to stumble on the office they'd have no idea just how secret it was. However, being so unbelievably secret, the ECIU often felt forgotten, which didn't really make sense because how can anyone forget something they never knew about in the first place?

Still, the ECIU wasn't known for its high morale, and because it was so secret, none of its employees were allowed to speak to a DOPS psychiatrist or participate in softball, merengue lessons, the office pet program, or any of the other morale-building activities the DOPS offered. In short, the ECIU was the most miserable, lonely, and forlorn department in an organization that prided itself on being able to make even the most hopeless job worse by following the motto *Obscurity, Perplexity, Tuna Fish*, the phrase, in itself, designed to make anyone contemplating it for too long feel woozy and feverish.

"Anything?" said Vargas.

"I'm still looking," said Zulawski.

Vargas tapped a pencil on his desk. No one in the ECIU was allowed to use a pen because objects in the archive occasionally turned ink sentient and vicious. They'd lost more than one unit member to a stray grocery list forgotten in a pocket.

"Take your time. You're just proving my point."

"Aha!" shouted Zulawski. "I found one."

"Let me see," said Vargas.

Zulawski marched over to Vargas and tossed a pencil-scrawled note onto his desk. "Convinced now?"

Vargas picked up the memo, gave it a quick glance, and tossed it back on his desk. "That's two months old."

"Really?" said Zulawski. "I thought it was more recent."

"Wishful thinking. I'm telling you. They've finally, completely forgotten us."

Zulawski picked up the memo and stared at it. Vargas was right. It was two months old. He went back to his in-box and pawed through the papers. "This one is from last week. I think," he said. He handed it to Vargas for confirmation.

Vargas read the memo with great suspicion. He was certain that Zulawski wasn't above planting a piece of correspondence in his in-box, just to prove him wrong. He also suspected Zulawski of dulling his pencils when he wasn't looking, overwatering his fern, and being the magician who put the crusts back on the sandwiches he brought from home that he was absolutely *certain* he'd cut the crusts off of. Some nights, Vargas wondered if he might be going a little mad, but he knew there was nothing he could do about it. Madness in the ECIU was also classified and, rumor had it, could result in a promotion to ECIU management, which was supposed to be even worse than his current position. It was easier and safer to continue blaming Zulawski for any unexplainable occurrences in the office.

Vargas read the correspondence over twice. Indeed, it was dated from the previous week. "Congratulations. They approved your requisition for more size-six erasers. You must be so proud."

Zulawski snatched the memo off Vargas's desk. "Well, it's something. And it proves you're wrong. They haven't forgotten us."

"I'm coming to terms with the obvious reality that we've fallen completely off the books, while you seem extremely invested in the idea that we haven't. Is there something you're not telling me?"

Zulawski put the memo back in his in-box. "It's nothing you don't already know about. It's because of the parcel."

Vargas went rigid for a second. "I thought we agreed not to talk about that."

"But that's the problem. We need to talk about it. We have to do something about it. Something *with* it."

"No, we don't. We don't have to do a single thing."

Zulawski looked around, then whispered, "I'm afraid of it."

"You think I'm not?" said Vargas. "It's ghastly. I don't want to know it exists, let alone that it exists in this office."

Zulawski looked at a set of gray metal shelves not unlike the gray metal shelves you'd find in any storeroom anywhere. The parcel, a simple flat rectangle wrapped in butcher paper, lay ominously atop the nearest set of shelves.

"It's like it's watching us," Zulawski said.

"It's not watching us," said Vargas. "You're being paranoid."

"Do you think it knows we're talking about it?"

Vargas experienced one of the brief episodes where he doubted his sanity. They never lasted long, but they were coming more frequently. But he couldn't let Zulawski know this for fear of management training.

"It's just a *thing*. A thing in a box," he said. "A hideous, awful, evil thing, but still just a thing."

"It scares me," said Zulawski.

"You already said that."

"It doesn't scare you?"

"I already told you it did!"

"Sorry. I'm just . . . Should we do something about it? Maybe hide it. Pretend we don't know anything about it."

Vargas picked up his pencil and examined the point. It was still sharp. For now. "What if someone who knows we have it comes looking for it? What then?"

"We can worry about that when we have to," said Zulawski.

"Too late. I'm already worried just talking about it."

"What if it's why we don't get messages anymore?"

"Don't be ridiculous," said Vargas.

Zulawski picked up a stepladder. "I'm hiding it."

As Zulawski carried the ladder to the shelves, Vargas grew suspicious again. "Why are you so obsessed with the parcel all of a sudden? I know there's something you're not telling me."

Zulawski stopped in midstride. He put down the ladder and sat on top. "It's my birthday. I haven't received a single card, not even from management. And they always send a little something."

"It's your birthday? Since when?"

"Since yesterday."

"How come I don't know anything about it?" said Vargas.

Zulawski jumped up from the ladder. "You say that every year! 'How come I don't know about it?' How do you not know about it? It happens every year on the same day."

"Don't get so upset. I'm sure you don't know my birthday either."

"June seventeenth. I gave you a card with a cat on the front. It said 'I'm *pawsing* to wish you a happy birthday.'"

"Oh yes. I sort of remember that," said Vargas. "Sorry. Happy birthday."

"Thank you," said Zulawski.

The more Vargas thought about it, the clearer the memory of the card became. Which began to make him suspicious again. How could he be sure his birthday was really June seventeenth? It could be a trick. If Zulawski was magician enough to make the crusts on Vargas's sandwiches reappear after he knew he'd cut them off, maybe he could change his birthday. Or maybe make him remember the wrong birthday. Vargas became determined to keep an even closer watch on his office mate.

Vargas glanced at his watch. Zulawski looked at his own.

"It's past your lunch break," Zulawski said. "Aren't you going to eat?"

Vargas had already examined his sandwich and seen that the crusts were firmly back in place. "No," he said. "I'm not hungry."

"Do you mind if I eat my lunch?" said Zulawski.

"Not at all," Vargas said graciously. "Go ahead."

Zulawski took a bag from under his desk and removed an apple, a small container of potato salad, and a turkey sandwich. The crusts were gone.

Vargas looked away, terrified. Had Zulawski magically transferred the turkey crusts onto *his* sandwiches? That was the only explanation. Well, there was another one, but he didn't want to examine it too closely.

I've completely lost my mind.

11

In was early in the morning when the phone rang. Or maybe it was very late. Coop wasn't sure because his head felt like a box of nails packed in a box of cotton balls, which itself was packed in an even larger box of nails and clamped into one of those paint-mixing machines you see in hardware stores. The kind that take the cans of paint and shake them like a cast-iron terrier with an extremely unfortunate rat. In this state, he lurched for his phone on the nightstand and kept going, rolling onto the floor with a thud.

Coop thumbed his phone on. "Ouch. Goddammit," he said before his alcohol-soaked brain remembered the more traditional phone greeting. "Hello."

There was no one on the line. His head and back hurt. And the damned phone rang again, insistently, it seemed, to him.

He heard Giselle roll over in bed, then the beep as she turned on her phone. "Hello?" she said.

He listened for a moment to confirm that the call wasn't for him. Then he tossed his phone on the floor and crawled back into bed.

"What? Really?" said Giselle. "Okay. Great. Thanks. Bye."

"Who's great thanks bye and why did they call at such an idiot hour of the morning?" Coop said.

"It's not morning anymore. It's after noon. And great thanks bye was Woolrich's secretary calling to say that he wants to see the whole team from last night. You know what I think?"

"What do you think?"

"I think he might be giving us a commendation or something. I mean, has there ever been a smoother operation in DOPS history? Maybe it's a promotion."

"A promotion. Yippee," said Coop into his pillow.

Giselle swatted him on his ass. "Get moving, you. I've waited a long time for these people to recognize how hard we work."

Coop sat up blearily. "I thought we were taking the day off. Job well done and all that crap."

"You can sleep after Woolrich kisses our butts. I'm going to take a quick shower. You wake up Morty and put on coffee."

"Okay. I hate everything right now, you know."

"You'll hate everything a little less once you've had coffee."

Coop staggered to his feet and frowned. "Someone threw my phone on the floor."

"You did. In a fit of pique. Now go make coffee."

"I don't have fits of pique. I dispense swift, hard justice."

"Yes, dear."

As Giselle disappeared into the bathroom, Coop got to his feet and went into the living room, where Morty was asleep on the couch. He started to wake him, but it seemed too cruel right then. Instead, he went into the kitchen and put on a pot of coffee. When it was close to done, Morty sat up.

"Is that coffee I smell?"

"It better be or I put oatmeal in the coffeemaker."

Morty pressed his hands to his forehead. "I think I'm hungover," he said.

"We're all hungover," said Coop.

"Then why are we awake?"

"Woolrich is giving us blue ribbons for being the prettiest pigs at the county fair."

Morty looked at him with red eyes. "What?"

Coop turned off the coffeemaker and got down three mugs. "It's a commendation or something for the bang-up job we did last night."

Morty smiled. It clearly hurt, but he kept on anyway. "Wow. I've never gotten a commendation before. Is it a piece of paper or a plaque, you think?"

"I think coffee is ready is what I think."

"Maybe it'll be a bonus."

"Coffee."

Morty came over and dropped down onto a stool by the counter. Giselle soon joined them. Later, they decided that no one was in shape to drive, so they called a cab to take them to DOPS headquarters. Giselle put the ride on her company credit card. Why not? It was their day and she was going to make the most of it.

Coop was feeling a bit more human when they got off the elevator on the management floor, but his mood had turned a little sour. He hated being summoned and his head still hurt enough that the mazelike corridors were more aggravating than usual. He took a small penknife from his pocket and made a tiny slice on the corner of the hallway junctions each time they turned. If he couldn't memorize the layout, then he'd leave a trail of bread crumbs for himself. Each cut made him feel a little bit better. He might never need the trail, but he was vandalizing government property and that was satisfying all by itself.

Like last time, when they reached Woolrich's office, Giselle opened the door and walked in without waiting. The others followed and Woolrich politely ushered them to seats by the desk. Giselle and Morty were all smiles. Coop tried to join in, but the best he could do was a pleasant grimace. Dr. Lupinsky stood by the window. The cat on his screen jumped up when he saw them and walked back and forth meowing quietly.

"How is everyone today?" said Woolrich. "All rested up from last night's adventure?"

"We're feeling great, sir," said Giselle.

"Never better," said Morty.

Coop quietly shielded his eyes from the light and wished he'd brought welding goggles or a sombrero.

Woolrich raised his eyebrows. "What about you, Cooper? Feeling bright-eyed and bushy-tailed?"

Coop nodded. "Are rats bushy-tailed?"

"No."

"Then I feel like a rat. A hungover rat."

Woolrich's smile broadened. "It's nice to see that you were celebrating a job well done. Even Dr. Lupinsky here."

They gave me some extra mice to play with. It was fun.

"Have you heard anything about the museum?" said Giselle.

"Oh, they're going quite insane," said Woolrich brightly. "Heads are rolling. Insurance companies are having nervous breakdowns. They've brought in new security. The press is having a field day, of course."

"Well, as long as you're satisfied, sir, that's all that counts," said Morty.

Coop sat back and tried to keep his eyes open, waiting for the spiel about what a credit they were to Uncle Sam, puppies, and the baby Jesus. He'd heard similar things from the warden while he was in jail. It was the main reason compliments of any kind put him in a bad mood. What they usually amounted to was a vague homily, extra pudding at dinner, and then an ass kicking by everyone who hadn't qualified for the nice dessert. However, instead of a speech, Woolrich laced his fingers together and stared down at his desk.

"Satisfied? Well, you see. There's a small problem with that."

Coop felt an unpleasant jolt of energy. Woolrich's tone didn't sound remotely like a commendation or extra pudding, unless the latter was laced with arsenic.

"There was an incident with the mummy last night," Woolrich said.

"Oh? What kind of incident?" said Giselle.

"It left."

Left? appeared on Dr. Lupinsky's screen.

"Yes. Quite abruptly and with an overabundance of violence."

"Can you go into a little more detail?" said Coop, not really wanting to hear any details at all.

"Of course," said Woolrich. He picked up a remote from his desk and pointed it at the wall, which slid away to reveal a large flat-screen monitor. On the monitor was a lot of smoke and people running around screaming, which was followed by a number of loud *bangs*, a little more screaming, a lot more running, and then a final hollow thud.

"The sound at the end, that's my favorite," said Woolrich. "Do you know why?"

Morty started to reply and Coop said, "Don't answer. It's a trick. If we all stay very quiet, maybe he'll forget we're here."

Dr. Lupinsky's cat walked offscreen and was replaced by the test pattern.

"Where do you think you're going, Doctor?" said Woolrich. "You're as much to blame as anybody."

"Blame for what? What happened last night?" said Giselle.

"About an hour after you brought Harkhuf to us, he reanimated. Once he'd done that, he appeared to remember that he had business elsewhere. The final thud you heard on the video? That was him breaking through a wall and out into the street."

"Where is he now?" said Giselle.

"We have no idea," said Woolrich. "We think he was using some sort of ancient Egyptian magical system, one we aren't familiar with. Once he was out of the building, we couldn't track him."

"So, he could be anywhere," said Coop.

"Exactly."

"So, do we get the promotion now or after lunch?"

Giselle looked out the window. Morty tried to make himself very small. Dr. Lupinsky remained out of order.

Woolrich set down the remote. "Not only won't there be any promotions, the reason I wanted all of you here today was to emphasize how incredibly much this is all your fault. Especially you, Cooper. And you, Dr. Lupinsky."

Coop sat up. "How is this my fault? We took the mummy you told us to take."

"Yes, but obviously it was the wrong one."

"It was the one you wanted."

"But it was the *wrong one*," said Woolrich, shaking his head. "I don't see why you can't understand that."

"If it's the wrong mummy, then what mummy is it?" said Giselle.

"We're not sure. The Harkhuf we wanted was an engineer from one of the later dynasties, supposedly knowledgeable about the ancient forms of temporal and spatial folding the Egyptians were famous for."

"There's a dry cleaner around the corner from our place that will fold anything you want. Maybe you should talk to them," said Coop.

"Don't make things worse for yourself, Cooper," said Woolrich. He leaned back in his chair. "Dr. Lupinsky. Do you have any thoughts you'd care to share on the matter?"

Dr. Lupinsky's cat poked its head around the corner of the

screen. Slowly, it slinked out and sat down, its tail wrapped around its feet.

I'm not sure what to say.

"Why blame us?" said Coop. "The doc was there and he said the mummy was all right."

"Is that true, Doctor?" said Woolrich.

The cat cocked its head to the side. Its tail twitched.

The cartouches were all correct. They indicated that the mummy was Harkhuf, an engineer of high social rank.

"Then why is my mummy gone, Doctor?"

There was more tail twitching. Coop felt a little sorry for Lupinsky right then. First an Egyptologist. Then a cat. Then a TV. Then an octopus. And now being told he's no good at any of them. Still, him getting grilled for a while gave Coop time to think. Mostly what he thought about was getting out of there, but in between fantasies of running a one-minute mile, he went over everything that had happened the night before.

Perhaps the sarcophagus markings are a forgery. Or, more likely, the sarcophagus is real, but the mummy isn't who we thought it was.

"Forged by whom?" said Woolrich.

I have no idea.

"And why would someone do it?"

I don't know.

Coop looked at Woolrich and said very quietly, "Maybe this is *your* fault."

"What was that?" said Woolrich.

Coop cleared his throat. "You don't know what's going on now, so maybe you never knew what was going on. Maybe the guy in the box was the real Harkhuf. Maybe he wasn't. Whoever he is, if he busted out, I bet there's been something he's wanted to do for a long time and he's doing it right now. Maybe that's why you're blaming us. The DOPS didn't do its homework."

Giselle put a hand on his. "Why don't you calm down a little, Coop?"

"Yeah. We're all friends here," said Morty. "We can work this out."

Coop didn't want to work anything out. He wanted his hangover to kill him, but it refused to do anything but make his eyes hurt.

"Dr. Lupinsky," said Woolrich slowly and precisely. "You didn't see anything unusual when you examined the sarcophagus?"

Nothing.

"And, Cooper, there weren't any snags when you were relieving the museum of the mummy?"

"No. It popped right out of the case like a Pop-Tart from a toaster."

"After we cut him out," added Morty.

"Right. After we cut the stuff off his hands and feet."

Dr. Lupinsky rose up on his tentacles.

What kind of stuff exactly?

"You know. Loops of that mummy wrap held together with wax."

Was anything written or printed on them?

"Yeah," said Morty. "There were pictures."

"One was a dog," said Coop.

Anubis. And the other?

"It had kind of a long snout," Morty said.

"It looked like an anteater in a dress."

Set.

The cat lay down and put its paws over its head. Coop wanted to do the same thing.

"Are those names significant, Dr. Lupinsky?" said Woolrich.

The cat didn't move, but at the bottom of the screen it said, *Whatever Harkhuf is going to do, it's going to be very bad.*

"And why didn't you notice anything amiss when you were at the museum?"

I . . . I don't know.

"Maybe it was his batteries," said Morty.

Everyone looked at him except for Woolrich. He was looking at Coop.

"You didn't change Dr. Lupinsky's batteries before taking him into the field?"

Coop had a sinking feeling in his stomach. "No one told us to."

Woolrich raised his hands and dropped them on his desk. "It's basic procedure when working with a Class Three necro-mecha system this old."

"Remember the part where I said that no one told us?"

"Don't try to make this somebody else's fault."

"But it *is* somebody else's fault. That's exactly whose fault it is," Coop said. He looked at Dr. Lupinsky. "Why didn't you say anything?"

My batteries were low. I forgot. I'm sorry.

Woolrich tapped a pen on his desk. "So, to sum up. You, Cooper, brought us the wrong mummy . . ."

"*We* brought the wrong mummy. *We*," he said.

"So you admit it. Good. And you didn't even follow standard procedures to ensure that the one person who might have helped to avoid this mess— Dr. Lupinsky—was in working order."

"Once again, I have to point out that this is a *we* situation."

"I don't have to explain to you how grave this is, do I?" said Woolrich.

"Grave? Which part? The building exploding, the killer mummy escaping, or how you're trying to make this all our fault?"

"*Your* fault."

"A minute ago it was Lupinsky's fault, too."

"Clearly the doctor was impaired. That leaves you."

Coop opened his mouth, but Giselle put her hand over it. "What can we do to fix things?" she said.

Woolrich took a folder from a desk drawer and dropped it on the desk.

"Another folder. Great. That's how this all got started," said Coop.

Woolrich gave Coop a fatherly smile. "Be nice now. This is your lucky day."

"That's what everyone says right before they try to sell you the Grand Canyon."

"I had a meeting with the folks down in thaumaturgic antiquities . . ."

"The people who had us steal the wrong mummy? That's encouraging."

"They said that in cases like this, there will be certain charms, sacred objects, and whatnot with significance to the mummy. And the right one will be able to control it."

Coop closed his eyes. "And you want us to get it."

"No. I want *you* to get it. But you'll need help, so you can bring your miscreants along. Just try not to drag them down with you again."

Coop slouched in his chair. "What is it you want?"

Woolrich opened the folder and laid out a photo of an amulet.

"That," he said.

"Where is it?"

"That's the one bit of good news in all this mess."

Coop slouched a little lower. "Please don't tell me it's in the museum."

"It's in the museum," said Woolrich. "Near the sarcophagus."

Morty picked up the photo and studied it. "I think I saw this the other night. We could have taken it then."

"But we didn't need it then," said Woolrich.

"Which is also our fault?" said Coop.

"Yours. And yes."

Coop took a long breath and stood up. "No. That's how I met you people. Stealing that damned box over and over. I'm not going through that again."

"But you're not stealing the same thing," said Woolrich. "You're stealing something different, just from the same place."

Coop ran a hand through his hair. "We just did the best, cleanest job of our careers and you want us to go back and do it again, only now the security setup is going to be different, there might be cops around. Maybe even new curses and wards."

"Wonderful. Those are your specialties, aren't they?"

"Yes, but we have no idea what to look for."

"Fine," said Woolrich. "If you're going to be insistent, you can bring along a poltergeist assistant. What about Phil Spectre? You two have worked together before, as I recall."

Coop sat back down feeling like he'd dodged a punch in the face just in time to shoot himself with a shotgun full of bees.

Morty handed him the photo of the amulet.

"Cooper?" said Woolrich.

"When do you want us to go in?" Coop said.

"Let's see, there's a homicidal mummy on the loose with vast magical abilities and an unknown agenda, so whenever is convenient for you."

"We're going to have to work on a plan. The day after tomorrow?"

"Did I hear tomorrow? That will be fine," said Woolrich.

Coop pointed a finger at him. "You know things are going to get messy this time, right? We don't know what the hell is waiting for us in there."

"Just bring back the amulet. Requisition what you need, but remember . . ."

"I know. Don't go over budget."

Coop looked at Dr. Lupinsky. "Your wish has come true, doc. You're going in with us this time."

The cat stood up, walked to the edge of the screen, and fell over.

Excuse me while I go and soil myself.

12

There was a knock on the door to Nelson's office. He cursed quietly.

Nelson was busy making a long list in a notebook. Every now and then, he would copy a group of items from the list and put them in a specific square on a grid he'd drawn at the back of the book. He was creating a handwritten database, handwritten because he couldn't chance creating one on his computer. The audit department swept those at regular intervals, checking for viruses, malware, peeking at browser histories, etc. Nelson thought that it must be a tedious way to spend your days.

Of course, those audit creeps ought to come down here and try this job. Then they'll know what tedious is.

Nelson, however, had become an expert in ways to make his job less tedious. His games of reading, losing, rerouting, and holding back memos and mail helped keep his job semilively and periodically engaging. But he couldn't keep all of the clandestine traffic in his head, so he had to create his paper database. It was dangerous, painstaking work, but if he did it right, it would pay off big in the end. Patience was what he needed now, but he'd never had a lot of it. It was doubly hard now that alcohol no longer had any effect on his mook system. However, some of his smaller-scale and petty meddling in the information flow through the DOPS helped compensate for it. Every missed meeting, every wrong assignment, every bit of research material lost—while pinning the blame on someone else—was a personal victory. It wasn't the same as getting loaded or being alive, but the resulting chaos buoyed his spirit enormously.

The knock came again. Nelson put away the notebook and locked the drawer.

"Come in," he said.

The door opened and McCloud came in with a brown paper bag. When Nelson saw it, his spirit did a malevolent little pirouette. But he was careful not to show it.

"Yes, McCloud?" he said in the tone of the management book when referring to "Harried Enthusiasm," which was meant to convey that while you were very busy, you were glad to make time for the employee's no doubt fascinating idea, news, or query. Because he despised everyone he worked with, it wasn't Nelson's strongest management voice. He made a note to work on it when he wasn't completing the database.

"I have the items you wanted," McCloud said.

"And no one saw you collect them?"

"No, sir. I was very careful. You made it clear how important it was to keep things on the TQ."

"QT," said Nelson.

"Sorry. I'm dyslexic."

"I know. We've discussed it before."

"Have we? I don't remember."

"Trust me, we have."

The reason McCloud didn't remember was that the discussions always took place when he was under hypnosis. During some of those trances, Nelson had tried to rewire McCloud's brain several times, always with disastrous results. He started speaking backward. He broke into sea shanties. He forgot English completely and spent a whole work shift inventing a new language that consisted mainly of obscene hand gestures and chasing his fellow workers around with a fire extinguisher. Still, the dyslexia worked in Nelson's favor. As long as other mooks innocently followed his instructions to divert a message here and there, McCloud could collect them without being able to read any. It made McCloud an integral part of his plans.

"You are plausible deniability personified," said Nelson.

McCloud thought for a minute. "Is that good?"

"Wonderful. Now what do you have there?"

McCloud set the bag on the desk. "The correspondence you asked for. I hope it's the right ones."

Nelson upended the bag. Several corporate and even a few personal birthday cards fell out. All were addressed to Zulawski.

"Perfect," Nelson said. He put the cards back in the bag. "Now, here's what you're going to do next. Remember the squid you took from Bayliss's desk?"

"Yes. I have it in a tank in the storage room."

"Good. At the end of the shift, when everyone else is gone, you're going to pack up the squid. Then tomorrow, you'll get someone else to route it to the ECIU."

McCloud looked puzzled. "All right," he said finally. "Is there anything else?"

"Yes. When you're done packing the squid, you're going to take all of Bayliss's office supplies that we've been gathering, box them up, and send them to the audit department."

Now McCloud looked distressed. "I don't understand why you want me to do that."

"Of course. Let me explain it to you," said Nelson, coming around the desk.

He put a finger on McCloud's forehead. "Macho Taco Guy Lombardo," he said. McCloud blinked vacantly.

"Now, I want you to forget the conversation we just had, but I want you to remember to pack the boxes I told you about."

McCloud smiled. "Sure thing, boss."

"Once you've packed them, you're going to feel refreshed and happy. When you do, you're going to forget about the boxes, too. Understand?"

"Sure thing, boss."

"Good."

Nelson put his finger on McCloud's forehead and repeated the hypnotic phrase. McCloud sagged for a second, then straightened and looked his usually idiotic, chipper self.

"Did you want anything besides the bag?" he said.

"Nothing. You did a great job," said Nelson. He steered McCloud to the door, following him out to the mail room. As soon as McCloud went back to his regular duties, Nelson took Zulawski's birthday cards to the shredder and tossed them in.

The crazier I can make one of them, the crazier he'll make the other.

Nelson stood by the machine until every card was thoroughly sliced, diced, and chewed to bits.

That's Zulawski taken care of for the moment.

Now, what can I do to Vargas?

13

There wasn't much light in Minerva Soleil's storefront psychic reading parlor. There were, however, heavy drapes, crystal balls, tarot cards, Tibetan prayer flags, and statues of a dozen saints. The walls were festooned with pictures of Orishas, Bodhisattvas, a Kabbalah Tree of Life, and old spirit photos with the ghosts of lost loved ones leaking ectoplasm into the air. Around them, in the subtly unsubtle pattern Minerva had worked hard at, were yellowing images of her with big-name movie and television stars of the fifties and sixties. On her good days, she felt that the space projected an air of calm but powerful spiritual power. On other days—most days, actually—it felt like she was running a flea market in the Wicked Witch of the West's garage. But the knickknacks hid the cracks and water stains in the wall plaster, so they were a dusty necessity.

"Are you in contact yet?" said Mrs. Caroline Barnett. "Is Scotty there? What does he say?"

Probably "Quiet, you old bat." He probably danced a jig when he died.

"He's close by," said Minerva in a low, soothing voice. "I can see him."

"Oh, good. What does he want me to do with all that jewelry in the safe-deposit box? I mean, diamond rings and pearl necklaces. He didn't steal it, did he? He promised he'd given up that kind of thing."

"She's quite the Chatty Cathy, isn't she?" said Dross, Minerva's spirit guide. Dross was a ghost and spoke to Minerva in her head. He was the only dead person she could stand.

Minerva answered him in her head. "Will you tell me something useful already? Mrs. Methuselah is giving me a rash."

"I'm working on it," said Dross. "Scotty isn't as spry as he used to be. Neither am I, come to think of it."

"Cry me a river. We need this job."

"Calm down. I . . . Wait. Here he is."

"Thank fucking Jesus," said Minerva without thinking.

"But Scotty is Jewish," said Mrs. Barnett. "And an atheist. Why would you be talking to Jesus?"

Minerva heard Dross snigger.

Just my luck. The old biddy hears like an airedale.

"Not Jesus," Minerva said. "Jeeves. Jeeves-us. An old Roman spirit guide. Very powerful. Very wise."

"My goodness. The people you know. It must be very exciting."

"It's like being shot out of a spiritual cannon into a net of angels."

"My goodness."

Dross sniggered again. And coughed. Minerva never heard a ghost cough before. If she wasn't so busy trying to keep Little Miss Chatterbox here happy, she would have asked him about it.

"Tell her Scotty says, 'What does she want?'" said Dross. "And, 'Oh God, I can't shake her; even here?'"

"Scotty says he loves you and misses you."

"Really?" said Mrs. Barnett. "He never talked that way when he was alive."

Minerva nodded sagely. "Death has a way of giving some people access to the true emotions they didn't have in life," she said.

"Ask him about the jewelry. It makes me nervous. I thought about having it appraised, but knowing Scotty's past, I'm afraid that might not be wise."

"I'll ask him."

"He wants her to go away," said Dross. "He's whining up a storm."

"Oh, and find out about the air-conditioning warranty. I looked in the filing cabinet, but I can't find it," said Mrs. Barnett.

Let this work or kill me now, God, thought Minerva.

"I think she's kind of sweet," said Dross. "Tell her I think she's sweet."

Minerva thought, "Listen, I want those jewels, but we need to convince her it's Scotty's idea."

"Hey. We've been doing this for fifty years. I know the scam."

Minerva was about to tell him to get his ectoplasmic ass in gear when he broke out into another coughing fit.

"And is Peaches there with him? She loved to curl up on Scotty's lap," said Mrs. Barnett.

"Hmm," said Minerva.

"Quick, ask him about Peaches," Minerva thought. "I need to give Mrs. Dingbat something."

"Peaches is fine," said Dross. "Barking and humping angel legs in the celestial dog park."

"Your little dog is fine. She's with him right now," said Minerva with a reassuring smile.

Mrs. Barnett looked at her quizzically. "Peaches was our cat," she said.

"Really?" said Dross. "Hang on." He disappeared. There was nothing in Minerva's head but a deep dismay. Still, there had been other hiccups over the years. Nothing she couldn't handle.

"I didn't mean *your* dog. I meant Scotty's dog. The stray he adopted in Heaven."

"Scotty was allergic to dogs. He hated them," said Mrs. Barnett. "Our neighbor's Pomeranian brushed against his leg and I had to take him to the emergency room."

"But he likes them now," said Minerva hopefully. "And so does Peaches. They play together."

Mrs. Barnett's eyes narrowed. "Peaches hated dogs more than Scotty."

Shit. Shit. Shit. Shit. Shit. Shit. Shit.

When Dross popped back into Minerva's head, she could swear he was out of breath. "Here's the thing," he said. "And don't be mad."

"What about the warranty?" said Mrs. Barnett.

"I think he's the wrong Scott Barnett," said Dross.

Minerva's dismay expanded like a panicked puffer fish.

"It's funny when you think about it," Dross said. "I mean how many Scott Barnetts can there be that are married to a Caroline? Well, at least two."

"Ask him if he knows anything about an air conditioner or jewelry," thought Minerva.

"I'll be right back."

"Yes. Do that."

"Well?" said Mrs. Barnett. "What does he have to say?"

"It will take just a minute. He's thinking. Sometimes these earthly matters slip the spirit's mind when they've been gone for a while."

"It's only been two weeks."

"That's a long time for ghosts."

"Is it?" said Mrs. Barnett, impatience and perhaps something darker in her voice.

Minerva's puffer fish of dismay was growing into a hammerhead shark of dread.

"Okay. I double-checked. He never stole anything," said Dross.

"I doubt if he was ever sober enough. He's just a lush who wants to play cards with his buddies."

"Have you checked *behind* the filing cabinet?" said Minerva. "Scotty thinks the warranty might be there."

"That was the first place I looked after I couldn't find it," said Mrs. Barnett.

"Also, you should bring the jewelry to me so I can do a spiritual cleansing . . ."

Mrs. Barnett jumped to her feet. "I knew it. That's all you wanted all along, you faker."

"No. You don't understand. I'm not a faker," said Minerva. "I'm talking to the dead right now."

"You don't talk to anyone," said Mrs. Barnett, snatching up her purse.

"I'm psychic. I have a spirit guide and everything."

"Psychic? So, you can see into people's minds?"

"Oh! I'm good at that, remember? Quick, tell her yes," said Dross.

"Of course," said Minerva. "What would you like to know?"

"What's my middle name, my favorite food, and the number I'm thinking of?"

"Annette, pizza, and seven," said Dross.

"Annette, pizza, and seven," repeated Minerva.

"Louise, Thai fried rice, and four," said Mrs. Barnett.

"Wow," said Dross. "First the wrong ghost and now this. It's not my day." He broke into a coughing fit.

Minerva's dread, dismay, and everything else deflated. It wasn't like this in the old days. There had been limos. Parties in the hills. Invitations to movie premieres. Steve McQueen and Elizabeth Taylor never asked her about air-conditioner warranties. Why did she have to deal with this kind of crap now, at her age?

"I'm going to lay it on the line, Mrs. Barnett," said Minerva.

"When a woman finds a secret stash of jewels in her dead husband's safe-deposit box, they're stolen. Period. Dot. End of sentence. But I know people that's not a problem for . . ."

"That's what this whole thing has been about, isn't it? The jewels?"

"Pretty much," said Minerva wearily.

Mrs. Barnett walked to the front of the parlor and flung the street door open. The L.A. light that flooded into the place was blinding. Minerva put up a hand to shield her eyes.

"What do you say, Mrs. Barnett? I can set up a meet for tomorrow."

Mrs. Barnett was a blur in the light. "I ought to call the police, you big faker." Then she walked out, disappearing into the light like a ghost.

"Fuck me," said Minerva.

"Well, that was rude," said Dross. "Huh?"

Minerva didn't reply.

"Oh, don't be like that. Look, I'm sorry," Dross said. "It's just that it's all getting harder these days."

"What's getting harder?"

"This. The gags we pull. The gaffes. The cons. The old switcheroo."

"We didn't always have to play tricks on people, did we?" Minerva thought. "We imparted great spiritual truths."

"Well, we told them if their movie was going to bomb and if their spouse was banging anybody on the side. But yeah, it was the truth."

"Good times," thought Minerva.

"We were great back then, but . . ." Dross broke into another coughing spell. "Neither of us is what we used to be."

"Your point being?"

"I'm thinking about hanging up my spirit-guide spurs and retiring."

"You're a ghost. What are you going to retire to?"

"Ghosts can retire. They retire all the time."

"To do what?"

"Ghost stuff. You wouldn't understand."

Minerva's dismay returned, this time in hobnail boots.

"You're serious?"

Dross wheezed. "I'm afraid so. Look, we had a good run . . ."

"Stop right there," thought Minerva. "You sound like Carl when he handed me the divorce papers."

"Ouch. Sorry."

"I just need one big score. Stick around that long."

"I can't, Minerva," said Dross softly. "I have to go."

"Can you give me the lottery numbers, at least?"

"I couldn't even tell Thai fried rice from pizza in an old lady's noggin. You think I'm up to lottery numbers?"

"How about a horse? I'll get the racing form."

"Good-bye, Minerva."

"Wait . . ."

She felt a void in her head where Dross usually was.

Minerva walked to the front door, closed and locked it. From a tin Santa Muerte on her altar, she took out a fat joint. She lit it off a candle with Saint Jude on one side and a picture of Keith Richards taped to the other.

"To better days, boys," she said.

Over the next half hour, Minerva puffed away. She let her mind drift back to happier, more profitable times. But they refused to stay there. *These young stars today,* she thought. They were all vegans. They all did yoga. Or they went to Beverly Hills quacks for thousand-dollar high-colonics. And when one of them did come by, on the drunken advice of some fossil of a star as old and washed up as Minerva herself, it was always with a dozen friends. They laughed and never listened to what the cards or the crystal ball had to say. Dross, of course, loved them. *The ridiculous starfucker*. And as much as the kids laughed, they tipped big, so she gave them the whole swami bit.

Minerva smiled, remembering the time she managed to slip a ring off one little starlet's finger during a palm reading. That was slick. Now she wondered if she could slip a Hula-Hoop off a skeleton.

Someone knocked at the door. She went up front and peered out. It was Kellar. When they'd met in the early sixties he'd been a buff body builder and run with a rough crew of bikers. Now he was as pale and round as the moon, but with a magnificent comb-over. She undid the lock and let him come in.

"Well?" he said anxiously. "How did it go with the jewels lady?"

Minerva shook her head. "No dice."

"Damn," said Kellar.

"And Dross took a powder. Forever."

"Bummer." He plucked the joint from her mouth, took a couple of massive puffs, and handed it back.

They sat down at Minerva's reading table.

"How did your real estate scam go today?"

Kellar waved his hands at her. "Don't ask. A disaster. A total disaster."

"Yeah. We're getting good at those."

"We're getting old," said Kellar.

"We *are* old. We're ancient. Archaic. Antediluvian."

"Speak for yourself. I'm not a day over primeval."

Minerva laugh-coughed out a mouthful of pot smoke. Kellar laughed at her choking and slapped her on the back a few times.

"I'm okay," she said as her throat cleared. "I'm okay."

Kellar sat back. "Maybe we should get into sideshows."

"Do they even have those anymore?"

"Ironic ones, yes. It's these rock-and-roll circus types. They get a few tattooed freaks, a couple of sexy contortionists, and some masochists who'll do awful things to themselves and call it a circus. There's always a little freak show on the side."

"You said sideshow."

"Did I? Freak show. Sideshow. What's the difference at our age?"

Minerva's buzz ebbed substantially at that thought. "I'm not joining any freak show."

"I might," said Kellar. "If I don't get some actual money coming in, I'm going to lose my mystical hovel out by the airport."

"Still in that strip mall?"

"Between a computer repair shop and a massage parlor that smells like sandalwood and shame."

Minerva looked at him. "Who repairs computers these days? I thought people just chucked them and got a new one."

"I'll tell you who repairs computers," said Kellar. "Old people. I thought about going in and asking them for a job."

"You can repair computers?"

"No," he said quietly. "Sweeping. Cleaning up."

Minerva puffed out some smoke. "You mean cleaning them out. Were you just going to steal the cash register or were you planning on hammering the safe out of the wall? If there's not a lot of heavy lifting, I might join you."

Kellar crossed his arms on the table and laid down his head. "We just need a break. One damned break."

"More than one, but I'll take one."

"Have you reconsidered my idea . . . ?"

"I'm not burning the place," said Minerva. "I live here. Besides, those insurance companies, they have all kinds of machines and tests these days."

Kellar sat up. "You're right. Arson just isn't fun anymore."

"Remember the old days when people still played cards? Dross would look at everyone's hand and we'd clean them out."

"He was a good ghost."

"He was. The asshole."

Kellar took another hit off the joint. "I'm going down to Hollywood Boulevard to let tourists hit me with their rental cars."

Minerva pinched the end off the joint and put the rest back in the tin. "Are you going for an insurance settlement or a quick bribe from the drivers?"

"Sadly, the latter. Want to come along and be my witness? Do a little screaming?"

"Why not? If that old biddy calls the cops, I don't want to be here."

As Minerva got her bag she said, "I swear, I'd shake down the pope if I thought it would bring me just a smidgen of luck."

"You should have fucked over Keith Richards back when you had the chance."

"No, him I should have fucked."

Kellar laughed and they went out. As she locked the door, Minerva thought, *Send me one good mark, Saint Jude and Saint Keith. Just one.*

They took the bus into Hollywood and spent the rest of the evening bouncing off rental cars and screaming. After the fourth car, Minerva began to think that the sideshow idea might not be so bad after all.

14

The break-in team was in Coop and Giselle's apartment. Giselle, Morty, and Dr. Lupinsky were huddled in the kitchen. Smuggling the doctor from the car into the apartment had taken some time. It was less like sneaking in the back door and more like trying to discreetly maneuver a tap-dancing refrigerator through a wedding reception.

Coop sat alone in the far corner of the apartment, staring into space. Blueprints and coffee cups littered the floor around him.

"How many cups has he had?" said Morty.

Giselle put a finger to her lips for quiet. "I don't know," she whispered.

Dr. Lupinsky's cat paced nervously back and forth.

It looks like a lot. Is that good for him?

"Definitely not," said Morty.

And he's always like this when he's making plans?

"Not always," said Giselle.

"Just when he's onto something."

"Or not."

Morty shifted uncomfortably in his seat. "Yeah. Sometimes he's like this when he's completely stumped."

Is he stumped now?

"It's hard to tell."

"He's busy being enigmatic," said Giselle.

"But superfocused."

It's a little unnerving seeing him there all evening not talking.

"Don't be scared," said Coop. "Panicked is a much more reasonable response. In fact, feel free to scream. We don't much like the neighbors."

"Have you got something?" said Morty.

Coop shook his head. "I've got nothing."

"What are we going to do? We can't use the same plan as last time, can we?"

"Why not?" said Giselle. "They don't know how we did that job. We just cut the power and do it all again."

Coop shook his head. "It won't work. The first thing that's going to happen is someone moves in an emergency generator."

"We can blow that, too."

"Maybe."

"If we can't go through the back, how are we getting in?" said Morty.

Coop looked at them. "I have one terrible idea. The roof."

"Why there? And bear in mind, I'm a bleeder."

"They'll have the roof locked up, so it's the last place they're going to worry about. If there are cops or worse—armed security—they won't be up there."

Why is armed security worse?

"Cops deal with crooks and have to fill out forms when they shoot people, which they don't like doing," said Giselle. "Armed security are basically velociraptors with guns."

"One look at you, doc, and they'll be setting off nukes," said Coop.

"So, he can stay on the roof," said Morty.

"No way. He's our Egypt expert. I want him right there with us."

Giselle said, "How do we get on the roof? A helicopter?"

Coop stared at the plans. "No. Someone might hear it." He looked over at Dr. Lupinsky. "You walked up Woolrich's wall pretty good. Think you can do that at the museum?"

Of course.

Coop pointed to Lupinsky. "There you go. The doc goes up, lowers a line, and we follow. Morty takes care of the locks."

Morty hunched his shoulders and slid his hands into his pockets. "I still think we should cut the power."

Coop came to the kitchen and ticked off items on his fingers. "Here's how I figure it. If we cut the power, people get antsy, and if anything goes wrong, we're going to get shot. If we try a smash and grab—with whatever new alarms they've set up—we get shot. If we try to infiltrate the cops or security and get spotted, we get shot."

"You're an inspiring leader," said Morty. "You need to know that. I feel inspired."

Giselle looked worried. "I can cloud a lot of minds, but if there are too many people too far away, I don't know. If we go in with the lights on, someone is *going* to spot us."

"Yeah. They will . . ." said Coop, trailing off.

Dr. Lupinsky's cat stopped pacing and sat up on its hind legs, its front paws against the screen.

What are you thinking?

"How are we going to stay hidden?" said Giselle.

Coop stared into space again. "We're not. They're going to see us. It's the only way."

"Are you crazy?" said Morty. "You just said we'd get shot."

Coop came over and poured himself more coffee. "Giselle, can you get us some of that government amnesia gas?"

She handed Coop the sugar. He started pouring. "Sure, but you know that stuff isn't a hundred percent," she said. "People are going to remember things."

"I'm counting on it," he said, absentmindedly pouring sugar.

"If they can see us, how are we supposed to do the job?" said Morty.

"We'll be in disguise." Coop set the sugar down.

"I love disguises," said Giselle. "What kind?"

"Horrible. Terrifying. The worst thing imaginable." Coop took a sip and set his coffee down. "Who made this? It's terrible."

Dr. Lupinsky's cat paced again.

If it isn't too late, I think I'd like to panic.

"It's never too late to panic," said Morty. "I do it every morning with my cornflakes."

"It's better exercise than jogging," said Coop. "But so is drinking."

Dr. Lupinsky's cat walked offscreen.

Excuse me. I'm going to have a hot toddy and scream for a while.

"You can drink?" said Giselle.

The cat poked its head back on-screen.

No, but it seemed like the polite thing to say.

The cat disappeared again.

"Take care, doc," said Morty uncertainly.

Across the bottom of the screen appeared: *AAAAAAAAA!*

15

Froehlich winced. Rockford, the insurance investigator, was back and he was dragging two of the museum's most irritating board members with him. He'd spent a lot of time with them over the last twenty-four hours, ever since Rockford made it clear that Froehlich was a prime suspect in his break-in investigation. Finessing a chat with the three of them was like navigating a runaway kiddie pool between Scylla, Charybdis, and Darth Vader.

Besides those nosy nuisances, Froehlich was surrounded by a police forensic team and a heavily armed squad from an outside security firm that seemed to recruit mainly—judging by their size—professional wrestlers and the mutant offspring of humans and redwood trees.

And then there was the investigator's name. Rockford. Why did the nosy bastard have the same name as a TV detective? There was something nightmarish about it. Like it was a trap. Or a hallucination. *Oh God,* Froehlich thought. *I'm going crazy.* He pinched himself. It hurt. Was that good or bad? Was self-pinching itself a sign of madness? There were so many questions, each one worse than the last.

The three museum representatives stopped in front of him.

"Froehlich," said Rockford.

"Rockford," said Froehlich.

"Froehlich," said Mr. Klein.

"Mr. Klein," said Froehlich.

"Froehlich," said Ms. Baxter.

"Ms. Baxter," said Froehlich.

Every time the trio got near him, Froehlich wanted to duck out to the loading dock for a drink, but with so many people around it was hard to slip away. Having no access to vodka, he settled for being light-headed with fear.

"What are you doing here?" said Rockford.

"You've asked me that twice today," said Froehlich. "I work here. I'm still head of security."

"We'll see about that."

"You said that, too."

Rockford tapped a pencil against a small spiral-bound book in which he obsessively scribbled notes. "You have a pretty good memory for a guy who doesn't remember anything."

"What am I supposed to remember? I wasn't here during the robbery."

"That's convenient."

"How is going home convenient?" said Froehlich. "I do it every day."

Rockford scribbled something in the notebook. "I'm going to check that."

"I bet you go home every day, too."

Rockford pointed the pencil's eraser at him. "You know who else goes home every day? The Mafia. Al-Qaeda. John Dillinger."

Froehlich thought for a minute. "Hasn't John Dillinger been dead for something like eighty years?"

"So, you're intimate with the criminal underworld," Rockford said, making another note.

"No," said Froehlich. "We had an exhibit on famous American criminals a couple of years ago." He looked at Klein and Baxter. "Remember it? It was very successful."

"Yes. We did quite well with that one," said Baxter in a frigid tone that said, *Nice save, but you're not fooling anyone.*

"Of course," said Klein in a more jovial tone. "The Jesse James snow globes were a big hit." He turned to Rockford. "You shook him up and all these little bullets would float down around him."

"Cute," said the investigator in a tone that made it excruciatingly clear that he thought it was anything but.

Over Rockford's shoulder, the forensic team worked in overalls that reminded Froehlich of space suits. Between them and the behemoth guards, it was like watching aliens about to abduct a herd of dinosaurs.

"None of that gets you off the hook for this little escapade," said Rockford to Froehlich.

"Yes. What about the surveillance cameras?" said Baxter.

"What about the alarm?" said Klein.

"What about the lack of guards?" said Baxter.

"And what about the guard who hasn't reported for duty?" said Klein.

"Yeah. Where is this . . . ?" Rockford flipped through his notes.

"Gilbert," said Froehlich.

"This Gilbert character?"

Froehlich felt like a dead jackrabbit being eyed by a trio of hungry buzzards.

"I don't know," he said. "But Gilbert couldn't plan a robbery with a copy of *How to Rob a Museum*, Albert Einstein, and a tunneling machine."

Rockford's eyes locked on his. "Who's this Einstein?"

Suddenly Froehlich was very tired. "A smart guy."

"Just like you," said Rockford.

Klein stepped a bit closer to Froehlich and to his surprise

said, "Really, Rockford, Mr. Froehlich has been a loyal museum employee for nearly twenty years. I doubt he has anything to do with this business."

"I'm not so convinced," said Baxter. "Mr. Rockford makes a very convincing argument for an inside job. Why weren't there more guards on duty, Mr. Froehlich?"

"The board—that is *you*—cut the budget."

"And the surveillance system?"

Froehlich shook his head. "I don't know. That's a mystery."

"A mystery. Yes," said Baxter. "It's all a mystery, isn't it?"

"Robberies usually are," said Froehlich.

"I told you," said Rockford. "He knows all about how criminals work."

"I—I mean . . ." Froehlich stammered.

"I've got my eye on you, Froehlich."

"Me, too," said Baxter.

"Don't try to leave town."

"I wasn't planning on going anywhere."

"Good. See that you don't," said Baxter.

"I just said that I wouldn't."

"You've got an answer for everything, don't you?" said Rockford.

"Yes?" he said. Froehlich felt like a tipsy bull trying to maneuver through a china shop in high heels.

Baxter harrumphed. "Head of security indeed. I've never entirely trusted you or the lack of security around here, Mr. Froehlich."

Froehlich looked around at the three of them. "But the cuts were *your* idea. The board's, I mean."

Klein nodded to the others. "Why don't we let Mr. Froehlich get back to work and check in with the other security?"

"Don't go anywhere, you," said Rockford.

"I'm supposed to make my rounds in a few minutes."

"Make sure you do."

"How can I if I'm not supposed to go anywhere?"

Rockford made another note in his little book. "Always with the smart answers."

"No, really," said Froehlich. Looking from Klein to Baxter and back to Klein. "I don't know what . . ."

"It's fine," said Klein softly. "Go and make your rounds. It'll be all right."

The trio started walking away, leaving Froehlich with the dizzying sensation of floating out of his body, a perplexed ghost in dire need of a drink.

Klein stopped and said, "Excuse me," to his companions. "I'll catch up with you in a minute."

As the others went on, Klein came over to Froehlich. A moment later, it was clear to Froehlich that Klein was going easy on him.

"Are things all right with the situation out back?" Klein said.

Froehlich looked past him, making sure the others were out of earshot. "You mean with Gilbert's body?"

"Shh!" said Klein.

Froehlich flinched. "Don't worry. The truck came last night and took everything away."

Klein took a deep, relieved breath. "Good man. With all this mummy nonsense, a dead body is the last thing we need."

"But what if someone finds out about the borrowed mummies? The fake artifacts?"

Klein waved to Baxter and Rockford. "No one cares about anything except Harkhuf," he said. "They're not even looking at anything else."

"If you say so. Anyway, the Gilbert situation is all squared away."

"I knew I could count on you. And don't worry about that detective or the police. I've got your back."

"Yeah, but Ms. Baxter wants my neck," Froehlich said.

"Yes. Too bad *she* couldn't take a header into the trash," Klein said.

Froehlich stared after the other two. "Accidents *do* happen," he said, picturing a delightful scene in which Baxter was sinking below layers of crates and cardboard boxes. "Just one little push . . ."

Klein cocked an ear. "Sorry. I didn't hear that last part."

"Nothing," said Froehlich, almost, but not quite, dismissing the idea. "Thanks for looking out for me."

Klein shook Froehlich's hand. "Don't worry. This will all blow over soon. Oh, by the way, that drink truck you suggested is coming by today."

Froehlich raised his eyebrows. "Why? We're closed. There's nothing to sponsor anymore."

"Too late to stop it, I suppose. Deal with it when it gets here, will you?"

"Of course."

Klein clapped him on the back. "All right. Chin up. Don't worry about a thing."

"Thanks."

The moment Klein and the others disappeared around a corner, Froehlich headed out the back to the loading dock.

Outside, he made a quick circuit of the area to make sure no one was there. Seeing that it was all clear, Froehlich ducked behind some crates left by the exhibit load-in crew. Alone, he took out the miniflask he kept in his inside jacket pocket and unscrewed the top. The antiseptic perfume of vodka greeted him like an old friend. He took a quick pull off the flask and thought about Baxter. What would it take to lure her back here? And how could he do it without anybody knowing it was him? It was a puzzle, but maybe one worth solving. He put the cap back on the flask and slipped it into his pocket.

Froehlich took out a piece of xylitol gum and chewed it vigorously, trying to get the scent of vodka off his breath. Sighing, he leaned against the dock wall. However, instead of feeling brick on his back, he hit something that was softer and more brittle. Like sticks or balsa wood. It cracked under his weight.

"Shit."

Sure he'd broken a no-doubt-important crate, he turned around to inspect the damage.

It wasn't a crate he'd crushed. It was a mummy.

Froehlich stared at it for a minute, wanting to make sure that he wasn't hallucinating something out of wishful thinking or panic. He reached out a hand and touched the dead man's wrappings.

Nope. Those are real.

He stepped back for a better look. A giddy little thrill danced in his gut.

I found Harkhuf. I solved the case. I'm a goddamned hero.

Then the eternal flicker of despair at his core did what it always did at happy moments like this. It roared up and barbecued his hopes and dreams like a careless marshmallow at a cookout.

He looked again. The mummy wasn't Harkhuf.

Is an extra mummy better or worse than finding the right one? If I found Harkhuf, that creep Rockford will think I stole him, then chickened out and brought him back. But if this one isn't Harkhuf, it means there's an extra mummy, which is bad because it means someone was screwing around with mummies before the robbery while I was still in charge.

Froehlich took a drink to settle his nerves. Not that it helped. His heart pounded against his ribs like it was trying to start a fight with them. He took a few deep breaths and went over the situation in his head a few times before making a decision.

He checked the dock again. When he found it empty he sidled

up to the mystery mummy, grabbed it, and ran to the Dumpster. It arced beautifully through the air. The moment the mummy left his hand he had an even better, if ill-timed, idea. Clambering clumsily down into the Dumpster, Froehlich piled papers and crushed boxes on top of his inconvenient discovery. Just before the damned thing disappeared from sight, he broke off one of the mummy's index fingers and put it in his pocket. Climbing back onto the dock, he shoved another piece of gum into his mouth. He was sweating badly from both fear and exertion.

If anyone asks, I was in the back looking for the truck Klein told me about.

Froehlich wiped away the sweat from his face with his jacket sleeves, which left damp streaks down his arms. After patting the dirt off his clothes, he went back into the museum. He paused by the door, hoping he looked relatively normal and not like someone who'd been busy burying a three-thousand-year-old pain in the ass.

Rockford appeared to be gone and no one else was interested in what a disgraced museum flunky was up to. He took the elevator up to the top floor and wandered the exhibit halls alone, pretending to do his rounds. Instead, Froehlich's mind raced in the special way that only the mind of a man full of vodka and dread can. It would have been perfect if it had been Baxter he'd tossed into the Dumpster, but that didn't mean he couldn't help her halfway in.

Froehlich hurried down a floor, into the restricted area of the building, where employees ate lunch and some of the board members kept small offices. He went straight to Baxter's and knocked lightly on the door. There wasn't an answer. He turned the knob and the door opened. The office was empty. Stepping quickly inside, he closed the door behind him.

From his pocket, Froehlich pulled out the mummy's finger. Crushing it in his hand, he left mummy dust on the edge of Baxter's desk and the carpet beneath. When he was done, Froehlich dropped the finger into her wastebasket.

Let's see what the cleaning crew makes of that when it falls out. Rockford will forget all about me and go straight for her.

Froehlich made it out of Baxter's office just as his walkie-talkie crackled. It was one of the new security men. Carlson? The one whose neck bulged like a boa constrictor that had just swallowed a sheep.

"Froehlich, get your ass down here."

"What is it?"

"There's a truck out back. The driver said he's supposed to talk to you."

The sponsor's truck. One more piece of bullshit to deal with . . .

"I'll be right down."

"Make it fast. I have better things to do than babysit your asshole buddies."

"He's not my buddy," said Froehlich. "And you can't talk to me like that. I'm head of security."

Carlson laughed. "And I'm the security your boss hired to watch you and your Teletubbies. Now move your ass."

"Listen to me, pal . . ." said Froehlich, but Carlson was gone.

He took the elevator downstairs and hurried to the dock. The mummy exhibit sponsor's garish logo, all tentacles and lightning bolts, covered the whole side of the truck. KRAKEN ZAP, it said. As he signed to accept the now useless sport-drink banners and display cases, Froehlich took a discreet look at the Dumpster. Someone had piled more garbage inside, burying the superfluous mummy even deeper. He happily handed the forms back to the driver. As the Kraken Zap crew loaded drinks and T-shirts onto handcarts, for the first time all day, Froehlich felt vaguely human.

He wandered calmly back and forth between the museum's interior and the loading dock, making sure he was seen by as many people as possible while being as boring as he could be. *Nope. Nothing to see here,* he thought. He was just a lowly museum drone carrying out his dull duties and not at all the kind of person who would wish a board member dead or plant damning evidence in her office.

A half hour later, he gave the truck a jaunty wave as it pulled away from the loading dock. On his way back inside, Froehlich spotted a can of Kraken Zap that had fallen from one of the carts. He took it behind a pile of crates and opened it up. It wasn't so bad after all, he thought, especially when he fortified it with a little vodka.

Back inside the museum, Froehlich made a big deal out of piling up the cardboard displays and cases of Kraken Zap in a corner of the lobby.

Carlson came over to watch him. He picked up a T-shirt.

"I've had this stuff. It's swill," he said. He unfolded the T-shirt, at least six sizes too small for him. "Who's Ozzy?" he said.

"Harkhuf, the metal mummy. It was my idea. What do you think?" said Froehlich.

"Are you fucking kidding me?" Carlson said.

"Not at all."

The security behemoth wadded up the T-shirt and tossed it with the rest of the Kraken Zap display. "You are the biggest loser I ever met."

Froehlich did an exaggerated sigh. "You might be right."

Carlson went over to a cluster of other security men. He pointed at Froehlich as he refolded the T-shirt. The giants laughed at him.

Normally, a moment like this would crush Froehlich's already minuscule spirit, leaving him bitter and broken for the rest of the day. Instead, he hummed as he worked. The more people who saw him working the better. Everything was working out great.

"Come to me," said someone behind him.

Froehlich turned around, but there was no one there. He went back to work, but soon the voice came back.

"Weak and soulless one, obey me."

He spun around this time. The lobby was full of busy people going back and forth, but there wasn't anyone near him. No one was paying him the slightest bit of attention.

Froehlich set down a last case of drinks on top of a stack he'd made in the corner. When he was done, he went back into the mummy exhibit. Sometimes things echoed weirdly off the museum's marble walls.

"Hello?" he said.

Nothing. But just as he was walking away, Froehlich heard something. This time the voice seemed to be coming from inside his head.

"Worthless mortal cur."

He turned in a slow circle. "Who is that? Ms. Baxter?"

The voice seemed to be coming from the far corner of the room, by one of the sideshow mummies.

"Wretched dog."

When Froehlich got closer, his mouth fell open. It wasn't a cheap, flea-bitten stiff in the corner. It was Harkhuf.

"Hello? Who's there?" Froehlich said to the room.

"Come closer," said the voice.

He went right up to Harkhuf and stared into his empty eye sockets. They suddenly seemed like the most interesting things in the world.

The voice said, "Be my thrall."

Without thinking, Froehlich took out his flask and drained it. Still mesmerized, he stared at the mummy. It felt like it was staring back at him.

"Your will is mine. Your body is mine," said the voice.

Froehlich's eyes fluttered shut. He felt great. Better than he'd felt in years. It was like being drunk, but even better.

"Be my thrall."

A goofy smile spread across Froehlich's face.

Someone tapped him on the shoulder. He turned and saw Klein.

"Are you all right?" said Klein. "I was calling you."

"Sorry, but doesn't that mummy look like—"

"Never mind. Come along. I need you."

Klein started away. Froehlich glanced back over his shoulder at Harkhuf. He could swear that the mummy winked at him. He winked back.

"Are you coming?" said Klein.

Froehlich's goofy smile widened. "I live to serve."

"What an odd thing to say."

Froehlich's consciousness snapped back into sharp focus. "Sorry. My mind wandered."

"Hurry along. There are things to do."

"Yes," Froehlich said. "There's so much to do."

16

"Shouldn't we *all* have cop uniforms?" said Morty.

"You're wearing your uniforms," said Coop.

"Yeah, but what if we get stopped? You look fine, but the rest of us aren't exactly in standard cop issue."

"If we get stopped, you're my prisoners."

"You think that will work?"

"I can always handcuff you."

"Yay. I volunteer to be handcuffed," said Giselle.

Morty looked from her to Coop.

"Coop, you dirty old man," said Phil Spectre inside everybody's head.

"Everyone pipe down. If we get stopped, I'll just hit them with some of the amnesia gas."

Giselle crawled up to the front of the van. "So, no cuffs?" she said in mock disappointment.

"Later, dear."

She flopped down between the seats. "Promises, promises."

The break-in team prowled through the city at four A.M. in a police van courtesy of the DOPS. Not that it was a real LAPD vehicle. It was Coop's understanding that the DOPS had 3-D printed it. It was also his understanding that they could print human organs, five-lens spider-friendly glasses, robot parts, and—for office picnics—geometrically perfect s'mores.

"These giant shoes are killing me," whined Morty. He took off his round red nose, sneezed, and put it back on.

"You think I'm happy dressed like T. J. Hooker?" said Coop.

"Yeah, Coop. You look like you're about ten seconds away from tossing yourself in the pokey," said Phil.

"Shut up, Phil," said Morty. "You and Coop are the only ones not dressed like Bozo's hillbilly cousins. I hate wearing makeup."

"You look fine, Morty. You could have a second career making balloon animals at kid parties," said Giselle.

Morty looked back at Dr. Lupinsky. "I bet you're happy you don't have a regular body tonight."

Wait a minute.

Dr. Lupinsky's cat walked offscreen and came back wearing what looked like a pointy party hat.

"Is that supposed to make me feel better?" Morty said.

"Looking at you idiots is making me feel *great,*" said Phil.

"What should make you feel better is messing with cops so they have to write the worst robbery reports in history," said Coop.

"All I'm saying is we should have been ninjas."

"Ninjas don't give people nightmares. Clowns do."

Morty considered it. "I guess that makes sense. But next time you come up with a plan like this, *you* get back here in the floppy shoes and I'll drive."

There was a flash from the back of the van.

"What was that?" said Coop.

"Nothing," said Giselle.

"Did you just take a selfie?"

"Of course not."

"Fibber," said Phil.

Coop shook his head. "I can't take you people anywhere."

"But I'm adorable like this," said Giselle. "I just wanted to commemorate the moment."

Coop just shook his head and steered the van into a parking lot.

"No more class pictures or complaining," he said. "We're almost there."

They drove around the very edge of the museum's lot until they were behind the building. Coop stopped the van in a regular parking spot under one of the still-broken streetlights.

He turned around in his seat. "Everyone suited up? Wigs on? Noses in place?"

"This is humiliating," said Morty.

"At least you're not stealing office supplies," said Phil.

"Yeah," said Morty, brightening a bit. "You need to tell me about that sometime."

"When we're in the old-folks home," said Coop. He looked to the back of the van. "How are you doing, doc? Got your new batteries?"

I'm feeling fine. A little nervous.

"We're all nervous," said Giselle. "You're going to do great."

Thank you.

"Stick with me, Optimus Prime," said Phil. "I won't let you pop a rivet."

Speaking as a fellow spirit, you're very optimistic. How exactly did you die?

"Yeah, Phil. You've never talked about that. What's your story?" said Giselle.

"I was rescuing a damsel in distress when a dragon got me," he said.

"Or you got shot by a trumpet player in Sonny Brisco's big band when he caught you climbing out of his girlfriend's window," said Coop.

"It's true. I died for love."

"And the trumpet player's gold cuff links."

"Just how old are you, Phil?" said Morty.

"Well . . ." said Phil.

"The way I heard it, at least one of you was wearing spats," said Coop.

"Wow. You're like ancient," said Morty.

"At least I don't look like I escaped from Captain Kangaroo's basement," Phil sputtered.

"Down, boys. Let's get to work," said Giselle.

"She's right," said Coop. "Here's how it's going to go. The doc and I'll get things set up at the museum. When he lowers the line, you run like hell over to us. And don't forget the gear."

Everyone nodded in jittery agreement. Giselle honked her bicycle horn. Coop gave her a long stare, then lowered the ramp on the back of the van. He and Dr. Lupinsky bolted across the parking lot to an unlit area of the museum wall.

"You ready for this, doc?"

Dr. Lupinsky's cat paced, its tail twitching nervously.

What if I fall?

"My advice is don't."

That's good advice. Here I go.

Dr. Lupinsky put one of his tentacle-like legs against the wall, then another. When he had three legs on the stone, he gingerly lifted himself off the ground and curled the rest of his legs onto the wall. Once secure, he tiptoed up the side of the building like an ambivalent spider. A few minutes later, he disappeared over the lip of the roof.

"This isn't terrifying at all," said Phil.

"A walk in the park," said Coop.

"It's like old times, isn't it?" said Phil. "You and me on the job, about to snatch some big shot's solid-gold shoe trees."

"Except now we're on a salary and have to give everything back."

"Yeah, that's a drag. Still, it's great working together again."

"Don't take this the wrong way, but I'd rather be literally anywhere else in the world right now." Coop checked his watch. "What's taking him so long?" He looked back at the police van. If they ran now they could make it to Mexico by dawn, ditch the van, steal a car, and disappear into the desert by lunch. Coop knew it wasn't his best plan but, he thought, *It can't possibly be any worse than this.*

"I'm giving him two more minutes," he said.

"You don't have to. Watch your head, dummy," said Phil.

Coop stepped out of the way just as the end of a length of heavy rope thudded to the ground beside him. He gave the cord a tentative pull and it felt solid.

"Looks like Robocop did his job after all. See? You're always so worried about things," said Phil.

Coop climbed the rope a few feet and jumped down. "I haven't been shot by a trumpet player yet and I'd like to keep it that way."

In his head, he quickly went over his plan again, hoping to find something he'd missed, some other way into the museum that didn't involve dangling like a dying flounder at the mercy of a windup toy.

"Coop . . . ?" said Phil.

"Okay," he said, and waved to the van.

Morty and Giselle dashed out of the back, duffel bags slung over their shoulders. In their odd costumes, it took a little longer than normal for them to cross the lot. Morty was the slowest, high-stepping in shiny blue shoes that extended a good twelve inches past the end of his foot. Eventually, they reached the wall.

As soon as they got there, Coop said, "Everybody ready?"

"You're not," said Morty. He thrust a spiky green wig and red round nose into Coop's hand. "Join the clown club, Officer Twinkles."

Coop reluctantly pulled the wig over his head and stuck the nose over his.

"Satisfied?" he said.

Giselle sniggered.

"Getting there," Morty said.

Coop grabbed the rope and stuck his foot into one of the loops tied down its length. "I'll go up first. The rest of you grab on when the doc pulls. Oh, and don't ever call me Officer Twinkles again."

"Sergeant Sparkles is more like it," said Giselle.

Coop didn't say a word. He just took a duffel bag off her shoulder and tugged twice on the rope. It slowly pulled him into the air.

The whole way up, Coop kept telling himself that Dr. Lupinsky knew what he was doing. Besides, why was going up this wall so different from others? He'd climbed plenty of walls and ropes in his criminal career. Of course, those times he'd been *climbing*, not hanging on for dear life hoping he wasn't going to pull a walking clothes dryer down on top of him. At around the third floor, he closed his eyes. Coop wasn't big on praying, but he did mention God's name several times on the way up—mostly to curse everything and everyone around him.

Finally, he made it to the roof. Coop pulled himself over the edge and dropped the duffel bag. Dr. Lupinsky continued to wind up the rope around two of his metal tentacles. Coop gave him a quick nod.

Meow, said the television cat.

Coop hung over the edge of the roof and helped pull up the others. First Giselle, then Morty. Their wigs were askew, one of

Morty's shoes was half off, and the enormous plastic carnation in Giselle's striped lapel drooped as though it had lost the will to live. Giselle gave Coop a hug. Morty leaned against an air duct and gave them a gasping wave.

"Coop," he said.

"Yes?"

"Your plan sucks."

"That was the hard part. The rest is going to be a lot easier."

"Ahem," said Phil.

"Yeah. That's why we have Phil with us?" said Morty. "Because it's going to be easy?"

"Easier," said Coop. "Not easy. *Easier.*"

"Can't we just stay up here for the rest of our lives? We can drink rainwater and eat pigeons."

"I like Morty's idea," said Giselle.

"Me, too. That's three votes for living up here. You're outnumbered," said Phil.

"We can't stay here," said Coop.

"Why not?" said Morty.

"Because the doc needs batteries. You don't want the pussycat to die, do you?"

"Aw. You do like kitties. I knew it," said Giselle.

Thank you, Coop, appeared on Dr. Lupinsky's screen as he pulled up the rest of the rope.

Coop ignored the chatter and looked around. "Who has the amnesia gas?"

"It's over here," said Giselle, unzipping one of the duffels. She took out several soda-can-size canisters with little bat wings tucked underneath.

"How do they work?' said Coop.

"It's easy. They're like grenades. You pull this pin and it turns them on. Then you just point them where you want them to go and off they go."

"They look like party favors."

"They'll make everyone inside loopy as a ferret and as dumb as a goldfish," Giselle said.

"Sounds like a party," said Phil.

Coop scratched his scalp through his wig. It just made his head itch more. "We want the things inside, on every floor from here to the lobby. Can they do that?"

"Easy," Giselle said brightly.

"Don't say 'easy.' You'll jinx it," said Morty.

"Doable."

"Thank you."

Coop went to where Morty leaned on the duct. "You're in charge of any locks between us and the museum. We need to get the bats all the way inside."

Morty gave him a thumbs-up. "You look good giving orders again. Like your old self."

"My old self would have punched me for a rickety plan like this," said Coop.

Dr. Lupinsky set down the rope and crept over.

What about me?

"You stay with me and Phil until we get to mummy central." Coop looked around once more. "Anybody have any questions?"

"I have one," said Giselle.

"What?"

She took out her phone. "You look ridiculous in that nose and wig. Can't I take just one picture?"

"There's no way . . ." said Coop before he heard the sound of a camera shutter. "Are you happy now?" he said.

"Very."

"Finish with the bats."

"Just two shakes of a lamb's tail," she said.

"Did everybody take their anti-amnesia pills?" said Morty. "I have some more."

"I'll take another," said Coop.

"How many is that for you?"

"This'll be my third."

"Maybe you ought to lay off after this. There might be side effects."

"I'm in a cop getup with a green wig and a rubber nose. How much worse can I get?"

Morty shrugged. "Maybe I'll have another, too."

"Finished," said Giselle. A dozen of the winged canisters lay in a neat pile next to her.

"That's enough for the whole museum?" said Coop.

"Are you kidding? That's enough for Las Vegas."

Coop turned to the others. "I know this plan is sketchy as hell. If anyone wants out, now's the time. No hard feelings."

"I don't have hands per se, but if I did, they'd both be raised," said Phil.

"A minute ago, you were all gung ho," said Coop.

"A minute ago, I was on the ground. Now I'm in the air with Cirque du Soleil and some bottle rockets."

"Tough. You don't get a vote."

"We have no idea what's inside."

"We will in a minute. Anyone else?"

"Will you quit it with the dramatics?" said Morty. "No one's going anywhere, so let's get the rodeo started."

"Okay. Thanks," said Coop. "Morty, you're up. Get us inside."

With Morty in the lead, they went to a door over an enclosed staircase at one end of the roof. The others followed with the gas bats and bags. Morty took a breath and touched the door. Locks popped. He pulled, and the door swung open.

Timidly, Morty stuck his head inside the staircase. There was nothing but cinder-block walls and metal steps. He edged down a flight to another door and listened for a few seconds.

He looked back at Coop and touched the door with one finger, jumping back as it came open.

The lights on the top floor were all out. Morty took a quick skulk around the gallery and came back.

"You were right, Coop. Everybody is downstairs."

"Great. Let's send in the bombers," he said.

Giselle took one of the gas bats, pulled a pin on its rear, and tossed it.

"Fly, my pretties!"

Silently, the bat's wings began to flap. It rose, almost to the ceiling, before zooming down the stairs.

Coop and the others smiled. The television cat meowed. They pulled the pins from the rest of the bats and tossed them into the dark. They swooped and fluttered downstairs, leaving trails of white mist behind. As the last one disappeared, Coop pulled the door closed and checked his watch.

"How long will the gas take?" he said.

"Not long. Give it ten minutes," Giselle said.

"What are we going to do to pass the time?" said Phil.

"You can tell us more about spats, Uncle Phil," said Morty.

"What do you know about dressing well?" Phil said. "You're a guy who probably buys his clothes by the pound."

"Touchy. Why don't you sing us one of Sonny Brisco's big band tunes?"

"Do *not* encourage him to sing," said Coop. "He's impossible to turn off."

"Don't worry, Coop," said Phil. "I wouldn't waste my pipes on these philistines. But just so you know, I *own* Roy Orbison on karaoke night. I'll sing 'In Dreams' and make you cry like I banged your mom."

"Don't threaten me with karaoke," said Morty. "I have more Sinatra in my little finger than you have in your ectoplasmic whatever."

"Are you calling me out, Clarabell?"

"Are you challenging me, Casper?"

"Don't call me that!" said Phil. "Ghosts hate that name."

"Sorry," said Morty.

"It's okay. Just watch it with that stuff."

"Okay, Sam."

"Why are you calling me Sam now?"

"He's the ghost from that movie."

"What movie?"

"*Ghost.*"

"Never heard of it."

"Come on. Every ghost must know that movie."

"Nope. I'm drawing a blank."

"It's got Demi Moore and a pottery wheel."

"Now it's arts and crafts. Settle on a topic, Emmett Kelly."

"I think he's messing with you, Morty," said Giselle.

Morty's eyes narrowed. "Is that true? You screwing with me, Freddy Krueger?"

"Maybe just a little," said Phil. "Every ghost knows that goddamn movie. And we hate it almost as much as we hate Casper. Ever since that thing came out, spirits are supposed to look like that Swayze asshole. All pecs and six-pack abs. You think there's a lot of gyms over here? Let me tell you, there's not. If you were a fat fuck when you died, you're pretty much a fat fuck as a ghost. Does that sound like fun?"

"Sorry," said Morty. "I didn't know it was so hard being a ghost."

"Aside from being dead?"

"Yeah, aside from that."

"It's not that bad most of the time," said Phil, calmer now. "At least I have a job. I'm not some stir-crazy phantom stuck in a Gothic mansion out on the moors somewhere."

"Does that really happen?"

"All the time. And then some prick knocks the place down to put up a mall and the last microscopic bit of dignity you had left goes out the window because now you're not haunting the tower where you were murdered by your jealous lover. No, now you're the spook in the haunted nail salon. On a good day, maybe you get to throw some cotton balls at a soccer mom."

Dr. Lupinsky nodded his bulky body.

It's true. Being dead is complicated. It took me a long time to convince anyone that I was still here, trapped in this television. For years, everyone just thought I was stuck on a crappy nature show that never ended.

"That's so sad," said Giselle.

It wasn't all bad. Unlike Phil, I never got the hang of fashion. Being dead during the seventies means I missed a lot of terrible clothes.

"Flared jeans," said Phil.

Paisley.

"Nehru jackets."

Puka shells.

"A velour tuxedo to your prom," said Morty.

Giselle looked at him. "You sound as old as Phil."

"No. It was a seventies theme. Though, in retrospect, the tuxedo was maybe a little much."

"Velour could be. With girls, there's a fine line between ironic and unfuckable."

"I overshot ironic by a mile."

"You poor boys. Such sad stories," said Giselle, putting on a pouty face. "Want to hear a really crappy one about Coop?"

"Yes!" they said.

"No," said Coop. He turned away from the group and looked at his watch. "It's ten minutes. Let's move."

"There's no way it's been ten minutes," said Phil.

"Yes. It's absolutely been ten."

Dr. Lupinsky's cat rubbed its side on the television screen.

Thank you for bringing up the subject of the ghosting experience, Phil. I seldom get to talk about it.

"Anytime, doc. It's good to have another spirit around when I have to work with these meat buckets."

Dr. Lupinsky's cat knocked its party hat off and batted it around happily.

If you ever want to come over and visit my television, you're welcome.

"Thanks, but I'm allergic to cats."

I understand.

"Let's move," said Coop.

"There's no way that was ten minutes," whispered Morty.

17

Across town, Vargas was getting home before dawn, an unusual event for him. As much as he hated leaving work early, he just had to get away from Zulawski. The man's obsession with the parcel was getting worse. Of course, Zulawski loved to accuse *him* of being the one obsessed. Tonight, though, Vargas had nailed him. Coming back from the restroom in the middle of their shift, he caught Zulawski in a welding mask and gloves, poking the parcel with a cardboard mailing tube covered in aluminum foil.

"Exactly what are you doing?" said Vargas.

Zulawski shushed him and crooked a finger for Vargas to follow. They backed all the way to the office door before Zulawski would speak.

"It's talking," he whispered.

"What? The parcel?"

"No. The pencil sharpener. Of course I mean the parcel!"

"All right. Calm down," said Vargas, who was beginning to feel less and less calm the more Zulawski talked. "What did it say?"

"I don't know. It wasn't speaking English."

"What was it?"

"Something old," said Zulawski gravely. "Something . . . eldritch."

Vargas scratched his chin as if deep in thought. Really, he was looking around for something to hit Zulawski with if he kept on his current trajectory and went completely insane.

"Eldritch, huh? Well, that does sound unsettling."

"Unsettling? It's horrifying. I can't stand being near it anymore."

"I can understand. It being so eldritch and all."

Zulawski peered at him appraisingly. "You don't believe me."

Vargas held his hands up, still speaking quietly. "I didn't say that. But tell me one thing, please."

"What?"

"What's with the foil scimitar?"

Zulawski clutched the silver-wrapped tube to his chest like a homemade life preserver. "It's to keep away the rays when I touch it."

Vargas continued to keep his voice low. "Which rays are those?"

"The thought rays. The ones that put the voice in your head."

"You mean like a tinfoil hat that people wear so the CIA can't read their thoughts?"

"Yes. Like that."

"Those are crazy people," said Vargas at full volume.

Zulawski took a step back, holding the tube at him like a sword. He looked at the parcel over on the shelf. "What have you done? I think it heard you."

"That's it," said Vargas. He went to his desk in as calm and nonthreatening way as he could and put on his jacket. "I'm leaving. If I stay, you're going to make me as crazy as you."

Zulawski came over to his desk. "You can't leave me alone with that thing," he said pleadingly. "Please."

Vargas stepped around Zulawski, but stopped by the office door. "I'm going home. I suggest that you do the same. Tomorrow we'll call someone who knows about haunted whatnots."

Zulawski went back to frantic whispering. "That's the insidious part. It's against the rules for us to tell anybody! We're trapped with it."

Vargas opened the door and stepped out. "Go home. You're overwrought. We'll figure out something tomorrow."

"Maybe you're right," said Zulawski. He set down the tube just long enough to snatch his jacket off the back of his chair. Then he grabbed it again and pressed it to his chest. "But I'm taking my tube with me. If you want one, you'll have to make your own."

"I'll get right on that," said Vargas. "Good night."

"Good night," said Zulawski, coat in one hand, tube in the other, still staring at the parcel.

Living on a government salary in a city like L.A. wasn't easy and Vargas didn't much like the seedy building where he lived, his grim apartment, or his odd neighbors. Like that Brad guy on the first floor. The earnest loser who stuffed animal rights pamphlets into everyone's mailboxes. Sometime in the last few days, he'd nailed crosses and hung rosary beads all over the hall near his apartment door. As he picked up his mail, Vargas thought, *The guy is as batty as Zulawski.*

At that precise moment, he looked up from a gas bill to see a bewildered-looking Brad in the hallway in a T-shirt and boxer shorts.

At least he doesn't have a damned tube.

Brad looked at Vargas a little wide-eyed. "Hi," he said tentatively.

"Hello," said Vargas equally tentatively.

He noticed something white squirm in Brad's hand, and when he looked at the floor, he saw more white things on the hall rug. Vargas looked back at his neighbor.

"I'm sorry. They got out again," said Brad. "Please don't tell anyone."

Vargas pointed at the floor. "Those are mice. With ears on their backs."

"Yeah."

"They're yours?"

"Sort of," said Brad.

"So, you stole them."

Brad scooped up a couple more mice. "We liberated them from a research lab."

"You might want to liberate them back. They might have diseases or something."

"No. They're fine. I've been with them for days."

"I'm not sure if 'fine' is the word I'd use. I mean, the ears."

"They're funny-looking, aren't they?"

Vargas looked at Brad. "Hysterical. But please try keeping them out of the hall," he said.

Vargas carefully sidestepped the mutant horde and headed for the stairs thinking, *First Zulawski and now the Pied Piper. When it rains it pours mice.*

"Please don't tell the landlady," called Brad. "I think she thinks they're demons or something."

A tiny switch clicked in Vargas's head.

Two crazy people in one night? Maybe it's not a coincidence. Maybe it's something more.

Vargas stopped at the bottom of the stairs and turned back to Brad. "I'll make you a deal," he said.

"What kind of deal?" said Brad suspiciously. "I don't have any money."

Mice wandered aimlessly around the hall. A few scratched at the apartment door, clearly as sick of the crosses and incense as Vargas was.

"I don't want money. But in exchange for not telling the landlady, I want some of your mice. Six should do it."

Brad took a step back, scattering a mob of mice. "What for?"

"Don't worry," said Vargas reassuringly. "I'll give them a good home."

"I don't know if I'm allowed to do that. We're sort of a collective . . ."

Vargas started up the stairs. "Oh, well. I'm sure the landlady knows a cheap exterminator."

"No. Wait," Brad said, clutching his mice the way Zulawski had clutched his tube. "You'll take good care of them?"

"Like they were my own mutant kiddies," said Vargas. "And they'll have more room to run around than in your shitty apartment."

Brad frowned. "How do you know my apartment is shitty?"

"Because my apartment is shitty. Odds are your apartment is just as shitty. Plus, it's full of deviant rodents."

"I guess it is. Okay," Brad mumbled, looking at the furry swarm. "Six, you said?"

"Yes. Three males and three females."

Brad shooed the remaining mice back into his apartment. "Wait? You want babies?"

"Lots," said Vargas.

"What for?"

"They're for a friend. He's not feeling so well right now, but I think these furry little beauties will brighten both of our lives."

"Okay. But don't let them escape. People freak out. They're just too weird."

Vargas reached out and gently petted the mice in Brad's hands. "Trust me, where they're going, they'll fit right in."

Brad scratched his ass through his boxer shorts. He clearly wasn't happy about any of this.

"Well?" said Vargas. "It's me or the landlady."

Brad looked dumb and blank, which Vargas took for him thinking. "I'll get a box," he said finally.

"Remember. Boys *and* girls. Just like Noah took on the Ark."

As Brad went into his apartment he shook his head. "You're kind of a strange guy, mister."

"Shh." Vargas pointed to his ear and then at the mice. "They're listening."

"I'll be back in a minute," said Brad.

"Take your time," said Vargas. He sat down on the stairs thinking, *Wait until Zulawski gets a look at these.*

18

They took the elevator down to the first floor, but Coop kept a finger over the button for the top floor in case anything had gone wrong with the gas.

It hadn't. In fact, it had worked better than any of them hoped.

The lobby was full of what at first looked like a scene from a zombie movie, except that no one was eating anyone and everybody was immaculately coiffed. Dazed, glass-eyed security guards wandered listlessly across the room or sprawled on the floor like exhausted two-year-olds. Every now and then a couple of them would collide and ricochet off in different directions. They'd stagger or laugh and get right back to wandering like it was part of their job description.

"Holy shit. These people are huge," said Morty. "It's like André the Giant had a litter of little Andrés."

Coop watched the zombies on patrol. "Even stoned, they're on the clock," he said.

"You have to admire their work ethic," said Giselle.

"No, I don't. I resent it. Why can't they lie down like regular people when they're high?"

"The gas doesn't work like that. It just wipes their brains. It doesn't turn them into a freshman dorm."

"I suppose we have to go out there and see just how wiped they are."

"I hope by 'we' you mean 'you,'" said Phil.

"I guess so," Coop said. "But don't you dare bail on me. There might be traps or alarms I can't see."

"I'm right with you, pal."

"Good."

"Until circumstances dictate otherwise."

"I knew I could count on you."

Coop took a few cautious steps out of the elevator, grabbed one of the museum stanchions, and dragged it back to the elevator.

"I don't think anyone noticed you," said Giselle.

Coop looked around the room. None of the wanderers seemed the least bit interested in them.

"They could be biding their time," he said.

"For what?" said Morty. "Half of them are drooling and the other half are about to join the first half. These people aren't planners."

Coop put the stanchion in front of the elevator doors so they wouldn't close. Picking up one of the duffel bags, he said, "I guess we'll know in a minute."

"Good luck," said Giselle.

"If I make it to the exhibit room, the rest of you follow me."

Dr. Lupinsky's cat cocked its head.

And if you don't?

"Rescue me."

How will we do that?

"You went to college. Think of something."

Coop took a few tentative steps from the elevator. He moved carefully around the caroming guards, trying not to come into contact with anyone. But the lobby was crowded, and his creeping turned into a nervous, jerking square dance. Inevitably, a woman with an earpiece and the bulge of a gun under her arm tripped and fell into Coop's arms.

He froze, eye to eye with the armed guard. She stared at him hard. Then frowned and pushed away. Coop tensed, ready to retreat to the elevator. Swaying slightly, the guard reached out a finger and touched his red rubber nose.

"Boop," she said. And broke down laughing.

"Boop," said Coop, and she dropped to the floor, giggling. He waved to the others.

The rest of the team followed Coop to the exhibit hall. Stacked against the wall on the way in was the Kraken Zap display. Morty stopped in front of it.

"'Kraken Zap: Release the Serpent,'" he said. "What the hell is this?"

"It's an energy drink," said Giselle.

Morty pointed to the kraken's tentacles shooting lightning into the sky. "Hey, doc. He kind of looks like you."

Ha ha ha.

Giselle looked annoyed. "This is dumb. Krakens were mythical creatures that dragged ships to the bottom of the ocean. Plus, they're cephalopods. Cephalopods don't zap."

"It's poetic license," said Morty. "Like it's a superhero."

Giselle shook her head, unimpressed. "You can take all the poetic license you want; it still doesn't make a kraken Batman."

Coop gestured impatiently for them to follow him inside.

"Wouldn't it be cool if Batman had tentacles?" said Morty.

"I'd watch the hell out of that," said Phil.

"Me, too."

The group spread out around Coop, who stood a few feet back from a circle of police tape surrounding Harkhuf's sarcophagus. Stoned security guards pinballed into them or slept on the floor by the room's remaining mummies.

"Okay, Phil. Earn your keep. Do you see any illusions, wards, or supernatural traps?" said Coop. He felt the poltergeist squirm around inside his skull for a few seconds.

"Nothing. Not a thing. These nimrods don't have so much as a spooky black cat."

Coop slowly approached one of several slender metal cylinders set up around the sarcophagus area.

"But they have a regular alarm system," he said. "It looks like a motion detector. If anything goes inside the police tape, it goes off."

"What are we going to do about that?" said Giselle.

"We could lower you on a zip line like *Mission: Impossible,*" said Phil. "Who has a ladder?"

Three or four grinning guards stood around the group, staring at their funny wigs and floppy shoes.

"Are we okay?" said Coop.

"Look at them," said Giselle. "They think it's the circus."

Coop looked over the closest one. His eyes were big and dumb, like a taxidermied guppy. Giselle was right. As far as they were concerned, Coop and the others were a kiddie show come to life.

"We should have brought cotton candy. We could sell it to these dopes and make a fortune," he said.

"So, how are we getting around the alarm?" said Morty. "I could pop the lock on one and maybe turn it off."

"I don't want to drive the *Titanic*. I want to crash it and get out," said Coop. He pointed to the exhibit. "Hey doc, is that the amulet over there?"

Dr. Lupinsky looked past Coop.

Yes. The round object in the center of the jewelry collection.

Coop and Morty looked at a small display case within the ring of motion detectors.

"It doesn't look like much," said Morty. He took a pry bar

from one of the duffels. "Ten seconds with this and we'd have it."

"But how do we get to it?" said Coop.

The security guards that had been staring at Coop and the others had gathered around Dr. Lupinsky.

"Doc, can your cat do a trick or something so they stay out of our way?" said Coop.

Dr. Lupinsky turned to the group and the cat disappeared. It was replaced by a grainy black-and-white movie of a mummy wrapped in rotting linens and carrying a beautiful woman through a painfully obvious cardboard set. The security guards crowded around to watch.

"So, this is the job?" said Phil. "We get a bunch of security lugs stoned and set them up with their own drive-in theater? Morty was right, Coop. Your plan sucks."

Coop took the pry bar from Morty's hands. "Why get clever now?" he said. "They've already seen us. We can do this fast and dirty and make it their fault."

"I like the sound of that," said Giselle.

Coop looked over the alarms. "It'll take the cops three, maybe four minutes to get here when the alarm goes off. I'm going to get the amulet. When I do, the rest of you clear a path through the mimes so we can get back to the elevator."

"Good. It's hot in this clown suit and I think I'm allergic to this nose," said Morty.

"Ready?"

"Not at all," said Phil. The others nodded.

Coop grabbed a beefy security guard with a neck like a tree trunk, and shoved him backward. He fell through the police tape, knocking over one of the motion detectors. The moment the guard hit the floor he began to snore. Coop jumped over him as a pulsing siren alarm went off. Jamming the pry bar into the top of the display case, he put his weight on it. It only took a few seconds for the case to pop open. Coop grabbed the amulet and threw it into one of the duffels. He took a few steps toward the elevator, but the other jewels sparkled so beautifully. *Screw it,* he thought, and grabbed everything in the case.

"Let's go," he said. "The cops are on the way."

He hoisted the duffel over his shoulder and went to follow the others. But they weren't moving.

"Coop," said Giselle. "Look behind you."

He turned, but wasn't sure what he was seeing at first. It looked like a scene from Dr. Lupinsky's Karloff movie, but it was in color and right in front of him in the museum. A mummy had stepped away from the wall and was lumbering toward them.

"Does anybody else hear that voice?" said Phil. "It's like it's in my head."

"You don't have a head," said Morty.

"Still."

As the mummy closed in on them, a security guard dragged himself unsteadily off the floor. His name tag said FROEHLICH. The mummy pointed. The security guard pointed.

"Oh, man. He's in my head," said Phil.

"Who?"

"Cooper," said Froehlich. "Charles Cooper. Give back to me what is mine."

"The mummy," said Phil.

"Crap," said Coop.

"Run!"

They shouldered their way through the careening mob of confused guards as Froehlich pulled a pistol from the holster of the guard on the floor. Coop and the others were almost out of the exhibit area when he started firing. Bullets pinged all around them, gouging holes in the marble walls and floor. Morty kicked over a couple of cases of Kraken Zap. As Froehlich staggered after them security guards slipped on the cans, pulling other guards on top of them. Froehlich tripped and cannoned into the pile, but kept firing.

"There's no time to get to the roof," said Coop. "Out the front. Giselle, do your thing. Doc, open those doors."

Giselle concentrated. If any of the guards were lucid enough to notice that kind of thing, the group would have seemed to disappear. Dr. Lupinsky slithered on his tentacles through the chaos and kicked open the front doors. They ran down the museum steps and around the back as shots flew over their heads.

Coop took out the van keys and activated the ramp. With Dr. Lupinsky still in the lead, they charged inside and got the back of the van closed just as the first few police cars pulled into the lot.

"What do we do?" said Morty.

Coop got in the driver's seat and tossed his nose and wig on the floor.

"Nothing. We sit tight. We're cops, remember?"

"Oh, right."

"See? Your plan doesn't suck entirely," said Giselle.

"Thanks," Coop said.

"Wow. That was close," said Phil. "But exciting, right?"

"What the hell happened back there, Phil?" said Giselle.

"Happened?"

"You said someone was in your head, then that security hump all of a sudden knew my name," said Coop.

"Oh. That."

"Yeah. *That*."

"That strolling mummy? It's kind of alive. And it's got power."

"And now it knows my name."

"Sorry about that."

Coop drooped back against his seat. "I told Woolrich going back a second time was a bad idea."

Dr. Lupinsky's cat returned to the screen.

I know things didn't go entirely to plan, but I have to agree with Phil. It was exciting.

"I'm glad you had a good time," said Morty.

I've never been shot at before.

"You have a strange sense of fun, doc."

I'm bulletproof. It helps.

"What do you think was going on with that guard who shot at us?" said Giselle. "His badge said Franklin or Frodo or—"

"Froehlich," said Coop.

"It should have said Renfield," said Phil. "I've seen this kind of thing before. Dead things on the prowl? They usually need a fall guy."

"What does that mean?"

"Do you think mummies can drive or wander down Sunset in broad daylight? They need a stooge who can do that for them."

"A stooge with a gun," said Giselle.

"In this case."

"Let me get this straight," said Coop. "I have a mummy's curse on me?"

"I'm afraid so," said Phil.

"And the mummy has a chauffeur."

"Probably Netflix and pizza delivery, too."

"How is this even possible? I'm immune to magic."

"From what I heard, it's using old stuff. Prehistoric shit."

"And that makes a difference?" said Coop.

"Let me put it this way," said Phil. "Were you fucked ten minutes ago?"

"No."

"Are you fucked now?"

"Yes."

"Then I guess it makes a difference."

Coop looked at Giselle. "I should have gone to Mexico when I had the chance."

"I should have let you," said Giselle.

"Never mind. I have an idea."

"Another?" said Morty in a not-entirely-encouraging tone.

"I'm keeping the amulet."

"What?"

"Coop, you can't," said Giselle. "Woolrich will send you back to jail."

"Or you'll end up as one of those heads on his wall," said Phil, then added, "But, hey, if you're dead, you, me, and the doc can work together all the time."

"I'd rather haunt the baboon house at the zoo. They have more class," said Coop.

"Well, now my feelings are hurt."

"Good," said Giselle and Morty.

"Okay. Woolrich can have the amulet," said Coop. "But I'm keeping everything else. Maybe something in that junk has power to keep the mummy off me."

"Now you're thinking," said Morty.

"Giselle, do you know anyone at the DOPS who can get rid of curses?"

"No, but I can ask around."

Coop started the van, hit the siren, and burned rubber out of the lot. The other police cars just watched them roll by.

As they turned out of the lot Coop said, "I just want you to know, Phil, that this is it. We're never working together again."

"Oh, stop whining," said Phil. "It's a mummy. Bones and beef jerky wrapped in tissue paper. What's it going to do? Stagger at you menacingly? Morty does that when he's had too many beers."

"*I'm* never menacing," said Morty.

"You are sometimes," said Coop.

"Yeah. You are," said Giselle.

"Huh. I never knew," Morty said. "That's upsetting."

"Well, you're not a hundred percent *menacing*," Coop said.

"Maybe more like distressing," said Giselle.

"Like a two-hundred-pound-baby-bear-looking-for-its-mom distressing."

"That's better?"

"Don't worry. You couldn't menace a kitten in those floppy shoes," Giselle said.

"Yeah. Can we take these damned costumes off?" said Morty.

"I forgot you were wearing one," said Phil. "You look so natural that way."

"Shut up, Phil. You don't get to be smart tonight," said Giselle.

"Fine. I'm leaving."

"So leave. Just be around tomorrow when we meet with Woolrich."

"Sure thing. I'll be right there," said Phil, and popped out of everyone's mind.

Dr. Lupinsky's cat lay down.

I don't think he's going to be there.

"Not a chance in hell," said Coop.

19

As predicted, there was no sign of Phil at the morning meeting.

"I can't help but notice that one of your team is missing," said Woolrich.

"Phil is probably halfway to Fiji by now. Maybe Uranus," said Coop.

Morty giggled.

"Traumatized, was he?" said Woolrich.

"*I'm* the traumatized one," said Coop, pointing to himself. "He told a three-thousand-year-old dead guy my name."

"Don't worry. We'll get to that."

Coop sank down a few inches. "I don't know if I need therapy or an exorcist."

"I can recommend good ones of each," said Woolrich.

"A DOPS shrink? No thanks. I'd rather face the mummy."

"So would we."

"What does that mean?" said Giselle.

"We'll get to that."

Coop looked at Giselle and Morty, who now looked as uneasy

as him. Dr. Lupinsky's cat lurked right at the edge of his screen, ready to skitter off at a moment's notice.

Woolrich glanced at some papers on his desk. "I'd like to congratulate you all on a job well done," he said.

"Thanks," muttered Coop.

"I'd *like* to congratulate you . . . but I can't, in all good conscience."

Coop sat up. The cat disappeared.

"Why? We got you the amulet," he said.

"Yes, but the ruckus. We're a *secret* organization. You practically drove a tank through the front door with 'robbers' painted on it in Day-Glo pink."

"That's not a bad idea," said Morty.

Giselle nodded. "No one would be expecting it."

"We didn't have a lot of time to be delicate," said Coop.

Woolrich picked up the amulet. "At least your bacchanalia worked. All the police reports are the same. The guards—the ones who can remember anything—swear that the museum was invaded by a small army of jesters and *War of the Worlds* Martian machines."

Morty perked up. "Yeah? I really liked that movie."

Coop looked at the heads on the wall and wondered what it felt like to be stuffed and mounted.

"What about Harkhuf?" he said. "He knows me. I need protection."

Woolrich stacked his papers. "I wouldn't worry about it. We have the amulet now. Plus, we sent in a recovery team with the police last night."

"So you have him?" said Coop hopefully.

"Not at all. Harkhuf was gone by the time we got there."

"Then I should be worried," said Coop. "Worried is exactly what I should be."

"Look for a guard named Froehlich," said Giselle.

"We know about him, but he's also missing. Too bad for him, too. He's a bit of a hero, having single-handedly chased the Bozo brigade out the front door."

Coop put his head in his hands. "But he's the one working with the mummy. Find him, find Harkhuf."

Woolrich steepled his fingers. "Now, why didn't I think of that?" He unlaced his fingers and scribbled a note on a piece of paper. "With luck, we'll have him in a day or two."

"With luck? That's very comforting," said Coop, his head still in his hands. Giselle reached over and patted him on the back. "I brought you the amulet. Why can't you use it to get Harkhuf's ass over here?" he said.

"We don't know how it works yet, do we?" said Woolrich.

"Isn't there someone on staff who knows how to break mummy curses?" Giselle said.

"I take it that Dr. Lupinsky hasn't been any help there?"

Everyone looked, but the cat didn't come back.

Sorry, appeared at the bottom of the screen.

"As are we all, Doctor," said Woolrich. "But have no fear. I've sent for the heads of thaumaturgic antiquities. If anyone knows about mummy curses, it will be them. They'll be here in just a moment."

They sat in an uncomfortable silence for a minute. The little brain in the bowl swam a few silent laps. Woolrich pushed a dish of hard candies forward on his desk. Coop and the others shook their heads. Everybody looked around so they didn't have to look at each other. Dr. Lupinsky's cat crept back onto the screen and lay down with its back to the room. Morty cleared his throat.

"So, Mr. Woolrich. What's with the monster museum on your walls?"

Coop and Giselle looked at him. Morty shrugged. "Silence creeps me out," he said.

"Oh, you know," said Woolrich airily. "Some people have snapshots and vacation slides. I have heads."

"No one has vacation slides," said Coop.

"Really? Since when?"

"Since humans gained the power of speech and could say 'I don't want to see your vacation slides.'"

"Hmm. We used to love them when I was a lad," he said.

"We invented the wheel since then. People can go places and see things for themselves."

"Not a bunch of heads like that," said Morty, craning around to get a look at all of them. "I've never seen anything like it before."

"Thank you."

Morty stopped abruptly and frowned. "That's not a person up there, is it?"

Woolrich glanced over his shoulder. "No. That's a windigo. They can mimic all sorts of species."

"What was it mimicking there? It's pretty horrible."

"My wife, actually," said Woolrich.

"Oh," said Morty.

"And that's what happens when you talk about heads on walls," said Coop.

Woolrich turned in his seat to look at the windigo. "She's my ex-wife, actually. She didn't look like that all the time, of course. Just during the full moon."

"She was a werewolf?" said Giselle.

"No. Just moody. I keep the windigo around to remind me of why we're not together anymore."

"Where's your wife now?"

"She's hanging in a museum in Vienna."

Coop sat up. Giselle and Morty gasped. The cat left again.

"She's not mounted," said Woolrich irritably. "She hangs paintings. Really, I think you're a lot more obsessed with my heads than I am."

Coop looked around the room. "Trust me, we're not. The only thing I ever obsessed over on my wall was Miss July when I was fifteen."

"I thought you were obsessed with your hamster," said Giselle.

"Leave Shamu out of this."

"Shamu?"

Coop held up his hands. "Let's just have a moment of reflective silence until the antiquities people get here."

They sat quietly.

"Hamster freak," whispered Morty.

There was a light knock on the door.

"Come in," said Woolrich.

The door opened a few inches and a plump woman stuck her head into the room. She was wearing a white lab coat and cat glasses on a chain around her neck.

"Cooper, this is Dr. Buehlman. One of the heads of thaumaturgic antiquities," said Woolrich. "Isn't Dr. Carter with you?"

"Hello," said Dr. Buehlman with a slight German accent. Then, "Dr. Carter couldn't make it."

"A work issue?"

"Um . . . yes . . ."

"Why aren't you coming in?" said Coop.

"No reason," said Dr. Buehlman with a charming smile.

"It's the curse, isn't it? That's why Carter isn't here. You don't want to get near me."

"Of course not," she said. "I just don't like . . . rooms . . . ?"

"Is there anything you can do about the curse?" said Giselle.

"Harkhuf is using an ancient spell system we're not entirely, that is *at all*, familiar with."

"In other words, I'm stuck with a homicidal corpse who wants me as dead as him," said Coop.

"We don't know that it's homicidal," said Woolrich.

"You think it wants to buy us lunch?"

"There is some good news," said Dr. Buehlman, ignoring the question. "Old Egyptian curses tend to follow patterns. You might only get boils."

"Boils?"

"Or ravaged by jackals."

"You're safe there, Coop. There aren't any jackals in L.A.," said Giselle.

"These would be the magic kind of jackals, so, yes, they could be here."

"Oh."

"There's also locusts. Or your soul could be sucked out through your eyes."

"Mom always said it was the drinking that would get me. She never mentioned jackals," said Coop.

"Or locusts," Morty added.

"But consider this," said Dr. Buehlman, smiling. "None of these things is irrefutably fatal, so there's a slight chance you'll live."

"I'll just be half-eaten, covered in boils, bugs, and minus my soul. That *is* good news."

"Of course not. The good news is that it's usually only one or two of those things."

"Do I get to choose?"

She slowly shook her head. "Not really."

"Thank you, Doctor," said Woolrich.

Half of Dr. Buehlman's head had disappeared behind the door when she stopped.

"Are you a religious man?" she said.

"You're kidding, right?" said Coop.

"Maybe you should consider it," said Dr. Buehlman. "Prayer can be such a comfort."

"So's bourbon."

"Good luck," she said, and slammed the door closed.

Coop looked at Woolrich. "That was fun. Who else is out there? Vlad the Impaler? Because I'd rather see him right now than any more of your doctors."

Woolrich brushed the comment aside. "Don't exaggerate, Cooper. Clearly the curse hasn't manifested itself yet, so you have plenty of time."

"For what?"

"To start with, do you have a will?"

Coop sat back, exhausted. Then something occurred to him. "Why was Frau Blücher so afraid and you're not?"

Woolrich leaned back and opened his hands. "I don't let trifles like curses bother me."

Coop lay down on the floor and looked under Woolrich's desk. "Ha!" he said, and popped back up on his knees, pointing to a powdery white circle around Woolrich's chair.

"What is that?"

"Salt," said Woolrich.

Coop got back on the floor.

"Please don't break the circle," said Woolrich through gritted teeth.

Coop got up and went back to his chair, wiping salt off his hands. "I have a funny feeling about this whole setup," he said. "You don't want to use me as mummy bait, do you?"

"That's absurd," said Woolrich. "But maybe you should take a few days off. Stay away from the office until this whole thing blows over."

"I was right. You're not even looking for him, are you? You want him to come to me."

"Of course, your time off will be with pay. And it won't count toward your vacation days."

"He's not even listening to me," Coop said to his friends. He dropped his hands in his lap. "I'm like one of those hams they hang up to dry."

"We'll have you under twenty-four-hour-a-day surveillance."

Coop got up. "I'm getting out of town."

"Yes, I'm sure that will help," said Woolrich drily. "This is a curse after you, not your neighbor's Schnauzer."

Dr. Lupinsky's cat prowled the screen.

He's right. You can't run from something like this.

"I'm not running. I'm fleeing. And I'm really good at it," said Coop.

"Sit down, Coop," said Giselle.

"Yeah," said Morty. "Listen to the man."

"And you, getting chatty with the heads," said Coop, pointing to Morty. "You think I want to end up there?"

"Really, Cooper, you're in good hands. We can't afford any more employee homicides until the next fiscal quarter," said Woolrich.

"If you try just a little harder, I think you can be even less reassuring."

"Think about it. Where would you go?" said Giselle.

"Yes. And with Harkhuf on your trail, your friends are in as much danger as you," said Woolrich.

Coop looked at the others, wondering what kind of danger he'd leave Giselle and Morty in if he ran. Finally, he took a breath and dropped into his chair. "Okay. I'll be your bait," he said. "But the cavalry better come charging in or I'm haunting your office."

Woolrich took a bag of salt from his desk drawer and closed the circle again. "What makes you think it's not already haunted?" he said.

Coop turned his eyes up at the heads.

"If you want to haunt me, you're going to have to get in line," said Woolrich. "I tell you what, I'll even put you down for hazard pay. Time and a half."

"Great. I can buy some boil cream," said Coop.

Woolrich took a pinch of salt and tossed it over his shoulder, then put the bag back in the desk. "I think that's all for now. Thank you again for the amulet. I'll be forwarding it to our bewitching and allurements boys. When something develops, we'll be in touch."

Coop and the others started out. Coop stopped by a set of old weapons Woolrich had on display in a corner of the room.

"Is that a bear trap?" he said.

"Yes, it is."

"I want time and a half *and* that."

Woolrich looked at him. "What for?" he said dubiously.

Coop picked up the bear trap. "We have a squirrel problem."

"If it's for Harkhuf, I doubt it will help."

"But I'll sleep better."

Woolrich waved a hand at him. "Be my guest."

Coop took the trap and they left the office.

In the hall, Morty said, "You're really just going home?"

"Hell no."

"What are we going to do?" said Giselle.

"If Harkhuf is using magic, I'll use magic, too."

Dr. Lupinsky's cat jumped up.

Wonderful. What kind?

Coop shook his head. "I have no idea."

Gisele took his hand. "You always come up with something."

"Maybe a disguise," said Morty.

"Like I should dress up like a pirate?"

Morty crossed his arms. "It couldn't hurt."

"I'll give that all the serious consideration it deserves."

"Come on. I'll take you home," said Giselle.

"No. It might be dangerous. I'll take the bus."

Won't that be just as dangerous?

"Yeah, but it's an L.A. bus. Everyone sort of wants to die anyway."

"It's true," said Giselle.

"It is," said Morty.

Coop stepped away from Giselle. "Maybe you should stay in a hotel for a while."

"Don't be stupid. I'll see you at home."

What's the trap for?

"I'll tell you if it works," said Coop. He took off his jacket and wrapped it around the vicious metal jaws.

"I'll see you guys later," Coop said to Morty and Dr. Lupinsky. He nodded at Giselle. "Want to go hunting?"

20

Bayliss was at her desk writing a report about Irvine Laing, the chancellor of a popular technical online university. Ostensibly, the university specialized in computer science and engineering degrees, but in reality it was a front for a sect of ancient demon worshipers. The homework projects each student was assigned—while appearing to be ordinary design and programming work—were, in reality, all parts of one monstrously intricate summoning spell for Amduscias, the lord of the Seven Extremely Unpleasant Legions. The group had been working on the spell constantly since well before the fall of Rome, with no end in sight. That's when Laing came up with the idea to outsource the spell work to the best and brightest minds he could find that were, one, good enough for MIT, but didn't have the money, and, two, had just enough money to steal.

What Laing hadn't revealed to his fellow Amduscias worshipers was that sometime during the two thousand years they'd been working on the summoning spell, Amduscias had retired to wherever it was that hoary beasts of the netherworld went to spend their golden years. Maybe Miami. Maybe Antarctica.

Laing had spent the last ten or so years skimming millions from both the group and the minor demons they employed on a contract basis.

Bayliss wrote a report detailing all of this, assuming that the DOPS was about to swoop in and arrest Laing, unaware that they were preparing to make him a job offer in Unfathomable Disbursements, a division for staff members who were paid in items a bit more chthonian than cash. After all, anyone who'd worked out how to embezzle from this world *and* the next and not have his skin used as a cocktail napkin in a demonic dive bar was, in the opinion of management, excellent DOPS material.

Bayliss was in the process of printing her report when two men appeared in her cubicle and began to loom over her. Not stand, but specifically loom. The men were pale and, as far as she could see, entirely hairless. They wore matching suits and looked so much alike that when she first saw them shoulder to shoulder, Bayliss thought they might be conjoined twins. In fact, they weren't. At least, not physically.

"Agent Bayliss?" said the one on the left.

"Yes?" she said.

"I'm Agent Night."

"And I'm Agent Knight," said the one on the right.

"You have the same name?"

"No. He has a *k*," said Night.

"I have a *k*," said Knight.

"I see," said Bayliss. "How can I help you?"

"We're from internal auditing and . . ." said Night.

". . . we'd like to ask you a few questions," continued Knight.

"About what?"

"Your office . . ." said Night.

". . . supplies," said Knight.

"We have them."

"Oh," said Bayliss.

"Do you have any . . ." said Night.

". . . supplies in your desk?"

"Some," said Bayliss.

"Are they authorized DOPS . . ."

". . . supplies?"

"Yes, they are," said Bayliss.

"And did you obtain them through . . ."

". . . normal . . ." said Night.

". . . channels?"

"You mean through a requisition?"

"Yes," said Night.

"Yes," said Knight.

Bayliss said, "You see, someone was stealing them and—"

"Did you . . ."

". . . report it?"

"I wanted to, but I was afraid."

"Of . . ."

". . . what?"

"Well, you," said Bayliss.

"Hmm," said Night.

"Hmm," said Knight.

"You should come . . ."

". . . with us."

"For auditing?" said Bayliss.

"Yes."

"And bring your desk squid," said Night.

"We'd like to examine it."

"I'm afraid it was stolen, too."

Night and Knight leaned together, whispering rapidly in each other's ear.

"You should come with us," said Night.

"Everything is going to be all . . ." said Knight.

". . . right. There's nothing to worry . . ."

". . . about."

"Let me get my things," said Bayliss.

"Of course."

"Of course."

Bayliss picked up her shoulder bag from under her desk, pausing for a minute so that the Auditors wouldn't see her hands trembling. She took a breath and prepared to leave when from behind her she heard, "Hi. Who are your friends?"

She looked up and saw Coop and Giselle shoulder to shoulder with the Auditors.

Night looked them over. "Who are . . ."

". . . you?" said Knight.

Giselle said, "I'm Agent Petersen."

"I'm Coop," said Coop.

"Ahhh," said Night.

"Ahhh," said Knight.

"The thief, yes?"

"Yes, the thief?"

Bayliss looked down at the bag in her lap. "They know about the office supplies."

Coop raised his eyebrows at the Auditors. "You think maybe I took them?"

"Who . . ."

". . . knows?"

"You remind me of a couple of Auditors I heard in the lunchroom," said Coop. "They were clones. Are you clones? Are you *all* clones?"

"What makes you ask . . ." said Night.

". . . that?" said Knight.

"That," said Coop.

"What?" said Night and Knight.

"That. What you said. What you both said."

The Auditors shook their heads vigorously.

"We're not clones. My name has an *n*."

"My name has a *k*."

Coop looked at Bayliss. "That certainly clears everything up."

"Where were you . . ." said Night.

". . . when the office supplies were . . ." said Knight.

". . . stolen?"

"I don't need office supplies. I don't write reports," said Coop.

"Everyone writes . . ."

". . . reports."

"I don't. I just steal things."

"Hmm," said Night.

"Hmm. Do you have a . . ."

". . . desk squid?"

Coop shrugged. "I don't even know if I have a desk. I used to have a hamster. A cat ate him."

The Auditors put their heads back together, whispering and taking quick glances at the three of them.

Giselle leaned over to Bayliss. "Are you all right?"

"I don't know yet. I've never been audited before."

"We'll be looking out for you."

"Thanks."

The Auditors stood apart abruptly.

"We'll be . . ."

". . . in touch."

"That's quite a speech impediment," said Coop. "You ought to have it checked out."

The Auditors looked at each other.

"What do you . . ."

". . . mean?"

"Of course, maybe you're just possessed. Woolrich knows some good exorcists. You'll love it. It's like an enema for your brain."

The Auditors frowned.

"We have to . . ."

"Go," said Coop.

"Yes. Agent Bayliss is . . ."

"Going with you."

"Yes. We'll be in touch with . . ."

"Me," said Coop.

"Soon."

"Okay, but you should know that I'm cursed. Anyone around me is in mortal danger."

"Cursed?" said Bayliss.

"Cursed?" said Night.

"Cursed? Is it an . . ." said Knight.

". . . authorized cursing?"

"If the guy who did it kills me, I'll ask," said Coop.

"This is all . . ."

". . . extremely irregular."

Bayliss stood up. "Please, Coop. I just want to get this over with."

He nodded to her, then looked back at the Auditors.

"It was swell meeting you. Don't be strangers. Any stranger than you are, I mean."

"Come, Agent . . ."

". . . Bayliss."

"We'll see you later," said Coop to Bayliss.

"Take care," said Giselle. When they were gone she added, "Those guys are scary."

"Poor Bayliss."

"I wonder if there's anything we can do."

"This, for a start," said Coop. He took the trap out of his jacket and put it in Bayliss's top drawer.

"Going bear hunting, are you?" said Giselle.

"I don't know. Let's see if I catch anything."

21

It was the end of another long and particularly dull shift in the mail room. Nelson had spent the best part of the night working on his spreadsheet. Some parts were filling in quite nicely, but there were holes and blank spots everywhere. He sat back and looked at his work. It wasn't exactly the plans for the Normandy Invasion. In fact, the more he stared the more it looked to him like the seating chart at a particularly hostile wedding reception.

Technically, it was progress, but he was frustrated and confused. No matter how much correspondence he controlled, it didn't seem to be getting him any closer to *it*. The book. He tapped his pencil on the desk. As much as it infuriated him, there was nothing to do right then but follow the mook work credo mounted on the wall over his desk:

THERE'S NO DREAD WHEN YOU'RE DEAD,
LET'S NAIL IT ON THE HEAD, SO WE CAN PUT IT TO BED.

At some point in the past, the phrase must have stirred old memories in an especially dim mook's brain, because someone played

the game where you add "in bed" to the end of a fortune-cookie fortune. The sign over Nelson's desk actually read . . . SO WE CAN PUT IT
TO BED. IN BED. The additional words didn't fill Nelson with despair
so much as a kind of slow-burning alarm. Yes, there was nothing to
do but carry on with his plans, but if they didn't work out, Nelson
wondered if he might end his days wandering the bowels of DOPS
headquarters adding *In bed* to the end of every sign he came across.

IN CASE OF FIRE, PULL ALARM. IN BED.

EMPLOYEES MUST WASH HANDS. IN BED.

IN THE EVENT OF A SHOGGOTH OUTBREAK, USE TORCHES AND ABOMINA-
TION REPELLENT PROVIDED. IN BED.

Someone knocked on his door. He put his spreadsheet away.
"Come in," he said genially, trying to mask his inner turmoil.

McCloud shuffled in. Nelson took his spreadsheet out again.
He'd already hypnotized the mook earlier in the evening, so
there was no reason to hide anything from him. And there were
his extremely limited reading skills.

Nelson started to say, "What can I help you with?" in a tone
the management handbook called "Convivial Engrossment,"
meant to convey "exuberant fascination to mask existential
panic." However, he only got as far as, "What c—"

What stopped him from completing his carefully crafted greeting was McCloud's right arm. Most of it was missing and what
was left seemed to be attached to an old-fashioned bear trap.

"I think I goofed up," McCloud said. "Sorry, boss."

Nelson just stared. Even in the sometimes lethal confines of
the DOPS, it was an unusual sight. Finally, he said, "Come here."

McCloud came around the desk, and after several minutes
of pushing and wrenching with every implement Nelson could
find in the mail-room toolbox, he managed to pry open the trap's
jaws enough for McCloud to pull out his mangled limb.

"Thanks," McCloud said as if Nelson had just given him a
puppy for his birthday.

"What the hell happened?" said Nelson. "Actually, forget that. I can see what happened. *Where* did it happen? *How* did it happen? And most importantly, did anyone see you?"

McCloud's eyes got glassy as he contemplated that many questions at once.

He took a breath and said, "Bayliss's desk. I put my hands in one of her drawers. And no one, because everyone had gone home."

Nelson put the bear trap on his desk and looked it over. It was a rusty, pockmarked antique with little shreds of McCloud between its teeth. There weren't any markings or serial numbers on it to indicate where it had come from. But that didn't matter. The trap had come from Bayliss's desk, but it was nothing she would have ever done. But she had a friend who would have.

"Coop," said Nelson.

It's not enough that he dropped me down in pinhead central, now he's going after the only assets I have to get me out of here.

Nelson moved the filing cabinet and put the bear trap in the secret compartment where he'd been hiding Bayliss's office supplies. McCloud was still standing by his desk, right arm dangling by a few spaghetti strands of meat, but without a care in the world.

"Come on," Nelson said.

"Where are we going?" said McCloud.

"We're shoving your arm in the shredder. It's the only safe way to explain how it got that way."

McCloud headed for the door. "You got it, boss," he said merrily.

Nelson pictured Coop's smug face as he contemplated the man's fate.

Your time is coming. The moment I get the book . . .

"Hey, look," said Nelson. He twitched his shoulder up and down so that his mangled arm bounced like a yo-yo.

"Please stop that. You're getting gristle all over my floor."

McCloud stopped, but inertia made it bounce a few more times. He gave Nelson an awkward smile.

"Sorry, boss," McCloud said, and began looking for the broom.

"No. I'll do it," said Nelson. "It's more important that we take care of your situation first."

"Thanks. You're the best boss ever."

"I know," said Nelson wearily.

He held the door open, but McCloud looked down at his one functional hand and held up a small box.

"Oh. I forgot. I found this going to allurements," he said.

Nelson leaned on the open door. "What is it? A rabbit's foot? A monkey's paw? I have a whole drawer full of monkey's paws."

"I don't know what it is," said McCloud. "But it's very pretty. There's a note inside that mentions that guy Pooc you don't like."

"Who? Do you mean Coop?" said Nelson.

McCloud thought about it. "No. I'm pretty sure it was Pooc."

Nelson slammed the door and snatched the box out of McCloud's hand. Inside, he found an amulet, along with a note explaining what it was. Nelson felt more alive than he'd felt since he'd stopped being alive.

"This is good work," he told McCloud. "You get an A-plus tonight." Nelson slid the secret compartment closed.

"Now let's go and chop off the rest of your arm."

"Yay," said McCloud.

Things are falling into place. I just have to hang on long enough for management to get so fed up with Coop that they make him a mook. Maybe it's time to push up the timetable on that.

Nelson thought about the amulet and wondered if he could use it to get closer to the book. It would take some research, but time was one thing he had plenty of.

In a singsong voice, Nelson said, "Let's nail it on the head, so we can put it to bed."

"In bed," said McCloud.

Nelson opened the office door. "Get to the shredder."

22

Coop stepped out of the cab like a drunken ballerina. While he didn't quite pirouette, he did turn in a series of fast, clumsy circles trying to keep an eye on the street, the alleys, and all of the empty store-fronts. Really, anyplace big enough to hold an angry mummy. To the untrained eye, he would have seemed irrational or deliri-ous, but Coop felt more like a giraffe in a sports coat chasing its own tail. At the moment he was okay with that. He continued this dizzying sprint all the way from the curb to the door of a psychic reading parlor.

The taxi remained at the curb. "Are you all right, man?" called the driver.

"Just great," said Coop.

"Do you need a doctor?"

"Yes, but not the kind you mean."

The cabbie leaned closer to the window. "What kind do you need?"

"Someone who can do a body transplant. Put my brain in a whole new, unrecognizable body."

"Oh," said the cabbie. "I don't know any like that."

"I bet they have some at work, but I'd probably just end up jammed inside a Game Boy attached to whatever robot legs they had lying around."

"Is that so?"

"If you had to choose, would you rather have tentacles or chicken feet? I'm leaning toward chicken. They can run fast and tentacles are just creepy."

The cabbie scratched his head. "You look very together for a crazy person."

"Thank you. That's what I'll be putting on my tombstone."

"I got to go. You be careful. Don't let any ghosts sneak up on you."

"Why? Do you see any ghosts?"

Coop did another quick turn and came to rest with his back against the psychic parlor's door.

"See you around, Froot Loops," said the cabbie as he merged into the sunny and resolutely unspectral traffic of Sunset Boulevard. The flat L.A. light, the smog, and newspaper bins full of abandoned sandwiches and strip-club flyers were suddenly very comforting. Coop managed to turn around and slowly open the psychic parlor's door.

Bells overhead tinkled in the curtained gloom. The mingled aromas of incense, herbs, and cigarette smoke made his eyes water. It smelled like someone had burned a witch and tried to cover it up with a gallon of patchouli oil.

"Minerva?" Coop shouted into the dark back room.

A cheerful voice called back. "Hello there, friend. I'll be out in just a minute."

Coop threw the dead bolt on the front door and checked for undead pharaohs through the front window.

"Almost there," came the voice again.

Coop turned around to find a .44 Magnum pistol shoved in his face. At the other end of the pistol was an older woman in a big flowing seventies dress with a lot of scarves. She looked like Stevie Nicks carved out of a dried apple.

She shouted, "All right, fucker. You have ten seconds to get out or you're going to have more blowholes than a dolphin gang-bang."

Coop threw up his hands.

"Minerva, don't shoot. It's me, Coop."

Stevie Nicks considered this for a second and with her free hand put on a pair of glasses she had tucked into the top of her dress. She squinted at him.

"Coop," she said in the same cheerful voice she'd used before. "It's been a dog's age."

"How are you, Charles Bronson?" he said, his hands still high in the air.

Minerva lowered the pistol and put it in her pocket.

"Don't let this bother you," she said. "I just keep it around to shoot people with. How are you?"

"You're the psychic. You tell me."

He lowered his hands. She looked him up and down.

"I don't exactly need my crystal for that. You lock my door and your knees are shaking like a Chihuahua banging a snowman." She shook her head. "This isn't a social call, is it?"

"I'm afraid not."

"Come in the back," Minerva said.

She fished around in her pockets until she came up with a cigarette and a cheap plastic lighter. As she lit up she said, "Forgive me for being mercenary, darling, but I don't suppose you have any filthy lucre in the pockets of those quivering slacks?"

"No money," said Coop. "But I have jewelry. Shiny stuff. Antiques."

Minerva gave him a wicked half smile. "Want to give me a gander?"

"Let's talk first."

"You were always a slick one."

Minerva led him through a curtain to the inner room where she did her readings. She sat on some cushions and puffed her cigarette. To Coop, the setup looked like one big stoner firetrap.

"Where the hell have you been all this time?" she said.

Coop was still taking in the room. The candles. The paisley drapes. The black-light astrological posters. Soft cushions and low chairs. It was like a pretty little bunker decorated by a teenage hippie Hobbit.

"I've been all over," he said. "Down on my luck for part of it. Then in jail for a while."

She listened, and then nodded. "The curse of those of us on the job. But you're out now and it doesn't look like you're starving."

"I ran into Giselle a while ago. We're back together."

Minerva leaned back in the pillows. "After she tore out your heart and burned it in the public square? You really are the forgiving sort."

There were a lot of shadows, nooks, and crannies in the Hobbit hole, but he didn't see anything mummy size. Still, he had to suppress the desire to twirl.

"There's something else—and don't hate me for it . . ." he said.

"Here it comes," Minerva said cautiously. "Out with it."

"I'm a fed."

She turned white and stubbed out her cigarette. Carefully clasping her hands, she spoke to him sweetly, like an old lady in a pastry house trying to lure him into the oven.

"Coop, dear, if you're here to bust me, how about giving old Minerva a head start? For old times' sake?"

"Relax," he said. "I'm not that kind of fed."

She curled her lip. "Then what kind are you?"

Coop leaned across the table and said, "We don't do bank robberies or heists. We're on the enchantment end of things. Naughty vampires. Crooked ghosts. That kind of thing."

"You're a spook hunter?"

"Me? Never. You heard about the museum job a couple of days ago? I'm that kind of fed."

Minerva's eyebrows arched. "That was you? How delicious. Tell me all about it."

He flashed on the image of the mummy and the tired-looking rent-a-cop pointing at him hungrily, like the last éclair in a gas-station donut bin.

"Things went great the first time in. But they went south fast the second."

"Wait. You went back for sloppy seconds? That's bad luck, you goose. I suppose you had a good reason."

He sighed. "We forgot something."

"What?"

"This." Coop took a handkerchief from his pocket and dumped the loot from the Egyptian exhibit on the table.

The feeling that welled up in Minerva's gut wasn't greed but the certainty that if her eyes weren't rooted into her brain, they would have grabbed everything, shot the place up, and been on a plane to parts unknown before either of them could say, *Well, you don't see that every day.*

"Be still, my heart," she said.

"It's a lot to take in, isn't it?" said Coop.

"Might I . . . ?" said Minerva, pointing to the glittering gold and jewels.

"Be my guest. It's all the real thing."

She picked up some rings and a small necklace. "It certainly is. Oh my. Some of these baubles are practically vibrating with metaphysical power."

"Really? Don't kid around," said Coop.

"No, there's some powerful stuff here. But I'm curious. Why bring it to me? Why not just fence it?"

In his head, the mummy said, *"Coop."*

"I've got magic troubles, Minerva."

"You? Bull. Now me, I've got magic troubles. My spirit guide just dumped me like I wouldn't put out on prom night." She took out another cigarette and lit it.

"I've got *real* magic troubles."

"What are you trying to drag me into?" she said guardedly.

"A curse," said Coop. "A real-life holy-shit Boris Karloff mummy curse."

Minerva put out a hand and pushed the jewelry back to Coop's side of the table.

"It was lovely seeing you. My door is always open, but why don't you get the hell out of here? Go and try . . . I don't know . . . Professor Moony."

Coop frowned. "I checked. Moony's on the county-fair circuit. He does a mind-reading act with a pig."

"Not anymore," said Minerva. "He got booted out for drinking. Had to eat his partner."

"Then why did you tell me to see him?"

She shrugged. "I figured neither of you has much to live for."

Coop pushed the jewelry back to her side of the table. "I need help, Minerva."

"I don't know," she said with a little shudder. "Old Egyptian curses. That's rough stuff. Did you ever hear of Preston Casey?"

"No."

She gave him a dreamy little smile. "He was a gorgeous MGM up-and-comer. Broke the heart of a local chippy while shooting *The Swingin' Legionnaire* in Cairo back in '56."

"What happened to him?"

"You know about the Seven Plagues of Egypt?"

"I recently made their acquaintance."

"He got all of them. Down south, if you get my drift," she said, pointing to her lap.

Coop made a face. "Did he get cured?"

"Sure, in the sense that he died. They say he still haunts the bar at the Cairo Princess Hotel—a wailing wraith with an eternally empty martini glass searching for a drink and his balls."

Coop crossed and uncrossed his legs. "Balls-wise—that's exactly the kind of thing I'm trying to avoid."

"Here's some advice: if you're visiting the pyramids, don't screw the help. That's the best I can do for you. Now why don't you run along?"

Coop picked up each bit of jewelry and set it down separately, like a window display. "See, I figured if I couldn't buy off a mummy, maybe I could find someone who could do it for me. I'm willing to pay."

"Go on," said Minerva.

"At work, there's an amulet they think can control the mummy. But I don't trust them. I'm wondering if there's something in this junk that can help me."

Minerva drummed her fingers on the table nervously. "You left out the payment part."

Coop waved his hands over the table like a carny magician. "Take something from the pile. Anything you want."

"Anything?"

"Anything. But if there's something here that will get King Tut off my back, that one I keep."

"That sounds reasonable. But I'll need to check some of my books," Minerva said.

She reached under some pillows and came back with a glass that had probably been clean once and a bottle of Jack Daniel's. "Feel free to commune with the spirits while I'm in the back."

Minerva disappeared and Coop poured himself a shot.

What am I doing with my life? How the hell did I get here? Maybe I need to get into another line of work.

He drank a shot at the thought of each job he could come

up with. Dog walking. Cable-TV installation. Putting restaurant menus under windshield wipers. Those all seemed peaceful, and they were about the only things he might be qualified for besides stealing.

How many shots is that? That can't be all I can do.

Maybe he could do the reformed crook bit and put on seminars about robbery and sorcery for cops.

No. Scratch that. The only law enforcement that deals with magic is the DOPS. Regular cops would have me locked up as a fraud or an escaped schizo.

He put the bottle down, hopelessness welling up inside him. He couldn't work in the straight world and he knew it. The closest he'd ever come was working at a movie theater one summer when he was around twelve. He didn't steal from the box office—that would have been too easy—but he watered down the butter for the popcorn. With the money he saved, he bought his first set of lockpicks.

Maybe I can be an Igor for an old-school conjurer. A straight nine-to-five gig and the only downside would be wearing a hump all day. Or volunteer for medical experiments. Vaccines and sleep deprivation. Maybe they'll hit me with some gamma rays and I'll Hulk out. Would Giselle still like me if I was green?

It sounded scary, but not much different from working for the DOPS.

Minerva came out of the back with a huge old book bound in cracked leather and closed with silver clasps. She dropped it onto the table. The bottle and glass jumped like they were startled.

"You are one lucky son of a bitch," she said.

"You found something?" said Coop, his stomach no longer boiling with tension, but merely simmering.

Minerva picked up a few pieces of jewelry and compared them to illustrations in the book. Coop got up and walked around to Minerva's side of the table. She slammed the book closed.

"Your balls are at stake, boy. Don't annoy Minerva."

"Sorry." Coop went back to his side of the table and poured himself another drink.

"Okay," said Minerva thoughtfully. "Some of this junk is junk. Some has magical properties, but not the kind you want."

"Get to the lucky-son-of-a-bitch part."

She set down the book and handed him a thin lapis lazuli necklace.

"This is it, kiddo. If anything is going to save your bacon, it's this little charmer here."

"What do I do with it?"

Minerva scowled. "It's a necklace, Dumbo. You put it on."

Coop shrugged off his sports coat and put the lapis around his neck.

"I look like I'm selling pot brownies at Woodstock," he said.

"You wear it under your shirt."

"The magic can get out?"

"Yes. That's why they call it magic."

He unbuttoned his collar and pushed the necklace down inside. "Okay. What do I do now?"

Minerva looked over Coop's loot. "I don't know. Go home. See a movie. Learn the banjo. Just don't take the necklace off for any reason until this thing blows over."

Coop was doubtful. "This little thing is going to protect me?"

Minerva looked at him. "It's this or you can go to Egypt, find a bigger, meaner mummy, and bring him back to fight the first one."

"But then I'll have an even worse mummy on my hands."

"It's a pickle, isn't it?"

"I'll stick with the necklace."

"Good boy. You're so sharp I could slice bologna with you."

Coop pointed to the jewelry. "Okay. Your turn. Pick anything."

Minerva pursed her lips and let her hand drift over the baubles. She reached down and picked up a small gold ritual knife.

"That's it?" said Coop. He showed her something else. "This ankh thing is a lot bigger and has more jewels."

She waved a hand at him. "That's all right. I feel a kinship with this little darling."

Coop took a breath. Maybe it was the Jack Daniel's, maybe it was the lack of oxygen from all the patchouli fumes, but he actually felt relaxed. He put the rest of the jewels in his pocket and touched the necklace under his shirt.

"I don't know how to thank you, Minerva."

She came around the table and gave him a hug. "Don't be such a stranger. Keep in touch and let me know how you're doing. If you need any more help, my door is always open."

"I feel a lot better."

Minerva took his arm and led him to the front of the parlor. "Please give Giselle my warmest regards."

"I will."

"Are you still in touch with Morty?"

"Sure."

"Tell the little shit he never thanked me for setting him up with that hottie dental assistant."

She gave him a motherly smile and unlocked the door.

"I'll see you around, Minerva," Coop said. He felt no desire to pirouette, gyrate, or whirl like a dervish down the street. He walked like anyone else—one foot in front of the other, not worried about mummies or looking for a new job. He was okay now. Maybe better than he'd been since he got out of jail. He went to the corner and even got a cab after just a couple of minutes. Outside in the afternoon was suddenly a great place to be. He was protected and on top of the world.

In her parlor, Minerva was on the phone in the back room that served as her library, kitchen, breakfast nook, and, with the addition of a television she bought off the back of a truck, home entertainment center. The phone rang a few times and a man answered.

"Kellar. Get your ass over here right now," she said. "I don't care if you have a hot prospect; mine's hotter. Oh. Really? That *is* good. Fine, but get over here when you can. That break we've been looking for? He might have just walked out. Why did I let him go? I put a mystical Kick Me sign on him before he left. He'll be back."

23

Vargas got to work early to make up for having fled the previous day. Considering Zulawski's recent behavior, he looked forward to having the office to himself for a few minutes to settle in and prepare things. However, when he opened the door, there Zulawski was, seated at his desk. Before Vargas could say anything, Zulawski held up a small cardboard box.

"Look. We actually received something today."

Vargas came in and put down his own package. "How exciting. What is it?"

Zulawski pulled apart the top of the box to reveal its writhing contents.

"Oh."

"Yes. Oh."

"Did you request a squid?" said Vargas.

"Of course not. And if I had, I would certainly have mentioned it."

"Hmm."

"Really."

Vargas went to his desk and sat down, already feeling

apprehensive—and the day had barely begun. The best cure for that, he remembered from his training, was to seize control of the moment. With a box cutter, he carefully sliced away the tape that held together the top of his own box. Before he could say anything, however, Zulawski came over and put out his hand. Puzzled, Vargas shook it.

"I want to apologize for my behavior yesterday. You were right. I was overwrought."

"Apology accepted."

"I'm sure you'll be happy to know that I've even destroyed the tube and put the aluminum foil in the recycling bin."

"That is good news," said Vargas. He looked at Zulawski, trying to gauge his state of mind. From where Vargas sat, it seemed shaky with a sprinkling of tenuous.

"However, I do stand by one thing," Zulawski said. "You have to admit that things are getting stranger down here. I know I sounded irrational yesterday, but I truly believe that the parcel is exerting a bad influence on the entire room."

Vargas peered at the shelves.

"The bad news is that I agree with you. The good news is that I plan on doing something about it along with our general neglect down here."

"You have a plan?"

"Indeed I do." Vargas opened his box. "Behold our salvation."

Zulawski looked inside. "Are those mice?" he said, clearly disappointed.

"Maybe you were expecting someone from management or perhaps the president?"

"Of course not. It's just . . . our salvation? Please explain that."

"I'd be happy to," said Vargas, his confidence returning. "Mice are small, they don't eat much, and they breed quickly."

"So do my brothers, but they wouldn't be much help."

Vargas took one of the mice from the box and stroked its

whiskered head. "We release the mice in the office, see? They'll breed and start a vermin explosion. Everyone is afraid of mice. They carry plague."

"I believe that's rats."

"Are you positive? Anyway, I'm sure you get my point. When a certain vermin-to-human ratio is achieved, someone will have to come down."

Zulawski scratched his ear nervously. "I'm not sure about this."

Vargas put the mouse back in the box. "What's wrong with the plan? Please. Poke holes in it if you can."

Zulawski glanced back at his desk. "I can't. But we already have a squid to take care of."

Vargas raised a finger. "That's the beauty of this. They're mice. Just leave out some food and they'll take care of themselves. Once they start breeding, we'll have all the attention we need."

Zulawski peered down into the box. "They are kind of cute." He turned his head to an odd angle. "Is that an ear on its back?"

"Yes."

"Can they hear us?"

"I would assume so."

Zulawski stiffened. "This isn't a trick by management, is it?" he whispered.

Vargas smiled confidently. "For management to be involved, it would have to be diabolical on a scale known only in Dante's Hell and Casual Fridays."

Zulawski turned his head straight again. "We have Casual Fridays?"

"The last Friday of every month."

"Why didn't you ever tell me?" said Zulawski. He went back to his desk to check on the squid.

"It was for your own good," said Vargas. "You once showed me a photo of you in a Hawaiian shirt. The last DOPS employee who wore a Hawaiian shirt is now hunting CHADs down in the sewers."

"What are CHADs?"

"Carnivorously Horrifying Abysmal Denizens."

Zulawski pondered that. "Shouldn't it be 'abyssal'?"

"Should what be?"

"'Abyssal' instead of 'abysmal.' 'Abyssal' means 'underground.'"

Vargas crossed his arms. "Have you ever seen one?"

"No."

"Then I don't see how your opinion has any bearing."

"Good point. Sorry. Have *you* ever seen one?"

Vargas shrugged. "Just pictures. They look a bit like a lamprey someone turned inside out a million years ago and they're still holding a grudge."

Zulawski made a face like he'd swallowed what he thought was Turkish Delight and then realized it was jellyfish. "It sounds horrible."

"One might even say . . ."

Zulawski nodded. "I know. Abysmal."

"Exactly," said Vargas triumphantly.

Zulawski stuck a finger into the box with the squid. "I suppose the mice are no stranger than anything else down here. You know the mirror that shows you your true self, but always being dragged away by dingoes?"

"Yes. Who would invent something like that?"

"I don't know, but last night one of the dingoes tried to bite me."

Vargas brought his fist down on his desk lightly so as not to disturb the mice. "I told you not to go back there without adequate protection."

Zulawski looked down at the floor. "Doggie treats and a big stick. I know."

"Maybe now you'll listen to me."

"Ow."

"What happened?"

Zulawski held up a finger. "The squid bit me."

"They *are* mighty hunters of the deep," said Vargas.

"If it does that again, it will be a mighty hunter in my lunch," said Zulawski crossly.

"Where do you think we should keep it?"

"It's a desk squid. I suppose we should—"

"Not it," said Vargas quickly.

"Fine," Zulawski said, shoulders slumping. "I'll keep it in mine." He got up and put on a fencing mask and hockey pads. Picking up a chisel on the end of a collapsible pole, he said, "I'm going back to clean the haunted toaster oven."

"Don't upset it," said Vargas. "I brought pizza rolls and I don't want them getting burned."

"I'll be careful," said Zulawski, his voice muffled by the fencing mask.

Vargas started taking the mice out of the box. "And put the gargoyles and dingo mirror and anything else with teeth on a higher shelf. I'm releasing the mice."

Zulawski, who'd been heading to the back of the office, stopped. "Why am I always the one on gruesomes duty?"

"You're right. I'll do it," said Vargas, setting the mice on the floor. They scurried away in all directions. "But you have to milk the mole people."

Zulawski took off the mask and pads. "All these years and no one has ever once requested mole milk."

"I know. But it's our duty."

"True," said Zulawski. "And knowing that someone will be down here soon makes it all easier."

Vargas pulled on the hockey pads. "And then the parcel will be someone else's problem."

Zulawski started to follow him into the back.

"Don't forget ear protection," said Vargas. "The mole people are screamers."

Zulawski went back to his desk. "Thanks, Vargas. If I'm stuck down here, I'm glad it's with you."

"Ditto," said Vargas.

Armored and chisel in hand, he walked into the shadowy recesses of the storeroom. Zulawski followed with ballistic ear-muffs in one hand and a clean bucket in the other. Just another day at a, now, much happier office.

24

Sheriff Wayne Jr. strutted into the back office in a tailored Stars and Stripes cowboy suit that would make Captain America look like a commie stooge. Donna was signing invoices. She set down her pen with great care and looked him over.

"You have got to be kidding me," she said.

Sheriff Wayne did a turn like a model on a catwalk and shot out his hands. "What do you think?"

Donna looked down at the pile of invoices. It wasn't just that the car lot cost a fortune to keep open, but Sheriff Wayne was actually losing money on the stolen cars. *What kind of lame-ass outlaw loses money on hot cars?* Donna took a deep breath. She'd chosen to be with a manic little boy when she'd left Roy for Sheriff Wayne, and now she had to live with that decision. She wondered if she could explain that to their creditors.

You see, I made certain life choices and I would love to have paid the electricity bill this month, but the sheriff needed neon underwear to go with his neon Frye boots or he might have looked silly on the playground with the other children. I'm sure you understand.

"You're making another commercial?" she said. "I swear, with the money you've spent on those things, you could have made a whole movie."

Sheriff Wayne cleared away the papers and sat on the edge of the desk. "With my Gary Cooper good looks, maybe I should."

Donna looked up at him. "You look like Gary Cooper like I look like Princess Di."

He put a hand under her chin. "You always look like a princess to me, darlin'."

"Thanks. But you still look more like Alice Cooper than Gary Cooper."

He jumped up. "Nonsense. We can do it in black and white like *High Noon*. My old enemies—high prices, lousy financing, and no guarantees—come back to town. I try to get the other car dealers to stand up with me, but they turn chickenshit and run, so I have to face the gang down myself. And I blast them all to Kingdom Come!"

"Oh my God. You're serious." For a brief second, she wondered which would pay off bigger, shooting him or burning the whole place to the ground.

"Why not? That piece of shit Johnny Newman did a whole series of ads like *Casablanca*."

"Yeah, and he looked like Howdy Doody in his dad's overcoat."

"And Ed Clay did one like *King Kong*."

"'Cause the big ape looks the part. Christ, that guy is hairier than gorilla shaving day at the monkey house."

"The bastard *is* a tad Neanderthal," said Sheriff Wayne. A thought crossed the desert of his mind like a stray tumbleweed. "Did Ed ever bother you?"

Donna looked away. "Once, a long time ago. It was a New Year's party over at Zoom City. It was no big deal."

Sheriff Wayne sat back down on the desk. "I wonder if he knows what a tire iron tastes like? Maybe I should send some boys over to show him."

Donna immediately forgot about shooting Sheriff Wayne. "You'd do that for me?" she said. If it came down to it, she could burn the place and make it look like an electrical fire.

"Bash old Fred Flintstone around? Hell, I'd do that just to see if I could knock some of the ugly off him."

"You're so sweet." Donna looked out the office window. "I think your boyfriend is here."

Sheriff Wayne turned. "Chris? I don't see him."

"He's over talking to the guy with the eagle."

Sheriff Wayne looked at his watch. "That little art school faggot is late. Do you have any idea how much it costs an hour to rent an eagle?"

Donna nodded at the suit. "How much did that Uncle Sam onesie cost?"

Sheriff Wayne put his thumbs under his lapels. "This is an *investment*. I can wear it every July Fourth. Presidents' Day. Christmas."

"Christmas?"

"Santa is a patriot first and toymaker second. How do you not know that?"

Donna smiled up at him. "I'm not a genius like you."

"Maybe I ought to do an Einstein ad," said Sheriff Wayne thoughtfully.

"Hotrod Al. E equals MC squared," said Donna, holding up a hand like she was painting in the air. "*M* for low mileage and *C* for even lower cost."

"Holy shit balls. That could work. Who's the genius now?"

Donna pointed to herself. "That would be me." Okay. She'd pay what bills she could this month, lose the rest, and save the fire for a less romantic moment.

"But Einstein did not have your ass," Sheriff Wayne said.

"Too bad for Mrs. Einstein."

"Damn straight." Sheriff Wayne took off his hat and smoothed down his hair in the office mirror. "Okay, I've got to go and make some movie magic."

"Knock 'em dead, Bogey," said Donna.

"I'm going to knock someone dead if he makes me do more than three takes today."

Donna picked up her pen. "I'll keep the ice ready for your knuckles."

She blew Sheriff Wayne a kiss. He caught it and put it in his pocket. Then he checked his pistols and went out to the lot.

"Okay. Everyone fan out and look for the llama," said Tyler.

They'd only arrived at the car lot a couple of minutes earlier and he was already taking command. Heather squeezed in next to him. She couldn't be happier. Leave it to her idiot brother to ruin the moment by opening his stupid mouth.

"What are we planning to do if we find it?" said Dylan. "It's not exactly a cageful of mice."

"Speaking of which, how are the mice doing?" said Sarah.

"They're fine," said Brad, trying to sound casual. It would have been more convincing if his throat hadn't closed up on the word *fine*.

Warren held up two fingers to make a cross. "Your landlord didn't send Super Jesus over to purge the demon rats?"

"Nope. They're doing fine. However, there's a lot more of them now. I wouldn't mind handing a few off to people."

"One thing at a time," said Tyler. "Today's mission is entirely llama-oriented."

"Okay, but I kind of feel like whenever I bring up the idea of someone else taking the mice, the subject changes."

"Who wants to get ice cream?"

"Shut up, Warren," said Tyler. He turned back to Brad. "We'll discuss your situation immediately after we've secured the llama."

"Back to my question, what do we do when we find it?" said Dylan.

Tyler looked out over the lot like he was searching for the source of the Nile. "Let's rendezvous back right here in twenty minutes. In the meantime, try to look like you're really thinking about buying a car."

"Who'd sell Warren a car?" said Sarah. "He'd just try to eat it."

Warren smiled. "It's true."

"Just do your best," said Tyler.

"All these cars look new," said Linda. "Are you sure we're at the right place?"

"Of course I'm sure we're at the right place. I printed out the directions from Google," said Heather. She took a piece of paper from her back pocket and unfolded it.

Dylan snatched it out of her hand and looked it over. "Let me see."

"Dick," she said.

He folded the paper and handed it back to her. "You took us to Detective Jesse's. We want to be at Sheriff Wayne's."

"Sheriff Wayne *Junior.*"

"Shut up, Warren."

"So, this isn't the guy with the camel?" said Heather.

"Llama," said Brad.

"Actually, they're in the same family," said Linda.

"Wouldn't it be awesome if Detective Jesse had a camel *and* a llama?" said Dylan. "Then this wouldn't be a complete goddamn waste of time."

Tyler put a finger to his lips for silence. "Calm down. We've had bigger setbacks. Now, does anyone know where Sheriff Wayne is?"

"Sheriff Wayne *Junior.*"

"Shut up, Warren."

Sarah held up her phone. "I've got it."

A smiling salesman in a neat blue shirt and gold tie with money signs on it came over. "Hi. Can I help you folks?"

"We're spotted," said Brad.

"They're onto us," said Dylan.

"Onto what?" said Tyler. "We haven't done anything."

"Run!" shouted Heather.

They ran back to Dylan's Land Rover and fishtailed out of the parking lot.

"Why did we just do that?" said Linda.

"We panicked," said Brad.

"Heather panicked," said Sarah.

Heather turned around in her seat. "You ran, too!"

"No, I didn't. I was just swept up in the wake of your fat ass."

Silence fell on the car like a skydiving rhinoceros that didn't realize until too late that without opposable thumbs it couldn't pull the rip cord.

"Um, Sarah. Can you give me the directions to Sheriff Wayne's?" said Dylan.

"Sheriff Wayne *Junior,*" said Warren.

"Turn left up here."

It was a very solemn ride.

It took another forty-five minutes for the crew to set up the lights and camera before they could begin shooting the commercial.

Sheriff Wayne looked impatiently at his watch. "Let's go, Fred Zinnemann. I haven't got all day."

Chris had come off back-to-back shoots for *Thar She Blows 1* and *2* (rather loose porn interpretations of *Moby-Dick,* with Dixie Calhoun as a sexy, but murderous she-whale) and he was not in the mood for this cowboy bullshit. "Who?" he said, a bit more testily than he intended.

"Fred Zinnemann," said Sheriff Wayne. "He directed *High Noon.*"

All the speed Chris had taken to get through the overnight shoot had left his brain active but somewhat nonlinear. He tried to make words come out of his mouth, but as soon as he got hold of a few, they skittered away like hyperactive gerbils.

Sheriff Wayne closed in on Chris. "You call yourself a film-maker and you don't know the greatest western in cinematic history?"

Finally, the words got together and came shooting out of Chris's mouth all at once. "I think you'll find that most critics consider *Once Upon a Time in the West* to be—"

Sheriff Wayne grabbed Chris's shoulder and jammed a finger in his face. "Mention that Italian piece of dog shit one more time and I'll chop you up and personally feed you to this magnificent animal that's costing me a goddamn fortune every second you waste with not knowing about *High Noon*."

Chris felt something very strange. All the speed had amped up his system to the point of aggression, and it waged a fierce battle with his lifelong and innate fear of all physical confrontation. He wasn't exactly a coward, but he had recently left a Slayer concert when he refused a passing joint and two girls called him a "little bitch."

"I'm very sorry," he said. "Look, I'll rent *High Noon* and we can talk about it the next time we shoot."

"Next time? Son, I have grave doubts about your making it through this time."

Chris retreated to his video monitor. "Maybe we should get started."

"That would be awfully fucking nice," said Sheriff Wayne.

Across the parking lot, Donna, who couldn't stand looking at the accusing faces of invoices anymore, had come out to do a little sales work. She escorted an older couple and their little rat dog around the lot.

"Have you decided on a model you like?" she said.

"Something big. I like legroom," said Walter, the older man. He reminded Donna a little bit of Roy. That man scowled like he thought it would make his dong grow six inches.

"We talked about this," said the woman. Her name was Doris. "It's not 1965 anymore. The kind of cars you like go too fast and are too big. We'll never find parking."

Walter made a growling sound in the back of his throat. "A big car, you don't want to park anyway. You just drive until you or it dies."

Doris put a hand on Donna's arm. The little dog yapped. "Something small. Something compact."

"Like the damned dog," said Walter.

"It's very cute," said Donna.

"I wanted a husky. Instead we got a tribble."

"She's a teddy-bear Pomeranian," said Doris.

"I can see that she likes you," said Donna.

"Thank you. Now, about the car?"

They walked across the lot, moving from sedans to compacts.

"Nothing Japanese," said Walter. "I don't trust them."

Doris scowled back at him. "He got sick at a Benihana's a few years back. He blames the food, but he doesn't talk about the eight beers he had before dinner."

"I've been drinking beer my whole life. It was the food."

Visions of an electrical fire were coming back to Donna.

Doris can live, but if I could figure out how to get Walter to hold a can of high-test next to a spark, I'd burn down the whole San Fernando Valley.

"We have a large selection of European compacts," she said.

Doris looked back at her husband. "See? European. Just like James Bond."

"You have any compact Aston Martins?"

"I don't know if they make a compact," said Donna.

"There goes that theory," he said.

"Let me show you what we do have."

"Thank you, dear," said Doris. "Come on, grumpy bear."

Donna smiled and ushered the couple along, wishing she had a flamethrower or at least some oily rags for Walter to hold near a bonfire.

Dylan parked his Land Rover and the group piled out. This time they were careful to keep low and prowl through the car lot using vans and pickup trucks as cover.

"All right. Same plan as before," said Tyler. "Fan out and look for the llama."

Brad said, "It just occurred to me, I mean we were so worked up about having a target—"

"You mean having a chance to friendmancipate," said Linda.

"Sorry. How do we know he still has the llama? It was just a commercial. Maybe he just only had it for a couple of days."

"Still, we should look around. Even if the llama is gone, he might be oppressing another animals," said Tyler.

"Beings," said Linda.

"Right. Other beings."

Sarah pointed at a red, white, and blue figure halfway across the lot. "Is that him? It looks like he's shooting another commercial."

"He has a bald eagle," said Linda.

"They're endangered," said Heather.

"The bastard," said Tyler.

"I hear they taste like chicken."

"Shut up, Warren."

"Should we try to grab it?" said Sarah.

"An eagle?" said Brad. "It will claw your face off."

"And Sheriff Wayne *Junior*," said Dylan, cutting off Warren, "is wearing guns."

Warren perked up. "Cool. Do you think they're real?"

"A monster like him, who knows?" said Linda.

Dylan moved the group one lane closer. "Let's wait and look for an opening."

"Okay, Sheriff. We're ready to roll," said Chris.

"Finally." Turning to the eagle handler, Sheriff Wayne said, "Okay, Jungle Jim. How do we do this?"

The handler gave Sheriff Wayne a heavy leather glove that covered most of his arm.

"You just put this protective glove on your arm and bend your arm a bit. The eagle will hold on. All you have to do is worry about your lines."

"Sounds good to me."

Sheriff Wayne pulled on the glove, which pissed him off a little, considering how much he'd paid for every damned stitch of his suit. Once he was covered, he bent his arm and the handler brought over the eagle. He held it by the legs and just as he was transferring it to Sheriff Wayne, the bird let out a wild screech and viciously flapped its enormous wings.

Sheriff Wayne staggered back a few feet. "What the fuck was that? I swear if that pterodactyl puts one claw in me, you'll end up on the barbecue with the porno king over there."

The handler got the eagle settled on his arm again. "I'm sure he was just startled by the traffic. He's a professional. He'll be fine."

"He better be."

"He scared the bird," said Linda with a little catch in her throat.

"I think the bird scared him," said Warren.

"I know I'm scared," said Brad.

Heather hated herself for saying it, but she couldn't help it. "Maybe we should think this over a little more."

"Seize the moment," said Tyler.

"Who's going to seize the bird?" said Dylan.

"It will sense that we're here to save it and come to us," said Linda mistily.

"Really?" said Sarah. "You really believe that?"

"Gaia is a lot smarter than you, smartass."

"Sheriff Wayne has the eagle," said Brad.

Dylan looked at Warren. "I swear, if you say *'junior'* again, I'll buy that pickup truck over there just so I can run you down."

"I don't know what you're talking about. You're hearing things again," said Warren, smirking.

In the distance they could hear, "Hi. I'm Sheriff Wayne Jr., home of low, low . . ."

"It's started," said Tyler in a way that made Heather wish that everyone but the two of them would all drop dead at once.

"This is an Audi. It's small, so parking is easy, but it has a lot of power," said Donna.

"See? Little cars can have power," said Doris.

Walter's normal scowl turned into a menacing glower. "What's that smell?"

All three of them looked around for where the stink might be coming from.

Walter laughed and pointed at Doris. "I think Rin Tin Tin is doing his number ones on you."

"Oh, Pepper, not again," said Doris. She put the dog down and took a wad of tissues from her purse. As she dabbed at her blouse, Pepper went to the Audi and pissed on the tire.

"Atta girl," said Walter. And for the first time since they arrived, Donna saw him smile.

Sheriff Wayne Jr. was just wrapping up a perfect first take with, ". . . So, come on down to Sheriff Wayne Jr.'s. We're at the Livingston exit off the 101 near . . ."

A gust of wind came up and blew off his red, white, and blue hat. He whirled around to see where it went, knocking the eagle off balance. It cawed and snapped at him.

"Goddamn fiend," he shouted, and shook his arm free. The eagle flapped its majestic black wings and took off across the parking lot.

"It looks like she's all done now," said Doris.

"Good girl, Pepper," said Walter.

Doris shielded her eyes and looked into the distance. "What is that?"

A second later, what Doris would later describe as a "black-and-white hell beast" shot between them and took off into the sky.

Doris looked around. "Pepper?"

The three of them looked at each other, and then at the black dot disappearing over the horizon.

Sheriff Wayne Jr., Chris, the handler, and the video crew watched the eagle fly away.

"Boys," said Sheriff Wayne, retrieving his hat, "I'm definitely shooting someone today." He looked at Chris and the handler. "You two work out which one of you it's going to be."

Across the lot, Linda and the others gasped.

"It . . . it . . ." she said.

Tyler drew himself up heroically, something he'd wanted to do since seeing Chuck Norris in *Good Guys Wear Black* as a kid. "We've got to get this guy."

Warren waved at the receding dot. "Fly, Falkor, fly!"

"Shut up, Warren."

25

Froehlich and Harkhuf were staying in a caveman-styled cabin in the Hollywood Golden Bungalows on Sunset Boulevard. The walls and ceiling were made of Styrofoam with a rigid gray material on top that resembled rock in the same way that a dusty plastic fern in a dentist's waiting room resembles the Amazon rain forest. While the Hollywood Golden Bungalows had been built during the Hollywood heyday of the forties and were used to house rising stars and the occasional movie-magnate mistress, the years hadn't been kind to the place.

By the seventies, the movie studios had lost interest in the Hollywood Golden and it quickly became a hangout for the endless waves of starry-eyed musicians that washed up on L.A.'s shores like so many dead whales.

By the eighties, it had become a hot destination for punks, runaways, celebrity Satanists looking for a discreet place to hold their monthly black masses, and the coke dealers who supplied them all. This led to a brief revival of the Hollywood Golden's fortunes. But it all came crashing down when Phantom Ball Sac, a speed metal band from Pensacola, OD'd while bingeing on what they thought was a kilo of stolen Colombian nose confetti. In fact, it had been misplaced by a particularly lucky Satanist. Lucky because what he thought was coke was really a mix of angel dust and crystal meth, all cut with a kind of animal tranquilizer that would have been more appropriate for larger rhinos and, if they still existed, woolly mammoths.

Rumors soon began circulating that Phantom Ball Sac haunted their French Revolution–themed room, with its guillotine bed and Parisian sewers decor. The LAPD closed the bungalows soon after and the place fell into disrepair.

When the Hollywood Golden finally reopened, the only people interested in its abandoned carnival ambience were hookers and ghost hunters, along with a few lost souls hiding from jilted lovers and the police. Froehlich had once visited a Vegas-themed bungalow in the company of a hooker who always brought her pet Gila monster along in her purse. On one occasion, the lizard escaped the bag, crawled onto the bed, and bit Froehlich on a tender area of his body at a particularly frantic moment of coitus.

He'd had a soft spot in his heart for the Hollywood Golden ever since.

Froehlich's romance with the bungalows only increased now that Harkhuf had taken control of him. He expected to hate being a slave, but the truth was that ever since he'd relinquished his will, the flicker of despair that lay at the center of his being was nothing but a smoldering ember. This puzzled him and led to some serious self-examination.

First, he'd given up his will easily.

Second, he didn't mind as much as he thought he should.

Third, he had to admit that he sort of liked it.

Maybe that's been my problem my whole life, he thought. *I wasn't called a cur enough. What's next? Am I going to be in a collie costume paying a lady dressed like Eleanor Roosevelt to spank me with a rolled-up newspaper for not doing my business outside?* Froehlich didn't like how easily the idea popped in his head—or how much it appealed to him—but he didn't dislike it either.

A commercial for auto insurance came on the television. He got up from the bed with its faux-tiger-skin duvet and used a Swiss Army knife to unscrew the room's air vent. Carefully, he slid Harkhuf from the vent shaft and set him down next to a caveman chair. It was supposed to look like it was made of the bones of some small dinosaur, but to Froehlich it looked like what serial killers did on weekends as a hobby.

Froehlich dusted Harkhuf off a little and then took a step back from his master.

"I told you you would fit," he said. "And it wasn't any worse than that sarcophagus, I bet. Are you comfortable over there? If you could bend your legs, I could put you in the chair."

"I am adequate where I am," said Harkhuf inside Froehlich's mind.

The commercial ended and a game show came back on. There was a lot of screaming. Froehlich sneaked a glance at the screen.

"Serve me, soulless one," said Harkhuf.

"I am serving you. But I was also watching TV. In case you're interested, our set only gets two channels. One is all Hitler all the time. The other is a foreign game show where girls have hamburgers strapped to their asses and guys crawl around trying to eat them while the girls have a pillow fight." Froehlich held up the remote. "Do you have a preference?"

"Wretched dog," said his master.

"The game show it is."

Froehlich looked from Harkhuf to the game show and back again. He waited for a reaction, but got only silence. He looked at his master and dropped the remote on the bed.

"How exactly am I not serving you? I got you out of the museum. I got you across town, and I got us this room. And I found a nice vent for you to hide in. I even paid in cash, so no one can track us," he said with as much pride as worthless scum like him deserved.

I may be getting too comfortable with this too fast. I might be scum, but I'm not worthless. I'm worthful. Except . . .

"Is 'worthful' a word?" Froehlich said.

Harkhuf's voice filled his head. "I have need of objects of power. With them, I will find my beloved Shemetet and we shall change this wretched world forever."

A little piece of fake rock had fallen from the ceiling. Froehlich picked it up and tossed it in the trash because he knew Harkhuf liked the place tidy.

See? You're doing it again. Don't be such a pushover.

"Why is everything so wretched all the time?" Froehlich said. "I'm wretched. The world is wretched. Earlier, you said the room was wretched. Be happy. You're in L.A. You hit the jackpot."

"How dare you question me, cur?"

Froehlich kicked another piece of rock under the bed while discreetly taking a quick look at the pillow fight. "I admit it. The room isn't that great. But I'm not made of money. And you didn't even have cable three thousand years ago, so I think it all evens out, don't you?"

Harkhuf turned to him and slowly raised an arm. "You are my thrall."

Froehlich nodded, sighing. "I know. We've clearly established those boundaries. But I haven't eaten since I helped you escape. I'm your tired, hungry thrall."

"Retrieve my objects immediately!"

"I would, master, but the museum isn't open. I can't get in until tomorrow. But I will. First thing in the morning."

"Bring the objects to me or your suffering will be endless."

Froehlich took another peek at the game show. The more he

watched the more he really wanted a hamburger. "I gave up a promising career for this, you know."

"You gave up nothing," said Harkhuf. "I have given you your true life in eternal servitude."

Froehlich saw the collie costume clearly in his mind's eye. Eleanor was glaring at him with the rolled-up newspaper in her hand. Now he wanted a hamburger and to be told he couldn't have it.

"Maybe 'promising' isn't the word for my career. But after helping out Mr. Klein, I was moving up," he said. "Now look at me. Hiding in a fleabag motel, I'm starving, and I can't even watch girls have a pillow fight."

Harkhuf moved closer to him ponderously. "I must have the amulet. With it, wretched mortals could have power over me. This cannot be allowed."

Froehlich sat down, his mind racing. "Really, Master? An amulet that gives mortals power over you? That's interesting."

Pain that felt like a monkey with an ice pick shot through his head.

"Ow. Okay. Don't jump to conclusions," he said. "I wouldn't use it. I was just asking." He took a long drink from his flask.

"You must bring it to me," said Harkhuf.

Froehlich's ears rang. "Is there anything else you want?"

"A figurine. The goddess Isis herself. She will lead me to Shemetet."

Froehlich looked up at his master. "Don't take this the wrong way—I'm only asking as your wretched thrall—but how the hell am I supposed to walk into the museum and stroll out with a pile of artifacts under my arm?"

Harkhuf said, "I will be with you in spirit. I will see through your wretched eyes, hear through your unworthy ears. I will grant you power when needed. You will do this for me."

"Power? That could be fun," Froehlich said.

"Fun? Beguilement is not for the likes of you. You will serve me and my beloved until the flesh falls from your unworthy bones."

Don't think about the collie costume. Don't think about the collie costume . . .

"I will, Master," said Froehlich. "But I've never been on the lam before. It's more exhausting than I thought it would be."

"Then eat. Drink. Fill your dog belly, for tomorrow you shall serve and die for me if necessary."

"That's not going to give me nightmares. Thanks. Maybe I should be the one who hides in the vent tonight."

Someone knocked on the door. Froehlich looked through the peephole in the door. "Finally!" he said. "Let the feast begin."

He'd taken his jacket and work shirt off earlier and was now just in his guard pants and a white T-shirt. He thought about putting the shirt back on, but this was the Hollywood Golden Bungalows, he thought. *They're lucky I don't come to the door in nothing but a devil mask and Mary Janes.* Froehlich found the image not quite as compelling as that of the collie, but it wasn't bad. He decided to file it away for later, and opened the bungalow door.

A guy with hungover red eyes and a guitar-toting rooster on his T-shirt shirt was waiting outside. "I've got a delivery from Dr. Rock's Chickenpalooza for a Mr. Smith."

"That's me," said Froehlich. The delivery guy handed him a large white bag. It smelled like deep-fried heaven.

The delivery guy looked at the other bungalows. "A lot of Smiths out at this place, if you know what I mean."

"It's a family reunion," said Froehlich.

"You must have a really big family, Mr. Smith."

Before he could say anything, the delivery man went on.

"That's one Sammy Hagar Rockin' Barnyard Special, with extra gravy and napkins."

Froehlich signed for the bag and dug around in his pocket for a tip.

"Looks like you've got your own Barnyard Special going on, Mr. Smith," said the delivery guy.

Froehlich looked around and realized that Harkhuf was clearly visible just a few feet behind him.

The delivery guy did a mock salute. "Evening, ma'am. I hope you enjoy the chicken. And whatever else you're doing in there."

Froehlich grabbed some bills from his pocket and shoved them into the delivery guy's palm. "Thank you. You didn't see anything," he said.

The man looked at his hand. "Wow. Five bucks. I can finally quit my job and go to beauty school."

Froehlich slammed the door.

"Sorry about that, Master."

Harkhuf walked away. "When Shemetet and I rule this world, he will be dealt with."

"Him?" said Froehlich. "Don't worry about him. He's seen plenty worse."

He tore the bag open and spread the Barnyard Special on the tiger bedspread.

"Eat your fill, dog," said Harkhuf. "Tomorrow I shall find my beloved."

"Damn, this chicken is good," Froehlich said. He wondered what it would be like to get bitten downstairs by a Gila monster while eating chicken and how much it would cost to arrange.

Damn. My mind is all over the place tonight.

He was well into his second chicken thigh when Harkhuf said, "What is that man doing to that woman?"

Froehlich looked at the television. "I told you. He's eating a hamburger off her ass."

"It is wretched to behold."

Froehlich licked grease off his fingers. "She doesn't seem to mind."

"No, she does not," said Harkhuf. "This is a strange world in which to awaken."

"Sorry. I'll switch to Hitler."

"I said it was strange. I did not say turn it off."

Froehlich wiped his mouth with a napkin and with as much nonchalance as he could muster said, "When you were a big shot back in Egypt and a thrall was bad, did you ever hit him with a rolled-up newspaper?"

"What is a newspaper?" said Harkhuf.

"Silly question. Never mind."

Harkhuf got closer to the television, then looked at Froehlich. "And what ass will you eat *your* dinner from? Surely you do not have the temerity to think I would permit—"

Froehlich put up his hands. "No, Master. That's a contest. This is regular life."

"Good. Shemetet would not approve."

"Plus, it would get your wrappings dirty."

"Indeed. Now be quiet. I'm watching."

Froehlich finished the second thigh. On television, men on their hands and knees gnawed on burgers.

He said, "If you wanted, I could crawl around a little. Would you like me to crawl around while I eat?"

"Why would I want that?"

"No reason," said Froehlich quietly, his appetite suddenly spoiled.

26

Froehlich drove his Camry to the museum early the next morning. The banners for the Egyptian exhibit were still up, but there was a large Not Open to the Public sign at the front door. He parked and approached the building nervously. His master had told him that everything would be all right, and who was Froehlich to question the boss? Of course, it was easy for him to say from the comfort and safety of his own personal caveman bungalow. Froehlich's ass was hanging way out in the open, a pockmarked Macy's Thanksgiving Day Parade balloon just waiting for a gust of wind to blow it into the power lines.

Froehlich peered through the front-door glass and saw that the place was full of security guards. He took a deep breath, went over his story in his head one more time, and knocked.

Carlson scowled at him through the window and straightened his tie. His neck strained against his tight collar like someone pulling a bedsheet around a veiny fire hydrant. He took a slow and leisurely walk to the front door and opened it a crack.

"What do you want?" he said.

"I'd like to come in," said Froehlich.

"Why?"

"I work here."

"Where have you been since the robbery?"

"Am I a suspect?"

"I don't know. It depends on where you've been."

Froehlich moved around, trying to see past Carlson. However, every time he moved, Carlson took a step to block his view.

"You didn't answer my question," Carlson said.

"Which question was that?"

Froehlich caught a glimpse of Mr. Klein in the lobby.

"Where have you been since the robbery?"

He didn't have much time. Froehlich looked at Carlson. "Banging your mom."

Carlson shoved the door open, but before he could crush Froehlich's skull in one of his manhole-cover-size hands, Froehlich ducked and shouted between the big man's legs.

"Mr. Klein! Hey, Mr. Klein!"

Klein stopped and headed for the door. "Froehlich? Is that you?"

"Yes, sir. I'd like to come inside, but I seem to be encumbered."

Klein came up beside Carlson saying, "Step aside and let the man in. He's a hero."

Carlson took a grudging step to the right of the door, a colossal gargoyle looming in Froehlich's peripheral vision. Klein, all smiles, grabbed Froehlich's hand and pumped it hard several times.

"There you are. We've been worried about you," he said. "After your heroic gun battle with the thieves, you disappeared. We were afraid you'd been kidnapped."

Froehlich plastered on the smile he'd been practicing all morning as other security guards came over, many of them wanting to shake his hand. "Nope. Not kidnapped. Just a little dazed is all. It's hard to remember anything."

Klein and some of the guards nodded.

"Yes, everyone seems to have memory problems. The police theory is that the thieves somehow drugged everyone. Have you ever heard of such a thing?"

"Gosh no. I guess I got lucky and got a little less of the gas than some people."

"It's not just that," said Klein. "You fought back. None of these overpriced Barney Fifes did that. We found most of them asleep or wandering around like zombies."

"I know the feeling."

Klein put an arm around his shoulder and pulled him to the exhibit hall. "You did good the other night, but that's not what I wanted to talk to you about. There are big things happening here. Some serious opportunities for advancement after what happened to Baxter."

Baxter. After his exciting new job as a slave, Froehlich had forgotten all about her. As innocently as he could, he said. "Ms. Baxter? What happened to her?"

As they reached the Egyptian exhibit Rockford, the insurance investigator, headed their way.

Klein said, "I have to get to a meeting. Rockford can give you the overview. Big things are happening and some of them have your name attached."

"Thanks, Mr. Klein. That sounds great," said Froehlich. For the briefest of moments he reconsidered his job prospects. Be a slave for all eternity to a scarecrow in a fleabag vent shaft or become a big wheel at the museum with a desk and a 401(k).

Pain shot through his head like a monkey with a steak knife.

Ow. I get it, Master. Bad dog. I got distracted for a second, but I'm back on the job now.

The monkey gave him one last poke and disappeared. Froehlich rubbed a knot out of the back of his neck. He wanted a drink, but Harkhuf had made him leave his flask back at the bungalow. Of all the mummies in the world that he could have become enslaved to, he had to get a buzzkill. The flicker of despair in the center of his being grew from an ember back into a small flame as Rockford got closer.

I swear, someone better hit me with a goddamned newspaper or I'm not going to make it to lunch.

Just as he was settling in for a new round of dread, Rockford came by and looked him over. "Good to see you, Froehlich. It seems I had you figured all wrong."

Rockford put out his hand and Froehlich shook it, sure the other man was going to slap cuffs on him. Instead, Rockford gave him a sympathetic look.

"What happened to you after the gunfight? Where have you been?"

Froehlich froze, not so much like a deer in the headlights as a hang glider who'd just set a new altitude record being sucked into the engine of a 747.

"I don't know," he stammered. "I barely remember the night at all."

Rockford tapped a pen on his notebook and looked around. "Neither does anybody else. And have you heard their stories? I suppose you saw clowns, too?"

"Yes. And something else . . ."

"A Martian?"

"No," said Froehlich. "More like a TV set. I think it was showing a nature documentary. There was a cat. A lion? Yes. A documentary about lions?"

Rockford made another note.

"Lions? First time I heard about that, but it's not anything stranger than what we already have."

"Mr. Klein said something had happened to Ms. Baxter?"

Rockford smirked. "She's under arrest. We found irrefutable evidence of her involvement in the mummy theft in her office."

Good. The old biddy, thought Froehlich.

"You mean you found the mummy?" he said lightly.

Rockford shook his head. "Just part of one. But it's enough. Airtight evidence."

"That does sound pretty damning," said Froehlich, trying not to laugh. His despair flame was shrinking back down to a flicker the more he thought about Baxter's demise.

"She denies everything, of course," said Rockford.

"What else is she going to do? Do you know what she did with it?"

"Not a clue. What can you do with a mummy?"

I threw the extra one I found in the Dumpster. I wonder if it met Gilbert in Dumb-ass Heaven?

"You can't put it on eBay," said Froehlich, trying to sound serious and thoughtful. "My guess would be she'd sell it to a private collector."

"Really? There's a lot of calls for mummies?"

"You know rich people. Half the stuff they buy is so they can show off to their friends," said Froehlich. He shook his head disapprovingly. "The freakier the better. I mean, look at that movie star with a T. rex skull. What does a person do with something like that?"

Rockford made a note.

"A dinosaur skull. Who is this again?"

Froehlich looked around trying to spot his master's objects of power. "I don't remember, but there's a million like him out there. And if it's not rich movie stars, maybe it's a cult," he said gravely. "Charlie Manson types. God knows what someone like that would do with a mummy."

Rockford looked serious. "You think Baxter would sell to someone like that?"

Froehlich leaned in and said in a low voice, "Hell, she might even be *in* the cult. With her money and connections, she could be a high priestess."

Rockford looked dubious. "A society lady like that? I don't know."

"What about Patty Hearst? What about Elizabeth Báthory? She was a society lady."

"Who's that?"

"A demented countess who used to bathe in the blood of young peasant girls."

"I think I saw a movie about her. Hungarian. What do you expect?" said Rockford evenly. His eyes narrowed. "You think Baxter could be mixed up in something like that?"

"I don't know," said Froehlich. "It depends on what kind of cult she's in."

"This case just gets stranger and darker."

You have no idea, thought Froehlich. He noticed bullet holes in the wall and remembered that he was the one who made them. He tried not to smile.

"Grill her hard," he told Rockford. "I've read about these cult types. They don't give up their secrets easily."

"Don't you worry. I'll get them out of her."

Rockford slapped his pen into his notebook and put it in his pocket.

Froehlich walked casually into the Egyptian exhibit. "So, what all did they get the other night?" he said.

He stopped in front of the empty display case.

"Everything in here. I have a list," said Rockford. "A necklace. A knife. Various statues of dogs and falcons and whatnot. An amulet . . ."

Froehlich's head whipped around. "An amulet? You're sure it's gone?" When he spoke the question, he felt his head tighten as something alien entered it.

"Why? Do you know anything about it?" said Rockford.

Storm clouds formed in Froehlich's skull. *It's not going to be a fun night at the bungalow,* he thought.

"No. I just remember seeing it. It was pretty."

"I suppose," said Rockford in a distracted tone. "Just between you and me, this is out of my field. I usually work on stolen art, diamonds, vintage cars. You know, real things. All of this . . . stuff . . . it's just annoying. Dogs and birds. Who comes up with it?"

"Some of it is very beautiful. Let's go over here," Froehlich said.

They went to a display case that was still full of artifacts. It was unlocked. There were small cards next to each item with an inventory number on each.

"Don't you think some of it is pretty at least?" Froehlich said.

Rockford shrugged. "Heathen crap."

The monkey reappeared and tickled Froehlich's skull with the point of the knife.

"Ow."

"You okay?"

"Just a cramp," he said. He pointed to a statuette in the front of the case. "What about her? She's not an animal. She's a person. Isis, I believe."

"Yeah, but she hangs out with all these barnyard rejects. What's her story, some kind of Tarzan-and-Jane thing?"

"Maybe we should take a closer look," said Froehlich conspiratorially. He started to lift the display-case lid. Rockford laid a hand on top.

"Whoa. We can't do that. All that stuff has to be accounted for."

Froehlich's head snapped toward him. He looked at Rockford hard because he had to.

Rockford's face went slack.

Feel free to use me like a sock puppet, Master. There's nothing weird about me standing here gazing into a detective's eyes like I either want to kiss him or eat his brain. I'm sure nobody's noticed us.

That's sarcasm, by the way. Did they have sarcasm three thousand years ago? I hope so because I'd hate for this to go to waste.

"Maybe you should open the case anyway," said Froehlich. "I'll wait over there. Get the Isis and the inventory slip." He wandered calmly over to the other side of the exhibit hall.

A minute later, Rockford brought him the statuette. Froehlich slipped it into his jacket pocket. Rockford's eyes were as blank as a fried cod's.

"I should go," Froehlich said. "But I've been dying to ask. Your name. Is it really Rockford? Like the TV detective?"

Rockford nodded. "Our mom changed our name. She said she 'knew' the actor." He said "knew" with air quotes.

"Please tell me your first name is James."

Rockford nodded. "Mom called me Jim."

"Is that why you're a detective?"

He stared straight ahead. "It was Mom's idea."

"What did you want to be?"

"A massage therapist."

Froehlich tried not to laugh. "Forget the detective game. Forget this case. Get yourself some New Age music and one of those folding tables. Boom. You're in business."

"You have to take a test. It's supposed to be hard."

Froehlich clapped him on the arm. "Start studying. I have faith in you, Jim."

Rockford blinked a couple of times. "Is that all?"

"One more thing. Grow a ponytail, too. That's mandatory in California."

"A ponytail," he said blankly.

Froehlich watched Rockford's eyes return to normal.

"It was nice talking to you, Jim," Froehlich said.

"You, too," Rockford said. He started to walk away and stopped. "Is there somewhere around here to get scented baby oil?"

"What for?"

Rockford frowned. "I'm not entirely sure," he said, and wandered off.

That was fun. Now I get the master-and-thrall thing. I could get used to this.

The monkey jabbed him.

Just kidding, boss.

Froehlich started back to the museum lobby when Carlson got in front of him.

"I saw what you did," the big man said.

Froehlich froze. Again. *I really have to get a better poker face if we're going to take over the world.* He touched the Isis in his pocket while calculating how far it was to the door and if he could he make it before being mowed down by a meat locomotive in a uniform.

"I don't know what you mean," he said.

"Big hero. Cozying up to Rockford. You think you're a detective now? Well, you're not. You couldn't protect bacon from a Chihuahua."

Froehlich could feel Harkhuf's annoyance as he stood there dithering. He pointed to the empty display case. "After the robbery, I heard that they found you counting sheep. I hope you kept a better eye on them than you did on the exhibit."

"That was *my* gun you stole to shoot at the clowns. Don't ever touch my weapon again," growled Carlson. He grabbed Froehlich by the arm. "Time for you to go, hero."

Froehlich finally stopped dithering and decided instead to be terrified. When Carlson grabbed him, he slapped his hand over his pocket.

The big man pushed Froehlich's hand away. "What have you got there?"

"Your mom's ass," said Froehlich as Harkhuf took control of his mouth.

Carlson grabbed him by the throat. Froehlich looked him in the eye and managed to croak, "You're my thrall."

Carlson's eyes went glassy. "I'm your thrall."

"First off, how about you stop choking me?" said Froehlich.

Carlson let him go. Froehlich took a couple of deep breaths, but kept his eyes on the big man.

"If anyone figures out that the Isis is missing, you're going to run away," he said. Then added, "And flap your arms and cluck like a chicken."

"If someone figures out that the Isis is missing, I'll run away."

"And flap your arms and cluck like a chicken."

"And flap my arms and cluck like a chicken," said Carlson.

"If Rockford questions you, tell him he should learn to work with his hands. Maybe carpentry. Or better yet, massage."

"Carpentry or better yet, massage."

"Good boy. And since we're having a moment here, I feel the need to confess something to someone and you look out of it enough to be safe," said Froehlich. He looked around. "I like being ordered around."

"Ordered around," said Carlson blankly.

"There. I feel better for having said it out loud. Now forget it. But remember Rockford's hands and the other thing."

From across the exhibit hall, someone said, 'Hey, is there something missing from this case?"

Carlson's eyes went wide. *"Braraaach!"* he yelled, and rushed away flapping his arms. The other security guards dashed after him.

Froehlich strolled out the front door and got in his Camry. He'd ruined just enough lives today to feel really good about the doomed direction he knew his had taken.

27

Minerva was dead tired. She'd barely slept the previous night, studying obscure old books, ancient pamphlets, medieval scrolls, and a used paperback of *The Black Arts for Dummies*.

It was all gobbledygook.

She just didn't have the head for putting the whammy on people. Even with Dross gone, she was reasonably sure she could pull off a crooked séance, and if she brushed up on some of the patter she'd bribed from a carny acquaintance, even do a *soupçon* of bogus mind reading. But actual magic? It was all invoking this and woo-woo that. Trying to understand it was like pushing soup up an escalator. If Kellar didn't get that wobbly sack of custard he called an ass up here soon, she'd be stuck reading the cards for morons like this bimbo . . . what was her name? Judy? Julie? Something with a J . . . for-fucking-ever.

"This card is your past," said Minerva.

"What do you see?" said J. She was a dye-job redhead and only pushing thirty-five, but she'd already gone through at least three nose jobs. And not great ones. Her perky little proboscis reminded Minerva of the bunny slope at a cut-rate ski lodge.

"Love," said Minerva in a slightly dreamy voice, careful not to lay it on too thick. "A love that didn't end the way you wanted."

"You mean Robert?" said J excitedly.

Bingo.

"Yes, Robert."

"What do the cards say about him?"

This was too easy, thought Minerva. That many nose jobs and the reading is always about lost love. At least one of those nose jobs was for Mr. Wrong.

"This is your future," Minerva said, carefully dealing a card from the bottom of the deck. It was the Lovers, a couple of naked morons being watched over in the sky by a winged peeping tom. Or maybe it was Cupid or Glinda, the Good Witch. Who cared? It always worked.

"The Lovers," she said.

J brought her hands to her mouth and said, "Robert is leaving his wife after all?"

Oh God. One of these. Minerva kept her cool and stared at the cards like a wise gypsy she once saw in an old horror movie. After a nice dramatic pause, she raised her eyes to meet J's.

"You're all he thinks about."

"I knew it," J said, raising her arms over her head like she'd just won a stuffed bunny at the county fair. "What else do the cards say?"

Minerva dealt another card from the bottom. She'd loaded the deck earlier in the afternoon. There was a real art to stacking the cards just right so they'd tell a story that would reel the suckers in. She turned over what she knew was the World, with promises of good times to come. Only it wasn't the World. It was Death.

"Oh," said the bimbo.

"Oh," said Minerva, thinking, *Fuck. Fuck. Fuck. Fuck. Goddammit. Fuck.*

J's hands went back to her mouth. "Oh my God. Is Robert going to die?" she said. Her voice dropped an octave. "Am *I* going to die?"

The bell over Minerva's door tinkled. She looked up and saw Kellar standing by the curtains, one eye cocked at her. Minerva knew that he knew that she'd fucked up.

She slapped down a random spread of cards on top of Death and did her gypsy stare.

"What does it say?"

"Reply hazy. Ask again later," said Minerva.

J looked puzzled. "Isn't that something from a Magic 8 Ball?"

Minerva gathered up the cards. "Not at all. Sometimes the spirits just aren't ready to reveal their secrets. I'm afraid we'll have to conclude today's session."

"I have to leave? What about Robert? Isn't there something I should do to bring our love together?"

Minerva grabbed the candle closest to her, but spotted Keith Richards on the back.

"Oops. Not that one." She handed J a Virgin of Guadalupe instead. *Virgin,* she thought. *That's rich.*

"Here. Burn this."

J looked at it. "Is that all? It doesn't seem like enough."

Working hard to hide her annoyance, Minerva picked up her tin and pulled out a joint. She held it out to J, but withdrew it at the last minute.

"You're not a narc, are you?"

"Of course not," said J.

"Then here. Smoke this with the candle."

"What is it?"

No spring chicken, Minerva really was seriously fried from last night's cram session. She knew it was why she screwed up the card bit, and why she was experiencing a major brain fart that left her staring at J instead of answering.

Kellar stepped forward, delicately plucked the joint from Minerva's fingers, and handed it to J. "It's sage and rose petals," he said. "Very powerful for love. And health."

"Just don't drive or handle anything sharp," added Minerva.

J put the joint in her purse. "Can I come back tomorrow to see if the cards are ready to speak?"

"Sure. Tomorrow," said Minerva vaguely. "I'm certain the cards will be aflutter with good news."

"Thank you so much."

Minerva escorted J to the door. "Good-bye, my dear." She threw the lock and looked at Kellar. "It took you long enough to get here."

He crossed his arms and gave her a reproving look. "Really? The old lover bit? Nice money up front, but the rubes can get pretty testy when it doesn't work out."

"Money!" said Minerva. She unlocked the door and ran outside, following J, but the woman had disappeared. Minerva slammed the door when she came back in. "I forgot to get the damned money."

Kellar rolled his eyes. "Come on, Minerva. Hookers and psychics get paid up front. It's basic."

"It's *your* fault. I got flustered." She walked back into the reading parlor. Kellar locked the door and followed her in.

"Don't look for money from me," he said. "I'm skint. But I do have this two-for-one Red Lobster coupon."

"Then tonight we feast."

Minerva took another joint from the box, lit it, and passed it to Kellar. He took a long hit and said in a raspy holding-in-the-smoke-like-a-pro voice, "What are you going to do when Juliet returns tomorrow looking for Romeo?"

Minerva took back the joint. "I've got that covered. How's this: the boyfriend has a brain tumor and lost his memory—except of her. But he isn't well enough to leave his wife yet. In the meantime, she should come back once a month to check in on old Bob's condition."

"And pay up front."

"Cash on the barrelhead," said Minerva, slapping the table.

"Good girl. I'll have to steal that for one of my clients."

"Go right ahead," Minerva said. She drew in the smoke and let it out. "But with luck, we won't have to worry about crap like that anymore."

Kellar got a sly smile on his face when Minerva passed the joint back. "Tell me. What do you have?"

Minerva took the knife from the pocket of her flowing dress and set it on the table between them.

Kellar poked it with a chubby index finger. "Been shoplifting at Pier 1 again, have we? I suppose it's pretty. Is it real gold?"

"Of course it's gold, but that's not the point," Minerva said. "It's an ancient Egyptian athame."

Kellar rolled his eyes. "A magic knife? Please. I make PB&Js with those."

Minerva accepted the joint back. "Not this one. It's the real thing. Give it a squeeze."

He looked at her skeptically and picked up the athame. Kellar's expression changed. "Oooo. Those are some nice vibrations. What can you do with it?"

Minerva tapped some ash off the joint. "I don't actually know yet."

"Then why did you call me all the way over from the airport?" said Kellar sternly.

"I mean, I know what it does," she said. "I just need to work out how to do it."

"And what does it do?"

She leaned forward. "It sends a psychic text message straight into the brain of a mummy. A real live resurrected one that's walking around in L.A. right now."

"No!" said Kellar in a hushed voice.

"Yes. Remember Coop?"

Kellar thought for a minute. "The thief? Bit of a loser?"

"Exactly. He pissed the thing off and it's put a curse on him. I gave him a necklace to keep the mummy at bay and he gave me this lovely knife in return."

"But how does that help us?" said Kellar.

Minerva winked. "The necklace isn't to keep the mummy away. It's to draw the mummy right to him. All we have to do is get in touch with *Bubba Ho-Tep*, and make sure he knows that we're the Good Samaritans who helped out and offer our services for the future."

Kellar frowned. "That's a tad on the mean side."

"Would you rather spend the evening eating fried shrimp at Red Lobster or jumping in front of rented minivans?"

Kellar placed a hand on his chest. "My heart says leave the poor boy alone, but my knees and back say screw him."

"Good man," said Minerva.

"To be back on top again," said Kellar dreamily. "So, if we're going to cut deals with . . . ?"

"Harkhuf."

"It sounds like you're clearing your throat. If we're cutting deals with him, what are you going to ask for?"

Minerva stubbed out the joint and put the remains in her tin box. "I want it to be like the old days. I want those young show-biz punks who laughed at me to come crawling back. I want limos and five-star hotels and to go to the Academy Awards with Jack Nicholson."

"Does he even go anymore?"

"He will when I'm done with him."

"Bad girl."

"What do you want?" said Minerva.

Kellar clapped his hands together. "This is perfect. You do the stars and I'll do everyone else. I'll be the Dr. Phil of psychics with my own supernatural afternoon talk show. Maybe I'll write a memoir about my adventures in the occult."

Minerva chuckled. "It will be banned in all fifty states, you degenerate."

"And Oprah will pick it for her book club."

She raised her eyebrows. "Oprah. That *is* dreaming big."

Kellar's eyes narrowed. "Why are you cutting me in on this windfall?"

"We've known each other a long time," Minerva said. "And I need some help. You know how obscure those old mystical texts can be."

"Well, what do you have?"

"I was up late last night and I've made some notes. Should we go ahead and give it a try?"

"You're not going to summon the Devil or anything, are you? I mean, that little mix-up with the cards . . . ?"

"No, this is nothing like that."

"Then there's no time like the present."

"Good," said Minerva. She pulled out her bottle of Jack Daniel's and a couple of glasses from behind the cushions. "For toasts later."

"Now you're talking," said Kellar. "Okay. Make with the magic."

"Did you lock the door?"

"And put up the Fuck Off We're Conjuring sign."

Minerva went into the kitchen and came back with a cracked tea saucer piled high with herbs. She put a match to them until they burned and consulted her notes. With the athame in her left hand, she delicately dipped it into the burning herbs and pointed it to the four cardinal points while chanting something she'd written down.

Kellar waved his hand to keep the smoke out of his face. He

raised his eyebrows as she chanted. "Are you having a seizure, dear?"

"Shut up," said Minerva out of the side of her mouth. She went back to chanting.

Something formed in the air between them. It was a small ball of vapor at first, but soon it collapsed in on itself and began to glow. It pulsed and shot across the room like a thumb-size star, went to the curtains, and looped back toward them.

"What is that?" said Minerva. "That doesn't seem right."

Kellar pursed his lips and said, "I think what you have there is an *ignis fatuus*. A will-o'-the-wisp."

The star came to a sudden halt a few inches from Minerva's nose. On closer inspection, the light was a tiny woman with shaggy hair, a short dress, and what appeared to be tiny go-go boots. She reminded Minerva of a miniature Debbie Harry.

Minerva smiled at the will-o'-the-wisp apologetically. "I haven't had much sleep and I seem to have gotten my wires crossed. I'm awfully sorry," she said.

Debbie gave Minerva the finger, darted around her, and grabbed the Jack Daniel's. The go-go-booted star sped away with the bottle and they vanished with a cheerful little tinkle.

Kellar looked at Minerva. "I guess we've been put in our place."

"I'll check a few more sources," she said.

"As will I."

"So," said Minerva. "Red Lobster?"

"By bus?"

"Fuck it. It's a special occasion. Let's cab it."

"I thought you were broke, too," said Kellar.

"I always keep a little mad money in my sock."

"That's where I keep my coke."

Minerva opened her arms wide. "And now we have dessert!"

28

"Where is my amulet?"

Coop opened his eyes. It certainly felt like he did. The truth was that he was still in the strange netherworld between deep sleep and true wakefulness. It's that fuzzy zone where you're absolutely convinced you're up and ready to juggle barracudas, but in reality are more likely to put your eye out with a shoehorn.

Coop sat up in bed. "What? Who's that?"

"The amulet, dog. What have you done with it?"

The voice was deep and didn't sound at all like Giselle's. It was more like a cop who thought he had you dead to rights or a strip-club owner who's annoyed that you taught all of his dancers how to pick pockets. But the strangest part was that it felt like the voice was coming from inside his head.

"Where is my amulet? Return it to me!"

Okay, that I definitely heard.

Coop got out of bed and walked into the living room. He still didn't recognize who was talking, but it wasn't like he'd stolen so many amulets recently that he had to puzzle out which one the voice meant. He went to the window and peeked out through the blinds.

"Crap."

What Coop wanted to be able to say was *How weird is it that there's a mummy in the street?* but what he ended up thinking was *How weird is it that I'm in the street in my underwear?*

He did appear to be standing in the middle of Franklin Avenue in his boxer briefs, the ones that Giselle got him with the Millennium Falcon on the butt. He hated them, but they were a gift, so he made an effort to put them on every now and them. And now any neighbors who happened to look out their windows would know about them, too. Good thing this was all just a strange dream.

"Bring it to me," said Harkhuf. "It is mine, wretched thing."

Coop wiggled his necklace at the dead man. "You can't hurt me. I'm mummy-proof. See?"

"You are nothing."

"In that case, nothing is going to say good night."

"Halt," Harkhuf.

Coop stopped. He didn't exactly have to, but all of a sudden he really wanted to. *This really is a weird dream,* he thought.

"Be my thrall."

Coop yawned. "You know, if you got yourself a ukulele and a hat, you'd wow the tourists on Hollywood Boulevard. They love novelty acts."

"Dogs do not question their masters. They speak when they are spoken to."

Coop looked down at his stupid shorts. He looked at the empty street. He looked at the three-thousand-year-old jerk in the shadows by a dented VW Bug. He'd seen scarier scenes at the DMV.

"You, my friend, are nothing more than an anxiety dream.

I had one like this in high school when Angie Rodriguez said she'd go out with me. All week I dreamed I drove to her house without pants. 'Hi, Angie,' I'd say in nothing but socks and a T-shirt. Then I'd run home screaming like someone snapped a waffle iron shut on my rooster eggs."

"Cease your nonsense and come to me, slave."

"No, it's Coop. Remember? Charlie Cooper."

"Deliver to me what I want."

This was a pretty realistic dream, he thought. Lights came on in a couple of houses down the street and Coop stepped in something that felt like gum.

"You want the amulet? I don't have it, asshole. And if I did, I still wouldn't give it to you because you're nothing but bourbon, Ambien, and that extra-spicy pad thai that Giselle always orders. Personally, I think it's too hot, but it makes her happy."

"In the end I will come for you, and when I do, I will not be as kind as tonight."

Coop waved to Harkhuf. "Good night, Angie. You were the girl of my dreams, but now you look like someone tried to make a hobo out of greasy Fatburger wrappers and dirty diapers."

"Soon, dog. Soon," said the mummy as it faded into the shadows.

Coop turned around and pulled down his Millennium Falcon shorts. "Kiss my ass, dream date."

"Coop!"

It was Giselle. A cherry red El Camino was rounding onto Franklin, coming fast. With his underwear around his knees, all Coop could do was hop out of the way.

"Crap."

"What the hell are you doing out here?" yelled Giselle. "And pull your damned pants up."

"This really is a weird dream," Coop yelled back to her. More lights came on.

"This isn't a dream, Dorothy, and you're not the head of the Lollipop Guild. You're in the damned street. And you just about got run over. Plus, you flashed everyone on the block."

Coop pointed to her with one hand and pulled up his underwear with the other. "That's exactly what you'd say in a dream."

The El Camino came barreling around the corner again, heading straight for him. Giselle dashed down the apartment steps and pushed Coop out of the way. The car stopped, reversed, and stopped right next to Coop. A girl, maybe sixteen years old, leaned out of the passenger-side window.

"Nice ass, Grandpa," she said, and bounced an empty Coors can off Coop's forehead.

The El Camino sped away around the next corner. He could hear young laughing voices as it went. Coop touched his head and sniffed. "Ow. That smells like beer."

"That's because it is, Lady Godiva. Now come back inside."

Coop looked around. "This isn't a dream?"

"No, it isn't."

"Did you see Harkhuf?"

"The mummy? Of course not."

"Then maybe this isn't a dream, but that part was," he said. "Or maybe the mummy was really in my head, but it couldn't take me over." He gave the necklace a flick of his finger. "It means the rocks are working."

"Sure they are," said Giselle, pushing his wet hair back off his forehead.

"How about we say no more pad thai for a while?"

"Yeah. That's what's wrong with your life. Pad thai."

"What else?" he said.

"You're cursed, dumb-ass."

"I'm protected."

"If that's what you call protection." Giselle picked up the beer can and bounced it off his forehead.

"That felt real."

"Some protection."

"Maybe I should look into getting more."

Giselle pulled him back to the apartment. "Let's get you inside and cleaned up. You smell like cheap beer, Hot Topic lip gloss, and balls."

"So . . . your prom night."

"I'd throw this can at you again if you weren't so close to right."

More lights came on around them.

"You sure this isn't just an anxiety dream?" Coop said.

"If it is, it's mine," Giselle said. "Now get inside, Grandpa."

Coop stopped. "Do I really have old-man ass?"

Giselle pointed to the apartment lights up and down the street. "You don't need my opinion. The whole neighborhood saw it. Ask them."

29

The next morning, Coop spent the entire drive to the DOPS building lying under a blanket in the backseat of Giselle's car. She told him it had been woven by an old *bruja* in the hills above Bahía de los Ángeles in Mexico and that it guarded against the evil eye. This was only half-true. Yes, the package the blanket had come in had a Mexican postmark, and yes, it was woven, but she'd bought it on eBay, and for all she knew it could have been woven by a machine or indentured monkeys being paid in bananas. But it looked rustic enough and was covered in obscure squiggles that, while they were probably spots from a lousy dye job, could be mistaken for arcane magical symbols by someone freaked out enough to believe in magic blankets in the first place.

Coop had been up all night after his encounter with Harkhuf. Giselle told herself that she'd encouraged him to burrow like a badger in the backseat to keep him from bugging her on the drive to work. The truth was that she was even more unsettled than he was. He believed in his idiotic magic necklace, but all she had was the image of a half-naked Coop shouting at shadows while standing in front of moving cars. If that bunch of rocks around his neck worked, it wasn't working well enough. She was worried, and that was the last thing she wanted Coop to see, hence the fairy tale about a voodoo blanket. At least they agreed on one thing: he needed more help and maybe Bayliss was someone they could trust. It was worth a shot. She couldn't keep coming up with magic blankets or divine beach towels in which to ensconce him.

"We're here," Giselle said as she backed into a parking space in the DOPS underground lot. "You can come out, Sleepy Beauty."

Coop pushed the blanket down just past his chin and looked out. "Are you sure? It's pretty cozy back here."

Giselle came around and opened the back door. "Don't worry. It's safe to come out. Nothing can get you here."

"If you're sure," Coop said. He wadded up the blanket and crawled out of the open door.

Giselle brushed him off. "See? I told you you'd be safe as long as you stayed down. It worked like a charm."

"Yeah. That was some powerful shaman," he said. "Oh. I forgot something." Coop handed her a small cloth tab. Printed on it in crisp black letters was MADE IN CHINA in both English and Spanish.

"The next time you stick someone under an enchanted doily, you might want to give it the once-over."

"I thought I did," she said. She screwed up her mouth. "I guess I'm not that good a con man after all." She started to throw away the tab but Coop grabbed it from her.

"You don't get off the hook that easy. This goes in the family memory. We can show it to the grandkids."

"We don't even have kids."

"Well, someone's grandkids. 'Gather round, little ones, and learn exactly how not to pull off a con.'"

"Have I told you lately how truly hysterical you are?" said Giselle. She locked the car and headed for the elevators. "I was only doing it for your own good."

Coop followed her. "See, if you'd slipped me a mickey, I might have bought it a little longer. You should remember that when you're shanghaiing sailors down at the docks."

They got into the elevator and Giselle punched the button like it owed her money. "You're enjoying this way too much for a marked man," she said.

"I think I'm enjoying it just the right amount," said Coop.

"Remember to keep your voice and your swelled head down when we get inside. Woolrich doesn't want you here."

"I remember. And no one gets to know that his plan to use me as mummy bait is working."

"So much for the twenty-four-hour surveillance Woolrich promised."

"I'm happy they weren't there. The last thing I want to see is my ass and Millennium Falcon shorts in the company newsletter."

Giselle took Coop's hand. "It was very sweet of you to wear them."

"I know. And I'm never doing it again."

"I already threw them away. They're not really special now that a car full of marauding juvenile delinquents has seen them."

He shrugged. "I was never a *Star Wars* fan anyway."

The elevator stopped and Giselle let go of Coop's hand. She rounded on him. "You don't like cats and now you don't like *Star Wars*? What *do* you like?"

"Crouching in backseats under mystical throw rugs."

They headed for Bayliss's cubicle. Morty was waiting for them around the corner with a cup of vending-machine coffee.

"Hey, you two. How's tricks?"

"Coop thinks he's a comedian," said Giselle.

"He always makes me laugh."

"You should have seen him last night if you wanted a real laugh."

"What happened last night?"

"I'll tell you later," said Coop. "By the way, I saw Minerva. She says you're a bum."

"The fortune-teller? Why am I a bum?"

As they passed an unoccupied desk, Coop picked up a newspaper and held it next to his face as they walked. "She says she set you up with someone and you never thanked her."

Morty coughed and tossed the coffee in the trash. "You mean the cute Japanese girl? She was a *Jorōgumo*. We go back to my place and all of a sudden she sprouts eight legs. She wanted to lay eggs in my brain."

"At least you'd have something up there."

"I already do. It's where I keep my spare change."

"I saw the mummy last night in a dream," said Coop.

"It wasn't a dream," said Giselle.

"He was in my head trying to take me over like that guard in the museum."

"Did it work?" said Morty.

"What do you mean? I'm here, aren't I?"

"Not before he stopped off to flash the neighborhood," said Giselle.

"I had a cousin who was that kind of flasher," said Morty.

"What happened to him?"

"He lost his glasses and flashed a bull."

"How did the bull take it?" said Coop.

"Not well. These days he's flashing Saint Peter in Heaven."

Coop frowned. "I'm not sure flashers go to Heaven."

"They don't. I checked with the afterlife placement department," said Morty. "But saying Heaven is nicer than 'He's flashing sharks with chain saws in Hell.' Anyway, it sounds like the necklace protected you."

"I'm not convinced," said Giselle. "I think it was just Coop's natural talent for dodging magic."

"What did the creep want?"

"An amulet," said Coop.

Morty thought about it. "*The* amulet? The one we gave Wool-rich?"

Coop rubbed the back of his neck. "That's what I'm afraid of. Maybe there's some other way to get him off my back. Bayliss might be able to find out."

"Have you seen her since the audit?"

"No. We want to check on her," said Giselle. "How was she?"

"I've seen people in worse shape, but she's still a little on the fuzzy side," said Morty. He held up a bandaged hand. "When I asked her how it was going, she stapled me to her desk."

"You poor thing," said Giselle.

"Maybe she likes you and wanted you to stick around," said Coop.

"If that's her idea of a first date, I'll pass," said Morty. "Anyway, I bet she'll be happy to see you. Just keep your hands in your pockets."

They found Bayliss at her desk. Where her keyboard normally sat was a pair of sneakers filled with paper clips. The walls of her cubicle were papered with colorful Post-its. Each one had an inspirational quote and a tiny drawing in black ink, but they all seemed a little off. *Hang in there, baby* was at the top left of her cubicle. While the saying was normally accompanied by an image of a cat hanging from a tree branch, Bayliss's *Hang in there, baby* featured a dragon in an evening gown eating what appeared to be a washing machine full of bowling shoes. Next to that was *There's no I in teamwork,* with a drawing of an ice cream cone holding an ax chasing a bat with a machine gun.

"That one doesn't even make sense," said Morty. "Why doesn't the bat just shoot the ice cream cone?"

"It's probably a pacifist," said Coop.

"Shut up," Giselle told them both. She put a hand on Bayliss's shoulder. "How are you? It's me. Giselle."

"Hi," said Bayliss. She smiled and handed Giselle a small sculpture of a dog made from wooden coffee stirrers she'd glued together.

"Bayliss," said Coop. "Is this what they told you to do after the audit? Or did you come up with this on your own?"

Bayliss looked around her cubicle. She pulled down a couple of Post-its and stuck them to a map of Mongolia taped over her computer monitor. "I keep trying to work," she said. "But I get distracted."

"I'm sorry."

"It's okay. They want me to catalog all the office supplies for the building. It's pretty boring."

"Especially with shoes for a keyboard," said Coop.

Bayliss looked at her desk. "Not again," she said, exasperation in her voice. She put the shoes on the floor and took her keyboard out of the trash.

"Do you want some coffee or something?" said Morty.

Bayliss picked up her stapler and Morty jumped back. "Thank you. That would be nice," she said.

"I'll go," he said, and left quickly.

"The Auditors did this to you?" said Giselle.

"Who else?" Coop said.

"I don't think they mean to. It just works out that way," said Bayliss. "I'll be all right in a day or two. I just wish I had something to do that wasn't figuring out which department has too many binder clips and which doesn't have enough."

"Did you hear about our job the other night?" said Giselle.

Bayliss brightened. "Oh yeah. How did that go?"

"Great. We got everything Woolrich wanted. We confused a lot of guards, which was fun. And Coop got cursed by a three-thousand-year-old mummy."

Bayliss pushed herself back and forth in her chair for a minute. "What was that last one again?" she said.

"I've was cursed by a mummy," said Coop.

"Cool."

"Not really," said Giselle. "The mummy wants something. It wanted an amulet, but that's gone."

"I'm trying to figure out if there's something else it might want. Maybe if I can get it, the mummy will leave me alone."

"Wow," said Bayliss. "That's so much cooler than office supplies."

"Do you think you might be able to help us out with a little research? Who he was. Where he came from. What he wants."

Bayliss opened her mouth wide. "That sounds awesome. What's the mummy's name?"

"Harkhuf," said Coop, and he spelled it for her.

Bayliss wrote the name on a Post-it with an eyeliner pencil. "We have all kinds of records on dead people. Come back later today and I'll tell you what I found."

"Thanks a lot," said Coop.

"Is there anything we can do for you?" said Giselle.

"No. I'll be fine," said Bayliss. "I just need to dinosaur Jell-O escalator."

"I'm going to make sure the Auditors don't bother you again," said Coop. "I'm not sure how, but it will come to me."

"You're sweet. You're both sweet."

"Let's meet at six at the café around the corner. Is that all right?" said Giselle.

"It sounds fine," said Bayliss. "But can you tell me one thing?"

"What's that?"

"Who put all these Post-its on my walls?"

"We'll ask around," said Giselle sympathetically.

Coop put Bayliss's recycling bin on her desk. "If you're feeling better, maybe you should take some down."

"That's a good idea," Bayliss said. "And I'll do your thing, too."

"Thanks."

"Hang in there, baby," said Bayliss, reading each Post-it aloud as she pulled it down.

Coop and Giselle went back to the elevator.

"Is Bayliss going to be all right?" she said.

"She said the effects will wear off. Maybe it'll go faster if she does more interesting work," said Coop.

"I hope so. I don't like seeing her like this."

"Me neither. Do you think Woolrich sent the Auditors after her?"

"Woolrich? He hates them more than we do. He's tried to have them fired lots of times. He'd probably like to have one of them on his wall."

"Why did you have to say that? Still, now I hate him slightly less."

"Are you really going to do something to them?" said Giselle.

"I'm going to try. I'll need to know more about them first."

"I'll see what I can find out."

"Great."

"Okay. Now get out of here before Woolrich finds out."

"I'll see you at six."

Giselle headed for her office. "Try not to moon anybody on the way home."

"I make no promises."

McCloud and Nelson were locked in his office, which was piled high with all manner of arcane, hideous, dangerous, and plain awful objects. One might say that it looked like the horrors from Pandora's box, but that was locked safely in the ECIU archives.

"What's this?" said McCloud.

Nelson stopped pawing around in an old steamer trunk long enough to look up. "John Dee's skull."

"And this? It's just a blur." McCloud held up what appeared to be a framed photo of a gray smear. "There's something scribbled at the bottom."

"That's Woolrich's autographed picture of Death. I'm saving it for someone I want to get into terminal trouble, if you get my drift."

McCloud pursed his lips and set the photo gently onto the increasingly large pile of spell books, charms, weapons, wards, cursed objects, and stolen tchotchkes.

He picked up a feather. "What's . . . ow!"

Nelson looked over and smiled. "Careful. That's the Marquis de Sade's writing quill. It always tries to stab you in the eye."

"You might have said something sooner."

"Yes. I might have," said Nelson.

McCloud tossed the quill onto Nelson's desk and looked around at the mess. "Tell me again why we're going through all these old boxes?"

Nelson kept working as he answered. "I've told you twice. You need to learn to listen."

"I remember what you said. We're looking for something incriminating to use against Coop."

Nelson looked at him. "In order to . . . ?"

"Have him demoted to a mook."

"And then . . . ?"

"He'll be sent down here to work under you in the mail room."

"What's so hard to understand about that?" said Nelson, going back to rummaging.

McCloud picked up a tangled mass of black hair. "This is disgusting."

"That's Rasputin's beard. They use it upstairs to clone him for parties. He's a load of laughs. Denouncing all the men, trying to seduce all the women, drinking everyone under the table."

"What happens to the clones when the party is over?"

"They give them twenty bucks and let them go. The city is

full of Rasputins. I mean, who's going to believe them, right? Like I said, a load of laughs."

"Charming," said McCloud.

"Maybe you had to be there."

"I guess I keep asking you about Coop because what we're doing, it just seems a bit unethical." McCloud rubbed his stump.

"Is your arm bothering you?"

"No. It's just that I don't remember falling into the shredder. You'd think that's the kind of thing a person would recall."

"There's a simple explanation for that. Let me show you," said Nelson. He touched McCloud's forehead and said, "Macho Taco Guy Lombardo." McCloud's face went slack.

"Do you remember falling into the shredder the other night?" said Nelson.

"I sure do, boss. You pushed me," said McCloud cheerfully.

"No. You tripped and fell."

"Really?"

"Yes."

"Really?"

"Yes."

"Okay."

"Do you remember falling into the shredder the other night?"

"I sure do. Boy, am I clumsy."

"It happens to the best of us," said Nelson, and he went back to work.

"Wow. Look at all this neat stuff," said McCloud. "Whose is it?"

"It's ours. Look for interesting items. Dark, scary things we can send to dark, scary people."

"You got it, boss." McCloud pawed through the piles of deadly mystical detritus like a kid looking for a lost cupcake at the bottom of a ball pit. "Don't people miss these things?" he said.

Nelson held up a jar marked *mixed nuts that spat venom and tried to wriggle away.* He tossed it back into a box.

"Around here, people don't ask questions," he said. "If you didn't get something, you weren't meant to get it. If you sent it and it didn't get there, it wasn't supposed to."

"But it's us doing that," said McCloud, elbow-deep in a Happy Meal box.

"Only we know that," said Nelson. "That's what makes the system work."

"What's this?" said McCloud, pulling a glass jar from the Happy Meal.

"Einstein's brain. Don't drop it."

"Is it magic?"

"No, but it will stink the place up."

"What's this?" McCloud held a small metal box with a plastic handle on which someone had written PANDORA in Sharpie. "Wow. Is it Pandora's box?"

Nelson let out a breath and looked. "No. It's Pandora's lunch box. Put it down and don't eat anything from it," he said excitedly.

"What's special about these?" McCloud held out a fistful of red pens.

"Nothing. I've been looking for those," Nelson said, and tossed the pens in a desk drawer.

"Smile," said McCloud happily. A flash went off. Nelson closed his eyes, seeing a floating red dot. There was a tiny machine hum as a photo emerged from the camera. A few seconds later, Nelson heard McCloud softly say, "Eww."

McCloud handed him the Polaroid photo. The image was monstrous. A scaly man-thing with jagged fangs and hands sporting scythelike fingers.

"Yes. That's a special camera," said Nelson. "It photographs the subject's soul."

"Oh. Sorry," said McCloud.

"No. You did good," said Nelson, his mind a whir. "What if Coop stole the camera? What if he's using the photos to black-mail important members of the DOPS staff?"

"Is he doing that?" said McCloud in a hushed, shocked tone.

"Of course not. But what if he did? I have a copy of his fin-gerprints from one of his memos. They'd be easy to put on the camera. Yes. This could work," said Nelson, putting the camera in a box. "Hand me de Sade's pen."

McCloud picked up the quill with his fingertips and lobbed it to Nelson. "Why are you putting in the pen? Did Coop know de Sade?"

"No. It will just annoy whoever opens the box. We want them good and riled up. Where's the packing tape?"

"On the desk," said McCloud.

When Nelson reached for the tape he noticed that Pandora's lunch box was open. He peered inside and then at McCloud. "There was a chocolate bunny in here and now it's gone. Did you eat it?"

"No," mumbled McCloud through a full mouth. He swal-lowed. A moment later his one good arm fell off. "Oops."

Nelson sighed. He found a box full of electronic equipment and took out a couple of mismatched robotic arms.

"Cool," said McCloud. Nelson sat down and stared at him. "Is there something wrong?"

Nelson wiped some bits of cardboard from his pants. "Noth-ing is wrong. I'm just waiting to see if anything else falls off."

"I feel fine," McCloud said just before his eyes plopped onto the floor. "Oops. Spoke too soon."

Nelson went back to the box and found a couple of metallic eyes. "You wait here," he told McCloud. "I'm going to need some pliers and a soldering iron."

"I'll get them!" shouted McCloud. Leaning over, he twisted

the doorknob with his teeth and pushed the door with his feet. When it was open, he rushed excitedly into the mail room. A second later, there was a crash.

"Sorry," he called.

"Did you break anything?" said Nelson.

"I don't know. I can't see."

"You really need to stop moving around."

There was another crash, this one louder than the first.

"Sorry."

Nelson taped Coop's box shut.

"Boss?" called McCloud.

Nelson addressed the box to the Auditors.

"Boss? I think I might be on fire."

Nelson stamped the box SUPER PRIORITY and set it by his computer monitor.

"Okay. I'm definitely on fire."

"Coming," Nelson called, a small bottle of Pellegrino water in each hand. "I just want you to know that I was saving these for lunch, which you've now ruined."

"Sorry," said McCloud, more than a little aflame.

At six, Coop and Giselle went to a café down the street from DOPS headquarters. It was called Le Chat Bleu and the sign outside had a chalk drawing of a cat with a saxophone, presumably playing the blues. The interior was full of cat paintings and photos, with cat picture books at some of the tables. Giselle led them to a dimly lit table near the rear of the place.

"Lupinsky would fit right in around here," Coop said.

"Except for the thousand-pound octo legs," said Giselle, "you're probably right."

Coop looked around. "Is this payback for me saying I don't like cats?"

"Something like that."

Coop kept an eye out for approaching mummies and cats. "I don't really not like cats. They just give me the willies."

"Because of Shamu?"

"No. Because they always seem to know something I don't. Like if you're playing cards, a cat looks at you like you're always laying down the wrong cards. It's unnerving."

"So much for your alleged poker face," said Giselle mockingly.

"I have a great poker face. But cats have a better one. Never play Texas Hold'em with a tabby."

"I'll put that in *My Big Book of Things That Will Never Happen*."

"We just pulled a job with a bunch of jesters and a robot. Never say never."

"I refuse to admit you're right until I've had caffeine."

"I'll get us some coffee."

She pointed to the table. "No way. You sit here and don't make eye contact with anyone. You're not even here, sticky fingers."

"Understood, boss," he said, and sat back as far into the shadows as he could.

Coop watched her walk away, but kept her in sight, afraid a SWAT team might burst in and airlift her to a moon base or an extinct volcano or wherever the hell the DOPS was interrogating people this fiscal quarter. He couldn't live with himself if he got her arrested. He shook his head to clear it. He thought about cats. He thought about Woolrich. He thought about Harkhuf trying to get into his head. Who and what else was out there that he had to worry about? Probably a dozen things, but he was too jittery to come up with a list at that moment. Being this close to DOPS headquarters was making him nervous. Was the café serving coffee to mooks, cyborgs, and windigos in the patio out back? He didn't really want to know, and anyway, there weren't any exits nearby. If any dead people or interdimensional spiders headed his way, Coop thought that his best bet was to hide under the table and make sure any cute cat books were at least two tables away.

Giselle came back to the table with Bayliss in tow. She looked a lot more clear-eyed than when they'd left her in the morning.

"How are you feeling?" said Coop.

"A lot better. I think doing some real work has helped. I hardly feel lightbulb monkey at all," Bayliss said.

Coop and Giselle exchanged looks, but didn't say anything.

"That's great to hear," said Coop.

"And I've cleaned up my cubicle." She laughed. "What a mess. I just hope the recycling department doesn't notice all the Post-its."

"Come on. No one counts used Post-its."

"It's the end of the fiscal quarter."

"The same reason you're not allowed to die," Giselle reminded him.

"Oh yes," said Bayliss. "We have to keep you alive."

"It's nice to know that accounting cares. I'll send them a fruit basket," said Coop.

"I mean for other reasons, too, of course," said Bayliss quickly. "Sorry. I'm still a little fuzzy."

"It's okay. Did you find anything we can use?"

"Lots." Bayliss pulled a pile of printouts from her bag. "Harkhuf was once a powerful wizard in the pharaoh's court, though we don't know which one because they tried to destroy the records of his existence."

"Why?"

Bayliss shifted her shoulder uncomfortably. "He went a little rogue. Which gets back to you, Coop."

"Why me?"

"You want something you can give him so he'll leave you alone. I think I found it. It's a magical manuscript that Harkhuf wants to use to resurrect his dead lover, Shemetet."

Giselle stirred her latte. "That sounds kind of sweet. True love after three thousand years."

"Yeah," said Coop. "That's not so bad."

Bayliss looked uncomfortable. "Now we get to the rogue part.

You see, Harkhuf and Shemetet tried to start a magical war against the pharaoh. It seems that Shemetet is an Amazon-like warrior sorceress who wants to, and I quote, 'lay waste to all lands and people that will not bow before me.'"

Giselle made a face and set down her coffee. "All of a sudden it's not as romantic."

Coop pressed himself deeper into the shadows. "Harkhuf knows who I am. Is there anything in there about what he'll do if he gets hold of me?"

Bayliss took a couple of pages off the top of the pile and put them back in her bag. "Nope. Nothing."

"You're as lousy a liar as Giselle. Come on. I'm a big boy. I can take it."

Bayliss pulled the papers back out and spread them on the table. They were covered with distorted and broken hieroglyphics. She said, "Some of the details are missing, but it seems like after his resurrection, he'll peel the skin off a chosen enemy and wear it, and I quote, 'as a royal cloak.'"

Coop's stomach did a backflip. "But I like my skin. How do I get on his good side?"

Bayliss pushed a photo across the table. "Give him the manuscript so he can bring Shemetet back to life."

"Great. How do I get it?"

Giselle crossed her arms. "Did you forget the part where they plan on destroying the world and ruling whatever is left?"

"One problem at a time," said Coop. "I'll give him the manuscript and *then* we'll figure out the not-destroying-the-world part."

"There's a problem," said Bayliss. "There aren't any copies of the original manuscript left. They were all destroyed when the pharaoh defeated Harkhuf and Shemetet."

"Then I'm back to being screwed. Who else wants a muffin? If I'm going to die, I want a muffin first."

"Hold on," said Bayliss. "There aren't any original copies

left, but there is a translation by Forsythia Krumpf. She's a nineteenth-century English witch."

Coop's stomach, which had been trying to thumb a ride to Rio since the conversation started, suddenly settled down. "Great. Where is it?"

Bayliss pushed a photo of a jowly older man across the table. "It's in a private library belonging to Ramsey Fitzgerald."

"Who's that?" said Giselle.

"He's a billionaire publishing magnate who lives on a huge estate in Beverly Hills. The library is a separate building behind the main house."

"Now we're getting somewhere," said Coop. "I wonder how fast I can get the layout of the place. I'll go to City Hall in the morning."

"You don't have to. I printed you a copy," Bayliss said.

Coop took the pages she held out. "You are a goddess."

"Thank you," said Bayliss, blushing a little.

Giselle said, "You remember that you're supposed to be lying low, right? It's great that Bayliss can get you pictures, but she can't help you in the field, and neither can I, Morty, Lupinsky, or anyone else at DOPS."

Coop ran a thumb over his lower lip. "I know. I'll have to make some calls. The first thing I need to do is find out more about Fitzgerald. What does he do? Where does he go? I'll want him out of the house so I'll have time to work."

Bayliss read from another printout. "He's a movie freak and investor in a couple of studios. According to his schedule, he'll be at the Global Showcase International gala tomorrow night."

Coop took the paper and looked it over, happy but also a little disturbed. "Does the DOPS have this kind of information about *everybody*?"

Bayliss smiled shyly. "That's classified, Mr. Cooper," she said.

Then she whispered. "But no. Just the ones with important magical connections."

Giselle looked at Coop. "Magical connections?"

"That means the library is going to be a pain in the ass," he said.

"Probably," said Bayliss.

Coop looked over the layout of Fitzgerald's estate. "Tomorrow isn't much time. I need to start making calls."

Giselle held up her hands. "Don't say another word. Bayliss and I are innocent bystanders."

"She's right," said Bayliss. "Anything you tell us the Auditors can get at. You shouldn't say anything else."

Coop took the pages, folded them, and hid them under his jacket. "Thanks a lot for this. I owe you."

"No, thank you," said Bayliss. "It's fun going over to the dark side a little every now and then. And if you can stick it to the Auditors when you get a chance, that's all the thanks I need."

"Don't worry. I'll figure out something for them."

"Okay. Now you need to get out of here," said Giselle.

"Just one more thing. You said the manuscript was a translation. What's it called?" said Coop.

Bayliss handed him one more sheet, this one with a photo of a weathered old book. "It's disguised as a cookbook," she said.

In flaking gilt on the spine the book said, *Enigmatic Confections: An Entirely Unsinister Guide to Puddings, Cookies, Cakes, and Not-at-All the Dark Arts.*

"Forsythia didn't have much of a poker face, did she?" said Coop.

Bayliss shook her head. "They say she lost a fortune playing Twinkle Bat."

"What's that?"

"Everyone sits in a circle and tries not to think of a purple bat."

"I already lost," said Giselle.

Bayliss said, "Me, too."

"Not me," said Coop.

"Liar," said Giselle.

"Prove it."

"I guess you win. Okay, hit the bricks."

"Good luck," said Bayliss.

"Thanks," said Coop. Then to Giselle he added, "And the other thing you're thinking? No, I don't want to get a cat."

"Now you're just being spooky," she said. "Get out before someone burns you as a witch."

He'd started out when Giselle called after him, "Hey, poker face."

Coop stopped. "Yeah?"

"A wise man once told me 'never say never.' So, meow."

"Crap," he said, and went outside to look for a cab.

30

Froehlich didn't get back to the bungalow until well after three in the morning. He swayed on his feet as he brought in the bags, but he tried hard not to show it. He'd chewed some gum in the car before coming in, but he wasn't sure if it completely masked the smell of the six-pack.

Harkhuf was waiting by the dinosaur-bone chair. "Did you bring me what I commanded, thrall?"

Froehlich set the bags on the bed and sat down, a little out of breath. "As much as I could. You know it's been a few centuries, right? Some of the stuff you wanted isn't easy to come by these days. I had to make a few substitutions."

"How dare you?" said Harkhuf icily.

"I tell you what, you try finding three drams of dove's bile in Hollywood on a Wednesday night. But I didn't let it stop me. I went to Griffith Park and rounded up a bunch of pigeons." Froehlich held up a jar full of a green liquid.

"That will have to do."

"The park is lousy with cats, so the whiskers weren't hard. And dark beer, obviously, was a cinch." Froehlich hiccuped.

"Have you been drinking?" said Harkhuf.

"Have you been chasing pigeons in the dark all night? No. I have. So, yes, I've had a dram or two of beer," said Froehlich, then hastily added, "Master."

"I will allow this, but just this once. What else have you brought me?"

Froehlich pulled items out of the bag and set them on the tiger bedspread. "You wanted—what was it?—a vial of the finest scented balm to be had in this unholy land? Oddly enough, they don't stock the finest perfumes at Safeway at two A.M., so you have a choice. I got a bottle of Old Spice cologne. If you don't know what that is, old men use it because they think it makes them smell like Leonardo DiCaprio on the *Titanic*. To change things up a little, I also got a spray can of Spring's Evening Mist. Ladies use it on their privates when they don't feel so fresh."

"What of the ivory ewer?"

Froehlich stopped taking things from the bags. He looked around the room nervously. "Yeah. Ivory. That's kind of a problem these days—you can't get it. Period. Especially at Safeway at two A.M. That means you have a choice." He held up what looked like a large metal donut. "A cast-iron Bundt cake pan." He held up a plastic vessel covered in daisies. "Or a plastic party bowl. You know, for Chex Mix."

"What is Chex Mix?" said Harkhuf.

"The greatest food known to man," said Froehlich. "Damn. I should have bought some. You'd love it if you ate some. Or had a mouth."

"What else?"

"For the bone mortar I got a mint muddler for mojitos. Now, the sacred amber incense was also kind of a problem. As far as I can tell, it doesn't exist anymore. Maybe there's some kind of witch 7-Eleven, but I don't know any witches. So, the only place I could think of was a kind of specialty shop. It's what these days we call an 'adult entertainment emporium.'" Froehlich picked up two long, plastic-wrapped packages. "The ones that stank the least were Tropical Three-Way and Cleaved in Twain, which, honestly, smells like musk and guilt. Sorry. And I guess that's pretty much everything."

Harkhuf approached him. Froehlich moved back until he was pressed against the bungalow wall.

"Even among these blind, pathetic, soulless mortals, you are a wretch."

"Really? Gosh, I hadn't picked up on that. Master. By the way, my ATM card doesn't work anymore and I have about a hundred dollars left on my credit card. The good news is that we have the room for a couple of more days. But whatever your plan is, we better do it by the weekend or we'll be taking over the world in the comfort of my 2003 Camry."

Harkhuf hovered over the bed. He pointed to one last object. "What is that?"

"It's a rolled-up newspaper."

"What is its purpose?"

Froehlich picked up the paper and slapped it in his open palm. "See, I know I'm a wretch and a cur, and I'm fine with that. *Really* fine with it, actually. And along those lines, there's a woman who works at the adult emporium I mentioned. I think she might have a pretty good handle on what to do with a rolled-up newspaper. However, as I also mentioned, I'm about broke. Do you think you could see your way to doing the evil eye trick you did at the museum and have her discipline a very bad dog?"

Harkhuf went back to the dinosaur chair. "This has something to do with the women with the pillows and the men eating the hamburgers, does it not?"

"It's in the same arena, yes."

"Then no. You will serve me and my beloved Shemetet. This is the only pleasure you need or deserve."

Froehlich dropped the paper onto the bed. "You can't blame a guy for trying. What do we do next?"

Harkhuf thrust his arm out dramatically. "Bring me the image of Isis," he commanded.

"Sure. Here you go, Master," said Froehlich, taking the statue from where he'd hidden it in a bureau drawer. "This little thing is going to show you where Shemetet is?"

Harkhuf took the statue in his clumsy mummy hands and raised it up over his head.

"There is one more thing I will need to resurrect my beloved. Soon I will send you for a holy tome. Tonight, though, yes, the idol will show me where she is. Then the book will bring her back to me. Prepare the elements for the spell."

"Happy to oblige. Are we going with the Bundt pan or the snack bowl?"

"The snack bowl."

"Good choice. I'll get the other stuff ready."

While Froehlich worked, Harkhuf gazed at Isis. "Soon, dear Shemetet, I will behold your beauty and power and together we will bring the world to heel."

Harkhuf held the statue lovingly. As he gently stroked it, the head bent to the side. "Strange. That is not supposed to happen."

Froehlich stopped working and came over. "That does look a little weird," he said. He knelt down and looked at the bottom of the statue. "Uh-oh."

"You have made that sound before," said Harkhuf. "It is a bad sound. What does it mean?"

Froehlich tried to push Isis's head back into place, but it snapped off in his hand. Harkhuf touched Froehlich's shoulder and squeezed. It hurt. It hurt a lot.

"What did the bottom of goddess Isis say?"

"'Nontoxic material. Safe for children.'"

"What does that mean?"

Froehlich reached around his master and tried to force Isis's head back into place. "Here's the situation. And don't be mad," he said. "Not everything in the museum was on the up-and-up. Some of the mummies were a little on the artificial side and, I'm afraid, so were some of the mummy accoutrements."

Harkhuf let go of Froehlich. He crushed the statue in his powerful hands and threw it hard enough that it stuck halfway into one of the faux-rock walls. When his master swung at his head, Froehlich ducked and ran across the room to the far side of the bed. Harkhuf picked up the dinosaur chair and ripped it apart. Plastic bones flew in every direction. He went to the bureau and smashed it to pieces with his fists. Froehlich hunkered down on the floor, terrified and just a little more excited than he cared to admit.

Coming around the bed, Harkhuf looked down at him. "You have disappointed me, cur. For this, you must be punished."

Froehlich held out the newspaper. Harkhuf knocked it across the room.

"I don't know what you want me to do about it," Froehlich said. "I guard things and get rid of the occasional body, but I'm not an antiques expert. I just did what you told me."

Harkhuf dropped his hand to his side. He went to the television, where women dressed as rabbits threw darts at men dressed like fried eggs. "This world baffles me," he said. "It is cheap and brazen, fit only for hamburgers, snack bowls, and Tropical Three-Way. I pity you for the empty lives you have led and for the horrors my beloved and I will bestow upon you."

"Horrors?" said Froehlich, slowly rising to his feet. "Are those for *everyone* or are the loyal thralls and curs exempt because we're so busy carrying out your entirely reasonable orders?"

"Those who serve will be afflicted with the most minor torments," said Harkhuf magnanimously.

"That's great news. No torments is better, but minor is entirely doable. Thank you, Master."

"Now, I require silence from you for the rest of the evening. I must ponder the situation and plot a new way forward."

Froehlich slipped quietly from the floor onto the bed. "Just remember that Saturday morning they're throwing us out of here."

Harkhuf waved the statement off with one ponderous arm. "I will control the clerks as easily as the fools you spoke to this afternoon."

"You're right," said Froehlich, relaxing a little. "We could stay here forever. If we hang around, do you think we could move to a room with more than two TV channels? Between the siege of Stalingrad and half-naked girls, I'm simultaneously depressed, turned on, and deeply confused."

Froehlich's master stared at the television. "Let me contemplate our new situation and tomorrow we shall upgrade to a room that does not smell like sweaty socks and receives a panoply of pay channels."

"Thank you, Master. Thank you," said Froehlich. For the first time he felt like the end of the world might not be so bad after all.

Coop dialed a number. Someone picked up after just a couple of rings.

"Hi, Sally. It's Coop."

"How are you doing, Agent Cooper?" Coop didn't say anything. "You know, like on *Twin Peaks*? I've been waiting to hit you with that ever since you went over to the dark side."

"I suppose I deserve that."

"You definitely do, J. Edgar," said Sally Gifford. Like Giselle, she was a Marilyn. She was also a fellow thief with whom Coop had pulled many jobs. However, unlike Coop, Sally hadn't gone straight.

"What can I do for you?" she said. "I've paid my taxes and I haven't ripped off Fort Knox, so this can't be a work call."

"Actually, it sort of is. How would you like to help me on a job?"

"What kind of job?" said Sally suspiciously. "The last one you talked me into got me no money and, oh yeah, almost killed."

"This one isn't like that. It's a straight crooks-doing-crooked-things-to-rich-people job. I only want one thing out of it."

"What's that?"

"A book. The job is breaking into a library."

"Are you serious? If you're that hard up, I'll lend you my library card. They let you take books home and everything."

"It's not that kind of library," Coop said. "I've done some research. It belongs to a rich asshole with highly expensive antique books, art, plus who knows what all else lying around? You keep anything you can carry."

"Okay. I'm interested. The rare-books market is picking up Whose library is it?"

"Ramsey Fitzgerald."

"The publishing creep? Yeah. He probably has some good stuff. Who else is on the job?"

"No one else. It's just us."

"Not even Morty? Who's going to open doors and locks?"

"A guy like this, he's not going to use regular locks. It'll be all death curses and light shows."

"Stuff you can handle," said Sally.

"Exactly. But I need a Marilyn who can walk me in and out past guards, servants, and other riffraff."

"And we get to loot the place?"

"Anything you can stuff in your pockets or carry in your hands and teeth."

"Is anyone likely to have guns?"

"There's minimal chance of that."

"Which means maybe. I'd still feel better if we had a lock man."

"I'm telling you. It's not that kind of place."

"How's Giselle doing? Does she still have that great ass?" said Sally casually.

"She's great. She says hi. And yes, her ass is still top-notch."

"You sound a lot better now that you're getting laid. More like your old self."

"I feel more like my old self."

"If you're coming to me, I'm guessing this isn't an authorized federal job. Why are you back on the down low?"

"I have a slight problem with a mummy's curse."

"Are you fucking kidding me?" shouted Sally.

"I am not."

"Only you, Coop. Did you steal its magic beans? I swear, you have the most interesting problems."

"Then you're in?"

"For a chance to see you carry the one true ring up Mount Doom? Hell yes."

"With luck it won't be that interesting."

"But if there's any hot succubae, I'm going in first," said Sally. "When do we do it?"

"Tomorrow night."

"Fuck you. There better be some good stuff in this library."

"There will be," said Coop. "I'll email you the details."

"See you tomorrow, then."

"See you."

Coop looked over the plans one more time. They didn't specify any mystical traps or guardians. *But with guys like Fitzgerald, it's always about showing off,* he thought. High-priced protection—dragons and lava chutes—but it was seldom the most effective. Coop knew that Sally was a pro, and in a clinch, she was as fast as him if they had to bail.

He was only worried about one thing: Harkhuf. What if the prick showed up during the job? He didn't bother Giselle, which meant he probably wouldn't bother Sally. As Coop went over the details of the break-in he settled on one plan if Harkhuf appeared, and that was to keep his damned pants on.

31

Ramsey Fitzgerald owned the largest group of tabloid newspapers and conservative magazines in the western hemisphere. He was also the president of a television news network so far to the right that, as one writer put it, "While Fox News appeals to a conservative viewership, the Eagle Exposé Network seems to have been created by Lex Luthor for Mad Max villains and Vlad the Impalers who want to return to the gold standard, replace preschool with toddler coal mining, and balance the budget through Bigfoot hunts and free-market organ harvesting."

Like his hero, William Randolph Hearst, Fitzgerald collected paintings, statuary, books, antique furniture, and exotic animals, but with more money and worse taste, keeping it all in a diabolically designed ghost bunker behind the main mansion of his Beverly Hills estate. All Hearst ever had were a couple of part-time poltergeists, and they were there mostly to amuse his weekend guests.

Fitzgerald's life was the rags-to-riches story of a man who started out with only a few hundred million dollars of family money and managed to turn it into even more hundreds of millions by sheer force of will, insider trading, and blackmail, a formula he referred to in his autobiography as the "Torquemada Reach Around."

But Fitzgerald secretly harbored dreams of being a producer of show-biz spectacles in the mold of Walt Disney, Busby Berkeley, and Leni Riefenstahl. Someone respected and admired. He used his holdings in various movie studios to develop big-budget projects based on some of their surefire successes.

His first effort was a musical based on *The Texas Chainsaw Massacre* called *I Got Your Face, but You Got My Heart.* It closed and the theater was burned to the ground after three performances.

Later, he dabbled in television, developing an American period drama along the lines of *Downton Abbey. Laredo Acres* was about a family dynasty in the West right after the Civil War. Its first season met with good reviews, but when ratings slipped in season two, he brought in Indian attacks, a smallpox outbreak, exorcisms, a sexy ghost, a sexy werewolf, and a sexy lady gunslinger to fight the dinosaurs the family unleashed while mining for gold. Amazingly, it all worked. The ratings soared, but the reviews didn't. Fitzgerald made millions from the show, but was even less respected than before.

His final attempt at a prestige production was *K Street Huggables,* a conservative take on *Sesame Street* in which adorable animal puppets taught lobbying and payola skills to preschoolers. The show did modestly well until he introduced the character of Holly Babette, the Truth Rabbit. It turned out that *K Street Huggables* was in the wrong time slot for a Holocaust-denying bunny and the show went off the air in the middle of their holiday special, *Gold, Bullets, and Antibiotics: Prepper Jesus Saves Christmas.*

After this last failure, Fitzgerald retreated into his media empire and movie-studio investments. He seldom appeared in public except at film functions and the occasional congressional investigation into arms smuggling and currency manipulation. Fitzgerald and his fifth wife, Tatiana or Tilda or some damned thing—those confounded foreign names all ran together after a while—were looking forward to the Global Showcase International gala and planned on arriving early, leaving the estate in the hands of their capable security team.

Through his less-than-legal connections, Coop was able to borrow a carpet-cleaning van for the day. This let him and Sally spend the whole afternoon parked in Fitzgerald's neighborhood. Coop watched the mansion from the driver's seat, while Sally— who'd dyed her short, usually blue hair dollar-bill green for the occasion—was sacked out in the back with a bag of cookies and candy. Coop had his lunch in a small insulated cooler on the floor.

The sun was starting to go down. Coop adjusted his binoculars.

"Are they leaving yet?" said Sally.

"You asked that ten minutes ago."

"Sorry. Are they *exiting* yet?"

"No." Coop moved the rearview mirror and watched her eat a Snickers bar. "You know, it's all that sugar that's making you antsy."

Sally swallowed. "No. Sitting for three hours is making me antsy. Should we play twenty questions?"

"Is that one of the questions?"

Sally lay down in the back. "I can see it would be a barrel of laughs with you."

"We could play cards, but I have to keep an eye on the house."

"I wish you'd told me we would be cooling our heels all day. I would have brought my cat or my vibrator. Which would annoy you more?"

"I'll give you a dollar to leave both of those items home on all future jobs."

Sally rolled over onto her stomach. "That's right. You're afraid of cats."

Coop lowered the binoculars. "I'm not afraid. I just don't like them."

"You haven't met the right one yet," said Sally. "I knew when I met Purr J. Harvey that she was the girl for me."

"Have you been talking to Giselle?"

"Of course not."

"Has she been talking to you?"

Sally rolled onto her back. "No comment."

"This is a conspiracy," said Coop.

"We're a girlie cabal."

"A couple of schemers."

"The Harpies of . . . Harassment? Helpfulness?"

"That one was kind of a reach."

"I know," said Sally sadly. "Are they leaving yet?"

"You just asked that."

Sally kicked the back of Coop's seat. "I'm bored, Daddy. Read me a story."

"Fine," he said. "One day, Little Red Riding Hood went into the woods to visit Grandma's house. In her basket she was carrying nonfat milk, sugar, corn syrup, maltodextrin, propylene glycol monoesters, cellulose gel, mono and diglycerides, locust bean gum . . ."

Sally kicked his seat again. "Are you reading me the ingredients off a candy bar, you asshole?"

"Actually, it's an ice cream sandwich. Want to hear more? We haven't gotten to the exciting polysorbate-80 and carrageenan part yet."

"You're a real raconteur, Coop."

"I don't know what the word means."

"Liar."

"Prove it."

"Are they leaving yet?"

"Wait," he said. "I see movement. Someone is coming out the front door, heading for a limo."

Sally sat up. "Thank God. I was about to commit ritual suicide with an oatmeal raisin cookie."

Coop grabbed a duffel bag and slung it over one shoulder. Sally went out the back of the van and he followed her. They were dressed in white overalls with the carpet-cleaning company's logo on the back. Sally carried a clipboard, which she perused with extreme interest as they crossed the street hoping to throw off any locals who happened by. They kept up the act until they came to the side of a palm tree outside Fitzgerald's estate.

Sally flipped pages on the clipboard as she said, "It's still light out, Coop, and this place is probably going to have surveillance. I've got us covered, but what are we going to do about cameras?"

He pulled a box the size of a television remote from the duffel. "It's all taken care of, courtesy of the DOPS. You do your thing and I'll set this off when the Fitzgeralds are driving away."

Sally looked skeptical. "You're the boss, boss. Here we go." Sally closed her eyes and concentrated for a moment. "We're good. Any human-type people in the vicinity can't see us."

"Terrific," said Coop, trying to sound more confident than he felt. On the one hand, he kind of got a kick out of these improvised jobs. They were always exciting, and with someone like Sally, they could even be a bit fun. But his skin happened to be riding on what happened tonight. It knocked some of the amusement value off the enterprise. But there was nothing to do now except get in and get out with the book. He knew he could handle whatever was inside. Within reason. *Please no spiders*, he thought. Dragons, demons, ghosts, windigos, vampires, rabid poodles, ponds full of leeches, high school guidance counselors—he could deal with them all, but working with Dr. Lupinsky was as close as he wanted to get to any octo-creeps these days. Just thinking about the crawlers made his skin itch. He set down the duffel, took out a spray can, and gave himself a good going-over.

"What's that?" said Sally.

"My neuroses."

"Is there something in there I should know about? Give me a shot of that stuff."

"I just have a bug thing. If there are any inside, I'd like them to run the other way."

Sally snatched the can out of his hand and sprayed herself all over. "You're passing on your neuroses to your partner. Is this kind of leadership I should expect from you tonight?"

Coop shook his head. "Spiders and mummies. Those are my only weaknesses."

"And commitment."

"Don't start. You sound like Phil."

"Speaking of which, why isn't he here with us?"

"He's a fed. I can't chance them noticing any of that crew is missing."

Sally watched the house. "I'd still feel better with a lock man."

"Will you forget about the locks? This is going to be all ghouls and fireworks. Besides, I have my picks with me."

Coop watched through the binoculars as the Fitzgeralds got into their limo and headed down the circular driveway to the front gate.

"Let's get ready to go inside."

"Then you'll take care of the cameras?"

"The moment Daddy Warbucks and the missus are on the road."

"I hope Fitzgerald has some Caravaggios. I always wanted one of those. Have you ever seen his little naked Cupid or John the Baptist? Pure art porn."

Coop stopped. "Since when do you want naked guys on your wall?"

Sally shrugged. "I went to Catholic school. You end up with complicated fetishes."

"With luck, we can feed your habit."

Coop and Sally came to the gates just as they swung open. They grabbed each other's arms and waited for the black limo to pass. The moment it went by, they dashed up the middle of the driveway as the gates swung closed. Inside, they kept running until they reached a stand of oak trees and hunkered down. They smiled at each other.

"That was fun," said Sally. "Like sneaking into the back of a movie theater."

"Sometimes simple is the best way."

"Where do we head now?"

Coop pulled a printout of the mansion grounds from inside his overalls. "We circle around the main house to the one in the back. You can't miss it. It has a moat."

Sally looked over his shoulder. "I remember that. I wonder if the Fitzgeralds ever get drunk and go skinny-dipping. I would if I had a moat."

"Not in this one. My bet is that it's loaded with something you wouldn't want to be naked around."

"Lions, and tigers, and bears, oh my," she said.

"But please no spiders."

"Or nuns."

Coop looked at her.

Sally looked sheepish. "I told you. I'm Catholic. But don't get hung up on my neuroses. The cameras?"

Coop held up the small box Giselle had used at the museum. "You ready?" he said.

"What's going to happen?"

"If it works, not much. I'm cutting all their power. Worst-case scenario, some people will start wandering outside to check wires."

Sally looked the box over. "Is that a fed machine?"

"Your tax dollars at work."

"You bad man. Using it for nefarious purposes."

"My skin is not nefarious. It's very personal to me," said Coop, taking a quick look around for mummies.

"What are you looking at? Pull the switch, warden."

Coop pushed the button. The lights flanking the front door blinked off. In the upstairs windows, bulbs shut down and the glow of a television vanished as the whole house went dark.

"Let's move," said Coop.

He and Sally walked briskly across the mansion's manicured grounds, past Greek statues and marble fountains. The printout of the Fitzgerald estate didn't quite prepare them for the scale of the place. It was really two Beverly Hills estates that Fitzgerald had turned into one. Sally clearly loved the place. She ran a hand through the cascading fountain and touched each statue as they passed. Coop, on the other hand, panted as they went. Not from exertion, but from a slowly mounting fear that something dead and very old was hiding in each shadow. It would be a long way to run to get out of the Fitzgerald estate. In fact, from what he'd seen, the best way out, if things went sideways, was to keep going deeper into the estate and follow a stream at the rear of the place back to the road. That's assuming Fitzgerald hadn't loaded that with goblins or flamethrower-wielding guppies.

"You okay?" said Sally. "Your allergies getting to you?"

"Yeah," he puffed. "Allergies."

Sally pointed into the distance. "Thar she blows," she said.

The library was about fifty yards straight ahead. It had a round central room and four wings that spread out in each direction. In the dim light, they could just make out the moat and the drawbridge beyond it.

"Wow. It looks like someone has a hard-on for Disneyland. What do you think?" said Sally.

He had to admit there was something about it that reminded him of cartoon haunted mansions. That should have made him feel better, but instead it brought images of a rotting army of Mickey Mouses and demented Goofies in Death-like cloaks swinging razor-sharp scythes.

"It sure is cute," he said. "Okay, you keep us out of sight and I'm going to get started on getting us in."

"We've got to get over that drawbridge," said Sally.

"That's plan one. There's a key-card reader up ahead. It should lower it."

"Do you have the code?"

"Of course not," said Coop, feeling a little of the fun coming back. "But I have more technology." He held up a generic key card attached to a small gray box with the DOPS logo on the side. He smiled, but Sally took a couple of steps back.

"Fuck your little boxes. What are those?" she said. Coop turned to where she was pointing.

Six women in flowing white gowns rushed toward them across the green grass. They were beautiful, with long straight black hair and delicate, porcelain features. All you had to do was overlook their sharp teeth and scalpel-like fingernails and they looked like they would be fun to take to dinner and a movie.

"They're Pontianaks," said Coop.

"What's that mean?"

"Mostly, they want to eat our innards. But worse, they're screamers. They must be Fitzgerald's alarm system."

"Screaming isn't worse than innard eating," said Sally. "If anything is going to eat me, it's going to be my cat."

Coop handed her the duffel. "Wait here," he said, happy that there was finally something to work with that wasn't wrapped in moth-eaten linen.

"What the fuck are you doing?" Sally whisper-screamed. "Get back here."

Coop strode forward.

"Evening, ladies," said Coop. "Would any of you be interested in a subscription to *Sports Illustrated*? You get the swimsuit issue and a paperweight shaped like a traumatic brain injury."

The women formed a semicircle around him. They were so pale it almost looked like they glowed in the dying twilight. When the first one raised her head to scream, the others followed suit. Coop reached into his pocket and pulled out a plastic bag of black powder. As the women drew in a long prescream breath, Coop held his nose and threw the bag at them. It hit in the middle of the group and burst. The Pontianaks staggered back, rubbing their eyes. Furious now, they opened their mouths to shriek . . . but sneezed instead. A few coughed, but mostly they stood around sneezing. Their noses ran and it got onto their flowing dresses. With their eyes watering, they bumped into each other and were generally extremely grumpy.

Coop grabbed Sally and made a wide circle around the shoving, sneezing group.

"What the hell did you do?" she said.

"I seasoned them with a little pepper. It's good for muggers, screamers, and rib-eye steaks."

Sally shoved him. "That's your plan to deal with innard eaters? Give them allergies?"

"It worked, didn't it?"

"Please tell me you're not going to try and solve all our problems with condiments."

Coop took back the duffel and patted it. "Relax. I have everything we need in here," he said. "If that's the best Fitzgerald has, we're going to be fine."

"Okay. But you might have just killed me for Goth girls. From now on I want tan lines, straight teeth, and not a fingernail in sight."

Coop pointed into the dark. "The card reader is straight ahead."

He led the way across the lawn, feeling like this bullshit, thrown-together, fly-by-the-seat-of-your-pants nonplan might just work. But there was still the one lurking fear in the back of his head.

"If you see anything mummy-shaped, or vaguely mummy-shaped, or just plain dead and ugly, give me a holler, okay?" he said.

"Shriek if I see a corpse. I can handle that," said Sally. "You know, I'm a lot more used to banks and penthouses than this *Dr. Terror's House of Horrors* stuff."

"It will be fine." At the card reader Coop said, "See? We're practically inside. Piece of cake."

Sally nodded at the moat. "Yeah? We already had snotty emo chicks. What are we going to find in there? Rockabilly sirens? Giant dubstep spiders? Maybe a barbershop quartet of sea serpents."

"Let's find out," Coop said. He slipped his card into the reader and hit a button on the DOPS device. It began computing all possible permutations of entry codes as Coop and Sally waited.

Sally looked around. "Is this going to take long?"

"I have no idea. I've never used it before."

"Did you have to say that?" said Sally. She took a can of pepper spray from her pocket.

"I'm not sure that works on sea serpents," said Coop.

'It's not for them. It's for you, dumb-ass. I swear, if we get eaten, you're getting a faceful of mugger juice."

Coop glanced at the device as it ran through random number sequences.

"By the way, how is Purr J. Harvey?" he said.

Sally looked at him. "She's fine. She has a playdate tomorrow with a boy cat downstairs."

"Really? I didn't think cats had playdates."

She watched the device compute codes. "They met at the vet and got along. Her owner and I thought it might be nice to have kittens."

"That does sound nice," said Coop.

Sally stared into the dark. "If cat chatter is supposed calm me down, it's not. It's just reminding me how thrown-together this whole thing is."

The gray box pinged. Lights went on across the card reader.

"Does that make you feel better?" said Coop.

"A lot," replied Sally. She put the pepper spray back into her pocket.

"Were you really going to squirt me with that stuff?"

"In a hot second."

They watched the drawbridge lower like a fairy-tale castle.

"This is pretty," Sally said.

"It is, isn't it?" said Coop.

"But I can't help feeling that something bad is about to happen."

"You're probably right, but you let me worry about the library. You look around for—"

"I know," she said, cutting him off. "Anything that looks like a walking dirty-paper-towel dispenser."

"Exactly."

Sally looked past Coop. "I think the bad thing I was afraid of happening is happening."

Clinging to the top of the drawbridge were what looked like a horde of hairy, bearded old men. They were small, but there were a lot of them and their eyes glittered in the dark. As they whispered to each other, Coop listened as intently as a man about to fall over in a fetal position could listen.

"Coop?" said Sally.

He shoved the card reader into her hand and pulled a book out of the duffel. As the drawbridge lowered, Coop frantically turned pages. Finally, the bridge touched the ground. The old men crawled toward them across the pitted wood, moving slowly, knowing that they were close enough to their prey that they couldn't escape. Coop thumbed through the book ever more frantically.

Sally got her pepper spray out again. "This is it, Coop. I'm turning you into Cajun barbecue."

At a silent signal, the little men rushed forward. Coop held the book close to his face and whispered something long and complicated, with a few stutters and stammers along the way. The little men kept coming forward, but they weren't rushing now. They were listening. Coop kept reading and Sally kept the pepper spray up to his head. Finally, Coop turned and pointed to the mansion. With a whoop, all the little men ran off to the house.

"What the fuck did you do to them?" said Sally.

"When they were talking earlier, it sounded like Russian. I took a chance that they were Domovoi."

"I take it that you've dealt with Domovoi before?"

"I've never even seen one," said Coop.

Sally put the pepper spray away again. "Let me emphasize one more time: fuck you. Where did you send them?"

"To the mansion. I think."

"You think?"

"With Domovoi, the trick seems to be that, while they can be a real trouble, they're not so bad if you invite them inside."

"Now you speak Russian all of a sudden?"

Coop shook his head and held up the book.

Sally squinted in the dim light. On the cover was a cartoon devil riding the shoulder of a spiny demon. *Monster to English Dictionary with Handy Phrases and Emergency Spells, Revised Edition.* She took the book from Coop's hands and hit him with it. When she was done she handed it back.

"You're welcome," he said, and tossed the book back into his bag.

Sally looked at the library. "We've survived those assholes. I wonder what's waiting inside that?"

"Nothing," said Coop. "Do you think Fitzgerald is going to leave his booty with a lot of sprites and Munchkins running around? Nope. We get inside and it's easy street from there."

Sally half smiled. "I hope you're right. How do we get in?"

"Right up here. It should be easy. Nothing was supposed to get past the alarms and the little men."

They crossed the bridge and came to the library door. It was a simple wooden panel with a knocker, a small window at the top, and on the side what looked like a spiral conch shell.

"Crap," said Coop.

"What?" said Sally, getting out her pepper spray.

"Put that away. It's not more monsters. It's this," said Coop, tapping the conch shell.

"What is that?"

"It's a ghost lock. To open it, you need the ghost of an actual key that's been destroyed. And it can only be used by a poltergeist or wraith of some kind."

"You brought me all the way out here, almost got me eaten and trampled by tiny ZZ Tops, and we're stuck?" said Sally through gritted teeth. "I told you we should have brought a lock man."

"A lock man wouldn't help," said Coop. "This isn't designed for humans. Fitzgerald must have some pet spooks back at the mansion."

"So, my point stands. We're stuck."

"Nope," said Coop. He pulled a small case from the duffel and set it on the drawbridge. Inside was a collection of tools that looked like the play set of a particularly cruel demon dentist. "I can open it. It'll just take some time."

"Tell me the truth: Morty couldn't do this faster?"

"Cross my heart and hope to die. Now, why don't you sit down and keep watch?"

Sally sat cross-legged on the drawbridge with her back against the library. "I had a date tonight, you know. I blew her off for this."

Coop slid a small pick into the edge of a tiny screw and worked the top with a tool that resembled a terrified squirrel. "Yeah? Anyone I know?"

"I doubt it," said Sally. "You know Minerva, the fortune-teller? She set it up. A cute dental assistant, she said."

While pulling off the first screw, Coop said, "Then you ought to buy me a thank-you card. She would have eaten you and not in the nice way."

Sally's eyebrows went up. "How do you know?"

"'Cause she almost ate Morty."

Sally hung her head down. "Great. Someone with a career, only her career is eating people."

"Sorry."

She looked up at the sky. "It's okay. It just sucks being single in L.A., you know? Everybody lives fifty miles and an hour away from everybody else. We might as well be fucking hillbillies and not see another human being for months at a time."

"I remember," said Coop. "And if you do meet someone in your area, they can't hold a job or they want to lay eggs in your brain."

"Love is weird." She rested her head on the library and looked at Coop. "How's it going over there?"

"All right, actually. There's just a lot of parts to get through. I'll be another hour at least."

Sally chuckled. "Morty almost got eaten by the dental lady?"

"That's what he said. What he didn't say is how far along they got before he realized she had eight legs. I like to think he was buck naked when it finally hit him."

"Kind of like you mooning all of Hollywood the other night?"

"I was trying to scare a mummy. It's not the same thing," said Coop.

"Yeah, you keep telling yourself that, tiger."

A few minutes of silence passed while Sally stargazed and Coop worked on the lock. Finally, she mumbled something.

"What was that?" said Coop.

"I said 'shit,'" she whispered. "I see headlights. The Fitzgeralds are coming back."

Coop looked at his watch. "It can't be them. They haven't been gone long enough."

"Maybe the cotillion or whatever got canceled. Maybe the prince turned into a pumpkin, but I'm telling you they're coming in."

"Goddammit," said Coop. "I can do this. I just need more time."

"You don't have it. Wrap your shit up. We have to move."

Coop started throwing his tools back into the duffel, but stopped. "Wait a second. They can't be coming in. Without power, they can't open the gates. They're just sitting outside."

"Great. That means we can't get out either."

Zipping up the bag, Coop hoisted it onto his shoulder. "I can get the power back on, but we'll have to time it right."

Fifty yards away, the lights in the mansion flickered and came back on. Floodlights across the estate grounds lit up, catching Coop and Sally in a pool of light.

"Did you do that?" said Sally.

"No. They must have a backup generator."

"Shit.

In the distance, voices shouted at them. They could see men and flashlights heading their way.

"Are you still doing your Marilyn thing?" said Coop.

"Of course," said Sally. "They don't see us, but they do see the drawbridge is down."

"Then let's go."

They ran across the lawn as fast as they could, cutting in a wide circle around the ten security guards heading in their direction. It was all going fine until they drew abreast of the guards. Out of the shadows, a Pontianak reared up, sneezed, and punched Sally in the face. Both women went down. Coop grabbed Sally and got her on her feet, but it was too late. The blow had stunned her and the noise had attracted the guards' attention. They were visible to everyone. The guards rushed them.

"Crap."

Coop and Sally ran as fast as they could for the front gates, but the guards gained on them.

"Do something," shouted Sally.

Coop rummaged in the duffel. "I have something, but I only *kind of* know how it works."

"What is it?"

"A distraction grenade."

The guards closed in on them.

"Use it! Use it! Use it!"

"Cross your fingers," Coop said. He pulled the pin on the grenade and tossed it over his shoulder. There was a muffled *whoomp* followed by the sound of drums and trumpets. They slowed down just enough to look behind them.

A large military marching band high-stepped in an elaborate pattern across the mansion grounds, completely surrounding the guards.

Sally looked at Coop. He shrugged. "Let's just get out of here."

At the house, the generator failed and the power went off again, leaving the Fitzgeralds' limo stuck between the half-open gates.

"Are you okay enough to do your Marilyn thing?" said Coop.

"I'm already doing it," Sally said.

"Perfect." He took the television remote from his pocket and pushed the button. The house and the grounds lit up again. The gate slowly swung open, allowing the limo to pass through. Before the gate closed, Coop and Sally ran out and kept going until they reached the van. They jumped in the back and both fell on the floor panting.

Sally gave Coop's leg a kick. "That was your brilliant rescue plan?" she said. "Halftime at the homecoming game?"

Coop waved a hand in the air. "I told you I never used one before. I don't know the different settings."

Sally sat up. "Fuck," she said.

"What's wrong?"

"My nose is bleeding."

Coop took a clean rag from the duffel and handed it to her. Sally wiped her face and held the rag over her nose. She said, "I guess I've been on worse jobs, but none weirder."

"I just needed a little more time."

Sally shook her head. "Dammit, Coop, you promised me a payday this time."

He rummaged in the duffel and his hand fell on something unfamiliar. Coop pulled it out. It was a small plastic black cat. The note attached said, *For good luck. xoxo G.*

He looked at Sally, thinking. "Don't worry. I'm going to get you that payday."

Sally wiped her nose and handed the rag back to Coop. "How? Do the feds have a time machine so we can go back and not fuck things up?"

Coop smiled. "No. They have something better."

32

"Ah!" screamed Zulawski.

A mouse ran from under his desk, dragging a Tupperware container into the recesses of the storeroom.

"Are you all right?" said Vargas.

"All limbs are intact. For now."

Vargas watched the mouse go. "What was that?"

"Thai green chicken curry."

"Oh, that sounds delicious."

"It was my lunch," said Zulawski. "But the container was yours. I was going to clean it after I ate."

"Damn. That was a good container," said Vargas. "Have you noticed how the mice's eyes are changing? Not just red, but they seem to glow. And they're getting more . . . what's the word?"

"Horrifying," said Zulawski. He used a yardstick to probe for other whiskered thieves under his desk. "And what about the squid? It keeps growing. I had to take all the drawers out of one side of one desk just so it would fit."

"Have you been back by the true-self mirror? The dingoes ate some of the mice. Ever since, they've been trying to break out of the glass."

Zulawski went to the perpetually empty in-box. He picked it up and shook it. He looked behind the table for any fallen items. There was nothing. "Why hasn't anyone come down?" he said.

"I filed a report," said Vargas tersely. "But you know it won't help. There just aren't enough mice yet to infest the rest of the floor."

Zulawski went back to his desk and dropped into the chair. "We'll just have to learn to coexist with the little beasts awhile longer."

Vargas pointed at the shelves accusingly. "This is all the fault of the parcel."

"Agreed."

Vargas glanced around and scooted his chair to Zulawski's desk. He put a hand up to his mouth so no snoops, metaphysical or otherwise, could read his lips. He spoke in hushed tones. "I have an idea. Why not lock the parcel in the box where Mad Prince Nestor kept his lucky Hand of Glory?"

Zulawski looked puzzled. He spoke in an equally conspiratorial voice.

"Lucky? Mad Prince Nestor was murdered by peasants and his body was chopped up and fed to wolves. Then the peasants killed the wolves and fed them to other wolves. Then, for some reason, they fed those wolves to other wolves and on and on until they created an uncontrollable pack of rapacious superwolves that plagued the French countryside for the next hundred years. I don't see how Mad Prince Nestor's lucky Hand of Glory was lucky for anyone."

"It was lucky for the wolves," said Vargas.

"You mean the superwolves."

"They wouldn't have existed without it. I'd say that's damned lucky."

"From a wolf point of view," said Zulawski.

"Of course."

"From everyone else's, it was terrifying."

"Obviously," said Vargas. "It's a good reminder that truth is often a matter of perspective."

"It's also a good reminder that you shouldn't keep feeding wolves to wolves unless you want your descendants to be eaten by wolves."

Vargas got even closer to Zulawski. "Wolves aside, the box that held the Hand of Glory was said to possess magical protective powers. Maybe it could shield the animals and us from the parcel's influence."

Zulawski glanced up at the parcel with all the cheeriness of a meerkat being carried away by a lion. "I suppose we could try."

"What have we got to lose?" said Vargas in his normal voice.

Zulawski ticked off items on his fingers. "Our jobs. Our pensions. Our sanity. Our lives."

"We have to do something."

"If only we had some superwolves. Maybe we could get them to eat the parcel."

"Brilliant," said Vargas. "Then you'd have superwolves full of a malevolent preternatural force that flourished in the hellish realm of death and chaos before the stars were born and that seeks to return the universe to darkness—the ultimate evil. Is that what you want? Preternaturally malevolent superwolves? Because that's what you're going to get."

"I guess not," said Zulawski, chastened.

"Of course you guess not," sad Vargas contemptuously. He went to a nearby shelf and took down two large boxes. "Now stop this nonsense and put on this astronaut costume. I'm dressing as Frida Kahlo. That way, if the parcel is watching us, it won't know that we're the ones plotting its demise."

"That's very clever," said Zulawski, taking off his shoes so he could put on his astronaut boots. "I'm glad one of us can still think clearly."

Vargas nodded sagely. "Don't worry. I have this all worked out."

"Good, because when I ran out of squid food, I gave it some of the canned chili we have in the back, and now that's all it will eat."

Vargas put on his wig. "I haven't noticed any empty cans."

"It eats those, too."

"We should hurry."

"I agree."

Putting some discreet duct tape over the locks, Morty left one of the DOPS emergency exits open. Around one in the afternoon, Coop sneaked into the building and went directly to the thaumaturgic antiquities department. Inside, he found Dr. Buehlman talking to a scarecrow-thin older man he guessed was Dr. Carter. It was lunchtime and there was no one else in their large lab space. Coop came into the room quietly. He leaned against one of the long worktables and waited. Buehlman and Carter were busy examining a skull that looked human enough, except for the horn protruding from its forehead and what appeared to be around a hundred teeth in serious need of flossing.

"Nice unicorn," he said. "My cousin Carrie had one when we were kids. Of course, hers had skin. Well, fur. It wasn't a real unicorn. It was stuffed. I bet you have some real unicorns around here somewhere, don't you?"

Buehlman looked up. When she saw who it was, her eyes went wide and a rictus smile gripped the lower part of her face like jolly vise grips.

"Unicorns?" said Carter in a Texas drawl. "You're looking for xenobiology up on three."

"Thanks. I'll stop by the gift shop. Do you know if they have snow globes?"

Carter started to say something, but Buehlman whispered

something in his ear. When Carter looked back at Coop, he had the same alarmed smile.

"How nice to see you, Mr. Cooper," said Buehlman.

"You, too, doc," said Coop. He walked down the table in her direction. She and Carter backed up. They remained cheery, but kept the table between them and Coop.

"I don't suppose you and Dr. Carter have found out anything that might help out my situation?"

"Please sit down, Mr. Cooper," said Dr. Carter, holding his hand out to a lab stool on Coop's side of the table. Coop sat.

"If you'll give us just a minute," Carter continued. "There's something you must see." He and Buehlman went to the other end of the lab, far enough away that they had to shout.

"Can you hear us?" called Buehlman.

"Clear as day, doc," said Coop.

"Good."

Carter looked at an anatomical chart on the wall. Buehlman went to a clipboard and flipped through some pages. "Now, would you repeat your earlier question?" said Carter.

Coop drummed his hands on the top of the table. "Have you found out anything about the mummy's curse that might save my skin?"

Carter cleared his throat. "No," he and Buehlman said. Buehlman grabbed his arm and they ran out a back exit together.

"That's encouraging," shouted Coop. "I want you to know that I'm going to be kissing everyone with measles and mumps I can find. If my skin ends up down here, I plan on making you as miserable as me."

He left the lab and went back to the emergency exit. Morty was waiting for him with a metal lunch box. He handed it to Coop.

"*Star Trek*. Very classy," said Coop, looking the lunch box over.

"That's a classic," said Morty. "From the original series and in mint condition, so I'd appreciate it if you treated it with a little respect."

"If it saves my life, I'll marry it."

"No need for that. Just be careful with it. And with what's inside. If you lose it, we're both going back to jail."

"I won't lose it. And thanks again."

Morty shrugged. "I like my friends with their skin on."

Coop put the lunch box under his arm. "Want to hear something funny? Sally Gifford had a date with your dental-assistant friend."

Morty's hand went to his mouth. "Is she okay?"

"She's fine. But we had a bet. Just how naked were you when you spotted her extra legs?"

Morty put his hands in his pockets. "Let me see if I remember," he said. "I had less clothes on than you the other night, but I wasn't outside with my *Star Wars* panties around my ankles."

Coop gave him a look. "Did Giselle talk to you?"

"No. Sally. She called this morning to get the lowdown on Spider-Girl."

"My secrets aren't safe anywhere," said Coop. He started to the exit, but stopped. "And for your information, they weren't panties and they were only down to my knees."

"That's not how I heard it."

Coop pushed the exit open. "Thanks again for this."

Morty pulled the duct tape off the door lock. "Just remember to keep your shorts on, Grandpa."

Coop couldn't get the carpet-cleaning van again. He had to settle for a large flatbed delivery truck. The canvas dome that covered the truck's bed belonged to a landscaping company. The truck's owner had even given Coop and Sally a couple of small palm trees to stick out the back so the truck would look more legit.

"And here we are again," said Sally. "Waiting in a truck, hoping a rich dope goes out to dinner so we can go inside and get our innards eaten by Siouxsie and the Banshees."

"I have more pepper," said Coop.

"And I have my pepper spray."

"Just be sure to point it at them and not me."

"Let's see how the evening goes."

Coop turned to her in the passenger seat. "Your nose looks good."

"It's fine. Just a little tender." She smiled to herself. "Morty called me. You lied to him about us having a bet about him being naked."

"You told him my awful secret about the other night."

"You think that makes us even?" she said.

"I do."

"When I get a Caravaggio and a couple of Gutenberg Bibles, we'll be even. I have a whole list of expensive books from a dealer friend."

Coop nodded. "You're going to love this. When I'm done, we're going to have all the time we need with the library."

Sally reached over and shoved Coop's shoulder. "Why won't you tell me this secret plan of yours? There *is* a plan this time, right?"

"There is indeed. And I want it to be a surprise."

Sally looked at the Fitzgerald estate through the windshield. "Maybe the second time is the charm."

"It will be. Trust me on this."

"Okay, smart guy. Show me some smarts."

Coop checked his watch. "It's almost eight. They'll be going to dinner soon."

"How do you know the Fitzgeralds' schedule so well?"

"The DOPS knows it," said Coop.

"That's creepy."

"You don't want to know all the things they know or the stuff they have."

"Tell me one thing."

Coop thought for a minute. "My boss has his wife's head on the wall over his desk."

Sally's face curdled. "You're fucking with me."

Coop looked out the window. "It's actually just a windigo, but it looks like his wife, so it's sort of the same thing."

"Sort of?" said Sally. "I was going to get you and Giselle to introduce me to some of the local fed talent, but if they're the kind of people who hang exes on the wall, I'll stay home with my vibrating friends."

"Not everyone there is crazy. We'll have a party. You can mingle and see what happens."

"I'm bringing my pepper spray."

"I won't try to talk you out of that," said Coop. "I think I see something at the house. Let's go."

Like the previous night, Sally turned them invisible and she and Coop went through the gates as the Fitzgeralds left. Like the previous night, Coop killed the power to the house and grounds. Also, like the previous night, Coop spent a certain amount of time looking for mummies over his shoulder. Enough that Sally noticed.

"You keep your eyes on the prize, Coop. I'll look out for bogeymen," she said.

"Deal."

They ran across the dark lawn to the library. When they were halfway there, the Pontianaks began to approach through the dark. When Coop and Sally got close enough to see who it was, they stopped. Coop had his bag of pepper out and Sally had her spray. One of the Pontianaks, the one who led the pack the previous night, held the others back. She gave Coop the finger, but waved him and Sally on past. She sneezed as they went by.

They made it to the library in record time. It sat silent and massive in the dark. Coop took out his key-card machine and got it working. While it computed, Sally said, "We're here. Now will you tell me what's going on?"

Coop opened his duffel and showed the lunch box inside. "This," he said.

"Is that Captain Kirk?" said Sally.

"I think so," Coop said.

"You realize he's made up and can't really beam down to help us?"

"That wasn't Kirk, that was Scotty. And he's not coming either. The DOPS is," said Coop as he opened the lunch box. He removed something that resembled an old-fashioned video-game controller. There were little toggles, buttons, and wheels.

"Aw. We're going to play Ms. Pac-Man," said Sally. "That's almost as good as being rich."

"O ye of little faith. Just wait and see," said Coop.

"What is it?"

"A Tweak box."

"A what?"

"It tweaks things. Their physical makeup. It's called a Quantum Molecular Trans something Engine."

"That clears everything up."

"Hold on and get ready to be amazed."

"I'm right here, Dr. Strange," said Sally. "Impress me."

The card reader pinged. Lights lit up. Sally took the device and put it back in the duffel as the drawbridge lowered.

"Good. They haven't replaced the Domovoi," said Coop.

"Yes. Less monsters is good. Now do your trick and get us inside. I'm hungry."

"We're not going inside," said Coop. "That's the surprise."

"What are we doing here, then?" said Sally.

"This," replied Coop. He pressed a red button at the top of the game controller and turned one of the little wheels. Then he moved the toggle ever so slightly forward.

"This isn't like the grenade last night, right? I mean you know how to use this," said Sally.

"More or less," said Coop. "It's all about mass conversion and molecular something. You'll see."

A haze formed around the library and grew thicker by the second. Soon the building disappeared completely.

"A fog machine. We're at a KISS concert. And I didn't even bring my lighter."

"Relax." Coop kept turning the wheels and adjusting the toggle. "I read the manual this afternoon," he said.

Sally tapped her foot impatiently. "I'm filled with confidence," she said, followed a moment later with "Holy shit."

The haze around the library was beginning to shrink. The building's four wings withdrew from the edges of the moat and moved in on the round central chamber.

"It's getting smaller," said Sally.

"You ain't seen nothing yet," said Coop.

He cranked a wheel at the top of the controller all the way to the right, as far as it would go. The fog became denser and the building continued to shrink. By Coop's thumb, an LED went from white to green and the controller shut down.

Sally clapped his shoulder and laughed. "What the hell did you just do?"

"I quantumed the something and tweaked the molecules. Squeezed it down so we can take the bastard with us and open it at our leisure."

"You are a goddamn genius."

"Be sure to tell Giselle that part."

"I'll send her an ice cream cake with that on top," Sally said. "Can we go and get it?"

"Why not?' said Coop.

As they went forward the fog began to dissipate. A large shape loomed at the center of the mist.

"It still looks pretty big," said Sally.

"Maybe it's just the fog," said Coop. "Let's wait a minute."

As the fog dissipated, something trumpeted loud and long from the center of the library island.

"It's the goddamn marching band again," said Sally.

"No, it's not," said Coop.

The dark shape trumpeted again and moved across the drawbridge.

"It's an elephant," he said.

Sally walked away. "I'm going back and letting the Goth girls eat me," she said.

Coop put the controller back into the lunch box. "I guess that's as small as it could make something as big as a library," he said. "But look, it's coming to us. It transports itself."

"Oh, fuck," said Sally.

Coop went to the elephant. "All we have to do is walk it out, turn it back into the library, and take our time with it. I'm telling you, everything is fine."

Flashlights came on around the house. They moved in Coop and Sally's direction.

"I assume you can Marilyn both us and the elephant, right?"

"Probably. But what are we going to do with it? We can't walk an elephant across L.A."

"We have the truck. I know where we can stash it."

The elephant came over to them and put out its trunk. Coop petted it. "See? It's friendly."

Sally shook her head. "Let's just get Jumbo out of here so we can get our loot."

The three of them started back for the front gate as the guards rushed past them yelling and pointing to the empty island. When Coop and the others got to the front gates, Sally held up a hand in disgust.

"Great. You can use your other box to turn on the power, but unless a car comes through the gates, they won't open. We're stuck."

"You're never stuck when you have an elephant," said Coop. He walked it forward and put its trunk on the gate bars. It wrapped around them and Coop started walking it backward. The gates squealed and scraped across the ground. The metal bars bent. A moment later, the lock popped and the gates swung open.

"You are a strange crook, Coop," said Sally as they walked the elephant to the truck.

It took some coaxing, but in a few minutes Coop managed to get the elephant onto the flatbed. Both he and Sally were relieved when the suspension held. Coop tossed Sally the keys.

"You drive. I'm staying in the back with Tiny here."

"Where are we going, Tarzan?" said Sally.

"The San Fernando Valley. There's a car dealer there named Sheriff Wayne Jr. He loves weird animals. He won't mind us stashing the beast for a night or two."

"Is he the guy with the crazy commercials?"

"That's him. Maybe I'll let him use it in an ad so we can pay the rent for a couple of nights."

"And then we turn it back into a library and get our goods," said Sally.

"Exactly."

Sally went to the cab of the truck. "It's not easy doing business with you, Coop, but it's never boring."

"Just remember to stop for red lights and don't go over the speed limit."

"Fuck you. You're acting like I never drove a magic elephant across town before."

"I forgot. You're an experienced girl, Sally. See you in the Valley."

"You're going to owe me so many drinks before this is over."

I'm going to owe a lot of people, thought Coop as he climbed into the back of the truck. As they drove away, he hit the button to turn the power back on at the Fitzgeralds'. He could just make out people running back and forth across the perfect green lawn.

"I wonder if we'll make the news?" he said to the elephant. It stuck its trunk across his shoulders. They drove all the way to the Valley that way.

33

Minerva held an armful of herbs like a demonic Mother Nature while Kellar cradled a book the size of a Great Dane on his lap. He shifted it this way and that trying to keep his legs from falling asleep.

People had been coming by Minerva's parlor all afternoon. Tourists in shorts and Hawaiian shirts. The idiot redhead who wanted to know about her ex. A supermodel and her junkie friends, as skinny as a herd of praying mantises. Minerva's blood was up just like that time she and the Amazing Criswell got high with Jim Morrison and drove mopeds naked to a Samhain party on Venice Beach.

Those were the days . . .

Kellar had arrived in the afternoon, a bit flustered and with bruised knuckles. He wouldn't say what he had to do to get the grimoire, but if the old ex-biker didn't want to talk about it, Minerva decided she probably didn't want to know.

"Are you sure that's what the book says?" said Minerva, looking over Kellar's shoulder.

"Yes, I'm sure that's what the books says. My Latin is excellent. It wants henbane, hemlock, belladonna, and euphorbia."

She set each ingredient aside and said, "What's the other thing?"

"Tanna leaves," said Kellar. "But we toss those in last."

Minerva put the useful herbs on the table and tossed the others onto the floor. She and Kellar were crouched on pillows in her reading parlor.

"We just burn the herbs and it sends up a smoke signal to King Tut?" she said.

Kellar nodded, staring at the book. "Did you cut them up with the athame?"

"As per your instructions."

"Then, apparently, I just have to do a little recitation and we're in business."

Minerva shook Kellar. "Are you excited? I'm excited."

Kellar took a deep breath. "My heart is doing a fandango."

"You want some ice for those knuckles?"

"Later. All cracked like this, it makes me feel young again."

Minerva rubbed her hands together. "Then let's not fuck around. Get to it, maestro."

"Where's the brazier?" said Kellar.

"Right here." Minerva put what looked more like a battered chafing dish on the table and lit the little can of Sterno underneath. The temperature rose quickly. When it gave off enough heat to make the parlor uncomfortable, Kellar put down the book.

"Are you ready?" he said. "And please don't say you were born ready."

"I'm ready, Freddy," said Minerva.

"Then toss in the salad."

Minerva dropped a handful of each herb into the chafing brazier. They immediately began to smoke. Kellar closed his eyes and began a low chant. Minerva had never heard anything like it before. It started as simple Latin, but changed into something stranger, with sharp consonants and a lot of glottal stops. In other circumstances, she would have held Kellar down and shoved a wallet between his teeth, but as the old fatty spoke he gave off waves of dark power. Minerva hadn't seen anything like it since the time Jayne Mansfield started speaking in tongues when some friends had gotten together to raise Errol Flynn's ghost. No one was sure if Errol had really appeared, but after the séance Jayne was sporting a mysterious hickey.

Smoke began to fill the parlor. Kellar reached over and tossed in the tanna leaves. The smoke grew thicker and more acrid. As it rose to the ceiling, he took a doll from a paper bag and laid it on top of the burning plants.

"What the fuck is that?" Minerva said.

"It's Coop," said Kellar.

"It's a fucking Ken doll."

"It's an effigy. It doesn't have to be perfect."

Minerva waved away the smoke. "Whatever. It's stinking up my home."

"Greatness requires sacrifice. Now let me get back to business."

Kellar went back to chanting. However, it wasn't long before the doll started smoking like a brush fire. Kellar coughed and choked mid-intonation.

"Goddammit," he croaked.

"Did we fuck it up?" said Minerva.

Before Kellar could answer, the dense smoke became a small whirlwind in the middle of the room. It condensed into a long upright oval. Within the oval, figures formed. Animals. Water. Plants.

"It's a cartouche," Kellar whispered.

"What does it say?"

"Do I look like the UN?"

The cartouche drifted lower until it hovered in the air

between them. Soon it collapsed into a ball. The ball grew eyes and teeth.

"Is that a skull?" said Minerva.

"Uh-huh."

The skull hung there for a moment. When Minerva reached out, it snapped at her fingers. Then it shot up to the ceiling and burst into a white mist.

Minerva tried to say something, but both she and Kellar broke down into coughing spasms. She found the top of the chafing dish and slammed it down on the dish. The smoke in the room began to dissipate.

"My God," gasped Kellar. "I think it worked."

"Was the flying skull your first clue or the part where I just about peed myself?"

Kellar looked at her, a little green around the gills. "Minerva? What did we just do?"

"We hooked us a mummy."

"It tried to bite you."

"Rule one in magic: never try to touch mysterious floating skulls. I got excited and forgot."

Kellar flexed his injured knuckles. "I'm not so sure about this anymore," he said.

"There's no backing out now. We're in this together."

Minerva got up, took the chafing dish into the kitchen, and ran water in it to kill the last of the smoke.

"When does it get here, do you think?" said Kellar.

"It's a mummy," said Minerva, coming back into the parlor. "It gets here when it gets here."

Kellar wiped sweat off his brow. "We just wait, then?"

"I'll put up a sign that says we're closed for a private event," said Minerva.

"I'm scared."

"Think of your talk show. Think of your groupies. Think of Oprah."

"Oprah," said Kellar dreamily. Then, "Do you have any food in the house?"

"Just some brown rice and peanut M&M's."

Kellar looked down his nose at her. "Because they're healthier than regular M&M's?"

"Naturally."

"That's what I told myself and now I have three heart stents."

"My heart is just fine, thanks," said Minerva.

"I could go out and get something."

Minerva sat down across from him. "No one leaves until Omar Sharif shows his ugly face."

"I guess it's delivery, then. Time to break out the emergency credit card."

"You prick. You've had a credit card all this time?"

"Emergency card," Kellar said, drawing out each syllable. "*Emergency*. If we're going to end up insufferable billionaires, it seems like a good time to use it. Now the question is what should we get?"

"I have a drawer full of takeout menus in the kitchen. Should we play menu roulette?"

"Go for it, girl."

Minerva went into the kitchen and opened a drawer. Without looking inside, she reached in and pulled out a cardboard doorknob hanger. She called into the parlor, "How's Indian?"

"Do they have lamb samosas?" Kellar yelled back.

"Wait," she said. "Yes."

"Then it sounds divine."

She went into the parlor. "Give me your card, big shot."

Frowning slightly, Kellar handed it to her. Minerva ordered and gave Kellar back his card.

"What do we do until the food gets here?" he said.

Minerva thought it over. "Do you have any coke left?"

Kellar shook his head. "We snarfed it up."

"Want some weed?"

"I'll fall asleep."

Minerva looked around like she was hoping the drug fairy might appear. In fact, it sort of did. She held up a pile of herbs. "There's some belladonna left."

"Be still, my heart," said Kellar.

Minerva got some rolling papers and laid out the leaves on the table. Kellar handed her the athame.

"What if the mummy shows up while we're high?" he said.

"If we can deal with its bony ass, it can deal with us a little wasted."

Kellar looked into the air vaguely. "Are we really doing this?"

"We've already done it. Real, high-level magic. I haven't been this jazzed in years. It's like losing my virginity all over again."

Kellar began rolling a joint. "You always did like older men."

A half-dozen animal rights protesters stood on the curb by Sheriff Wayne Jr.'s dealership. They waved to passing cars, trying to get them to honk in solidarity. Every now and then one would, but mostly people gave them the finger or tossed soda cups at them. Coop felt kind of sorry for them. A bunch of young do-gooders taking a stand where no one needed or wanted them. There was something admirable about it, he thought. It was the kind of thing that would have melted Giselle's heart. He'd tell her about it when he got home. She'd probably send them some money. Why not? They looked like they needed it. Except for a couple at the end of the line. They were trying to dress down like their pals, but Coop had ripped off enough Beverly Hills mansions in his time to recognize a twelve-hundred-dollar jean jacket when he saw one. None of this really bothered him, though. What did was the fact that with the picketers there, it wasn't safe for him to get near the elephant.

Coop took out his phone and dialed an old number.

"Sheriff Wayne Jr.'s Motors, blowing away high prices in the sunny San Fernando Valley. How can I help you?" said a woman's voice.

"Hi. Is this Donna?"

"Who's this?" she said, her voice going suspicious.

"It's Coop."

"Coop? Charlie Cooper? I thought you were in jail."

"No. I got out a while ago. How are you and the Sheriff?"

He could hear her take a breath. "Same as always. My darling has his schemes and I try to hold things together. What are you up to?"

"That's what I'm calling about. I don't suppose you noticed an elephant in your parking lot this morning."

"That was you?" she said pleasantly. "Wayne'll be so relieved to hear it. He thought it was those idiot animal rights people trying to set him up. What the hell are you doing with an elephant?"

"It's a long story. I'm sorry to have to dump it on you without warning, but don't worry. There's a payout for everyone when I get things set up."

"I like the sound of that," Donna purred. "So, how long are we supposed to let Mr. Peanuts shit up our lot?"

"I'll come by and get it tonight. It will take me a day or two to get things set up, but then I'll call and tell you where to meet me for the payout."

"Are we talking about cash?"

"Antiques. Books. Paintings. Furniture."

"Oh," she said, clearly disappointed. "But no money?"

"There might be, for all I know. All I want is one specific book. After that, you and Sally Gifford can split the rest."

"Sally! I love that girl. She never took shit from any man that I can recall."

"Are things okay with you and the Sheriff?"

"We're just fine, and don't take this as me criticizing the dear, but as a fellow crook, how do you lose money on hot cars?"

Coop considered the question. "I didn't even know that was possible."

"Me neither. Maybe this payout of yours is what we need to get over the hump."

"Trust me. This is big-money stuff."

"I wouldn't normally trust a setup like this—having someone dump something on us and we have to wait for payment—but we go back, you and me. Please don't screw me, Coop."

"Never you, Donna. Besides, your boyfriend has more guns than the Marines."

"He polishes them more often than he does me," she said, then, "Oh, my goodness. Did I say that? What a slip of the tongue."

"I have to go. Tell the Sheriff hi for me and that I'll pick up the puppy tonight."

"Can you take a few of those asshole picketers with you?"

"Sorry. I'm strictly animal transport."

"I'm about to turn the hose on those animals."

"I'll call you about the meet-up. You be good. Talk to you later."

"Later, sugar."

Donna put her phone down and chewed her lower lip. For a fleeting moment, she thought about not telling the Sheriff about the call. A big payout? How big and how far would it take her? she wondered. She looked at the invoices and the hot cars still in the garage and let the feeling pass.

Like the man said, "Buy the ticket, take the ride."

She looked out the window into the parking lot. The Sheriff was pouring on the charm to a couple of out-of-town suckers. Donna could never resist him like that. She wrote down everything Coop had told her. Her one concession to her fantasies of Mexico and New York was to toss the note into a desk drawer. She could decide later whether or not to share it. But she knew she'd give in. She always did.

While Donna debated the possibility of not going down with the Sheriff's ship, Coop got a text from Woolrich telling him to come and see him right away. He wondered if Buehlman and Carter had ratted him out for sneaking in where he wasn't wanted. Coop was sure that Morty was a good enough thief that no one would have figured out that he'd taken the Tweak box. But if any of his worst-case scenarios were true, he should probably pretend that his phone battery ran out. The only non-awful possibility he could come up with, and it went entirely against every shred of instinct he had, was that it might be good news. Maybe the Bobbsey Twins had figured out some way around the curse after all. Or maybe they'd grabbed Harkhuf and were currently grinding him into a powder to help salt Alaskan roads in the winter. Coop knew it was a long shot, but how many ways could there be left for Woolrich to screw with him? *A lot actually*. But until he could move Jumbo somewhere safe and get into the damned library, what choice did he have? *And if Woolrich really wants me, he'll just send a load of blacked-out vans to the apartment. The neighbors would love that. First I'm a nudist and now I'm a terrorist. That would be fun for everyone.*

He got back on the Hollywood Freeway and headed for the DOPS.

34

When the elevator doors opened, the Auditors were waiting in all their pale and somewhat larval glory. Coop tried to step around them, but each time they stepped with him.

"Hello, Mister . . ." said Night.

". . . Cooper," said Knight.

"Hi, guys. I'd love to chat, but I'm supposed to meet someone," said Coop.

"Yes. We . . ."

". . . know."

"Crap. It wasn't Woolrich who texted me. It was you."

"Yes," said Night.

"Indeed. You should come with us."

"Don't worry. Everything is going to . . ."

". . . be just . . ."

". . . fine. Mr. Woolrich is well aware . . ."

". . . of the situation," said Knight.

"Nice try, but Woolrich wants you gone as much as me. This is just you having fun, isn't it?"

"No matter. You are a miscreant."

"Worse even."

"Worse."

They know about the Tweak box. I wonder if sea slugs understand begging?

"Look, if this is about the box—"

"It is indeed about . . ."

". . . the box," said Night.

"I can explain," said Coop. "I just needed it for a while."

"To blackmail?" asked Knight.

"For a while? That's your . . ."

". . . excuse?"

"Wait. What box are you talking about?"

"We have evidence of . . ."

". . . your criminal . . ."

". . . activities. Theft," said Knight.

"I *am* a thief. That's why you people hired me," said Coop.

"Extortion."

"No. That's not me."

"The camera . . ."

". . . says otherwise."

"What camera?"

"Yes. What . . ."

". . . camera indeed."

"You should come with us," said Night.

"Don't worry," said Knight. "Everything is going to . . ."

". . . be just . . ."

"Fine," said Coop. "I know."

Morty came up in the elevator across the hall. When he saw Coop he waved and came over. "Hi. What's going on?"

"Nothing," said Coop. "It's fine. Walk away."

"Look, if there's a problem . . ." Morty closed in on the group. The Auditors spun around and he stopped in his tracks. "Oh. Hi, guys."

They smiled identical smiles at him.

"And your name . . ." said Night.

". . . is?" said Knight.

"Never mind. Sorry, Coop," said Morty.

"Leave now," said Coop.

The Auditors stood on either side of him. "Come, Mr. Cooper. There . . ."

". . . is much to discuss."

They pushed him back into the elevator and took him to a room in a secret subbasement. The fact that there was a secret subbasement left Coop wondering if he was more scared or more consumed with a sense of irrevocable doom. Before that moment, he wasn't sure there was a difference. He had some time to debate the issue on the walk from the elevator. It took them down a dank corridor to a room with no name or number on the door.

"Doom," he said.

"What?" said Night.

"What?" said Knight.

"I just came to a conclusion. A couple of fun guys like you. A playpen that looks like Ed Gein's root cellar. I'm doomed."

"Only time . . ."

". . . will tell."

They ushered him into a wreck of a room that looked like the place where the Inquisition stored its equipment in the off-season. The majority of the DOPS was tidy to the point of inertia, so seeing anything out of place in the building was disturbing. Here, half of the ceiling lights didn't work. Broken furniture had been tossed in piles with junked equipment all over the room. The one thing that Coop had going for him was that while he'd been in jail, he'd spent some time in solitary and even more time with prison shrinks in their "calming" offices painted in "restful" colors. He knew a good psych-out when he saw one. But none of that made him any less freaked out, especially since the copious amounts of darkness were the perfect place for a mummy to kick back, relax, and peel a guy's skin off at his leisure.

"You know I'm cursed, right?" Coop said. "Technically, I'm not even supposed to be in the building."

"We know about your . . ."

". . . 'alleged' situation," said Night.

"Alleged? All right, asshole. Hang around me long enough and you'll see what's alleged. If Harkhuf takes my skin for pajamas, I hope he takes yours for slippers."

Night and Knight looked at each other.

"Do you think he's deluded or . . ."

". . . pretending? He's slippery and . . ."

". . . devious."

"And deviant," said Night.

"Yes," said Knight.

They took a simultaneous step toward Coop. Night, or maybe it was Knight, pointed across the room. "Look over there."

Coop craned his neck trying to see into the dark. As the needle went into his neck he felt like a complete idiot for falling for such an obvious trick. But he didn't feel bad for long. He was too dizzy to feel much of anything. Night pushed a gurney toward him and Knight shoved him down on top of it. Together, they secured straps across his body.

Knight, or maybe it was Night, pointed to a clock on the wall.

"We'll begin . . ."

". . . soon. Rest until . . ."

". . . then."

Coop wanted to say something, but all he did was gurgle.

And then he was asleep.

When he woke up, the first thing Coop saw was the clock. He'd been strapped to the gurney for nearly four hours. It was close to the time when he should be rounding up a truck to move the elephant, but there was nothing he could do about it now. *And I'm too stoned to drive anyway.*

"I'll just have to ride it out," Coop said out loud, startling himself.

"Indeed you . . ." said Night.

". . . will, Mr. Cooper," said Knight.

The Auditors stood over him. They looked happier than he'd ever seen them. One was holding a straight razor. The other held a power drill.

"What the hell is that for?" he said, nodding at the drill. "Did you use that on Bayliss, you pricks?"

"Of course not," said Night.

"She was merely naughty," said Knight.

"Not a criminal like . . ."

". . . you. Criminals require special . . ."

". . . handling."

One of them took an official-looking certificate out of his breast pocket and held it up where Coop could see it.

"As members of the federal . . ."

". . . government, we have the right to mandate your welfare . . ."

". . . by law. We will take good . . ."

". . . care of you. There will be no permanent . . ."

". . . damage, but . . ."

". . . it will . . ."

". . . hurt," said Night.

"A lot," said Knight.

The certificate disappeared into Night's pocket.

Coop tried to hold up his head. "Are you boys open to bribes? Because I'm very comfortable with offering you a bribe right now."

The Auditors looked at each other.

"A born . . ."

". . . criminal. Let's see what . . ."

". . . else we can find."

Night, or maybe it was Knight, used the razor to shave a patch of hair behind Coop's left ear. When he was done he stepped away. Knight, or maybe it was Night, stepped forward and brought the drill level with the shaved spot on Coop's head. He started the drill.

There was a strange pounding sound. The Auditor with the drill stopped it, listened, and hearing nothing, started it again. The pounding came back. This time, when he stopped the drill, the pounding continued. It was coming from the door.

"Who can that . . ."

". . . be? You should go . . ."

". . . and see."

"I'll go. You stay . . ." said Night.

". . . here," said Knight.

Night walked off into the darkness, leaving Coop alone with Knight. It was strange. He knew he should feel better only having one lunatic hovering over him, but staring up into a single hairless, snow-cone face was actually worse. As Knight looked into the dark for his partner he idly flicked the drill on and off. Coop watched the drill bit the way a mongoose watches a cobra with a switchblade.

"So, do you like sports?" he said. "Movies? I'm a movie fan myself. Let's get to know each other. Did you have any pets? I had a hamster. Actually, it was my brother's hamster . . ."

Knight put a finger to his lips. "Shh."

The drill went on and off.

"Did the other kids pick on you in school or did the feds grow you two in a jar like sea monkeys?"

Knight reached out and petted Coop's head.

"I'm guessing jar. You and Thing One have all the personality and animal magnetism of a couple of talking lobsters. I'd ask you about your parents, but I'm guessing they were boiled and served with butter."

Knight stopped playing with the drill. He stared off into the dark, looking annoyed.

"What is keeping him?" he said. Soon he looked down at Coop. "I think we should get started. Don't you?"

"Hey, you can say whole sentences. That's great. I mean, I wouldn't want to be tortured by a weirdo."

Knight touched the drill to the bare spot by Coop's left ear. The motor whined as the drill spun up. Night, or maybe it had been Knight, had been right about one thing. It hurt a lot. Coop's body tensed. He closed his eyes.

A few seconds later, the drilling stopped. Coop went limp, but managed to open his eyes.

Night was off whispering with Knight. They passed an official-looking form rapidly between them.

"Are you sure? We've . . ." said Knight.

". . . already begun the . . ." said Night.

". . . procedure. Nevertheless it . . ."

". . . looks as if he's summoned . . ."

". . . elsewhere."

Reluctantly, Knight set down the drill. He and Night unbuckled the straps that held Coop to the gurney.

Night gave him a small bow. "Mr. Cooper, you may go . . ."

". . . now. But we will be . . ."

". . . in touch. To continue our session."

"You will not be forgotten," said Knight.

Coop pushed himself upright and slid off the gurney limply.

"Thanks, boys," he said. He leaned into Night and spoke in a stage whisper. "By the way, you really should hear the shit Thing Two talks about you behind your back." He headed for the door. Before leaving, he called back over his shoulder. "See you later, guys. Remember, softball on Sunday."

Coop stumbled out of the room and into the corridor, where he collapsed against the wall. He looked up at the massive shape above him.

"Dr. Lupinsky? What are you doing here?"

Lupinsky's cat paced nervously across the screen.

Come with me.

Coop tried to stand, but didn't make it. Lupinsky reached down and pulled him to his feet. Together, they walked to the elevator. Lupinsky pushed a button. While they waited, he handed Coop a bottle with a couple of pills inside.

Take these. You'll feel better.

Coop dry-swallowed both. In just a few seconds, his head began to clear. He patted one of Lupinsky's metal tentacles.

"Thanks, doc. How did you know about me?"

Morty told me. He was concerned.

Coop touched a hand to the shaved patch behind his ear. He was still bleeding, but it was just a trickle. "Do you know why Johnny and Edgar Winter grabbed me?"

Apparently, the Auditors received incriminating evidence with your fingerprints. I suspect someone in the DOPS doesn't like you.

"That's a lot of people."

Enough to want someone to drill holes in your head?

"Nelson," said Coop. "But there's nothing I can do about him now."

Lupinsky's cat hissed.

"Thanks a lot," said Coop. "I owe you."

The cat rubbed itself against the screen.

You made my life more interesting and I'm grateful. Now you should go. The form said you were helping me with a dissection, but it didn't specify when I was to dissect you.

"Thanks. I have to see a man about an elephant."

An elephant?

"I'll tell you later."

The elevator arrived and Coop stepped into it. He leaned against the wall and pointed a still slightly trembling finger at Lupinsky. "We're going to have a party when this is over. You and your kitty cat are invited."

The cat arched its back and purred.

Thank you. We'll be happy to attend.

"See you later," said Coop, and he punched the button for the garage.

35

It was dark out when someone rapped on Minerva's door. She and Kellar were still tripping lightly on the belladonna. The guy outside didn't look like a tourist. In fact, he didn't look like much of anything. He was one of those doughy guys who might have been anywhere from his midthirties to his early fifties. From his rumpled uniform, Minerva immediately pegged him for a loser. The kind of guy whose highest career aspiration was to drive the kiddie train at the zoo.

He said, "It's Match.com. Your dream date is here," while tapping a knuckle on the glass.

Minerva pointed to the Closed sign and waved him away angrily. "Can't you read?"

"No," he said. "I navigated here by the stars."

"Listen," she shouted, pointing in one direction and then the other. "The bars are that way. The hookers are that way. Now fuck off."

The loser scratched his head in mock puzzlement. "Are you sure you didn't send a message to a certain special gentleman? About this tall. Charming personality. Just spent the last three thousand years in a box and doesn't like crank calls?"

Minerva shot Kellar a nervous look. "What should I do?"

"Open it," he said excitedly.

Minerva unlocked the door cautiously. The loser went to a dirty Toyota hatchback and popped the rear door. He slid something large and heavy from the back and pushed it upright. Whatever or whoever he had his hands on needed help getting over the curb. Minerva stepped into the street, but all she could see was a figure shambling toward her wrapped in a dirty trench coat, his face blocked by a blue trilby.

Just my luck. It's just a couple of crazies, Minerva thought. She stepped angrily back into her parlor and started to slam the door. It closed about six inches before a hand in dirty bandages caught it and pushed it open again with almost no effort. The shambler came inside while the loser closed and locked the door. Still swimming on the belladonna, Minerva and Kellar cowered in a corner of the room.

"I'm Froehlich," said the loser. He pulled the hat and coat off the bandaged figure. Minerva managed to stifle a gasp. Kellar didn't. Froehlich tossed the hat and coat onto a pile of cushions.

Froehlich waved them forward. "Don't be shy, folks. Say hello to the hardest-working man in show business, Harkhuf. He doesn't seem to have a last name, sort of like Cher or Madonna."

"Silence, thrall," said the mummy.

Kellar dug his fingers into Minerva's arm. She patted his hand.

Harkhuf turned slowly, taking in the room. "You summoned me. I came. For what purpose did you make contact? And beware. A wrong answer invites eternal torment."

Froehlich leaned against the wall. "My master gets this way when he hasn't had a nap. Also, he means it."

"Your master?" said Kellar.

"As in master and slave," said Froehlich. "I didn't get this job through craigslist."

"Speak, fools. I grow weary of this pointless chatter," Harkhuf said.

Minerva pushed Kellar's hand off her arm and came forward. "I'm Minerva Soleil. I know that you want someone. A man named Coop. I can help you find him."

Harkhuf took a step toward her. "Then you have summoned me for nothing and have doomed yourselves."

"Wait," said Minerva. "He was just here. He told me about the curse."

Harkhuf stopped. "That was before. I will deal with him at a time of my choosing. Now I have a much more important goal."

"What kind?" said Minerva. "Kellar and I are at your complete disposal. We have a lot of connections and can help you with anything you need."

The mummy didn't answer. Froehlich came over and stood next to him.

"My master is looking for another mummy. His lady love, Shemetet."

"Quiet, cur," growled Harkhuf. "I will deal with you later."

"Yay," Froehlich said softly.

"Not like that."

"Aw."

Minerva said, "We can help you there, too. Coop, he works for the government. They deal in deep metaphysical secrets. If we give you Coop, I know that he can find your Shemetet."

"And why would you offer me such a boon?" said Harkhuf.

Minerva lowered her head and put her hands together, going for a humble look. "A great man such as yourself with all your mystical power, all we ask for is a little consideration."

"What sort of consideration?"

Kellar pushed past her. "I want my own talk show. And she wants to be famous again."

Minerva waved him quiet. She smiled timidly at Harkhuf. "Yes, we request those pitiful things from Your Eminence, but if we can give you Coop, there is one more trifle we would ask for."

Kellar looked at her, confused.

"I grow weary of your begging, woman. What is it you seek?"

"Just a book. *The Mysteries of the Dead. Mysteriis Ex Mortuis.*"

Kellar put a hand to his mouth. "Minerva! Are you crazy? What do you want with *that*?"

She looked at him hard, her eyes gleaming. "I got a taste for real magic tonight. Think about it. If show biz doesn't work out, with the book we can become the darkest, most powerful wizards on the coast. If that doesn't get us money, groupies, and respect, nothing will."

"But, where is it?" said Kellar.

"It's in L.A., I know that much. And just like with Mrs. Tut, Coop should be able to track it down."

"And if he can't?"

She turned to Harkhuf. "With this glorious presence working with us, he sure as hell will."

Kellar looked from Minerva to Harkhuf. "Fuck it," he said. "I'm in."

The mummy raised a hand. "This Coop, he can provide this book, too?"

"Oh yes," said Minerva.

"And my Shemetet?"

"Absolutely."

"Then I agree to your terms."

Froehlich applauded quietly. "I should have brought party hats."

"Thank you for your generosity, O great one," Minerva said.

Harkhuf shambled forward until he was within a few inches of her face. "But hear me. If you have wasted even a second of my time or have deceived me, your punishment will be swift and awful."

"Promises, promises," muttered Froehlich.

"Hush, thrall," said Harkhuf. "Now, witch, how will you deliver Coop to me?"

She took Kellar's arm and pulled him to her side. "We have a plan. Since your disappearance, you've become quite a celebrity. Everybody wants you, including Coop's people."

"Are you absolutely sure about this?" whispered Kellar.

"With what Coop does for a living," she whispered back, "his people are just waiting to get their hands on this magnificent creature."

"I hope you're right," said Kellar in a nervous, singsong voice.

"My patience grows thin," said Harkhuf. "How will you deliver Coop to me?"

"We don't. We deliver *you* to Coop."

Froehlich cleared his throat. "I don't mean to interrupt, but is that chicken vindaloo I smell?"

"Yes," said Kellar.

Froehlich turned to Harkhuf. "Do you mind, Master? I haven't eaten since yesterday."

The mummy waved an arm contemptuously. "Fill your dog face."

Froehlich looked at Minerva and Kellar. "How about you? Do you mind?"

"It's a little cold," Kellar said.

"The microwave is right through there," said Minerva.

"Thanks," said Froehlich, patting his belly. "It's hard to destroy the world on an empty stomach."

"Destroy the what?" said Kellar.

Coop had to do some fast talking in order to borrow the truck again, but he finally got it. It was almost midnight when he hit the road for the Sheriff's car lot. He was furious about how many hours he'd wasted with the Auditors, and he wasn't all that choked up about the way Nelson was still playing games with him. Plus, his head hurt like someone had tried to drill holes in it.

When he pulled off the freeway, he could see that the lights were off in the dealership. This was fine by him. He didn't need the Sheriff or Donna getting in his way or asking stupid questions. The elephant had seemed to like him well enough the previous night, so he was sure he could get it into the truck by himself. Then came the little matter of turning it back into a library, but he'd worry about that when his head was clearer.

There was a metal barrier across the driveway into the car lot. Coop parked the truck next to it with the blinkers on and went to get the elephant.

But it wasn't there.

He looked around the front of the dealership and ran around back. He pressed his face against the garage door and found a room full of hot cars, but no elephant. There was some open scrubland behind the car lot, so he climbed through a break in the fence and looked around there. None of the grass was more than three feet tall, not really hide-and-seek country for elephants, but he was getting desperate. He ran back to the lot, sprinting up and down the rows of cars hoping to spot something that would point to where seven thousand pounds of walking meat might like to spend an evening.

Finally, out of breath and sweating like he'd run a marathon in scuba gear, Coop went back to the truck and got out his phone. He hit redial.

"Hello."

"Donna. It's Coop. What the fuck? I mean, what the fuck?"

"Coop? Slow down. You're talking like a crazy man."

"Did you take it? I thought we had a deal."

"Did we take what?"

"The elephant," shouted Coop. "It's gone."

"Oh," she said. "Let me get the Sheriff for you. Don't you go anywhere."

"I'm not budging. By the way, I'm at the car lot. I have a truck, and I'm prepared to become entirely unreasonable."

"Okay. I'm not going to tell him that last part," said Donna. "You hang on."

Coop ran through all the possibilities in his head. One, Sheriff Wayne Jr. was pissed about his coming by unannounced and dumping a shaved mammoth on his front steps. Two, something happened to the elephant and the Sheriff had it stashed somewhere. He wondered if he could even turn an injured elephant back into the library and, if he could, what shape the library would be in. Three, the idiot let it get loose and it was doing a Jack Kerouac, hitting the road and trying to thumb a ride to Kenya.

Or maybe something worse happened, Coop thought. Maybe he used the box wrong. Maybe the elephant kept shrinking right down to nothing. No elephant meant no library. It meant no payout for Sally or the Sheriff and Donna, and no book for him. There weren't a lot of scenarios he could come up with where he didn't end up skinless, dead, in jail, or all three.

"Coop. It's me," said a man's voice.

"Sheriff, it's Coop. Did Donna tell you that there's a situation at your car lot?"

"She might have mentioned something about it. You're sure it's gone? Did you check around back?"

Coop rubbed the sore spot behind his ear. "Yes, I looked around back. I peeked in the drawing room and under the rosebushes. It's fucking gone."

"Okay. Calm down, son. Let me ask you this: Are any of those assholes still hanging around?"

"I'm the only asshole down here. Which assholes are you talking about?"

"Those animal lib assholes. They were there all day and all evening, eyeing the beast. I wouldn't put it past those thieving little shits to have made off with your pachyderm."

Coop sat straight up, trying to picture the do-gooders from earlier. There had been, what, six of them? Four regular kids and two with more money than brains. A bunch like that could be just stupid enough to rent a truck with Daddy's credit card and take the elephant. But where? What the hell would a bunch of lunkheads like them do with a full-grown elephant?

"If it was them, I'm screwed," said Coop. "L.A. is full of groups like that. How am I going to track down one I saw for all of two minutes?"

"That's why you were smart to come to Sheriff Wayne. He's already solved your problem for you. I talked to some acquaintances in local law enforcement, hoping to get the little pricks evicted, and one of them came up with a name. The Animal Human Love Society. Tell me that doesn't sound like a German porno. These kids are sick. They're based out of, get this, Carrwood."

"That's something, but it's still going to take time to track them down," Coop said. "My skin is riding on this."

"How would you like an address?" said Sheriff Wayne, sounding very satisfied with himself.

"You're kidding me."

"One of the little dummies parked his Land Rover where I could see the plate. My peace-officer friend ran it for me. I have it written down over here. Hold on . . . okay, got it. It's registered to a Dylan Barker at 2206 Vieux Carré Lane in Carrwood."

Coop scrambled around the cab of the truck until he found a pad and pen in the glove compartment.

"Thanks for the info. This is why you're the Clint Eastwood of crooks, Sheriff."

"Gary Cooper, actually, but Clint will do in a pinch," said the Sheriff. "Now, when you find these little creeps, you remember our deal. Just because the elephant isn't here now doesn't mean you didn't dump it in my lap. I'm still owed something for that."

"Trust me. The moment I get hold of the monster, it's going to be a payday for everyone."

"That's what I wanted to hear. And remember, if it comes down to it and you need a little firepower, call me day or night. I didn't shoot a film director a couple of days ago and I'm still sorry about it."

"Will do. Thanks. I'll be in touch."

This is what happens when you do business with the mentally berserk, Coop thought. *Doc Holliday wants to go to the O.K. Corral on Richie Rich and the Osmond family. Why can't I do business with normal thieves who want to steal things and not have everybody know who did it? Of course, normal thieves don't rush across town so they can stake out a trust-fund hit squad with their stolen elephant.* The fact that he might be his own worst enemy had occurred to Coop before, but it had never come with actual names, times, dates, and an address. It was unsettling.

Oh, and someone drilled a hole in my head tonight. That happens to normal thieves, right?

The moment Coop put his phone back in his pocket, it rang. He pulled it out and saw Giselle's ID.

"Hi. How are you?"

"Coop. Where have you been?" said Giselle. "You weren't around when I got back. I've been worried."

"I'm sorry I missed you last night. You don't get to pull those sexy all-night jobs much. Was it fun?"

"Never mind about that. Where are you?"

"Sorry I didn't call. I got a little tied up at work," said Coop. "And I lost the elephant, but I'm hot on its trail now."

"Did you say elephant?"

"Didn't Sally tell you? We stole an elephant last night."

"Why the hell did you do that?"

Coop rubbed his neck. "We were going to run away with the circus, but they already had an elephant."

"Coop," said Giselle, the concern in her voice replaced by annoyance.

"Call Sally. She'll explain everything. I have a massive headache and I need to concentrate."

"Okay, but you should know one more thing. Bayliss did some more research on your mummies. She thinks she found Shemetet."

"That's great. Where is she?" said Coop.

"Downstairs. They have her in thaumaturgic antiquities."

Coop dropped back against the driver's seat, visions of conspiracies dancing in his head. "Now I'm feeling just a little paranoid. Do you think they knew about their connection all along?"

"The DOPS knows everything," said Giselle. "Woolrich had one mummy, so he's hanging you out like a worm on a hook to get the other one."

"Funny you should mention people who don't like me. Someone drilled a hole in my head tonight."

"What?" said Giselle.

"Don't worry," he said. "It's not very deep."

"Coop, please come home."

"I can't. I have to find the elephant."

"What elephant?" Giselle shouted. Coop had to move the phone away from his ear.

"Call Sally. I promise I'll tell you the rest when I get home."

McCloud practically clanked into Nelson's office.

By the time Pandora's chocolate bunny had finished with him, he'd lost his remaining arm, his eyes, his nose, one ear, his left foot, and his right leg. Nelson had spent an entire night and had to go through several boxes of purloined cyborg parts to put him back together again. In the end, he was quite proud of his work. True, McCloud set off metal detectors whenever he left the mail room, which slowed his work, and his artificial leg tended to buzz like a demented hornet when he bent down to pick up anything, but it was a small price to pay to keep a well-trained, and now perpetually hypnotized, assistant. Plus, it meant that he didn't have to use any tiresome management voices. That was a relief.

Nelson was admiring a large brass coin when McCloud came in with a handful of stolen mail and memos.

"What's that, boss? It looks pretty cool."

Nelson held the coin up high because McCloud was still getting used to his new eyes and focusing could take a while. "It's a good-luck charm. Seventeenth century, if I remember correctly. It's called a Rogue's Aegis."

"Wow. That's great."

Nelson looked at him like one might regard a stunned trout in the bottom of a rowboat. "Would you like to know its function?"

"Boy, would I."

"It's an enchantment shield. It will ward off almost any curse or spell. But there's a catch. It only works once. Back in the old days, men like us used to carry these things around by the pocketful."

Still trying to focus, McCloud moved his head forward and back like a chicken pecking seeds off the ground. "Awesome. I guess that makes us a couple of rogues?"

"Rogue. Scoundrel. Black sheep. Rapscallion," said Nelson. "That's me, of course. You don't have the brains for actual roguery. You're a rogue temp at best."

"Sounds like a promotion to me. Do I get a raise?"

"I already gave you yours, C-3PO."

McCloud wiggled his metallic fingers. "Oops. I forgot. Thanks again for these."

"You're welcome. Now, do you have anything interesting for me?"

"I don't know. I couldn't read much before and it's a bit worse now," said McCloud. "But I'll get better."

"I'm sure you will," said Nelson, thumbing quickly through the correspondence.

"Are you expecting something?"

"I was hoping to see something about Coop's demotion." He gave McCloud a sunny smile. "A little bird told me that the Auditors had a chat with him yesterday. He should be headed our way anytime now."

"I told you about that. Am I a little bird *and* a rogue temp? A rogue bird temp?"

"You're a birdbrain and that's not a temp situation. It's permanent."

"Thanks for clearing it up," said McCloud. "Anyway, they let him go."

Nelson tossed the correspondence to the side of his desk, hoping he'd heard wrong. "Who let who go?"

"The Auditors. They let Coop go."

Nelson grabbed the pile and went through it again. "Are you sure? Are you absolutely sure?"

"Yes. Everyone in security is talking about it. The Auditors never let anyone go before."

"Did they say why they let him go?"

"No. But they'd started the session," said McCloud warily. He couldn't see much, but he could hear well enough and could tell that the boss wasn't happy. "They'd even drilled a hole in his head."

"A hole? An actual hole?"

"That's what they said."

Nelson allowed himself a grim smile. "That's something at least. Too bad they didn't hit an artery or some bit of higher-brain-function meat," he said. But the more he thought about it the more he realized he was wrong. If Coop had truly flatlined, he might not be demotable. And if the Auditors had given him a lobotomy before he was inevitably transferred to the mail room, he wouldn't have the brainpower to truly suffer like the rest of them. No, letting the bastard go was the best possible outcome of a bad situation.

"I guess you and I will be having another box party soon. We're going to have to go through all of them again and see what else we can use to pin Coop to the wall."

"What about the picture of Death? You said you were saving that for someone."

Nelson tugged at his ear. Staring at McCloud's aluminum one made his itch. "That could work, but then I'll have used up the camera *and* the photo. Let's keep it in mind, but see what else might work. And good for you for making a useful suggestion for once. You get another promotion."

"Do I?" said Nelson. "Oh, boy."

"You're officially promoted from birdbrain to ferret brain. Congratulations. You're a mammal."

McCloud beamed. "Thanks, boss. There's one thing, though."

Nelson looked at him. "You're going to ask what a mammal is."

"Yes," said McCloud sheepishly.

"Sit down and I'll try to explain."

Coop sat in the truck down the block from the address on Vieux Carré Lane all night. The lawn was as perfect and emerald green as the one at Fitzgerald's place, though it was considerably smaller. While Fitzgerald was obscenely rich, it was clear that Dylan Barker's family was just annoyingly rich. Which didn't bother Coop in the least. He was quite fond of the rich. Who else was he going to steal from? It's like what Willy Sutton said when someone asked him why he robbed banks: "It's where the money is." He felt a pang of regret that due to his current employment situation, he couldn't pay the residents of Vieux Carré Lane a visit sometime in the future. Still, he could live vicariously through his friends. He made a mental note to pass on the layout of the neighborhood to Sally.

Around ten in the morning, a handsome young man with a three-hundred-dollar haircut and five-hundred-dollar jeans came out of 2206, got into a pristine Land Rover, and drove away.

Coop started the truck and followed him at what he hoped was a discreet distance. It was hard to be sure. He'd never followed anybody in a battleship before.

The drive didn't take long. In perhaps a quarter of a mile and just a couple of turns, the Land Rover drove into the parking lot of the massive Carrwood community recreational center. There was another truck already in the parking lot. It said SWEENEY BROTHERS LANDSCAPING on the side. Probably the people who kept the trees trimmed and the lawns so nice, Coop thought. But what caught his eye were two other matters. The first was that there was a large Closed for Remodeling sign in front of the rec center, but there were no painters or carpenters in sight. The second point was even more interesting than the first. While a normal person might expect a crew like the Sweeney Brothers to haul their lawn trimmings out of Carrwood to a landfill or recycling center, they seemed instead to be carrying large bags of grass *into* the rec center.

Rich people might be different, even a little crazy, Coop knew, but there was no way they were using lawn trimmings in a remodeling project. It wasn't much of a leap to figure that there was definitely something in the rec center that would appreciate a few hundred pounds of fresh grass.

One of Carrwood's finest drove past the truck slowly, giving it the once-over. Coop had seen similar cars all night and had been forced to move the truck twice before dawn. He knew there was no way he could confront a bunch of grass-toting do-gooders, get the elephant, and load it into the truck without attracting the attention of local security. As much as he hated the idea, he was going to need help with a job like this. Coop started the truck and headed out of Carrwood, admiring its clean streets, quiet ambience, and sense of order. Somehow he was going to have to get around all of them if he was going to get back the elephant.

By the time he hit the freeway, he had a plan. He called Woolrich and told him everything that had happened since he saw Harkhuf outside the apartment.

When Coop was done talking, Woolrich said, "You can't keep it, you know."

"The cookbook? Even if it means my skin?"

"We can protect you."

"Bang-up job so far. How soon before you can put together a team to get the elephant?"

"We won't be getting it," Woolrich said. "We'll report its whereabouts to the Department of Fish and Wildlife. Play up how neglected it is and how much danger it's in. Then, once they have it tucked away somewhere safe and warm, we'll take it from *them*."

"That way no one can trace the elephant back to the DOPS," said Coop.

"See? You're getting the hang of it here."

"I'm not sure that's a good thing."

"As for you, continue to see this as an extended vacation," said Woolrich. "When we have the creature in hand, we'll be in touch. Oh, and if it wouldn't be too much trouble, you should probably return the Twonker. The boffins downstairs have been beside themselves."

"You mean the Tweak box?"

"Is that what it's called? No wonder they were all looking at me like that."

"I'll give it to Giselle."

"Excellent. We'll call you when things settle down."

Like hell you will.

"Thanks, Mr. Woolrich. I'll talk to you later."

"Take care, Cooper."

After exiting the freeway, Coop decided to do some shopping. Woolrich was going to screw him again, of course, but that was the beauty of the plan. This time, Coop didn't just see it coming.

He was counting on it.

36

Carlson was by the door when the delivery arrived, so he was the one who signed for it.

"What is it?" he asked the delivery driver.

"A crate."

"Where's it from?"

The driver looked at the readout on his digital pad and the shipping paperwork on the box. "Toys 'R' Us," he said.

"Funny guy," said Carlson. "How about I report you to your bosses?"

"Look for yourself. It says Toys 'R' Us."

Carlson tore the paperwork off the crate and looked it over. Sure enough, in the return address field, it said Toys 'R' Us. "Are you sure you're at the right address?"

"Once more, I must direct you to the paperwork," the driver said.

Carlson checked. The museum was the correct address. "If this is someone's idea of a joke, they're in big trouble," he said.

"I'm delighted to know that. Just sign here and I'll leave you to your toys."

"The museum doesn't display toys."

"You sure?" said the driver. "From what the news says, Raggedy Anns and Furbys is all anyone is going to trust you with from now on."

Carlson signed for the crate and shoved the digital pad back at the driver a little harder than he had to. "Your job is a joke and you're a joke, do you know that?"

"You ever heard of Pavlov's dog?" said the driver.

"Who's that?"

"It was a dog a scientist trained to come running whenever he rang a bell."

"So what?"

The driver pointed to the buzzer by the museum door. "I might be a joke, but I ring the bell and you come running. What does that make you?"

The driver got in his delivery truck and drove off. Carlson was still trying to think of an excuse to shoot out his tires and tase him when Klein came up behind him.

"What's that?" Klein said.

"I don't know, sir," said Carlson. "It says it's from Toys 'R' Us."

Klein made a face. "Very funny. You're not having another psychotic break, are you? The museum can overlook one tension-related clucking incident, but it better not become a habit."

Carlson held out the paperwork where Klein could read it. He looked it over and crumpled the pages in his hands.

"Very funny," he said. "It's probably from those shits at the Getty Museum. They think they're so smart. We should carry this thing straight to the Dumpster."

"Shouldn't we at least open it first?" Carlson said.

"Hoping for some windup chickens for your barnyard, are you?"

Carlson didn't say a word, but he seriously didn't need this kind of shit from delivery drones and paper pushers like Klein.

He'd been in the Corps. He'd worked security in Iraq and Afghanistan. *This Klein prick has no idea how many ways I know to kill him.* Carlson ran over a few of his favorites while Klein looked over the crate's paperwork.

"Fine," he said finally. "Let's open it."

The straps that secured the crate closed were plastic heat-sealed together. Pulling them apart wasn't any harder than opening an envelope. By now, a crowd of guards and museum workers had gathered by the door. Carlson tore open the last strap and unlatched the crate.

Inside, it was tightly packed wads of excelsior. On top of it all was an envelope. Carlson took it out and Klein snatched it from his hands.

Carlson forgot about the list of his favorite homicide methods and switched to the ones that looked like accidents.

Falling down a flight of stairs. A few too many drinks and drowning in the tub. Eaten by Clydesdales in a carrot suit during Halloween.

Klein opened the envelope and read the message to the crowd. "'We thought you might like this back. Just needed it for a kegger. Sorry for all the trouble. No hard feelings?'" At the bottom was the seal of a college fraternity that had once rejected Froehlich. Since he was on a roll ruining lives, he figured what was one more or a dozen?

Klein pocketed the note and began pulling at the excelsior. He stopped at the third handful, looked, and began frantically scooping out as much of the stuff as he could as quickly as he could.

"Help me, you idiot," he shouted. Carlson got beside him and threw excelsior back at the museum door. A few more handfuls and Klein put a hand across Carlson's body to stop him.

Spontaneous human combustion. Poisoned by cut-rate fugu. Stomped to death in a tragic clog-dancing incident.

Klein stepped back. The crowd at the door was hushed.

"Call that idiot Rockford," he said. "Call the police. Call the museum directors. And get one of the trucks around here. I'm not leaving Harkhuf with you pinheads ever again. We're moving him to our secure warehouse in Pasadena."

"Yes, sir," said Carlson. "We're on it."

Plague. Stung to death by bees. Exploded while cleaning a cannon.

That evening, Sarah and Tyler were on shit-shoveling duty. As each bag of lawn clippings emptied, they used it to hold the elephant's copious droppings. In their excitement at liberating the poor downtrodden animal, the fact that material came out of the elephant almost as quickly as it went in hadn't crossed their minds. They were paying a heavy price for it now. But no one complained. It might be seen as shirking, and shirking could get you a time-out. If the Cultural Revolution had reeducation camps, the Animal Human Love Society had time-outs. It came with a hefty load of pamphlets, books, broadsides, and online screeds, some of them dry, some hysterical, and all tedious, so they would do anything to avoid having to read them. Even if it meant shoveling enough shit to fill an Olympic swimming pool.

Sarah looked at the elephant. "Do you think it looks sick? I think it looks sick."

Heather was sweeping up lawn clippings across the room. "I don't know what a sick elephant looks like."

"That's a good point," said Tyler. "We should have thought of that before we stole it."

"Friendmancipated it," said Linda.

"Whatever," said Sarah, exhausted.

"Who wants to do some elephant health research?" Tyler said.

Heather's hand shot up. Everyone looked at her.

"You don't have to raise your hand," Tyler said. "You can just say you want to do it."

"Right. I want to do it."

"Great. Thank you."

Heather's heart swelled. As always, it was her idiot brother who ruined the moment.

"How long is it going to stay?" said Dylan. "If anyone finds it here, we're going to be in big trouble."

"Now you know how I feel," said Brad.

"How are the mice, Brad?" said Linda.

"Do you want them?"

"No."

"Then don't ask."

Tyler finished his bag, tied it off, and carried it to the considerable pile of other droppings in the corner of the rec center. "How much is it costing us to buy lawn clippings from those guys?" he asked.

"The clippings are free," said Heather. "It's getting them to keep their mouths shut that's costing us."

"I think the group should share the expense. It's only fair," said Dylan.

There was a general groaning around the room.

"Everyone here with a fifty-thousand-dollar Land Rover and a trust fund raise their hands," said Brad. He looked around the room. "Oh. I guess it's just you two."

"That's not a very collectivist attitude," said Sarah.

A door slammed at the far end of the rec center, causing everyone to jump. It was Warren. He came running to the rest of them. "The T-shirts are here," he said enthusiastically.

"What T-shirts?" said Tyler.

"They're a surprise," said Warren, handing out shirts to everyone. "I thought that since the group really put itself on the map with our recent operation, we should make it official. I Photoshopped the logo myself."

Above the group's name was the silhouette of a man with the silhouette of a dog clinging to his back in what, from a certain vantage point, could be considered an amorous position. A few of the group members looked at each other uncomfortably.

"It's a little suggestive, don't you think?" said Sarah.

"Sure it's suggestive. Suggestive of *solidarity*," shouted Warren, pulling on his shirt.

Tyler went over to him. "I think what Sarah is saying is that while we appreciate this heartfelt contribution, maybe artwork isn't your strongest—"

This time a different door slammed open. "Everybody on the floor!" shouted a man in riot gear and a balaclava. "Do it now!" He pointed a rifle at the group. Three more armed officers stormed in after him. They spread out across the room, pushing members of the group to the ground. As each kid went down, the officers secured their wrists behind their backs with zip ties.

"What is this?" said Tyler. "Who are you people?"

The first officer stood over him and pointed to a logo on his riot gear. "We're with the federal Department of Fish and Wildlife. You're all under arrest for putting in peril the life and welfare of an endangered species."

"Fuck," said Brad.

Linda began to cry.

Sarah and Tyler stared mutely at the officers.

Dylan shook his head. "When Mom and Dad hear, we're dead."

"So dead," said Heather.

Warren rolled over. "Tell me the truth, Officer. What do you think of my shirt?"

"Shut up, Warren," said everybody else.

The Fish and Wildlife officers pulled the group members to their feet one by one and marched them out to an unmarked van. "Watch your head," said another officer as he pushed each kid into the van. When they were all secured, he locked them in and went back inside the rec center.

Through tiny slits in the blacked-out glass, the group watched the SWAT team gently walk the elephant outside and coax it into the back of a waiting truck. They worked with a minimum of words and practiced efficiency.

Two of the officers got into the truck with the elephant while the two others went to the van with the kids. A crowd of Carrwood residents was crowded around the rec center. By now, a security car drove up. One of the riot-geared officers went over, shook the cops' hands, and flashed his Fish and Wildlife ID. He explained the situation with the stolen elephant and the deluded group that had absconded with it. After a few minutes, Carrwood security cleared the street so the van and truck could drive away.

Officer Darrel Pratchett held up his arms trying to get everybody's attention. "Excuse me, folks. Can you all quiet down for a minute? Thank you. We want you to know that everything is fine now. You're all safe. What appears to have been a band of ecoterrorists was operating within our community, but they're being dealt with by the government. Please return to your homes. I'm sure we'll know more tomorrow. All of it will be reported in the community newsletter."

The residents all turned their heads in the direction of an approaching siren. A moment later, three vans screeched into the rec-center parking lot and men in riot gear and balaclavas leaped out, fanning around the building. Officer Pratchett approached them warily.

"Who the hell are you people?" he said.

A tall man at the center of the group flashed his credentials at him. "Department of Fish and Wildlife. We've been given information about an abducted animal on the premises."

"But you just took it," said Officer Pratchett.

"Who?"

"You. Department of Fish and Wildlife. You were just here."

The tall man leaned close to Officer Pratchett and sniffed.

"I'm sure you civilian officers are doing your best to protect your community, but just between you and me, have you been drinking?"

Morty was shouting gleefully at Coop over the phone from the truck with the elephant. "I swear to God, Coop, if you'd made that thing step on my hand, I was going to sue."

"Who? Who are you going to sue?" said Coop.

"The elephant. Who else?"

"Hush," said Giselle. "Those kids can hear you."

"Fuck 'em," said Sally, shouting through Morty's phone. "I say we dump them in the ocean and let them swim home."

"Remind me why I'm here again," said Phil Spectre in their heads.

"Because you deserted us when we could have used you back with Woolrich," said Coop. "Now, if we going down, you're going with us."

"I'm sad to see that after all these years of loyalty and, dare I say it, love, it's come to this."

"You're breaking my heart," said Coop.

"If you don't mind me saying so, you're some pretty weird cops," said Heather.

"What was the part about dumping us in the ocean?" said Tyler.

"Do it. Do it soon," said Dylan. "Before our parents get home."

They drove for an hour before pulling off onto a rural two-lane feeder road. Coop and Giselle pulled the kids out of the van and into the parking lot of an abandoned shopping center. Morty and Sally got out of the truck and came back to the group. Sally went through everyone's pockets, collecting their cell phones.

"Oh my God," said Linda. "They're going to execute us!"

"Calm down. No one is executing anyone," said Giselle.

Coop walked down the line and pulled out the saddest-looking kid.

"Oh God," said Brad.

"Hush," said Coop as he cut off Brad's zip tie. When he was done, he handed the little knife to Brad. "Once we're gone, you can do the others."

"Where are we?" said Sarah.

Coop pointed down the road in the opposite direction from where they'd come. "If you follow the road down for a couple of miles, you'll come to a crossroads. There's a gas station. I'm sure for enough cash, someone there will let you use the phone to call for a ride."

"We're going to report you assholes," said Sarah. "You're all going to jail."

"Maybe we'll be bunkmates," said Giselle. "Do you know the penalty for putting an endangered animal in peril?"

"Twenty-five years, pal," said Morty.

"Think about that before you get the cops involved," said Sally.

The four of them walked back to the vehicles.

"Is it really twenty-five years?" said Coop.

"How do I know? I never stole an elephant before," said Morty.

Giselle looked at the forlorn bunch by the side of the road. "They seem like nice kids. What's the name of their group? I'm going to send them some money when we get home."

After the truck and van drove away, Brad cut off everybody else's zip ties.

"Did anyone get their license-plate numbers?" said Tyler.

No one said anything.

"The guy said we should walk that way," said Heather. "Maybe we should get going."

"How do we know he was telling the truth?" said Linda.

"Why would he lie?" said Heather.

"Duh. He's the government."

Dylan scratched his chin. "So, your solution is that we should just stand here by the side of the road and hope a band of rescuers or maybe wandering minstrels happens by?"

"Let's take a vote," said Tyler. "All in favor of staying here and hoping for the best, raise their hands."

Linda got slaughtered.

"We're walking," said Tyler, and he started in the direction in which Coop had pointed them. The others followed.

"Now that we have a moment, can someone please tell me what's wrong with my shirts," said Warren.

Sarah stopped. "It looked like he was fucking the dog," she shouted. "That's what you made, Warren. A dog-fucking shirt. Are you proud of yourself?"

"Are you saying that I'm the only one here who fucks dogs?" said Warren.

Heather pointed at him. "You're out of the group! That's it. You're out of the group."

"Guys, I'm kidding," he said.

Linda shoved him into the driveway of the shopping center.

"Come on, everyone. Really, I'm kidding. I only fuck the deer in Griffith Park."

Tyler spun around. "Heather is right. You're out of the group."

They continued down the road. Warren trailed behind them.

"Should I have said chinchillas? Wildebeests? Lemurs? What about lemurs, guys?"

"Please shut up, Warren," said Brad quietly.

"Capybaras. Jackrabbits. Big-horn sheep. Stop me when I get in the right neighborhood. Wombats. Red pandas. Blue skinks . . ."

They drove another half hour to a disused hangar at what used to be a small private airport. Now it was just mostly where teens from the local agricultural college came to smoke weed and tag the place with Crips and Bloods signs hoping to scare off the high school kids. It didn't work. Planes still occasionally used the airport's single overgrown runway, but never with lights and seldom with anything inside that wasn't banned by the DEA, frowned on by the FBI, and/or wanted by The Hague.

Inside the hangar, Coop and the others took off their riot gear and changed into their regular clothes. They led the elephant down from the truck and into the middle of the huge, empty expanse.

Coop gave the elephant a couple of pats on the head. It draped its trunk over his shoulder. "So long, pal. You caused us a lot of trouble, but none of it was your fault."

"That's nice," said Giselle. "You two look so sweet together."

"I still don't want a cat," Coop said.

"You're being spooky again."

He moved the group back to the hangar's open doorway and pulled the Tweak box from his duffel.

"I hope you're better at that thing than last time," said Sally.

"Practice makes perfect," Coop said.

"Just don't turn it into a dinosaur," said Morty. "I have a thing about dinosaurs."

"How can you have a thing about dinosaurs?" said Giselle. "They don't even exist anymore."

"I just do. There was a traumatic incident with my cousin's triceratops. Tempers were displayed. Tears were shed. Dinosaurs were banned from all family gatherings."

"Do you make up these stories or did you grow up in the circus?" said Sally. "Coop, you knew this guy when he was a kid. Did half the stuff he talks about happen?"

"I don't remember," Coop said. "I got amnesia. It's a lot like Morty's uncle Ned. Tell them about your uncle Ned, Morty."

Giselle pointed at Morty. "You, not a word." She pointed to

Coop. "You, make the machine work so we can get out of here."

"She's right, Coop. I can tell you all about Uncle Ned on the ride back," said Morty.

Coop played with the wheels, buttons, and toggles on the Tweak box. A mist formed around the elephant. Soon it thickened and began to expand.

"Wow," said Giselle. "I know you told me how it worked, but I'm not sure I believed it. Now, wow."

The mist became a fog and the fog filled the hangar. Finally, a green light glowed on the controller and Coop powered it off. In the gentle breeze that came across the empty airport, the fog trailed away, revealing a Disneyland castle with four large wings.

"I'm with Giselle on this one," said Morty. "Wow."

"Yeah, it's impressive. Okay, Phil, this is the other reason you're here. You're going to get us through the ghost lock on this thing and help me past any curses or traps inside."

"Once again, I'll point out that I don't need to be here. This far from its source of power, chances are that any curses or enchantments are going to be null and void."

"What about regular traps?"

"I'm guessing it will be same with those, but why listen to me?"

"I still need you for the ghost lock."

"I could have talked you through that on the phone."

"If you'd stop whining, we'd be in there and done already," said Sally.

"Fine. Don't listen to me. I'm the expert, but apparently my opinion doesn't count."

"Not right now," said Morty.

"Just do your job, Phil," said Giselle. "Some of us have cats to feed."

"What?" said Coop.

"Just kidding, dear."

Even with Phil's help, it took Coop nearly an hour to work through the fiendishly intricate ghost lock. However, when they were through it, the library door swung open wide. No ghosts, Domovois, Pontianaks, Jersey Mothmen, or Himalayan yetis came running out.

As Phil pointed out, when the library was disconnected from its power source, there was no electricity inside and no lights. Coop and Phil went in first. They triggered a couple of barely functional killing curses, one by the painting wing and the other by the sculptures, but they were so feeble without power that they did nothing to Coop and at best would have just given the rest of the group a little indigestion. After twenty minutes inside, he went back to the front door.

"Grab your flashlights and have a look around. Phil and I are going on a book hunt."

"Lucky me. Whee," said Phil. "Remind me again what we're looking for."

"An old cookbook," said Coop.

"That's right. *Granny Smith's Unnatural Fondues and Flans.*"

"*Enigmatic Confections: An Entirely Unsinister Guide to Puddings, Cookies, Cakes, and Not-at-All the Dark Arts.*"

"Very clever. I've had migraines that were more subtle than that."

"You *are* a migraine, Phil."

"Now that we're alone, would you like to explore your commitment issues, man-to-man?"

"I don't have any commitment issues. Giselle and I are just fine."

"Are you sure?"

"Yes."

"Really?"

"Shut up, Phil."

"How's your sex life? I heard something about *Star Wars* underwear?"

"Now definitely shut up."

"I'm going to write that down in my notes. Very defensive when sex or *Star Wars* comes up. Based on my diagnosis, I'd advise you against a career in the space program."

When they finally reached the antique cookbooks, Coop played his flashlight over the shelves.

"What was that title again? *Perplexing Soufflés and Raising the Dead?*"

"*Enigmatic Confections,*" said Coop.

"I remember now. *Puzzling Cupcakes and Voodoo Tarts.*"

"Yes. That's it exactly. You look for that and keep quiet."

"Winner buys the first round of drinks," said Phil.

"You don't drink. You're dead."

"I'm going to have to add that to your notes, too. Defensive about drinking habit. Based on this further examination, I'll have to advise you against a career in catering, bartending, bootlegging, and alcoholism."

"Alcoholism isn't a career."

"Of course it is. Most people just don't do it right."

"Found it," said Coop. He grabbed a book from the shelves.

"Are you sure? I'm pretty sure it's *Cryptic Cobbler and the Funky Bunch.*"

"We're done. I'm leaving."

"All right, team," Phil said. "Good effort. Let's everyone hit the showers."

"Thanks for your usual high-level help," said Coop.

"Always glad to be aboard one of your little Voyages of the Damned. But I'm afraid I'm going to have to charge you for my psychiatric services."

"Send the bill to Woolrich. He's the one who made me this way."

"Listen to yourself. If self-delusion was an Olympic sport, you'd be Jesse Owens, Mark Spitz, and Yevgeniya Kanayeva combined."

"Who's that last one?" said Coop.

"Yevgeniya Kanayeva. She took the gold in Rhythmic Gymnastics in 2012."

"Rhythmic Gymnastics. I should have remembered."

"Patient also has a pathological fear of sports, the human body, and confrontation. Recommend immediate nude tetherball therapy."

Coop walked out of the library with the book under his arm. Sally was already busy loading paintings and a couple of big books into the back of the van.

"Did you find any Caravaggios?" he said.

She held up a painting of a bloody Medusa head.

"That's your fetish?"

"This one is big money," said Sally. "The personal ones are already in the back of the van, and if you look at them, I will nuke this place from orbit."

"I understand completely."

"I have a few more piles inside. Are you going to help me carry stuff or are you and Phil going to stand around looking goofy?"

"I'll be inside in a minute. I have to make a call."

Coop dialed Donna's number and told her how to get to the airport. She sounded a little funny on the phone.

"Let's just keep this between you and me for now, okay?" she said.

"What do you mean?"

"I mean . . ."

Through the phone, he heard the Sheriff in the background.

"Is that Coop? Does he have our stuff?"

He heard Donna sigh. "Yes, sugar. I have the directions right here."

"Good night, Donna," said Coop. "And good luck with whatever you're cooking up."

He thumbed off the phone and put it away. Giselle took the book from under his arm and looked through it.

"It's kind of pretty," she said.

"I haven't even opened it yet."

She closed the book and handed it back to him. "Are you really going to give it to Woolrich?"

"That was the deal. Besides, we're going to keep him happy so he'll let us slide for borrowing all this equipment."

"But you worked so hard for it."

"He can have the damned book. But not until I scan the whole thing."

Giselle patted his cheek. "That's my smart boy."

"A little help over here?" said Morty. He was buckling under the weight of all the books and paintings Sally was piling in his arms.

Coop put the cookbook in the van and then he and Giselle went over to help carry some of the loot. He couldn't help feeling a certain sense of contentment.

Just like old times.

37

Coop sat in Woolrich's office with his duffel in his lap. As usual, Woolrich was behind his desk finishing paperwork. Coop counted the heads on the wall. He got to twenty before he noticed a blank spot.

When Woolrich looked up, he turned to where Coop was staring. "Ah. You noticed it."

"Was that blank spot always there?" Coop said.

"Not until recently. I'm just making room for some fresh additions."

Coop didn't like the sound of that. "Anyone I know?" he said casually.

Woolrich put the cap back on his pen. "The DOPS is a big organization. At any one time, there are a number of candidates for the wall. And there's always room to move something old off and add something new, if you get my drift."

Coop looked for more blank spots while trying not to sweat. "I guess everyone needs a hobby."

"You seem to be becoming mine. I'm sure you can imagine how much I enjoy that. Now, do you have something for me?"

From the duffel, Coop pulled the cookbook. He had to get up

to hand it to Woolrich. His boss thumbed through it, looking delighted.

"Thank you. We've wanted this for a long time."

"I'm glad I could be of help."

Woolrich slammed the book shut and put it on a side table.

"I assume you've returned all of the equipment you borrowed?"

"Every bit of it," lied Coop.

"Good," said Woolrich. "Then I have something that I'm sure will make you happy. We have your mummy."

"Harkhuf? You have him here?"

Woolrich pointed to the floor. "Right downstairs. He showed up at the museum unexpectedly, and when they transferred him to their warehouse, we just helped ourselves. Thaumaturgic antiquities is quite excited to have him for their collection."

Coop stared at the heads. "I don't know what to say."

"'Thank you' would be a good start. You can follow that with 'yippee, my troubles are over thanks to the diligent work of the DOPS.'"

"Yippee," said Coop as cheerlessly as he felt. Was this another scam or did they really have Harkhuf? It probably wouldn't be a good idea to get into another game of tag with Buehlman and Carter. There had to be some other way to find out.

Coop said, "I guess that means I'll be getting some assignments with less chance of locusts and boils?"

"Not right away," said Woolrich. He steeped his fingers.

Uh-oh.

"While your little vacation is over, you won't be coming back to work for a while. For your recent escapades—unauthorized use of equipment and our elephant friend—you're suspended for two weeks without pay."

Coop waited for the part where Woolrich told him how soon he was going to end up on the wall. When Woolrich didn't give him a date, he said, "That's it?"

Woolrich clasped his hands. "Do you want me to say the usual? Be good or you'll go back to prison and all the rest of it? It never seems to do any good."

"Yeah. Sorry about that," said Coop, still not sure what the hell was going on. Except that he was getting more time off. That was a nice perk. He got up. "Okay. I'll see you in a couple of weeks, then. Should I go?"

Woolrich picked up his pen. "Please do."

Coop picked up his duffel and headed for the door.

"And, Cooper," called Woolrich.

"Yes?"

"If you go running off on your own again, I really will send you back."

"I know."

Giselle was waiting outside in the hall. "How did it go?" she said.

"I'm not going to jail."

"See. I told you."

"And I get two more weeks off."

"That's great."

"Without pay."

"That's not so great. But still, no jail."

"Woolrich says the corpse grinders downstairs have Harkhuf. Do you know how I could find out if that's true?"

They walked to the elevator. Coop was a little light-headed. He told himself it was from the hole in his head, but he couldn't stop picturing the blank spot on Woolrich's wall.

"Maybe Bayliss can find out," said Giselle.

"How is she?"

"She's fine now. She heard about the Auditors and was worried about you."

Coop pushed the elevator button. "Don't tell her about the hole in my head."

"I won't have to. Those bastards didn't exactly give you a professional trim. You're going to have to let your hair grow out for a while."

"I have two weeks to work on a comb-over."

"I'll tell Morty. He'll be relieved."

They got on the elevator and Giselle pushed the button for the garage.

"Maybe this is over now and things will get back to normal."

"Maybe," said Coop.

"You don't sound convinced."

Coop shook his head. "I can't help thinking there's more to this than we know about."

"Relax. Let's just assume Woolrich was telling the truth. That means Harkhuf and Shemetet are locked up tight. Problem solved."

"Harkhuf got out once before."

"I'm sure between the physics and witching departments, they've come up with something foolproof."

Coop smiled. "You're probably right."

"I mean, there's no way he could escape twice, right?"

"No way."

When they reached the garage level, Giselle gave him a quick kiss and got back in the elevator. "I'll see you at home later. Let's go out to dinner to celebrate. Something fancy."

"Sounds good," said Coop. "But you're paying—I'm a little tapped for the next few weeks."

"I'll trade you dinner for a cat," she said, smiling.

"We'll eat at home."

"Killjoy."

As he walked through the garage to the car, when he saw things moving in the shadows, he could tell himself it was just a trick of the light. Still, he didn't hang around any longer than he had to. With Harkhuf out of the picture, he only had one thing to worry about. Was his future going to be jail or the blank spot on Woolrich's wall? Even if there weren't things in the shadows anymore, something was going to go wrong.

Just because overhead lights are inanimate objects that can't feel fear or confusion, it doesn't mean that they can't appear to be having a nervous breakdown. And, in truth, who really knows what lights feel? There are no studies in which anyone has interviewed incandescent or fluorescent bulbs—or even an LED—to get their take on the state of their being. Maybe when lights flick on and off, they're trying to tell us something like, *Look at me. I have feelings, too*. Or *Please stop playing with the light switch, you're giving me a headache*. But while the subject of "Do Lightbulbs Have Feelings?" can be debated—most often by liberal-arts freshmen trying Ecstasy for the first time—what can't be debated is the effect that endlessly flickering lights have on humans. They can be terrifying. They can be confusing. And they can make it hard to read the want ads in a newspaper when you're afraid to look at them on your office computer.

Vargas and Zulawski were experiencing all three of these effects in the bowels of the ECIU. The mice had gnawed through the walls and were eating the power cables. Zulawski's computer lay in a heap on the floor, the cords and most of the circuit boards having been devoured in one night of vigorous mouse snacking.

Zulawski was perched in his office chair with his back to the wall staring at his wrecked work space. He was disguised as a Parisian mime, right down to the white face. "Your idea of putting the parcel in Mad Prince Nestor's box hasn't resolved the situation. If anything, it's made it worse."

Vargas was busy banging on his dead computer keyboard, refusing to accept that his machine was next on the menu at *Chez Souris*. His disguise was the helmet and leather jerkin of a Mongol warrior. "Are you blaming me for the situation?" he said.

"Situation? Let's call it what it is: a calamity," said Zulawski.

Vargas picked up his phone. It was dead, too. "Why hasn't anyone come down?"

"No one is coming down" said Zulawski. "Get that through your head."

Vargas looked around. Bloated, red-eyed rodents with ears on their backs were at home on almost every horizontal surface. "But the mice. Surely someone has noticed the mice."

"No one has noticed the mice because they're all in here. They want to be close to the parcel."

Vargas slammed his hand down on his desk, startling a couple of mice long enough that they stopped eating his modem for a moment. Then they got back to work.

"Stop calling it the parcel," he said. "It's time to call it by its real name."

Zulawski held up a hand. "Don't you dare say it. It's bad luck."

"How much worse can our luck get?" said Vargas. He plucked at his costume. "It's not like we have our dignity left."

"At least the mice aren't eating *us* yet."

"Exactly. *Yet.*"

"If you say it, I'm leaving," said Zulawski.

"Fine. Go."

"I'm afraid to go by myself."

"Of course you are. That's why we have to confront the evil head-on."

"All right," said Zulawski. He put his hands over his ears. "Do it."

"It's time we said your real name, you monster. *Mysteriis Ex Mortuis.*"

Zulawski opened his eyes. "We're still here."

"See? It wasn't as bad as all that. Now don't you feel a little better?"

"Yes. I do a little," said Zulawski. "*Mysteriis Ex Mortuis,*" he intoned in a deep basso voice.

"All right. Let's not get carried away," said Vargas, waving a hand at him. "And speaking of getting carried away, have you found your squid?"

Zulawski glanced back into the dim recesses of the storeroom. "I caught a glimpse of it between Orpheus's lyre and the demon Girl Scout cookies."

"The ones that taste like Hitler's mustache?"

"The same."

"Who thinks of something so awful?" said Vargas

"Demons, obviously."

"Of course."

"Anyway, the squid is now larger than I'm comfortable wrestling with. It was eating a garden gnome."

"One of the little ones that wake up and dance at night?"

"Yes."

"Poor thing."

"Better it than us," said Zulawski. He handed Vargas a ragged piece of translucent plastic. "I found this, too."

"What is it?"

"The remains of your Tupperware dish."

"Thank you," said Vargas. He opened a drawer and tossed in the plastic wad. A mouse popped its head out, caught the dish, and began snacking on it. Vargas quietly closed the drawer. "I also couldn't help noticing that the squid demolished your desk while escaping."

"Do you think management will blame me for that?" said Zulawski.

"I think if you show them the squid, they'll understand who the real culprit is."

A particularly large mouse stopped directly in front of Zulawski. Zulawski reached down carefully and found an as-yet-intact jar of aspirin that used to be in his top drawer. He tossed it over the mouse's head and it scampered after it down one of the aisles. He and Vargas could hear it ripping the jar apart with its teeth.

"To sum up," Zulawski said. "The mice have taken over the office. The squid has moved on from canned chili and is now hunting live meat. At least one of the dingoes has escaped the mirror. Oh, and the mole people seem to have acquired a large cache of axes and clubs. Do you know anything about that?"

Vargas nodded as two mice worked in tandem to drag his keyboard off the desk.

"I think we can lay that at the feet of the taxidermy fairies."

"But they're dead. And they're stuffed."

"Yes, that is the definition of taxidermy," said Vargas. "But it's never stopped them from making mischief before."

From the dark came a crack and the sound of twisting metal. Something huge collapsed at the far end of the storeroom.

"I'm going to propose something radical," said Zulawski.

"Please do," said Vargas.

"We leave. We lock the doors and walk away."

Vargas stared at him. "Desert our post? What will our superiors say?"

"What superiors?" said Zulawski. "No one knows we're down here. We're on our own. Robinson Crusoe without a Friday. Jane without a Tarzan. We're the lost crew of the *Flying Dutchman*."

Vargas whispered, "But what about the parcel?"

"The what?" said Zulawski.

Vargas made a face at him. "The *Mysteriis Ex Mortuis*. What do we do with it?"

"We abandon it the way everyone has abandoned us."

"I don't know. We took an oath."

From a high shelf, something—many things, in fact—growled at them.

"The other dingoes have escaped!" cried Zulawski.

Something that made a sloshing, dragging sound emerged from the dark.

"The squid!" yelled Vargas.

Zulawski looked at him. "Desertion, then?"

"Desertion indeed."

All the lights went out in the ECIU.

"Run!" shouted Zulawski.

They barely made it out. Things growled and pounded on the door as they locked it. They both backed away, trying to make as little noise as possible.

"Do you think the door will hold?" whispered Zulawski.

"For a while," said Vargas.

"Long enough for us to get to the elevator?"

"I'm sure."

"Still. We should run."

"I agree."

So they ran. The mime and the Mongol made it to the elevator intact and rode it to safety. They shook hands in the garage, pledging to meet again in a week to talk things over. Neither of them had any intention of going to the meeting.

However, six months later, Vargas used the money from an insurance settlement with the DOPS to open a supernatural book and curio shop in L.A.'s Fairfax district. When he advertised for an experienced assistant to help run the place, there was only one applicant: Zulawski, who was as shocked to see Vargas as Vargas was to see him. They ran the shop together for another thirty years with the understanding that, one, they would never speak of the DOPS and, two, everything in the shop that wasn't them would be completely, one hundred percent, entirely, and irrevocably dead.

Dr. Buehlman and Dr. Carter examined their newest acquisition in a lead-lined chamber riveted together with cold steel bolts.

The lead had been blessed by the pope and the bolts had been made by a sect of virgin blacksmith nuns in an almost unreachable chapel high in the Ural Mountains. The transparent panels in the walls that let outsiders observe their work were a thermoplastic composite not designed by earthly scientists. It could withstand a direct hit from a small tactical nuclear bomb. The door lock was one solid piece of molydarium alloy, harder than diamond and more heat resistant than the shielding on NASA rockets. In short, this was not a room to be fucked with.

"This has been a long time coming," said Dr. Buehlman.

"Indeed it has," said Dr. Carter. "I was just hoping to see Harkhuf on exhibit. I didn't dare dream that we'd actually get to examine him."

"I wonder if now that we have him, the curse will be lifted off Mr. Cooper."

Dr. Carter picked up a scalpel and frowned. "In retrospect, I'm not sure I buy the man's story at all. I've asked around about him. He sounds like an unsavory character."

"Is he? He seemed quite nice when I spoke to him," said Dr. Buehlman.

Dr. Carter chuckled. "That was from a bit of a distance, as I recall. Even a volcano is pretty if you're far enough away, but I wouldn't want to shake hands with one."

Dr. Buehlman gave him a smile. "I see your point. Shall we get to work?"

"Yes. Let's," said Dr. Carter. "I'm going to scrape some detritus from the linen on the chest area. Do you have a sample dish ready?"

"Ready. And when you're done, I'll do the arms."

"Perfect. Here we go," said Dr. Carter. "Harkhuf, welcome to the twenty-first century." He placed his scalpel over the mummy's heart. There was an electrical spark and a small explosion. Blue lightning shot from Harkhuf's body, arcing to the iron bolts in the walls. Dr. Carter was knocked across the chamber. His flight took him directly into the path of Dr. Buehlman. They both crashed to the floor.

When their heads cleared, they looked up to see a strange sight. It almost looked as if the mummy was moving its arms, trying to push itself upright. The doctors climbed to their feet and watched in amazement as it dawned on them that Harkhuf's movements weren't the effect of a concussion or blurred vision. The dead man had pushed himself into a sitting position and was slowly stepping down onto the floor of the chamber. When he was fully upright, Harkhuf took in the room and was pleased with what he found.

"The witches' spell was sound. They shall be rewarded."

Drs. Buehlman and Carter looked at each other.

"Do you hear him?" said Dr. Buehlman.

"Yes. In my head," said Dr. Carter.

"Me, too."

Harkhuf looked them up and down as if just noticing them. He raised a hand and said, "Be my thrall."

Dr. Buehlman blinked. Dr. Carter shook his head.

"Yes, Master," said Dr. Buehlman.

Dr. Carter looked at her. "Dr. Buehlman. Are you all right?"

Harkhuf pushed Dr. Carter aside and spoke to Dr. Buehlman. "You care for the dead, thrall?"

She nodded. "Care for, examine, and catalog."

Harkhuf held his head aloft. "I sense a presence. You have my beloved here, my Shemetet."

"Yes. We have her," said Dr. Buehlman.

"What are you doing?" said Dr. Carter. "Why are you listening to this monstrosity?"

"Bring her to me, cur," said Harkhuf.

"Yes, Master." Dr. Buehlman went to the impenetrable door and put the palm of her hand on the scanner.

"No. We can't let him out!" shouted Dr. Carter. He rushed the mummy and stabbed his scalpel deep into Harkhuf's desiccated heart.

"Ah. You are resistant," said Harkhuf, pulling out the scalpel. "I have seen your kind before. There is but one cure for you." He plunged the scalpel into Dr. Carter's chest. He was dead before he hit the floor.

During the struggle, the scanner had finished verifying Dr. Buehlman's handprint. The enormous lock thudded back and she held the door open for her new master.

A dozen members of thaumaturgic antiquities returned from a group lunch. What greeted them was a glassy-eyed Dr. Buehlman and a resurrected mummy with fresh blood splattered on his dirty linens. Not surprisingly, they found this alarming. Even as some of them began to scream and others to run away, Harkhuf raised his hand.

"Be my thralls," he said. As one, the staff stood together quietly and said, "Yes, Master."

Harkhuf looked at Dr. Buehlman. "You, remain by my side." To the staff he said, "Find Shemetet. Bring her to me. I will give her new life and together we will make this world kneel."

As the staff filed out to do their master's bidding Harkhuf said to Dr. Buehlman, "Tell me, dog. I hear that this place holds dark magic and vicious creatures. What abominations are imprisoned nearby?"

Dr. Buehlman said, "There are remnants of the robot uprising of '98. In the Unfathomable Evil Unit there are . . . well, unfathomable evils. Malignant spirits and various unstable monstrosities. It's not imprisoned, but there's also Ping-Pong next door."

"What sort of a creature is a Ping-Pong?"

Dr. Buehlman held up her fingers about an inch apart. "It's a little plastic ball—"

"Is it mad? Will it kill without mercy or warning?"

"I suppose you could hurt someone's eye with it."

"Then I will have this Ping-Pong for my army," said Harkhuf. "Come now. Let us release the other beings you spoke of. We will create the little chaos before ushering in the great one that will sweep this world away."

With Harkhuf's ancient power—and Dr. Buehlman's pass codes—they spent the next hour breaking into each chamber and releasing unspeakable horrors into the whole wing of the building. Alarms sounded. Lights strobed. All of the doors into and out of L Wing slammed shut.

Harkhuf looked at the monstrosities rampaging through the building and was satisfied. "This will keep the mortal fools at bay long enough so that I might complete my work."

"Yes, Master. What excellent carnage you have wrought."

"Thank you, slave."

"What superb havoc."

"That, too."

"What glorious decimation."

"That's enough for now, dog."

"Yes, Master. But really, good job."

"All right," said Harkhuf. "Now I have need of an arcane text. Without it, I cannot resurrect my beloved. Where would I find such a thing?"

"I'm not sure," said Dr. Buehlman. "A rare and dangerous occult text? There's a place where they keep things like that. It's been so long since I thought about it I've forgotten. What is it called? Super-Secret Enigma Department?"

"Think, dog."

"Double Mystic Mystery Division? It's somewhere downstairs. I'm sure the name will come to me."

"I have no time for your lollygagging. All who are not useful to me will suffer eternal torment."

"And those who serve you well?"

"More like eternal discomfort."

That sounded slightly better, so Buehlman said, "I can look in the DOPS directory. It's just this way."

Dr. Buehlman led Harkhuf into her office. She sat down at her desk and tapped the space bar to wake the computer.

Harkhuf pointed at the screen. "Stop, slave. This is not a television, is it?"

"No, Master. It's a computer. I use it to research information."

Harkhuf came around the desk and looked at the screen. "On this computer, there are no hamburger girls to distract you?"

"I don't know what a hamburger girl is, O great one."

Harkhuf went back around to the side of the desk. "Search, thrall. But be warned. If I see a single hamburger, your suffering will be . . ."

"Eternal, Master? You told me that already. I'm not criticizing, but you seem to be in a rush, so I'm trying to streamline the process."

"Very good, thrall. Continue."

After Dr. Buehlman had been typing for a few minutes, Harkhuf moved back around her. "When we are done with your search, you will then explain to me the allurements of a rolled-up newspaper. My other thrall simply will not stop talking about it."

"I'm afraid I don't know anything about that."

"Curses," said Harkhuf. "Continue your search, then."

"Yes, Master."

Nelson sat alone and glum in his office, boxes piled around him. He just couldn't come up with the right item to finally nail Coop. He just might have to use Death's photo after all, but he'd grown fond of having it around. It was a reminder of happier, more alive times. Ones he was determined to return to.

McCloud came in with a box in his metallic hands, knocked

over a pile of boxes that Nelson had just finished sorting, twisted, and landed on the desk.

"Sorry, boss," he said, scrambling to his feet.

"It's my fault for existing in the same space-time continuum as you," said Nelson.

McCloud held out the box. "Here's that package you asked about."

"What package? I didn't ask about any package."

McCloud took the box back. "Not this particular package, no, you didn't. But other packages, yes, you did."

"And what were those?"

"Those what?"

"What are those other packages?" Nelson said slowly and evenly.

"Sorry. I got lost there for a minute."

Nelson went back to sorting through boxes. "I just might have to demote you back down to birdbrain."

"Please, please don't," McCloud. "I really like being a mammal. I don't want to lay eggs and fly. Flying always makes me nauseous. Plus, beaks are kind of gross and my face is funny-looking enough right now."

"Fine. You get to stay a mammal. But you're demoted from ferret. You're a guinea-pig brain now."

"Thanks, boss!"

"Now tell me what package you're talking about."

"The package? The package. Right. You wanted anything that came through with a security code on it. This one is for ECIU, Double-ultra-security."

Nelson held out his hands and McCloud gave him the box. "You should have given it to me right away."

"Given you what?"

Nelson stopped opening the box and studied McCloud.

"Maybe it's keeping you hypnotized all the time that's the problem. It could be that your circuits are burning out."

"I'm hypnotized?"

"Isn't it fun?" said Nelson.

"It's swell," said McCloud happily. A moment later, he frowned. "So my circuits are burning out—is that a bad thing?"

"Burning out parts of your brain is never a good thing and the fact you'd ask that means I was right."

"Can you fix it?"

"I can think of a couple of solutions," Nelson mumbled.

"Will they hurt?"

"Undoubtedly. Just a minute."

Nelson got the box open and took out a battered old book. *Enigmatic Confections: An Entirely Unsinister Guide to Puddings, Cookies, Cakes, and Not-at-All the Dark Arts.*"

"That sounds nice. Now I'm hungry."

"Interesting," said Nelson. "It's trying to pass itself off as a cookbook, but you're not that at all, are you, gorgeous?"

"Is it something good, boss?" said McCloud.

Nelson flipped pages slowly, studying each one. "There's some powerful-looking stuff in here. Well, this is interesting. A whole section of resurrection spells. My, my. Tell me, birdbrain—"

"Mammal brain."

"Guinea-pig brain. How would you like to be alive again?"

"I don't know. Is that better than this?" said McCloud. "I mean I'm pretty happy right where I am working here with you."

"And that's another clue to the state of your brain. I'll have to remember this for the future. Brains need a day off from mesmeric groveling."

"Does that mean I get more vacation to go with my promotion?"

"It just might," said Nelson as he continued perusing the book. In the silence, McCloud became uncomfortable. He wouldn't have minded playing with some of the stuff he saw in the boxes, but he had a feeling that wasn't allowed.

"Have you heard about the commotion upstairs in L Wing?" he said. "I guess that new mummy got out. It sounds like all heck is breaking loose."

Nelson looked up. "Did you just say 'heck'?"

"Yes. Sorry if that was too salty. I'll clean up my act."

"Say 'hell.'"

"*H, E,* double hockey sticks," said McCloud.

"Much better," said Nelson. "And yes, I've heard about it, and yes, with this little beauty and the amulet, I just might join in the fun."

"It sounds dangerous, boss. I wouldn't want to see you get hurt."

"Sometimes you have to take a big chance for a big payoff. Roll the bones, as they say in Vegas."

"That sounds like fun. I'd like to go there someday."

"Maybe in your next lifetime."

McCloud gave him a thumbs-up. "It's a date."

Nelson grabbed the amulet from a box behind the filing cabinet and put it into his pocket. "I'm heading upstairs to see the show," he said.

"It's dangerous out there. I should probably come with you."

"No, I have something more important for you. Let's get you started on that vacation."

"Oh, boy. Where am I going?" said McCloud.

"I don't know. New York? Hawaii? Paris? Or you could jump into the shredder."

McCloud cocked his head to the side. "Didn't I do that last one once before?"

"That's not how I remember it."

"I think I'd rather go to Paris."

"Super," said Nelson. "How much do you have to spend on a plane ticket?"

"Nothing. Remember how you said I'm not very good with money these days, so I should give all of mine to you to take care of?"

Nelson's lip curled. "You remember that, do you? The one thing I was hoping you'd forget. Well, I'm afraid you don't have enough to go to Paris."

"Darn."

"Or New York or Hawaii."

"*H, E,* double hockey sticks."

"Let's see, there was one more choice on the list. What was it?"

"The shredder. I should jump in the shredder," said McCloud.

"Well, if it's your idea, it sounds great. Why don't you wait until I'm gone and do just that?" said Nelson.

"Are you sure? It's awfully loud."

"So is New York."

"I guess if it's all I can afford."

"Trust me. It is."

McCloud said, "Will I see you there, boss?"

"In the shredder?"

"Yes."

"Not this trip. This one is all about you. Have a great time," said Nelson.

"I'm sure I will. Thanks a lot for the time off."

"Remember. Wait until I'm gone. We wouldn't want the others who aren't going on vacation to get jealous."

"Will do, boss," said McCloud. "I'll send you a postcard."

"I doubt it, but thanks for the thought."

38

Coop was watching *Thunderball* on the sofa with a glass of bourbon and a plate of Fatburger chili cheese fries on the coffee table. When his phone rang and he saw that it was Woolrich calling, he considered letting it ring through to voice mail. On television, Sean Connery was soaring above France in a jet pack. *I bet they have jet packs at the DOPS. I wonder what the chances are of me ever getting my hands on one?*

Deciding that the odds of his ever getting close to a jet pack were better if he didn't piss off his boss any more than he already had, he answered the phone. Naturally, he regretted it the moment he heard Woolrich's voice.

"Cooper, you need to come back in immediately."

"I'm watching James Bond. *And* I'm suspended."

"To hell with the suspension. You're back on salary. Now get to the office at once," barked Woolrich.

With a deep sense that he'd already ruined his life simply by answering the phone, Coop decided to dig deeper and find out exactly what flavor his doom was coming in this time.

"I'll come in under one condition. You tell me what's going on."

"It's the mummy. Harkhuf. The damned thing is running amok in L Wing."

"Wait. Is this a rerun? I thought Harkhuf already ran amok and you'd fixed it so he wouldn't do it again."

"We thought we had fixed it, but we missed something. He seems to have mesmerized the entire human staff down there. The ones still alive. It's bedlam. Sheer, bloody bedlam."

"Okay," said Coop slowly. "What does bedlam have to do with me? I'm a thief. I'm the opposite of bedlam. We thieves are quiet as mice."

"Cooper, you just stole multiple vehicles, an elephant, a building, you kidnapped a group of ecoterrorists—"

"That's kind of a harsh description of the kids."

"You traumatized the citizens of Carrwood—"

"And that's a harsh description of me."

"And you may have permanently damaged our relationship with the Department of Fish and Wildlife. Oh, and I suspect that you took rather more Egyptian artifacts from the museum than you were told to. So, don't tell me what a fragile butterfly you are. You're a menace, and a loud one, which is exactly what we need, so get back here immediately."

By now, Coop was sitting up flipping through the news channels trying to see if the situation was so out of control that it was on television. To his relief, it wasn't. This made him feel just the slightest bit better. Not a lot, but it was up from suicidal.

"What is it exactly that you want me to do if—and that's a big if—I come in?"

"You're the only member of staff immune to dark magic and L Wing is full of it right now. We need you to go inside and handle the situation."

Coop got up and checked for blacked-out vans in the street. He turned off the television. He put the chili cheese fries in the refrigerator, the sure sign of a troubled mind since chili cheese fries—once cold—can't be resuscitated by even the most brutal microwave oven.

"You're asking me to capture the guy who wants to make my skin into a loofah? No thanks," said Coop.

"You don't have to capture anyone," said Woolrich. "We just need you to go and open the door from the other side. Our security team will take Harkhuf down."

"You've already had two chances to do that and you've blown both of them. You know that he's going to try and find Shemetet, right?"

Woolrich's tone shifted. "How do you know about that?"

"Let's say Wikipedia and leave it at that."

"For the moment."

"What about the blank space on your wall?"

"I went hunting with the ambassador of interdimensional spiders. The space is for a Metaluna fly, you idiot."

"You hunt giant flies?" said Coop.

"Giant spiders do. It was a diplomatic mission and I was being polite."

"How do I know you're telling the truth?"

"Because you're too valuable to put on the damned wall," said Woolrich. "At worst, I might send you to back to prison, where you'll be safe."

"Then you can yank me out and put me back whenever you want."

"That's a crude, but not entirely inaccurate way of putting it."

"Forget it," said Coop. "I'll stay on suspension."

"What if we amend your contract?" said Woolrich, his voice going softer. "We'll make you a full DOPS agent. Think of it. No prison hanging over your head. A pension. But you have to promise to behave yourself."

"You didn't hire me to behave myself."

"Just within reason, then. Behave yourself within reason. No more magic elephants, for example."

As much as he didn't trust Woolrich, Coop liked the sound of a no-prison future. He looked outside again. There were still no blacked-out vans coming to drag him away. He couldn't decide if that was a sign of good faith or of negligence. "Okay, but I want to see the paperwork before I go in."

"I can arrange that," said Woolrich.

"And I want Phil to go with me."

"It would be a pleasure if you took him. He's decided he's Carl Jung and is driving everyone crazy with his mad diagnoses."

"He told me I have intimacy issues and need to play nude tetherball. How about you?"

"I'm an autocratically abstruse narcissist who needs to take up Greco-Roman wrestling."

Coop watched the street. "I think psychiatry is Phil just trying to see how many people he can talk into doing something stupid with no clothes on."

"That might explain the crew in cyborg repair."

Coop grabbed his jacket. "You get the paperwork ready and I'll be right over," he said.

"Hurry. The situation is dire."

"You know, I wouldn't have to worry about stoplights if I had my own jet pack."

Woolrich's voice was muffled as he said something to someone else. All Coop could hear was "What?" and "Fiendish." A second later, Woolrich was back on the line.

"Cooper?"

"Yes?"

"I wouldn't give you a jet pack if Lucifer himself were crawling up my colon covered in lemon juice and razor blades."

"I'll take that as a maybe. Remember to have the paperwork ready."

Oh, crap. What did I just sign up for?

Instead of trying to remember the whole conversation, he just ran over the key words as he looked for the car keys.

Bedlam.

Bloody bedlam.

Running amok.

A rather breathy "What?" and an exclaimed "Fiendish." Was there a "hell on earth" in there somewhere, too? He was pretty sure he'd heard "hell on earth," he just wasn't sure if it was in relation to the situation at DOPS headquarters or what would happen to him if he didn't come in.

On his way out, Coop took off the necklace Minerva had given him and tossed it into the trash. Halfway down the stairs, he turned around, went back, and put the necklace back on.

Who knows? Maybe it would work on something running wild in L Wing. And if it didn't, he knew there was a good chance that something running amok would eat him. At least he hoped so. The last thing he wanted was for someone to find the damned necklace on his lifeless body and bury him with it. Spending all eternity looking like Jerry Garcia was Coop's definition of hell.

It wasn't so much an escort waiting for him at DOPS headquarters as it was a band of wild marauders who had decided to kidnap him like a fairy-tale princess. The moment he was out of his car, enormous men and women in black suits with guns under their coats grabbed each of his arms, not hustling him through the building so much as dragging him. Coop didn't want to be dragged, but he couldn't quite get into sync with their gait, which seemed to hover somewhere between a buffalo stampede and an out-of-control monster truck.

People pressed themselves against walls when they saw them coming. The ones too proud or too slow to get out of the way were trampled like the morons ambling to the lifeboats on the

Titanic because they knew a big ship like that would have plenty to spare.

It was only at the end that Coop's pride was truly crushed, as he was shoved along like a drunk at a wake from one linebacker to another all the way down the hall to Woolrich's office. The last agent in line was a woman for whom the word *Amazon* would have been a paltry description. Relieved that he'd come to the end of the line, Coop started to say, "Thanks. I've got it from here," but he barely got out "Th" before he was launched through Woolrich's door like a goldfish from a shotgun.

He landed on his knees on Woolrich's floor. There were several other executive types in the room with him. None seemed the least bit surprised to have seen Coop tossed through the door like a bony Frisbee.

"Cooper. At last," said Woolrich, signing some papers. When he finally looked up from his desk, he said. "Get up off the floor, man. This is no time for your high jinks."

Coop used the desk to pull himself to his feet. "'High jinks' is not the word for what I just went through. I feel like a marshmallow Peep in a cement mixer."

"You poor thing. Where shall I send flowers?"

Coop dropped down into a chair next to the desk. Woolrich shook his head.

"There's no time for that now. We have to get you ready for your grand entrance."

Several of Woolrich's people reached out to grab Coop, but he jumped up and got out of the way just in time.

"Before I get mauled like a ham sandwich in a grain thresher, do you have my contract?"

"That's what I was signing when you burst in here," Woolrich said.

"I didn't burst in here. In here was thrust upon me with extreme malice."

Woolrich ignored him. "We don't have time for your excuses. Your contract is on the desk. It's exactly as we discussed. You're promoted to a full DOPS agent with no threat of jail as long as you behave."

"Within reason. I need some wiggle room there."

"It's all in the contract," said Woolrich. "You're not allowed to assassinate anyone, foment revolution, or print your own money. Short of that, there's some behavioral leeway."

Coop picked up the document. It was the size of car manual. "It's going to take some time to read all this," he said.

"Dammit, man. There isn't time for that," Woolrich took the contract back and showed Coop the colored Post-its stuck here and there throughout the document. "I've highlighted all the important clauses. Everything you asked about."

Coop paged through the contract, reading each section Woolrich had flagged. The truth was that he understood about one tenth of the quagmire of legalese on each page. But he recognized just enough words to be certain that the DOPS had fulfilled its end of the bargain. He reached for Woolrich's gold-tipped Montblanc pen, but his boss gently glided his hand away to a nearby ballpoint. Coop picked it up and signed the last page.

One of Woolrich's men snapped up the papers and slammed a rubber stamp over his signature. The woman next to him used an embosser to mark the same page. She handed it off to another woman, who locked it in a leather case, and she handed it to the last man in the line, who left with it through a back door Coop would have sworn wasn't there before.

"Did I just sell you people my soul?" Coop said.

"That's absurd. I wouldn't spend government money on something I wasn't sure existed," Woolrich said. "Now, let's get down to business. In a few minutes you are going to be inserted into the outskirts of L Wing. All you have to do is make your way from the insertion point around the perimeter to the main entrance. You'll enter an override code into the keypad you'll find there. This will open all the doors in the wing so that our tactical squads can clean up Harkhuf's mess."

"What makes you think you're going to be able to do it this time?"

"Because we have a secret weapon."

"What."

"You. You'll be reporting back to us via radio everything you see, hear, smell, feel, and taste."

"That's very optimistic of you," said Coop. "Most of what you're probably going to get is a lot of screaming and cursing."

"Try to control yourself, Cooper," said Woolrich. "You're a full DOPS agent now. Act like it."

"Then I'll scream and curse in triplicate. In case you haven't noticed, I'm not the hero type."

"No one is asking you to be a hero. All you have to do is get from point A to point B. Hide in the shadows if it makes you feel better. Crawl on your belly. Swing from branch to branch. I don't care."

"You left out the most important part. The part where I don't get eaten."

"There's nothing down there that's going to eat you," said the woman with the embosser. "Not all of you anyway."

Coop looked at Woolrich. "Why don't I leave Phil with you and take her instead? She's fun."

"Are you going to fulfill your part of the contract? Yes or no?"

"Yes, I'm going to do it," said Coop, feeling the bottom of his stomach sink to somewhere around Antarctica. "How am I going in? Rappel from a helicopter? Get lowered down an elevator shaft? Or maybe I crawl through an air vent like in *Die Hard*?"

"Don't be ludicrous. That would never work in the real world."

"Then how am I supposed to get in?"

Woolrich pushed a button under his desk and part of the wall slid away. There was a clear plastic cylinder about three feet wide with a door set in the side. "We're going to shoot you down through a pneumatic tube."

Coop looked around the room. No one was laughing. "Aren't pneumatic tubes how people in the olden times used to send messages and little packages?"

"Exactly."

"And, if I remember right, it works because there's a vacuum inside the tube."

"That's basic physics."

"Speaking as someone who likes his lungs on the inside, no thanks," said Coop.

Woolrich went to the tube. "We don't just jam you in there like so much bacon. You'll wear a pressurized suit with a breathing unit."

Coop walked to the tube and tried to see down inside. The light didn't go very far before it became a black void. "Why do you have people-size pneumatic tubes in the first place if no one can use them?"

"That's classified," said the embosser woman.

"Wait," Coop said. "Is this how you get all the dead bodies around the building without anybody seeing them?"

"That's also classified," said the man with the rubber stamps.

Coop went back around the desk. "I'm not jumping down your garbage disposal. Aside from my neurotic fear of becoming suddenly dead, who knows what kind of diseases are in those tubes?"

"We give them a flush-out every now and then," said Woolrich. "Otherwise they start to smell."

"No. I'm not today's sacrificial turd."

Woolrich sighed. "Cooper, what did we talk about when you got here?"

"Your days as an Elvis impersonator?"

"Your career. You signed a full-agent contract, meaning you're whatever the DOPS needs you to be."

Coop frowned. "And I get hazard pay for this?"

Woolrich nodded. "Time and a half."

"I want double," said Coop.

"Too late. You should have read the rest of the contract."

"You said there wasn't time."

"There wasn't."

"Cute. Okay, Hugo Boss. Suit me up."

"Good man," said Woolrich. He touched an intercom on his desk. "Get a team up here to grease down this slider and squeeze him into a corpse bun." He let up on the button. "Don't worry about any of that. It's just technical jargon. You wouldn't understand."

"Unfortunately," said Coop, "I think I do."

A team of six people stripped Coop down and covered him from head to toe in a clear gel so that he could squeeze into a skintight carbon-fiber suit that made him feel less like a secret government agent and more like a bratwurst having second thoughts about his life choices, his sanity, and whether he would be able to keep down those chili cheese fries he'd eaten earlier.

As the team began the laborious task of fitting him with a miniature breathing apparatus, Phil popped into his head.

"That lube looks cold," he said.

"It is."

"I'm only asking because I couldn't help noticing a certain amount of shrinkage. Are you nervous?"

"No. Are you?"

"No. I just sensed that you were, so I was going to be sympathetic because you're such a big crybaby."

"You're the one who sounds nervous, Mr. Chatterbox," said Coop.

"You have to admit, this assignment is a bit more . . . well, *lethal* than your usual fare."

"That's why you're here."

"To shepherd you through danger. I'm touched."

"And to go down with me if I'm eaten like an after-dinner mint."

"In case you don't make it and I do, is there anything you want me to tell your loved ones?" said Phil.

"That it was all your fault and you should be burned as a witch."

"Love and kisses all around. Got it."

"I knew I could count on you."

A technician grabbed Coop's head and shoved different-size mouthpieces into his face in an apparent attempt to see which one hurt the most. Satisfied that he'd found the most agonizing size and shape, he let Coop go.

"Don't forget," said Phil. "When you're a DOPS ghost, I'll have seniority, so you might want to start buttering me up."

"When I'm dead, I'm off the clock. I'm not working for anyone."

"Did you even read your contract?"

"Parts."

"Obviously the wrong ones."

"I started at DOPS before you, so I'll have seniority," said Coop.

"Not as a ghost. In the afterlife, I foresee you doing a lot of coffee runs and filing."

"Who are you talking to?" said Woolrich. He was wearing galoshes so the lube wouldn't get on his Italian shoes.

"I'm just going over strategy with Phil," said Coop.

"You only need one strategy: keep moving and don't die."

"If Coop does die, I'll have ghost seniority, right?" said Phil.

"I started at DOPS before him. I should have seniority."

A flunky ran up to Woolrich and he signed more paperwork. "Did you even read your contract, Cooper?"

"You told me there wasn't time."

"And you listened? Good man." Woolrich clapped him on the arm. "Get ready for insertion."

"Don't go too far, Mr. Woolrich," said Phil. "Remember we have another session tomorrow."

As Woolrich walked away he said, "Try not to bring him back. There's a bonus in it for you."

It wasn't clear which one of them he was talking to.

Another technician pulled a clear skintight mask down over Coop's face while the sadist with the mouthpiece shoved it between Coop's gums hard enough to loosen a couple of fillings.

Do I even have dental? thought Coop. *I really need to read my contract.*

Breathing compressed oxygen through his mouth now, Coop was led by two of the technicians to the corpse disposal and opened the door.

"Can you hear me, Phil?" said Coop in his head.

"Yes?"

"Start screaming."

The technicians shoved Coop into the tube and slammed shut the door. Woolrich gave him a quick wave and pressed a button on his desk.

"I wonder if he has a go-fuck-yourself button on his magic desk," said Phil.

"If not, let's buy him one."

A second later, he was falling. It wasn't a regular fall. It was more like being a piece of spaghetti sucked down the gullet of a particularly long-necked monster. A ball-tightening death luge through an amusement park designed by Charlie Manson and Mr. Hyde blind drunk on moonshine. What Coop at first thought was the roar of the vacuum in his ears he later realized was Phil shrieking. Apparently, being dead and not having to breathe meant that once you got a good scream going, there wasn't anything to stop you except boredom.

As they were shunted from tube to tube, Coop lost track of time. "Phil?" he said.

The screaming stopped. "Yes?"

"Are you all right?"

"You interrupted a perfectly good wail to ask me something that stupid?"

"I'm just trying to take your mind off things so you'll stop with the noise for two seconds."

"Oh, I haven't even begun to scream. What you just heard was only the warm-up exercise. You want to hear a real scream? Get ready."

A second later, they slammed to a halt. Stopping was possibly more unpleasant than the fall because Coop's internal organs felt like they weren't done luging when the rest of him was. He wasn't sure his kidneys had really lodged themselves behind his knees, but he planned to use some of his DOPS insurance to get X-rays.

If I even have insurance.

"Is it over?" said Phil.

Through the clear walls of the L Wing's pneumatic tube, Coop watched a large blue lobster whose head bore a strange resemblance to Lucille Ball drag a legless body in a lab coat up a steam pipe and disappear into the overhead ductwork.

"No," said Coop. "I'm going out on a limb and saying it's not over."

"You can do what you want," said Phil. "But I'm not going out there."

"I am, which means you are."

"Coop, you don't have to do this. We can just stay in our cozy little tube until this whole thing blows over. I give it six months tops."

"I'll be dead by then," said Coop.

"And I'll be your boss, so everybody wins."

"Except me."

"It's always about you, isn't it? What about my needs?"

"I'm going out."

"Oh, man . . ."

Coop pushed the pneumatic-tube door open. The sound of air rushing in to fill the vacuum was deafening. He gingerly put out one leg, and seeing that it made it to the floor while still attached to his body, he put out the other. With both feet firmly on the ground, he pushed himself out of the tube and closed the door.

Safety lights flickered on and off. Alarms wailed. Coop pressed himself against the wing's metal wall and removed his mouthpiece. His first breath of fresh air wasn't as refreshing as he'd hoped. In his work, Coop had encountered the occasional banshee, werewolf, or swamp goblin—and more recently the Pontianaks and Domovois—but he'd never encountered them in large numbers and it had always been in well-ventilated surroundings. However, in the stuffy, hermetically sealed confines of L Wing, the heady odor of musk and the potent breath of a dozen species of crazed hell beasts mingled with the death in the stale air to form a perfect storm of stink.

"It's like someone filled a monkey house with farts and garlic," said Phil.

"I think we just found the DOPS's next superweapon."

"I think that we could be a little outgunned. Maybe you should check in with the people upstairs."

Coop touched the button to activate the radio in the suit's hood. "Hello? Mr. Woolrich?"

Nothing came back.

"Hello?"

"Is the radio broken?" said Phil.

"I think the radio is broken. We're on our own."

"What do you have in that bag they gave you?"

"The override code, and some medical stuff. Morphine."

"Now you're talking," said Phil.

"And some stuff I sneaked in."

"What?"

"Nothing we'll probably need. Last-resort stuff."

"You're not going to do something stupid like kill yourself, are you? Suicide ghosts are the worst. Imagine the most neurotic, most annoying person you know—"

"This sounds familiar."

"They won't shut up and they won't stop whining and everybody hates them and it goes on forever."

"You just described yourself, Phil."

"What? Nobody hates me."

"Besides, I'm not the suicide type. This is other last-resort stuff."

"Fine, but nobody hates me."

"If you say so. I'm going to start moving."

"Where?"

Coop pointed to his left. "That way."

"Why?"

"Because look what's the other way."

A smorgasbord of short-circuiting cyborgs accompanied by hairy, bony, scaly, fleshy, and furred monstrosities was walking, crawling, and slithering in their direction. Some carried pieces of wrecked equipment as clubs. Some carried the enormous bones of other beasts. Some gnawed on unidentifiable carcasses with their grotesque fangs, beaks, or feeding tubes.

"Do you really think you can outrun them?" said Phil.

"I'm going to try. They said there are spirits down here, too. They're your job. Mine is not to get us killed."

"I suppose this isn't a good time to bring up my abandonment issues. It all started when I was a kid . . ."

"Here we go," said Coop. He pushed off the wall as hard as he could and started running.

Death curses and killing and crippling hexes hit him from all directions. Some tickled, while others burned and scratched, but none were strong enough to slow him down. From the unhappy sounds of the mob behind him, this was considered as rude and a good excuse to eat him, probably slowly, and probably from several different directions at once.

"Can't you run any faster?" shouted Phil. "You're like a basket of kittens dragging a boxcar of dumbbells up a ski slope."

"The bunny trail or the advanced?"

"Advanced."

"Go fuck yourself, Phil."

"Be nice. There's a pack of poltergeists ahead."

Coop had never seen Phil deal with other ghosts before. It wasn't pretty. As the poltergeists got into Coop's head, Phil jumped them. To Coop's surprise, while Phil and most other ghosts were invisible, when they were bent on kicking each other's asses inside a person's head, they became highly visible streaks and bursts of light. Coop thought that under other circumstances—such as when he wasn't being pursued by a hit squad of demented ogres—the ghostly battle might be interesting to see. After all, Phil spent a good deal of his time being as useless as a cotton-candy life raft and it would be nice to see him actually do something for a change. At the moment, however, all the lightning flashes from Phil's ectoplasmic Bruce Lee moves did was blind Coop. He kept running, but the more ghosts that came at him, the less he could see. And the death curses and hexes kept hitting from all sides.

Coop turned a corner and smashed into a pile of plastic storage containers. He didn't fall, but he did manage a soft-shoe routine worthy of Fred Astaire. Some of the creatures behind him didn't do so well. He could hear them falling and sliding around the hallway as they ran into the containers.

"Phil," Coop yelled. "I can't see. What the hell are you doing?"

"Saving your bacon, porkpie. Now shut up."

Coop bounced off a ventilation pipe and rebounded off a steel support column. Blind and exhausted, all he could do was dive behind a piece of equipment that resembled an upside-down pizza oven with metal claws.

Fortunately for him, broken robots and preternatural horrors aren't big planners, especially when they're bunched together in a bloodthirsty mob. They ran right past the pizza oven, clanking, howling, and wailing.

All Coop could do was lie on his back while Phil finished off the last of the Jacob Marleys. When the flashing in his head stopped, he had no idea how much time had passed or whether he was still, in fact, alive.

"Phil?" he said. "You there?"

It took a minute, but finally he heard a terse, "Shut up and let me catch my breath."

"Okay," said Coop. "But tell me this, is it over? With the ghosts, I mean."

"I think so," Phil said. "I hope so."

"Are you okay?"

"No, I'm not okay. I barely got started on my abandonment issues."

"You're okay," said Coop. He got to his knees and looked around. "I think we're in the clear. I don't see anything. Do you?"

"No. But where are we?"

"We've run around most of L Wing. The keypad must be up there somewhere. I don't think it's far."

"Don't think or don't know? Where's the map?" said Phil.

"They didn't give me one. They were going to direct me over the radio."

"Of course they were. And they were going to get me tickets for *Cats*, but they didn't do that either."

Coop took another look around. The hall appeared deserted.

"I know the way out is just ahead. I just have to convince my legs so they'll move."

"I'll just kick back, shall I, until you decide whether you want to get up, trampled, or eaten?"

"Okay," said Coop. "I'm going for it."

"Run, Forrest, run."

Coop blasted out from his hiding place, and when he took the first corner, everything was clear.

"You're doing it, buddy. You're doing it," said Phil.

But it all went to hell around turn two.

While the beasts and cyborgs without working brains were content to run around and around L Wing eating and/or crushing whatever wandered into view, a few of the mob had just enough reasoning power to know that if they stayed put, dinner would come to them.

As Coop rounded the second turn he was elated. "I can see the keypad."

"Good job. Now shut up and keep running."

Behind Coop, the floor rumbled. He allowed himself one quick glance over his shoulder. It was a terrible idea. While technically, knowing that you're being pursued by a ravening horde is useful information, it isn't all that helpful when you're not sure you have a way out. As Coop considered running past the keypad and hiding again, a second monster troop dropped from the ceiling in front of him.

"So, this is what it's like to be actually doomed," said Phil. "It was always very abstract before, but now that it's here, you know what? It's so much worse than I imagined. Do something, you ridiculous meat clown."

Coop looked from one group to the other. "I can make it," he said.

"No, you can't. Hide somewhere."

"I can make it."

"No, you can't."

"I can."

"No!"

That's when a third group of horrors dropped off to his left.

"You're right. I can't," he said.

"It's been nice knowing you, but I'm jumping ship."

"There's nowhere for you to go. We're trapped down here."

"What are we going to do?"

"I have a plan."

"Then do it."

"I am."

"Do it faster."

Coop reached into the bag the techs had given him. He put the keypad code between his teeth and took out three little cylinders.

"What are those?" said Phil.

"Distraction grenades."

"Do you know how to use them?"

"No."

"Good. For a minute there, I thought we were fucked."

Coop pulled the pin on the first one and threw it back over his shoulder. There was a loud *whomp* and something descended from the ceiling.

"What is that?" said Phil.

"I think a UFO is landing."

"Swell. Throw another one."

Coop tossed one grenade to his left and the third at the group directly in front of them.

Snow floated gently from the ceiling over Santa and a group of graceful elves pirouetting and leaping over a pristine frozen rink.

"It's a goddamn Christmas ice show," said Phil.

Coop dashed for the keypad. "Did the third one go off?"

"Yeah. It's just a bunch of jugglers on unicycles."

"Are the monsters eating them?"

"Yes."

"Good."

Coop slammed into the wall that contained the keypad.

"Hurry. The jugglers and elves are almost gone."

Coop entered the override code and pressed himself against the wall. The doors didn't open. Nothing happened.

Phil said, "Did you press enter, fuck nuts?"

Coop slammed his hand down on a red enter key. There was a series of metallic scrapes and thunks as bolts retracted and heavily armored doors slid open. The moment the closest door was up, what looked to Coop like the entire Marine Corps, Air Force, and maybe some Transformers, stormed into L Wing, guns blazing. Coop didn't stick around to see who won the battle. He was alive, and better than that, the chili cheese fries had remained safely inside him. As far as victories went, it wasn't exactly the liberation of France, but he'd take it.

He went to the elevator, punched the button, and pulled off his hood.

"Nice job," said Phil.

"You, too."

"And remember, we're getting hazard pay. Time and a half," said Phil.

"I wanted double."

"What did I tell you?"

"I know. I should have read the contract."

"Always read the contract."

"I need a drink," said Coop.

"Me, too. Would you think less of me if I wept hysterically for a while?"

"I just might join you."

"On three, then. One. Two . . ."

39

The only place left in L Wing that wasn't overrun with robots and monsters—or covered in blood, machine oil, and ichor—was thaumaturgic antiquities. It was a quiet island of peace in the middle of the biggest shit storm to ever hit the DOPS, aside from that one New Year's Eve when a drunken mob of ghosts and robots stole a saucer from the aberrant aircraft department and mooned the secret CIA bunker in Disneyland.

The antiquities staff was taking longer to find Shemetet than Harkhuf liked. To show his displeasure, he tossed a few of them out of the office and into the melee, where they were last seen running into the dark pursued by a group of cyborgs wielding Ping-Pong paddles and something that looked like a Caesar salad but had wings and breathed fire.

Dr. Buehlman and Froehlich emerged from a back room in antiquities.

"You are here, thrall," said Harkhuf.

"Which thrall?" said Froehlich. "Her or me?"

"You, cur."

"Thanks for clearing that up. Yes, I'm here. Nina Hagen," he said, pointing to Buehlman, "let me in through an emergency exit out back. It's huge, Master. You could march a whole army through it."

"That is indeed good news. You shall be rewarded with long lives and only minor torments in the darkness to come."

"Try to stay on his good side," Froehlich told Dr. Buehlman. "He's big on torments, especially eternal ones."

"I noticed," Dr. Buehlman said. "But our master is wise and will only do what's best for us and all mankind."

Froehlich gave her a look. "Are you sucking up to him? Are you angling for my job? The master chose me first. I'm top thrall and don't forget it, lady. I stuck one idiot in the Dumpster and I knew him. Think of what I'll do to you."

"I only wish to serve the great Harkhuf."

"We all do."

"And as he completes his great work, I would never trouble him about rolled-up newspapers."

Froehlich looked at Harkhuf. "You told her about that? I thought we had an understanding. Who ran around Griffith Park killing pigeons for you, stole for you, and brought you porn-shop incense? Me. Not Angela Merkel. Me."

Harkhuf raised his hand. "Quiet, dogs. You weary me with your petty bickering. There is much to do and it will require the work of many thralls before it is complete."

"But I'm still slave number one, right, Master?" said Froehlich.

"We shouldn't trouble our master with these matters when there's so much to do. It's enough that he allows us to serve," said Dr. Buehlman.

Froehlich went to Harkhuf. "Let me hit her just once," he said. "You want to know what to do with a rolled-up newspaper? Let me show you."

"That is enough. You will both be silent until the even-more-useless peons I enslaved earlier bring me my beloved."

"Shemetet really is here?" said Froehlich. "I kind of thought Minerva and Kellar were idiots like Gilbert. Sometimes it's nice to be wrong."

Someone called to them from the door through which Harkhuf had recently jettisoned some of the antiquities staff. "Knock, knock," the man said. "Is this a private party or can anyone join in?"

Harkhuf, Froehlich, and Dr. Buehlman stared at the man as he entered the room. "I was just in the neighborhood and thought I'd pay my respects. I love what you've done with the area outside. Monsters *and* cyborgs wreaking havoc together. Very high concept."

"Want me to throw him out, Master?" said Froehlich.

"Let me," said Dr. Buehlman.

"Quiet," said Harkhuf. "We shall speak when this is over. Establish some clear boundaries." Before either could say anything, he turned to the stranger. "How is it you were able to travel through such a sea of destruction? My beasts should have torn you asunder."

"Oh, that," the man said lightly. "They ignored me for one simple reason. Like you, I'm dead."

Harkhuf gestured to the man. "Approach me."

The dead man came to Harkhuf and bowed. He had a book under his arm and something small in his hand. "My name is Nelson," he said.

"Your name means nothing, cur. Be my thrall."

"I'm sorry. I didn't quite catch that."

Harkhuf raised his hand and his voice. "Be my thrall, you wretched thing."

"I see the problem here," said Nelson. "You think I'm like these other dimwits. I'm not. I'm protected. I have a charm that won't let you take me over."

"All who resist must be destroyed. I will have my thralls kill you where you stand."

Nelson held up what he'd hidden in his hand. It was an amulet on a short metal chain. "Recognize this? I can do a lot more damage to you right now than you can do to me."

Froehlich lunged for Nelson, but Harkhuf threw an arm in front of him, knocking him across a table and onto the floor.

"You have the amulet that gives you power over me, yet you do not use it," said Harkhuf. "Why is that?"

Froehlich got up off the floor and limped back to his master.

Nelson approached Harkhuf. "We're not like these other idiots. We're dead as doornails. Coffin candy. Why be enemies? We should be pals. We should work together."

"And what would you have us do together? The world is already claimed by Shemetet with me by her side. What can a puny thing like you offer me?"

"How about Miss Thang's return to life?" said Nelson. He took the book from under his arm and held it up. "This, I believe, has the resurrection spells you need for your lady friend. All I want to do is set up a trade."

"A trade? What sort?" said Harkhuf. "And answer quickly. My patience grows short."

"Let it grow a tail and have puppies, for all I care. As long as I have this amulet, you're going to listen to me, you walking pile of dirty laundry."

"Speak, then."

"You want this book. Fine. I'll give it to you. All I want is another book in return."

"And what book is this?"

"Don't worry about that. I'd get it myself, only, as I mentioned, I'm dead and revenants like you and me can't enter the ECIU. But one of your pet poodles can."

"The Extra-Confidential Inscrutabilis Unit!" said Dr. Buehlman. "It was right on the tip of my tongue."

Harkhuf turned to Dr. Buehlman. "You know of this place?"

"Yes! It's right downstairs. It's very secret. No one is allowed. But, of course, who could refuse you, my gorgeous master?"

"Dial it back, sister," said Froehlich.

Harkhuf went to Nelson and put his hand out to take the book. "Yes. I sense its power. This is indeed the text I require."

"Then we have a deal? A book for a book?" said Nelson.

"Under one condition."

"Name it."

"Along with the book, you give me the amulet."

Nelson made a face. "There's a problem with that. I don't trust you any more than I'd trust month-old meat loaf. But I'll make you this offer. We go to ECIU. One of your boobs gets me my book and I give you this book. Then one of them comes with me. When we're far enough away that I feel safe, I'll give the birdbrain the amulet and you and I can go on our separate ways. How's that?"

"Let me take it from him, Master," said Dr. Buehlman.

"No, me," said Froehlich.

"Quiet, both of you," growled Harkhuf. To Nelson he said, "Your offer is acceptable. Can you lead us to ECIU?"

"Sure, but what about Lucy and Ricky there? They're alive. Those things you let loose outside will gobble them up like kettle corn."

"Not if they are with me. All of creation bows to me and my beloved—"

"Yeah. I know her name. You keep saying it. It's coming off as clingy."

Harkhuf leaned toward Dr. Buehlman. "What is this clingy?"

"It means wise beyond measure and glorious to behold."

"Oh, come on," said Froehlich. "She's blowing smoke up your cartouche, Master."

"Silence," Harkhuf said. "Your bargain is acceptable, dead man. Lead the way to ECIU."

"Step this way, ladies and gentlemen," Nelson said. He went to the door and exited last, making sure none of the three got behind him.

Neither Harkhuf nor Nelson was bothered by the walk through the abattoir that was L Wing. True, DOPS security had the ravening hordes on the run, but there were still plenty of stray monsters around to menace both Dr. Buehlman and Froehlich. The two thralls clung to Harkhuf like ticks on a poodle. The walk to the elevators wasn't far, but the sheer terror of it was more than Dr. Buehlman's heart could take. She collapsed just a few yards from safety. Harkhuf pushed Froehlich onward. The last thing he saw of Dr. Buehlman was her body being dragged off by a blood-soaked plush unicorn wearing a tiara.

A severed arm with a pistol still in its hand lay near the elevators. "Oh. Shiny," said Nelson. He pried the gun loose and put it in his pocket.

No one talked as they rode the elevator down to the ECIU; however, Nelson hummed the *Star Wars* "Imperial March" the whole way just because he saw how much it upset Froehlich.

"Were you this much of a dick when you were alive?" said Froehlich.

"Were you this much of a loser before you started sucking scarecrow's dick?"

"Say nothing, thrall," said Harkhuf. "We will part ways with this uncouth creature shortly."

"The sooner the better," said Nelson, who went right back to humming the march.

Froehlich thought about all the lives he'd ruined over the last few days and tried to come up with a scheme to fuck over a dead asshole. He was rattled enough that he didn't come up with anything right away, but as long as he was by Harkhuf's side, he knew he'd have time to come up with something. Something a lot worse than framing a rich lady, turning a detective into a baby-oil-stinking hippie, or getting body-cavity searches for an entire fraternity. This Nelson prick had something big and bad coming to him, and with just a little time and, of course, his master's permission, he'd make him cry buckets of baby-doll tears.

When they reached the ECIU level, Nelson led the way to the unassuming entrance. He kept back well away from the door. Seeing this, so did Harkhuf.

Nelson looked at Froehlich. "You're up. The two nimrods inside are Vargas and Zulawski. Tell them you want the *Mysteriis Ex Mortuis,* and if they don't give it to you, there's a man outside with a gun who'll shoot them so many times you can play them like an ocarina."

Froehlich looked at his master and Harkhuf nodded. Cautiously, Froehlich went to the door and turned the knob.

"It's locked," he said.

"It's not supposed to be," said Nelson. "Give it a knock."

Froehlich pounded on the door a few times. "Nothing," he said. "Great plan. Now what?"

Nelson walked up a few steps and pulled out the pistol. Froehlich scrambled out of the way as three shots flew past him, splintering the lock. "Try it now, princess," Nelson said.

Again, Froehlich approached the door cautiously, not so much worried about what lay behind it as how soon it would be before Nelson started shooting again. When he reached the door, he gave it a light push. It swung open silently.

"It's open," he said.

"We're not blind," called Nelson. "Now scoot in there and get me my book."

"The lights are off."

"Here," Nelson said, and he tossed Froehlich a flashlight.

"What does it look like?" Froehlich said.

"The book? It looks like a book, you idiot. Look around. They might have it in a box or something."

"Okay. I'm going in."

"Chop chop, pal. Your boss and me have dead-guy stuff to do." Nelson looked at Harkhuf. "It's just so hard to get good slaves these days."

"Indeed. In the old days, worthy vassals clamored to serve."

"Now you have to make do with Mr. Chicken and . . . what was the lady's name?"

"I do not know. She was a thrall. That was enough."

"Sure," said Nelson. "It's not like you were going to send her a birthday card."

"No. I was not. Still, she possessed intelligence."

"More than this clown? I've eaten buffalo wings with more potential."

"Found it," shouted Froehlich.

"Good boy, rover," said Nelson. "Now bring the ball to Daddy."

Froehlich sauntered out of the ECIU office with a wooden box under his arm. He started for Nelson, but stepped back into the doorway. "You want the book so bad, why don't you come and get it?"

"Very funny. Bring it to me or the deal is off."

"What? I can't hear you. Us buffalo wings are funny that way."

"First off, it should be *we* buffalo wings, you illiterate gnat. And second," said Nelson, pulling the pistol from his pocket, "bring me the goddamn book or kiss your balls good-bye."

"Do as he says, cur. I want his business concluded," said Harkhuf.

"Fine," said Froehlich in a tone more suited to a six-year-old who'd just been ordered to eat his lima beans. "Coming."

From somewhere in the distance came a sound. It wasn't quite a slither. It was more like someone dragging a fifty-pound sack of wet oatmeal over a tile floor. There was a crash. Froehlich turned around and peered into the ECIU office.

Ten-foot-long tentacles shot through the doorway, wrapped around him, and pulled. Froehlich grabbed the doorframe with his free hand.

"Toss the book here," shouted Nelson. Froehlich didn't. He was too occupied with being dragged into the office's cavernous darkness.

"Throw me the damned book!" screamed Nelson.

With one last jerk, Froehlich disappeared. The box with the book spun in the air and fell, sliding into a shadow just inside the doorway.

"You asshole," said Nelson. "You were so close to not being useless."

"Can you not simply reach in and remove the book?" said Harkhuf.

"I can't cross the threshold," said Nelson. "This is completely fucked."

"For some perhaps."

Harkhuf swung an arm with surprising speed, hitting Nelson squarely on the side of the head. Nelson spun and hit a wall. Both the cookbook and the amulet slipped from his hands and slid across the hall. By the time he came to his senses, Harkhuf stood above him, the book and amulet in his grasp.

"Our bargain is at an end," Harkhuf said. "As is your miserable existence." He raised a linen-wrapped foot and brought it down hard, aiming for Nelson's head.

Nelson rolled away and staggered to his feet. "We had a deal, you used-paper-towel-looking piece of shit."

"Your book is just there, vile thing. Retrieve it yourself."

"I can't!" he said. Then, "Give me back *my* book."

"Begone, cretin, or I will have my other thralls hunt you down and feed you to my beasts."

Nelson ran for the elevator. *I just cannot catch a fucking break,* he thought. *First Coop and then the book. Now I've got Boris Karloff on my ass and even McCloud is gone. I am so fucking fucked.*

The elevator pinged and the doors slid open.

Nothing to do now but get really ugly.

Instead of hitting a button to go up, he hit one to go down.

By the time Harkhuf returned to thaumaturgic antiquities, the remaining thralls had found Shemetet and laid her out on one of the big examination tables. He set down the cookbook and went to her. Touching her desiccated face tenderly, he ran his fingers down her cheek to her noble chin. "My beloved," he said. Turning to his cowering thralls, he said, "Who here is your master?"

"You are," they said to him.

"That's not what I mean, dogs. Forget it. You are worse than my previous thralls." He pointed to a short man in the front. He had a boyish face and wore round red glasses. "You. Come to me."

The thrall crept forward, but kept more than an arm's length of distance between Harkhuf and himself. He spoke barely above a whisper. "Yes, Master?"

"Shemetet must be in robes befitting a queen. You have raiment here?"

"Yes. In the back."

"Bring her the finest you have."

"Yes, of course, Master. Is there anything else?"

"You have weapons?"

"A few swords and knives from some of the tombs."

"Bring them all," said Harkhuf.

"Right away, Your Awesomeness. Anything more?"

"The other thralls will release all the other dead beasts and humans that exist here."

"Release, Your Vastness?"

"Remove them from whatever cases, chambers, or sarcophagi in which they now dwell. I will have need of them. Tell the others to do this while you clothe your new queen."

"Naturally, Your Enormity. I'm happy to oblige. My name is Kevin, by the way. If you need anything at all, just—"

"Be gone, Kevin."

"Yes, Your Noble Immensity."

"'Master' will do."

"Wonderful, O Master of Masters."

Harkhuf took Kevin by the throat. "Just 'Master.'"

"Just Master," he croaked.

Harkhuf released him.

While Kevin scuttled off to tell the other slaves their various tasks, Harkhuf opened the book he had taken from the other dead man. However, when he looked for the spells he required, the markings on the book's pages were unfamiliar to him.

"Kevin," he said.

Kevin ran over. "Yes, Your Colossalness."

"What did we just talk about?"

"Sorry, Master."

"Good," Harkhuf said. He laid his hand on an open page of the book. "Can you read these markings?"

"Easily, Master. What are you looking for?"

"I wish to bring life back to Shemetet. Find this for me."

"With pleasure, Master. Let your unworthy servant just check the table of contents." With a trembling finger, Kevin scanned down a page in *Enigmatic Confections*. "Excuse me, Master, but it says it's a cookbook."

"This cannot be. I sensed the power within."

"Naturally, you're right, Master, but this whole section is about blueberry tarts."

Harkhuf put a finger on the page. "And that?"

"Oatmeal raisin cookies."

"And that?"

"Gugelhupf."

"What is Gugelhupf?"

"It seems to be a kind of German marble cake."

"And there is nothing about—"

"Wait," said Kevin. "Here it is, right between Raspberry Grunt and Rum Platz. Revivification of the Departed. Does that sound right?"

"Indeed. Read me what is there."

"With pleasure, Master of Masters."

Harkhuf gave him a hard look.

"Sorry. Wow. There's a lot more kinds of raising the dead than I thought. It says you can bring them back with a mind or without a mind. With a soul or without a soul. And there's a whole section here about egg whites. No. That's about resurrecting a soufflé."

"I grow weary of your prattle, cur."

"Royalty. Revivification of Royalty. Is that it, Master?"

"Good, thrall."

"It says it's just like a Rejuvenation of an Aristocrat spell, but with . . . huh."

"Yes?"

"It wants an offering of grains, milk, salt, the sweetest honey, butter, and the fruit of the cacao tree."

"Do you have those things, thrall?"

Kevin read the rest of the list. Twice. "I think . . . I think . . . it wants you to raise the dead with a chocolate brownie," he said uneasily.

"Answer me quickly, cur. Do you have this chocolate brownie?"

"Give me one minute, Master."

Kevin stood in the middle of the room and screamed at the top of his lungs, "Did anyone bring back any brownies from lunch?"

A woman raised her hand. "I did."

"Susan? What kind?"

"Butterscotch."

"Fuck."

"I've heard this word before, Kevin. It is a word of defeat," said Harkhuf. "I promise you eternal torment if you do not deliver to me a chocolate brownie."

Kevin thought for a minute.

"I grow weary, Kevin," said Harkhuf.

"I got it!" Kevin said, and ran to where he'd left his briefcase. When he got back to Harkhuf, he was panting. He had a bar in his hand. "This is what we call a jumbo Snickers. It has chocolate. Maybe I can microwave the Snickers bar and the brownie together. Do you think a chocolate butterscotch brownie would work, O Great, Merciful, Even-Tempered Master?"

Harkhuf looked from Kevin to Shemetet. "If that is all there is, we will have to make do. Bring to me the chocolate butterscotch brownie."

"Right away, Master." Kevin ran to Susan. However, halfway there he stopped. "Snickers also has peanuts. In or out?"

"Shemetet has a nut allergy," said Harkhuf.

"Peanuts out. Give me just a couple of minutes, Your Immeasurable Hugeness."

Harkhuf started to say something, but he let it go. There would be plenty of time to kill Kevin later.

Just a few minutes later, with a much-too-hot chocolate butterscotch brownie burning his fingers, Kevin began reciting the strange words in the even stranger cookbook. As he spoke, the room dimmed and a single light glowed from above the area where Shemetet lay in repose. The more and the faster Kevin read, the brighter the light became. He felt possessed by the words and they came faster and louder until, just as his voice reached a crescendo, some of the brownie dripped onto Shemetet's linen wrappings. Harkhuf grabbed Kevin and was about to snap his neck, when light exploded into the room and the two of them were knocked back. Both Harkhuf and his thralls were blinded for a few seconds, but when they could see, they were amazed.

"My beloved," said Harkhuf.

"My beloved," said Shemetet.

He helped her down from the table. Like Harkhuf, she was still in her linen wrappings, but she moved with grace and ease. A couple of the thralls that had been in the back came running forward and draped a finely wrought dress around Shemetet's body. Another thrall brought knives and swords and laid them out on the table from which she'd risen. She ran a hand over all of the weapons, finally selecting a curved khopesh. Weighing the blade in her hand, she addressed the thrall that had brought them.

"What is your name?"

"My name is Terry."

With the barest flick of her wrist, she cut off his head.

"The proper answer was 'My name is Terry, my queen.' Do you all understand that?"

"Yes, my queen," said the thralls in various states of shock. She turned to Harkhuf. "Have you assembled my army, dear Harkhuf?"

"It is being gathered now, my love." He went to Kevin. "Take me to the other dead. And bring the book."

They went into thaumaturgic antiquities' back room, and when they emerged just a few minutes later, they were followed by almost a legion of other mummies, skeletal horses, lions, bears, and other wild things.

"It is a beginning," said Shemetet. "But it is not enough."

"Not nearly. But soon there will be more. Kevin, bring in the witches."

"Witches, Master?"

"By the emergency exit. An old woman and a fat man. If you are too blind to see them, kill yourself with this because I will not be so kind." He handed Kevin a dagger.

Kevin stared at it. "Okay," he said. Then, "Master."

To his immense relief, he found Minerva and Kellar huddled together by the exit, jumpy and edgy.

"He wants to see you," Kevin told them.

"What kind of mood is he in?" said Kellar.

"Mood?"

"Are things going his way?" said Minerva.

"If you mean did he just wake up his girlfriend, yes."

"That's wonderful," she said.

"Then she killed Terry."

"Oh," said Kellar.

"He was my ride home."

"My condolences."

"Anyway, come on. He wants to see you both."

They went into the front room, where the thralls and the royals were assembled. Minerva and Kellar tried not to look startled by the skeleton army or by the dead body by Shemetet's feet. When they reached Harkhuf and Shemetet, they made a big show of bowing so low that Kellar thought his vertebrae were going to blast out of his back like popcorn.

"It's wonderful to meet you, my queen," said Minerva.

"Me, too, my queen," said Kellar.

Shemetet looked from them to Harkhuf. "These are the ones who led you here so that you might revive me?"

"Yes, my dear."

"Then, as worthless as they appear, they may continue to serve."

"Thank you, my queen," said Minerva.

"I know where we should go next," blurted Kellar. Minerva gave him a look and he turned red.

Shemetet reached for her blade, but Harkhuf laid a hand on her arm. "Tell me, witch man. Where is it you would take us?"

"The natural history museum. You think this place is full of cool dead stuff? Wait until you see a T. rex skeleton."

"This is a beast of war?"

"A magnificent killer," said Kellar, adding, "Master."

"Bring us to the T. rex," said Shemetet. "I will be the judge of its worthiness."

Minerva set the grimoire on the table. "Kellar found a spell he says should transport all of us right to the museum. Then you can double your army, my queen."

"That will still not be enough. I require fighters who will die and whose numbers stretch from here to the horizon."

"To the horizon, huh?" Minerva mumbled.

"Forest Lawn," said Kellar. "After the museum. We can go to Forest Lawn cemetery. The dead things here? Wait until you wake up all the stiffs in Forest Lawn, my queen."

"Then we shall go to Forest Lawn."

"And Hollywood Forever. That's another cemetery," Kellar said.

"Why Hollywood Forever?" said Minerva. "It's full of show-business douche bags."

Kellar looked at the grimoire. "I always wanted to meet Maila Nurmi."

"Who?"

"Vampira. I had the biggest crush on her as a kid."

"Oh, for fuck's sake."

"Are there vast numbers to be had at Hollywood Forever?" said Harkhuf.

"Not as vast as Forest Lawn, but these are high-quality people. And there are lots of other cemeteries in L.A. We printed out a map." Kellar held up a Google map of L.A. County covered in red circles.

"We shall go to all these places of the dead and begin amassing our forces," said Shemetet. "But tell me, witch—and your life depends on your answer—where shall we gather the army away from the prying eyes of the unworthy?"

Minerva and Kellar smiled at each other. She said, "Fear not, my queen. I have just the place."

40

Coop and Phil's debriefing was long and thorough, with more than a little shouting. Mostly from Coop, and mostly about how the DOPS was run by a lot of idiots who couldn't even make a radio that worked. Even with all the screaming, they kept Coop all afternoon, and even after the L Wing got the all clear, they didn't let him go. They let Phil leave, but kept Coop a little longer. All his internal alarm bells went off, but he played it cool. In fact, it turned out to be nothing. The security department just asked him if he could identify either of the strangers they'd picked up on the surveillance system.

The first photo was of a heavyset man with a comb-over.

"Never seen him before," said Coop.

They showed him a shot of an older woman who looked like Stevie Nicks's stunt double.

"Minerva Soleil," he said. "What the hell is Minerva doing downstairs?"

"Nothing," said the head security officer. "She and all the rest of the freak show vanished into thin air. Do you have any idea where they would have gone?"

"Have you checked out Minerva's reading parlor?"

"We have a team there now."

"Then I don't know what else to tell you."

As Coop started to leave, the security officer said, "How is it you know the Soleil woman?"

Coop thought fast. The last thing he wanted to admit was that he'd gone to her with a pocketful of stolen Egyptian artifacts and that, in fact, he was wearing a piece of the evidence around his neck right now. All he wanted to do was get out of there.

"I used to work with her on a séance swindle. She'd make like she'd contacted dead Aunt Tessie or someone's favorite pet and I'd do the voices. Mostly we'd scam widows and orphans. They were the easiest."

The security officer gave him a look of utter disgust. "You make me sick. Get out of my office before I have to fumigate it."

"Whatever you say, Chief. Tell Mr. Woolrich that I'll see him bright and early tomorrow. Also, that your equipment sucks."

"Get out."

Even though he wasn't in trouble with the DOPS anymore, Coop knew he was right where he was before with Harkhuf. The mummy was out there somewhere, and now he had the beginnings of a small army. Whatever he was up to, Coop was sure that sooner or later, Harkhuf would swing back around to him.

The question is: Do I trust Woolrich to really have my back even though I signed the contract?

The answer to that remained "no." Coop now had firsthand experience of the DOPS body garbage disposal and knew how easy it would be for him to end up as Soylent Green. That meant that while he now had a retirement plan to fall back on in his old age, it looked increasingly unlikely that he'd have old age, arthritis, bad knees, and senility to look forward to.

If I'm ever going to be clear of Harkhuf, I'm going to have to do it myself. But I don't know where he's holed up, and if I did, I couldn't do anything about it myself.

A moment later, Nelson and the Auditors popped into his head. That was three more assholes to worry about.

His head hurt. Rather than think his way into a mood that wouldn't let him sleep and would have Giselle telling him to go see a shrink, he decided to go with Plan B.

Circus Liquor was on Vineland Avenue in North Hollywood. Out front was a thirty-two-foot-high neon clown so terrifying that over the years it had shocked drunks sober, and sober people into a bourbon spiral just trying to get the glowing image out of their minds. Coop planned on joining that latter group that night.

Inside the store, his mind swam with Phil's endless screams, and visions of monsters and ice-skating elves and monsters eating ice-skating elves. He was distracted enough that he couldn't make any hard decisions. In the end, he made an easy one. He wandered the aisles and secured an armful of Elmer T. Lee, 1792, Barrell, and Angel's Envy before heading to the register up front. His logic was simple and impeccable: Why have only one kind of hangover when you can have four?

There was a television on at the checkout area. He managed to ignore it until one of Sheriff Wayne Jr.'s car commercials came on.

Crap. Can't you people leave me alone long enough to pickle my brain?

The sky behind the Sheriff crackled with storm clouds and lightning. It looked like an ad from last Halloween. *Cheap bastard,* thought Coop. *No wonder Donna is having second thoughts about your horse-puncher act.*

The shot widened until the Sheriff filled half of the screen and an old woman dressed like a late-night infomercial fortune-teller filled the other half.

"What do you see in your crystal ball, gypsy queen?" said the Sheriff.

"I predict the lowest prices and the highest values in the San Fernando Valley."

"You're a spooky woman, Minerva, but you know your business . . ."

Coop's mind went crystal clear. He looked up just in time to see Minerva Soleil winking at him. "Come on down and see Sheriff Wayne Jr. If you're looking for something special, you just know he has it."

The guy in line behind Coop bumped him with his cart. "Hey, Einstein, fix the universe on your own time." He patted a twenty-four-pack of Pabst like a prize poodle. "I have things to do."

"Me, too," said Coop. He dropped his bottles into the guy's cart and ran outside to his car. By the time he time made it home, his headache was gone and he had a whole new plan, the worst one he'd ever come up with.

They'll never see it coming.

He dialed a number.

"Hello?"

"Morty, those guys you got the Tweak box from, didn't you say they had a little antigravity gizmo? Does it work? How would you like to steal it for me? One night. Oh, and a truck. By morning, I figure I'll either be dead or in the clear mummy-wise."

In the end, Harkhuf didn't kill Kevin. He and Shemetet didn't kill any of the new thralls. They just abandoned them to their fate in the L Wing. The good news was that by then, DOPS security had gained the upper hand and was beating back the hideous horde that had been on the loose all day. The bad news was that the antiquities staff had to explain how they helped resurrect a mad mummy and kick-start its army. Also, there was the Terry situation. Lastly, there was the brownie. No one, especially Kevin, wanted to have to explain how the world might be destroyed because he and Susan were cheating on their diets.

It was nearly midnight. Behind Sheriff Wayne Jr.'s car dealership, Harkhuf and Shemetet looked admiringly at their growing army. After just a few hours of work, they'd supplemented the DOPS mummies and animals with thousands of Forest Lawn's dead and the natural history museum's lions, tigers, bison, gorillas, and elephants. While they were there, they also picked up a T. rex, a triceratops, a couple of pterodactyls, a herd of velociraptors, and a Stegosaurus. Earlier in the day, they'd resurrected some skeletal celebrities at Hollywood Forever, but the latter were more concerned with contacting their now deceased managers and agents than in world conquest, so nobody paid much attention to them.

"I swear, Minerva, this is a bigger clusterfuck than when Coop dumped that tusked mongrel in my lap," said the Sheriff.

"And how did that work out for you?" she said.

"Fine at first. Donna and me loaded up a flatbed with all kinds of statues, paintings, furniture, solid-gold cutlery, and what have you. Then, in the morning, the truck was gone."

"And so was Donna. And what is the lesson in that?"

"Don't trust bitches?"

"No," Minerva said. "It's that investing in things is always a losing proposition. Things break. Go out of style. Exes walk off with them. What you really want to invest in is the future. And that's just what this is."

The Sheriff pulled her into his office, out of mummy earshot. "I don't know how I feel about this. All these dead things walking around? I was raised by good Baptist folks. If they could see me now."

"Save the sob story for your memoirs, Sheriff. If those good Baptist folks could forgive you for spending the last few decades plowing other people's wives next to a garage full of hot cars, and a parking lot full of lemons, they'll forgive you for this."

"But have you listened to those two, Horker and Shemp?"

"Harkhuf and Shemetet," said Kellar. "Personally, I don't care what you call them, but they're a little touchy about their names and complete shits when it comes to the queen and master stuff."

"He's right," said Minerva. "If you want a head to put your Stetson on, you better wise up and get on board. These two are the future. When they take over, we're going to be right there with them. They're going to need loyal humans like us to control their armies of thralls."

"What's a thrall?" said the Sheriff. "It sounds like something on your pecker you have to get shots for to make sure it doesn't come back."

"A thrall is a slave," said Kellar.

"Why didn't you say so?"

"I have no idea. I don't even know why we're talking to you."

"You want to rumble, butterball?" said the Sheriff. He held up a fist. "I've got a frying pan ready for a pile of fatback like you."

Kellar flexed his bruised knuckles. Minerva got between them.

"Now, boys, play nice. We don't want to make a bad impression on our new master and queen."

"And what's with the master and queen bullshit?" said the Sheriff. "I won't have it. Not on my own land."

Kellar laughed. "Go out and tell them, then. Go outside and tell the three-thousand-year-old Egyptian warriors and their army of the undead that you'd like them to mosey on down the road a piece so you can get back to whittling up a new butter churn."

The Sheriff slowly shook his head. "I don't like the way you said it, but I take your point. It would be a little awkward telling Ma and Pa Kettle that them and the kids have to sleep in the barn and not the big house."

"Let them nap wherever they want. And when this is over, the three of us will be sitting pretty and you can leave this car game behind."

"I wouldn't mind that, I'll tell you. Especially after Donna ran off with what was going to be our nest egg."

"Then it's settled," said Minerva. "You give our queen and master a place to lie low for a while and we three are going to be set up for life."

"Plus, I'm getting a talk show," said Kellar. "And maybe meet Oprah."

"Is that right? It's the end of the world and you want to be Jay Leno?"

"God no." He shuddered. "But, yes, something like that."

"And how about you, starlet? What's your over-the-rainbow?"

"Right now I just want to get through the next few days until Harkhuf and Shemetet get enough firepower to take over this burg. Then I'm going to put Jack Nicholson on a leash and ride him like a bucking bronco."

"Yee-haw," said the Sheriff. "Okay. Let's go out and make a deal." He put on his Stetson and checked himself in the mirror.

"Now, remember. Master and queen," said Kellar. "Trust me, you can't say it enough for these two." He shook his head, muttering, "You'd think taking over the world would fix your self-esteem issues."

"Don't worry about me, Sonny Jim. I've sold mobile homes to people with no jobs, and Jaguars to old ladies with cataracts the size of an extra-large with pepperoni. I think I can handle Mr. and Mrs. Skeletor."

"Let's go out and lay out the welcome mat," said Minerva. She put an arm out for the Sheriff and one out for Kellar.

When they got outside, a T. rex was methodically ripping the roofs off of the hot pickup trucks Lee had just dropped off. Across the lot, zombie buffalo were stampeding back and forth over a flattened row of what used to be . . . ?

Audis? Avantis? Porsches? Good thing these bony cocksuckers are taking over. There are so many hot cars on this lot I can't even fire-bomb the place for the insurance.

He doffed his hat to the T. rex as they walked by.

There's fucked, there's buffalo-fucked, and there's dinosaur-fucked. And I'm all three.

The Sheriff turned on his biggest salesman smile for Shemetet and Harkhuf.

I don't know what's going to be stranger, working for dead folks or working for foreigners.

Coop didn't want to take Giselle and Morty with him. They weren't even part of his original plan. But Morty wouldn't get Coop the zero-G device if he couldn't come and Giselle promised to have the locks changed if she couldn't.

And as much as he hated putting them in danger—again—he couldn't help feeling a bit relieved that they were by his side.

They drove north out of L.A. in the borrowed DOPS truck and turned onto a feeder road. The rest of this part of the plan was pretty easy.

"Want to see how the zero-G thing works?" said Morty.

"Yeah. I need to practice so I'll get it right later."

"I don't know why you won't let me run it for you."

"For the same reason I didn't want you and Giselle here in the first place. If this doesn't work out, jail will be the least of my worries."

"This is the screwiest thing you've come up with," said Giselle.

"Thank you."

"It wasn't a compliment."

Coop took the zero-G device and started playing with it.

"It's going to be fine," he said.

"How do you know?"

"On the count of three, don't think of a purple bat. One—"

"I already lost. How about you?"

"Nope. I'm fine."

"Liar."

"Prove it."

Coop pulled off the freeway and called Mr. Woolrich.

"Cooper. Do you know what time it is?"

"Mr. Woolrich, I'm going to confess something."

"Please tell me you're defecting. I don't care who to. Just go."

"First off. I'm alone. That's important."

"By your saying you're alone, I know for a fact that you aren't. You haven't involved your friends in something nefarious, have you? You're the only one with wiggle room in your behavior clause."

"That's why I'm officially telling you that I'm alone."

"Fine. You're alone. Where are you alone?"

"I'm at Sheriff Wayne Jr.'s car lot off the Hollywood Freeway."

"If you're looking for someone to cosign a loan, I don't think so."

"I'm about to start a war. If you want to get in on it, you might want to send some of those crack DOPS troops up here. And tell them to get some radios at Walmart. Theirs don't work."

"What kind of war? What's going on?"

"It's not that I don't trust you, Mr. Woolrich, it's that I trust me more."

"What does that mean, Cooper?"

"It means that if you want Harkhuf and Shemetet, you better get here. Maybe send some regular cops, too. There are some other jerks who need to get arrested."

"Cooper, don't you do anything—"

"Sorry, Mr. Woolrich. My battery is running out. You're breaking up. Remember, Sheriff Wayne Jr.'s."

He hung up.

"While you're making prank calls, why don't you call the president. There's another important person you can antagonize tonight," said Morty.

"Woolrich is fine," said Coop. "He loves my high jinks. He told me so."

"High jinks. He used the term 'high jinks'?" said Giselle.

"Yep. He can't get enough of them."

"Whatever high jinks you've got planned, now that you've called him, we should probably get them going?"

"We've all agreed to our jobs, right?" said Coop. "All you two are going to do is lower the rear so the elephant can get out."

Giselle and Morty said yes.

"After that, I want you both to disappear. Now, I know you're not going to do that, but I'm saying it because I want a clear conscience if Woolrich arrests us all."

"Are you done?" said Giselle.

"Yes."

"You're so cute when you're brave and terrified at the same time."

Coop drove the truck to the foot of the Sheriff's car lot. The bar was across the driveway again, but when Giselle and Morty lowered the rear of the truck, it fit right over the barricade.

Coop jumped down from the truck cab and ran to the rear. Morty and Giselle were already leading the elephant out. When it was on the ground, Coop patted its leg. It draped its trunk across his shoulder.

"Seriously now, go away," said Coop. "Hide in the truck. Go down the street. Just don't be near the lot for a while."

Giselle and Morty got into the rear of the truck and pulled the ramp up with them.

"Good luck, stupid. If you die, I'll plant daisies on your grave and tell everybody you were a florist," said Giselle.

"Good luck, pal. Don't be afraid to run away. It's a strategy that's always worked for me," said Morty.

Coop led the elephant up the driveway.

"What the hell is happening out there?" said Kellar.

"What do you mean?" said the Sheriff. He went to the window.

"Is that Coop?" said Minerva.

"And an elephant?" said Kellar.

"He's brought that goddamn elephant back?" said the Sheriff. "That's all I fucking need. I've got Lucifer's own circus around back and this dipshit thinks my car lot is mammoth day care. Where's my gun?"

Halfway up the driveway, Coop and the elephant stopped.

"Hey, Harkhuf," he yelled. "It's me, Coop. I thought I was your prom date, but you dumped me for someone else. Sure, she's got a nice figure, but does she have her own elephant? Come on out and see it."

Minerva and the Sheriff ran around the back of the car lot.

"Don't worry, you two. I've got this covered," said the Sheriff, strapping on his gun belt.

"We'll deal with him, my queen and my master," said Minerva.

Harkhuf pushed past them. "No. I shall deal with the fool." He turned to Shemetet. "Stay here where it is safe, beloved, and watch your army make its first conquest."

Harkhuf went around the side of the garage, followed by a legion of dead horrors ready to do battle.

Coop waved to Harkhuf. "I'm down here, ugly. Have you met Horton? Go say hi, Horton. Harkhuf looks like he needs a hug."

Coop pushed the elephant forward. It walked slowly toward the skeleton army and stopped. In the distance, a woolly-mammoth skeleton trumpeted.

The elephant moved restlessly and returned the trumpet.

"What the hell is going on?" said Giselle, coming up beside him.

"I wanted you to wait in the truck," said Coop.

"And I wanted you to bring home Thai, but here I am with a magic elephant and the cast of *Evil Dead*."

"I think it's a territorial dispute," said Morty. "The elephants. Not you two."

"Don't be so sure," said Giselle.

The mammoth trumpeted again and so did the elephant. With one more burst of outrage, they ran at each other through the lot.

"I can't look," said Giselle. She put her hands up, but peeked through her fingers.

Back at the garage, Kellar said, "Oh, good. It's summer camp and we're playing mine is bigger than yours."

Standing at the front with Harkhuf, Sheriff Wayne Jr. said, "Let me handle this." He pulled his gun and got off a couple of shots at Coop before Harkhuf slapped his arm away.

"Stay your hand," said Harkhuf. Shemetet came to stand beside him. He raised his arms and shouted a war cry that hadn't been heard on earth in three thousand years. And his army ran forward to meet the elephant.

Are those shots? thought Coop as bullets whizzed by his head. Giselle and Morty dove for cover.

"Do something!" yelled Giselle.

Morty said, "In case you hadn't noticed, you're about to lose."

"Just a little more . . ." Coop said, flipping on the zero-G device.

Just as the elephant and the mammoth were about to collide, Coop pushed the power up to full and the elephant sailed over the heads of the skeleton army. They came shuddering to a halt and watched the floating pachyderm climb higher into the air.

Back by the garage, Kellar and Minerva were also watching.

"What are you doing, Coop?" said Minerva.

The elephant flew higher.

"Coop, you are really pissing me off. Do whatever you're going to do," said Giselle.

"Think that's high enough?" he said.

"For what?" said Morty.

"For this."

Coop hit a switch on the Tweak box and the elephant disappeared in mist. A moment later, a green light flashed . . .

Sheriff Wayne Jr. pulled his other gun and took aim . . .

. . . just as the Fitzgeralds' library came crashing down on him, Harkhuf, and his entire army.

The crash felt like an earthquake. A hundred alarms on a hundred cars went off.

Minerva and Kellar stood by the garage, just staring.

"Minerva?" said Kellar.

"Yes?"

"Did I just lose my talk show?"

"At the very least. Come on. Let's disappear. Where's the grimoire?"

"Oh, fuck," said Kellar. "Shemetet had it."

Police cars and blacked-out DOPS vans pulled up around the Sheriff's car lot. Tactical officers fanned out around the library.

"Freeze!" someone shouted, and a dozen lights hit Minerva and Kellar.

The two froze. For a moment, no one moved, but then Kellar shouted, "It was all her idea. I just wanted to go to Red Lobster!"

Coop and the others missed all that. They were already on the freeway, speeding to the DOPS to return the equipment. They hoped that if they cleaned out the elephant shit from the truck, Woolrich would forgive them.

41

Nelson met the Auditors outside of the ECIU.

"I see you got my note," he said.

"Yes," said Night.

"Yes," said Knight. "Now that we are here . . ."

". . . please tell us what incriminating information . . ."

". . . you have on Mr. Cooper. We would . . ."

". . . like to see him . . ."

". . . again . . ."

". . . very soon."

"It's not exactly information," said Nelson. "It's evidence. And it's just inside the ECIU. Really. Just a couple of feet inside."

"You are a . . ." said Night.

". . . mook?" said Knight.

"Yes. So, I can't go inside and get it, but I know it's in there. It's a book. I saw it. If you bring it out, Coop is screwed."

"And why should we believe this?"

"A corpse's story? Your type . . ."

". . . is so . . ."

". . . unstable."

"Instead of debating my mental health, why don't you go and get the book? Then you'll see I'm telling the truth."

"Very . . ." said Night.

". . . well," said Knight. "Your name is . . ."

". . . Mr. Nelson?"

"Yes. I'm head of the mail room. It's a privilege and a sacred duty."

"Is it . . ."

". . . now? If you're not telling . . ."

". . . us the truth, we will be seeing . . ."

". . . you even before Mr. Cooper."

"We don't like . . ."

". . . being deceived," said Night.

"I understand completely. Just go inside. It's in an ornately carved wooden box, just a few feet from the door."

"Shall I or . . ." said Knight.

". . . shall I?"

"Why don't you both go? One can hold the flashlight and the other can get the book."

"A reasonable . . ."

". . . solution."

"We will . . ."

". . . do it."

"Thank you," said Nelson. "And please stop talking. You're giving me a stroke with the schizo act."

"What . . ."

". . . schizo . . ."

". . . act?"

Nelson put a finger in the air. "I almost forgot something. I had to go back to my office for it."

"What is . . ." said Night.

". . . it?" said Knight.

"A neutron flare. It's like a big firecracker. You might want to cover your ears."

Nelson tossed the flare into the ECIU, then ran back with his fingers in his ears. A moment later, there was an explosion in the office. Dust and debris blew out into the corridor. Nelson and the Auditors coughed, waiting for the air to clear.

"Why was that . . ." said Night.

". . . necessary?" said Knight.

"It's a storeroom in there and some dangerous animals got loose. A neutron flare kills living things, but leaves everything else intact. You should be perfectly safe when you go in."

Night and Knight looked at each other.

"You're sure . . ."

". . . it's safe?"

"I'd go in myself if I could."

"When this is over, I think . . ."

". . . we will request . . ."

". . . your presence for a . . ."

". . . session in our office."

"I'll be there with bells on, if you'll just get the fucking book."

Nelson handed Night a small flashlight and the Auditors went into ECIU. They were only in the office for a minute or so when Nelson heard them say, "Here . . ."

". . . it is."

"Great," Nelson said. "Now bring it to me and I'll show you how we're going to get Coop."

Night and Knight came out into the corridor, dusting themselves off. Night, or maybe it was Knight, coughed.

"Give me the book so I can show you," said Nelson.

The noncoughing Auditor handed Nelson the box containing the *Mortuis*.

"Now, Mr. Nelson. Show us . . ."

". . . what you . . ."

". . . promised. How will the book . . ."

". . . deliver Mr. Cooper to us?"

"It won't deliver him to you," said Nelson. "I lied about that part."

He took the pistol he'd found earlier and shot Night and Knight in the head.

Nelson set the book down and wiped his prints off the gun. "The pistol is what's going to get Coop. I just add his prints to this little baby and it's the mail room for Mr. Smarty-Pants."

Nelson put the gun back in his pocket and got the book.

"It's nice to know that a couple of guys whose only other career option was biting the heads off chickens could find government work."

He stepped over their bodies.

"Makes me proud to be an American."

Nelson was planning to spend the night studying the *Mysteriis Ex Mortuis*. However, when he made a detour through the garage, he found, to his delight, Coop, Giselle, and Morty hosing out a DOPS transport truck.

"Hi, Coop. What are you up to?"

"Hi, Nelson," said Coop. "You know. We're just cleaning elephant shit out of a truck."

"That sounds like fun. Hey, do you know what this is?" Nelson held up the box.

Coop squinted. "A very tiny hope chest? You're getting married. Congratulations."

Nelson looked at the box. "Okay, I'll give you that one. I should have opened it first. But it's what's inside that's important. It's a book. A very special book."

Coop turned off the hose. "Clearly you want me guess what book, but I'm too tired, so, please, tell me what book."

"*Mysteriis Ex Mortuis.*"

"What the hell is that?"

Nelson's shoulders slumped. "Seriously? You have no idea?"

"Sorry."

Nelson looked at Giselle and Morty. "Guys? You're intelligent people. Tell him."

Giselle shook her head. "Can't help you."

"I never heard of it either," said Morty.

Nelson rubbed his chin. "No wonder China is beating us at everything. The *Mysteriis Ex Mortuis* is the spell book to end all spell books. The darkest, nastiest, most fucked-up magic you can imagine is all in this book."

"Great," said Coop. "Speaking for the group, we hope you and the missus are very happy together." He turned on the hose and began spraying the back of the truck again.

Nelson held up his hands in a football time-out. Coop turned off the hose.

"You still don't get it, do you?" said Nelson. "I'm going to use it. Those idiot mummies gave me the idea. They had their little cookbook with the resurrection spells. My beloved this and my beloved that. What a crock. I'm going to do what they should have done. What all the magic creeps around here are too chicken to do."

"Talk my ear off?" said Coop.

"Waste my air?" said Morty.

"Make me get pruny hands?" said Giselle, holding up her wet, pruny hands.

Nelson looked around in frustration, then back at Coop. "Now that I have the real, ultimate magic, the Necro-fucking-nomicon, I'm going to use the magic on myself and become a god."

"Okay. Well, call us when you're done. We're almost finished cleaning the truck."

"I'm not done yet, Cooper. You're going to listen to me."

"What? It's late and I promised Giselle Thai food."

"It's true," she said.

"They said I could come along," said Morty.

Nelson came closer to the truck and pointed to each of them in turn. "Once I make myself a god, I'm going to kill you. All of you. I'm going to kill you. And I'm going to kill you. And, Coop, Mr. Cooper, I'm going to kill the ever-loving hell out of you."

"No, you're not," said Coop. "You're the kind of guy that still has a VCR and it's been blinking 12:00 all day and night since 1979. Now please. Seriously. We need to finish this before Woolrich gets here."

Nelson tore off the top of the box and threw it away with a dramatic flourish. He flipped pages in the *Mortuis*, desperate to show these idiots something they could really understand. Something that would make them soil themselves and collapse like little kids screaming for their mommies.

"Aha!" he said. "'To inhabitate Astarogothor, whose body is of the unbreakable stone that set all matter in motion at the beginning of time. He is eternal. Unstoppable. Invincible.'"

"Did you say a rock?" said Coop. "You want to turn yourself into a rock?"

"Not just a rock. He's *the* rock. The primordial rock," said Nelson. "You need dust and rocks to make planets and stars." He stopped and put a hand behind his head. "Oh, man, I wonder if I can get enough stuff to orbit around me that I become a star. How about that, Coop? I won't be a rock forever. In a few million years, I might be bigger than the sun."

Coop hopped down from the truck and turned off the hose. "Like I said, I'm very happy for you. We all are. But guess what? The truck is finished and we're going home. I suggest you do the same." He looked Nelson over. "Is that dust all over you? Woolrich is going to be here any minute and you look like hell."

"I won't for long," said Nelson excitedly. "In a few minutes, I'm going to be on my way to godhood."

Coop looked at his watch. "Okay, we'll go along with your little prank. You've got three minutes to show us you're serious."

"Oh, I'm serious."

Nelson looked at the *Mysteriis Ex Mortuis* and began to recite a language that sounded like someone trying to plunger out a toilet full of creamed corn.

Slowly, as he recited, Nelson's skin darkened and hardened. His hair fell out and was replaced with a skullcap of gray stone. He grew as he spoke and soon his head almost touched the roof of the garage.

Coop applauded. "Very nice, Nelson. While you're getting stoned, listen to this." He said a word that was just as odd as the ones in Nelson's recitation, only Coop's word sounded like someone dropping underripe watermelons down a spiral staircase.

Nelson's stony body continued to grow, but even faster. His body distorted. His left side expanded to almost twice the size of his right.

"Oh, shit," he said. "What is this?"

"I'm sorry. Maybe I did it wrong," said Coop. "Let me try it again." He repeated the watermelon word several times.

Nelson grew even faster. When his head smashed into the top of the garage, he began to spread outward.

"What's happening to me?" he yelled.

"You wanted to be a rock. I'm just trying to help."

"Stop it."

"Stop what? Saying this?" Coop repeated the word a few more times.

"I have to stop," said Nelson. "Where's the counterspell?"

"They're usually at the back." said Morty.

Giselle slapped his arm. "Don't help him."

"Sorry."

"Oh, shit," whispered Nelson. "Oh no." He held the book out in front of him. He'd managed to flip all the way to the back with his thick, clumsy stone fingers, but there was nothing there. Several red-eyed mice popped up their heads.

"They've eaten it," he said.

"Tough break, old man," said Coop. He repeated the watermelon word one more time.

Nelson dropped the box. The remnants of the book fell out, and the mice scattered. Coop went to the mound of dark stone that used to be Nelson and put out a hand tentatively. He knocked on the rock.

"Hello? Nelson? Are you in there?"

Nelson didn't answer.

Coop turned around. "Who wants Thai? I'm buying."

Giselle came over and touched the rock. "What the hell did you just do?"

"Oh, that?" he said. "Just some super-awesome magic."

"But you're immune to magic. You don't *do* magic," said Morty. He came over and gave Nelson a kick. "Ow."

"Don't kick the rock, Morty. You're going to hurt yourself," said Giselle.

"I think I already did."

"It wasn't really magic I did," said Coop. "It was a kind of . . . a mystical cheering section. See, I read some of that cookbook I scanned. Didn't understand a word of it, by the way. But at the back, it had a list of what it called Elemental Promulgations. They're not regular magic. They just kind of encourage magic along. I really didn't understand most of that stuff either. But I managed to learn two words. One stops spells."

"And the other speeds them up," said Giselle. "Why did you decide to memorize them in the first place?"

"For something like this. I didn't know if I could stop Nelson, so I did the other. If he hadn't gotten all bent out of shape, his spell might have worked."

"But *he* did, and *it* didn't," said Morty.

Coop put his arm around Giselle's shoulder. "Let's get out of here. I'm hungry."

"Cooper!" Someone yelled his name so loud that it echoed around the garage. "What the hell have you been up to tonight? There's a stolen library in the Valley, a museum and two cemeteries have been looted, and a car salesman has allegedly been crushed by a flying elephant," said Woolrich. He was flanked by some of the other people Coop had seen in his office when they'd packed him into the garbage disposal.

"Coop just saved the world," said Giselle.

"Twice in one day," said Morty.

"The other time I just saved the DOPS."

"No. Just now, too." Morty hooked a thumb over his shoulder at Nelson.

"I guess you're right."

Woolrich went to the mound of stone. "Is this your doing, too? What is it?" he said.

"It's Nelson."

"From the mail room?"

"I don't think he'll fit there anymore. You might want to look for a replacement," said Coop.

A man clanked out of the elevators. Half of his face and his arms were mismatched robot parts. "Excuse me. I'm looking for Mr. Nelson. I was supposed to go on vacation, but I couldn't get the shredder started. Do you know where he is?"

"Who are you?" said Woolrich.

"I'm McCloud. I'm Mr. Nelson's assistant."

Woolrich pointed. "That's what's left of Nelson. Congratulations, McCloud. You're head of the mail room."

McCloud's smile was blazing. "Oh, boy. Thanks, boss!"

"You three can go," said Woolrich, pointing to Giselle, Morty, and McCloud. "I'll deal with two of you in the morning. Cooper, come with me. You're going to explain everything from the beginning. And no lies or omissions this time."

"I'm right behind you."

They walked to the elevator together. "And what was that crack on the phone about not trusting me?"

"You did use me as bait to get Harkhuf," said Coop.

"I suppose."

"*And* you promised me round-the-clock protection, which you didn't do because it would have interfered with Harkhuf getting to me."

"Yes. All right," said Woolrich. "You've made your point. But understand, the Department of Peculiar Science is a harsh mistress. We've all been bait for something over the years. When I was a young agent, I had to jump from the top of the Hollywood sign just so that I could infiltrate a group of spirits selling DOPS secrets to the Russians."

"Wait. So, you died?"

"Yes, Cooper. That's generally how ghosts work."

"But how are you here and not a mook?"

"Obviously, they cloned me a new body and uploaded the rest of me from a backup copy."

"Obviously."

"The point is that at the DOPS you frequently have to sacrifice a few eggs, and then sometimes a few more eggs, but in the end, you end up with a lovely flan."

"I think I'd rather end up on your wall than be a government omelet," said Coop.

"There's plenty of opportunity for that, Cooper. I daresay you're going to be with us for a very long time."

42

Morty, Bayliss, Sally Gifford, and Dr. Lupinsky sat in Coop and Giselle's living room, drinking bourbon while their Fatburgers sat on the kitchen table.

"Who should we invite to the party?" said Coop.

"Everybody," said Giselle. "Everybody in the world. And they should bring their own food and booze. They owe us."

"I'm not sure we could fit them all in here," said Coop.

"You could have it at DOPS headquarters," said Morty. "They have a really nice ballroom . . ."

"No," said Giselle. "No. No. No. No. No."

"I'll ask for my deposit back, then."

"Thanks again for all your help, doc. On the job and helping keep my head in one very sore piece," said Coop.

Dr. Lupinsky's cat sat very tall, with its tail wrapped around its feet, looking quite pleased with itself.

It was a pleasure. I hope I can help again in the future.

"I'm sure you will."

"Guess what, Coop? I'm thinking of taking a trip with my ill-gotten gains," said Sally. "I applied for a passport and everything."

"In your real name?"

"Yeah."

"Brave girl," said Giselle.

"Where are you going?"

"Italy. Milan. It's where Caravaggio was born."

"Caravaggio?" said Bayliss. "I love Caravaggio."

"Yeah? I have a few over at my place," said Sally. "Want to come over and see them sometime?"

"I'd love to."

"All right. It's a date." She looked Bayliss over. "You didn't go to Catholic school by any chance, did you?"

"How did you know?"

"Why don't you come over on Saturday?"

"I'll bring some wine."

"Did you ever try grappa?"

"No," said Bayliss.

"You're going to love it."

"You know who I feel bad for is those animal rights kids," said Giselle. "I know they were a pest, but their hearts were in the right place. Now they're going to have criminal records."

"How?" said Morty. "We're the ones who arrested them and we let them go."

"You know. Some jerk at Carrwood who saw the elephant is going to report them to the real police."

"And what are the cops going to do?" said Coop. "Where's the missing elephant? There aren't any missing from any zoos or circuses. There's no way to trace it because it doesn't exist. With no evidence and rich parents, those kids will maybe get a fine for messing up the rec center."

"I heard you got spanked by your boss pretty hard," said Sally. "How did that work out?"

"I'm suspended for two weeks again, so I'll be watching a lot of movies and catching up with my day drinking. You ought to come over."

"That's my Coop," said Giselle. "If he isn't saving the world, he's keeping the sofa warm for me when I get home from work."

Coop held up a hand. "I might also read a book or two."

Giselle gave his hand a squeeze. "Coop likes books. He just doesn't like to admit it. You know. Prison tough-guy stuff."

"That's not true. Everybody read in prison. There wasn't anything else to do half the time."

"I thought you said there were fights over people reading."

"Only when the new books came in. And some of the magazines."

"That was it," said Giselle. "When I caught you reading and you got all flustered."

"That was one time."

"That's not how it looked to me."

"There weren't a lot of choices in prison."

"What was it?" said Morty. "*Sports Illustrated?* Is Coop a secret jock?"

"*Penthouse? Hustler?*" said Sally. "*Playgirl?*"

Dr. Lupinsky's cat jumped.

Scientific American. *Coop is a secret egghead like me.*

"It's none of that," said Coop. "And I don't want to talk about it."

"You're right," said Giselle. "It's a private matter between Coop and *People* magazine."

Coop shot her a look.

"Oops."

The room went awkwardly quiet.

"Like I said. There wasn't a lot of choice of reading material. After a while, things just became a habit."

"You big sissy girl, you," said Sally. "I should introduce you to my mom and the ladies in her choir."

"Okay," he said. "It's not like I have a subscription."

"No. It's sicker than that. He sneaks off in the grocery store and reads it where he thinks I can't see," said Giselle.

"When did this become kick-Coop-while-he's-down day?" he said. "I just saved the world, in case you forgot."

"Old news," said Morty.

"Yeah," said Bayliss. "What have you done for us lately?"

Coop got up. "I'm getting the burgers before they get cold. Drinks are on the counter." He looked at Dr. Lupinsky. "I feel kind of weird about eating in front of you, doc. Is there anything I can get you?"

No, thank you. I enjoy being around food and people eating. It reminds me of the old days.

"You know, we just saw a guy almost turn into a god," said Giselle. "What happened to that book, Coop?"

"DOPS probably has it stashed someplace. Probably down in . . . what the hell is that place called?"

"I don't know what you're talking about," said Morty.

"I can almost see it," said Bayliss.

"Whatever. It's probably buried down there somewhere."

"What about the cookbook? We could print out the photos and look," said Giselle.

Coop looked at Dr. Lupinsky.

"You up for this? I make no promises, but maybe there's something in the book that will get you out of that TV."

I'm always ready for an adventure.

"The DOPS might be pissed."

They're always pissed about something.

"True. I guess I'm going to have two weeks with nothing to do. I'll see if I can find anything."

Thank you.

"Aren't you going to get lonely with Giselle and everybody else at work all day?" said Bayliss.

Coop put his burger on the table. As he poured himself a shot of bourbon Giselle said, "He's not going to be lonely at all."

"Why's that?" Coop said.

Something went *meow* in his ear.

He stared down at the table as Giselle set down a kitten.

"What is that?" he said.

"A cat," said Giselle. *"Felis catus."*

"Whose is it?"

"Guess."

"Oh God."

Giselle sat down next to him. "Poor boy. He's having hamster flashbacks."

The kitten had a dark nose, a light tan coat, and a gray tail.

"What kind is it?" he said.

"It's a mutt, but I think there's a little Siamese in there."

"What's it called?"

"That's up to you," said Giselle. "She doesn't have a name yet."

"You're really putting the spurs to me, aren't you?"

"I am. I totally am."

The kitten came over to Coop's hamburger and began gnawing at the paper wrapper until it got to the meat. When it did, it lay down on its belly and chewed on the burger contentedly.

After a minute Coop said, "Willy."

"Willy is a boy's name," said Giselle.

"I knew a Willy for Wilhelmina," said Sally.

"See? Willy is a girl's name, too," said Coop.

"But you're not naming her for a girl, are you?"

Who are you naming her for?

"Willy Sutton, the bank robber, right?" said Giselle.

Coop nodded. "Absolutely." He picked up the cat. It dropped a wad of meat on the floor. He set her down and gave the meat back to her. She ignored it and went back to digging through the wrapper to get to his burger.

"You're Willy all right. A born thief if I ever saw one."

ABOUT
THE
AUTHOR

New York Times bestselling author Richard Kadrey has published eleven novels, including *Sandman Slim, Kill the Dead, Aloha from Hell, Devil Said Bang, Kill City Blues, The Getaway God, Killing Pretty, Dead Set, Butcher Bird,* and *Metrophage,* and more than fifty short stories. He has been immortalized as an action figure, and his novel *Butcher Bird* was nominated for the Prix Elbakin in France. The acclaimed writer and photographer lives in San Francisco, California.